BALLAD FOR JASMINE TOWN

MOLLY RINGLE

central
avenue
2024

Content Warnings:
Mild: consensual sexual activity, self-harm thoughts, drowning, nonconsensual sexual activity (mentioned, not shown), child abuse (mentioned, not shown)

Moderate: classism/discrimination against groups, violence (physical), natural disaster, mass destruction, trauma, torture, swearing, murder (attempted), death and grief

Published by Central Avenue Publishing, an imprint of Central Avenue Marketing Ltd.
www.centralavenuepublishing.com

Published in Canada
Printed in United States of America

1. FICTION/Fairy Tales   2. FICTION/LGBT

BALLAD FOR JASMINE TOWN

Trade Paperback: 978-1-77168-364-7
Ebook: 978-1-77168-365-4

1 3 5 7 9 10 8 6 4 2

Keep up with Central Avenue

BALLAD FOR JASMINE TOWN

EIDOLONIA WIKI

This page is part of the Eidolonian Intranet: protected by fae spells and certified Unhackable Crosswater by Eidolonian witches. Welcome!

Eidolonia

Eidolonia is an island country in the north Pacific Ocean, consisting of one large main landmass and more than one hundred smaller islands. Only about one-sixth of this area is inhabited by humans, nearly all of it along the main island's coast, the rest being fae territory.

The country has no close neighbors, lying roughly equidistant from Hawaii, the Aleutian Islands, and Japan. Its climate is temperate, but weather can depend on the whims of regional fae. Eidolonia is a constitutional monarchy, with a royal family as well as a prime minister and other democratically elected officials.

Eidolonia was entirely fae territory until the early 1700s, when the fae allowed a few sailors from various countries to find the island. They permitted a limited number of additional human immigrants over ensuing years, making deals to allow human settlements, which gradually grew to encompass the entire coastline. Eidolonia is undetectable to outsiders (_crosswaters_) due to concealment spells maintained by the fae, and humans who leave the island will not remember it, with false memories taking its place, unless they carry a memory charm that preserves their knowledge of the country.

An estimated two-thirds of Eidolonian humans have some fae ancestry due to intermixing. Approximately half of humans on Eidolonia, regardless of ancestry, are born with witch abilities, being _matter-witches_ (able to manipulate inanimate matter), _exo-witches_ (able to manipulate other living things), or _endo-witches_ (able to manipulate their own forms). Being more than one type is rare but is occasionally documented. The magical powers of the fae, in nearly all cases, are stronger than those of witches.

Each individual of mixed background is either _counted human_ or _counted fae_. This is an innate and unchangeable feature. Being counted human means being mortal and having limited magical power. Being counted fae means possessing greater power and being immortal, though nearly all fae choose to regenerate into a new form after many centuries of life.

Wanderers, humans who live primarily in the fae realm and are not on record as citizens, are thought to be rare, though tallying their numbers (or that of the fae population) is essentially impossible.

The *verge*, the border between fae and human territory, underwent select alterations in 2020 to revert certain parcels of land to fae territory (for example, see Miryoku) but otherwise has not changed since its previous adjustment in 1799, in accordance with the Prince Larkin Treaty. This truce also put an end to the only fae-human war in Eidolonia. The fire faery Ula Kana, who led the attacks, was captured by an alliance of humans and fae and put into an enchanted sleep along with Prince Larkin of the Eidolonian royal family, a deal brokered by court sorcerer Rosamund Highvalley.

Since then, occasional crime between fae and humans has still occurred, but at a low rate. Entering fae territory, however, remains significantly dangerous for humans.

Miryoku

Miryoku was a small city (population 20,816) on the Southwest Peninsula of Eidolonia. It was founded in 1762 by human settlers from Asia and was situated unusually close to the verge, its easternmost boundary just under 100 ft away in places.

On March 21, 2020, upon the awakening of Prince Larkin and Ula Kana, and the subsequent destruction instigated by the latter, Miryoku was invaded by fae and almost entirely destroyed. While most residents were able to flee, nine were killed, another six went missing and have been presumed dead, and as many as two hundred suffered enchantment damage, including one who was permanently transfigured. After the restoration of peace, the verge was redrawn around the former town. The majority of Miryoku in its original form no longer exists, having been overgrown by the fae forest.

CHAPTER I
MIRYOKU - MAY 2018

AN ORANGE FLAME GLIMMERED BETWEEN branches, a flare in the night. From the back seat of the van, Rafi leaned forward to look, his smile vanishing.

"Is that a will-o'-the-wisp hanging out in our garden?" Izzy asked, steering into the drive. Gravel crunched under the tires.

"Yes." Rafi's eyes stayed on the figure. "I know him. He's from Kepelo's haunt."

"If he's come to fetch you, let us know before taking off," Tash said. She brushed the tip of her green braid lazily against her palm. "We'll need to find a replacement for you."

Rafi himself was a replacement, standing in for the band's regular mandolinist, who was out of town investigating a new job. Or something like that. Rafi tended to be hazy on human-world details.

Izzy parked the van, and Rafi slid the side door open and jogged to the garden. He'd been gone all day with the band, on a trip to Dasdemir to play at a festival. If Figo, the will-o'-the-wisp, was seeking him, he could have been waiting hours.

Ignoring the couch on Jove and Izzy's porch, Figo sat atop an azalea shrub. Or hovered, really. He put no weight on it; its branches didn't even bend. His two skinny arms were crossed in reverie, his four insectlike legs folded beneath him. At the moment, he was about a quarter the size of Rafi or any average human, and his long body was multisectioned like a caterpillar. His bottom half glowed.

In his wide-set eyes and small mouth, Rafi read pity. His body turned cold.

"Figo. What are you doing here?"

"Akurafi." Figo unfolded his arms, as well as his oval wings. "You must come to the haunt."

"Why?"

"Someone awaits you there. A ghost."

Rafi blinked. "Whose?" His mind flipped through the short list of humans who might seek him if—if they died…

"Your grandmother. Hazel."

The breath skittered out between Rafi's lips.

But he'd seen her just last week.

But she was doing fine.

But he didn't have, or at least know, any other human relatives and therefore *it couldn't be her*. He couldn't bear that.

Ever since Rafi could remember, Figo had been one of the many who'd brought him fire-roasted meats and apples (or forgot to), laughed at his childhood babbles and songs, and shrugged off his adolescent furies and advised him not to care so much. Now he looked solemn. Tonight's news evidently saddened even a blithe will-o'-the-wisp.

"What happened?" Rafi managed to ask, his throat tight.

"She will tell you. Come."

Rafi flared his magic, heat streaking through him, then remembered he should undress first so his clothes wouldn't rip. He paused to yank off his shirt and scrabbled at the tie on his sarong. Then he pivoted. He needed to tell the band—Tash had just said—

She stood nearby, her eyes grave for once rather than narrowed in a smirk. "I heard," she said. "I'll tell Jove and Izzy. Go."

Rafi nodded. He flung off his clothes and let his fire flare. His shape changed: broader shoulders, shorter arms, nails becoming claws. He grew wings, a tapering tail, a snout. An orange glow rippled under his skin. He hooked the sarong with one claw and flicked it around his neck like a scarf— it would do for clothes once he got there. Then he shot off across the garden, Figo gliding in flight alongside him.

Despite his wings, Rafi couldn't actually fly, and though he sped through the night faster than his human legs could carry him, he couldn't reach the speed of his fire-fae relatives.

Still, faster was better. He needed to see his grandmother. Ghosts seldom stayed long.

They swooped across the public footpath, then into the forest. When they reached the land adjacent to fire fae territory, they shot across the verge in a crackle of electricity and arrived in Kepelo's haunt.

Warmth and a smoky, floral scent enveloped Rafi. He changed back to human form to preserve energy and tied the sarong around his waist. Barefoot, he walked with Figo along a path between boulders and scrubby trees. Clumps of purple catmint flowers spilled from cracks in rocks. Flames sparkled everywhere: lanterns in trees, bonfires on the ground, sparks dancing in the air. He tried to take comfort from the familiarity of the surroundings, but terror clouded his mind.

Like most fae, Figo couldn't lie. Which meant Hazel truly was dead. Even so, Rafi couldn't quite believe it until he got to his mother's cave.

There Hazel stood—vigorous thatch of short white hair, thin frame, daisy-patterned blue shawl. But now, when Rafi reached out, his trembling fingers slipped through her translucent shoulder and touched nothing but cool air.

A lump blocked his throat. "Lao Lao?"

"Hello, Rafi. I'm so glad you came." She smiled, looking sympathetic but not particularly sad.

"What happened?"

"A stroke." Hazel's voice wavered as if distorted by water. "I don't think I'll make a very good ghost. I don't plan to stay long as one. But I had to talk to you before I left. It's easier to make myself visible in the fae realm, that's why I came here."

"Yeah, I've…only ever seen ghosts on this side." His tongue felt numb.

Those ghosts he'd seen in the past had unsettled him enough. They'd been a rare occurrence, and never anyone he knew well.

"I told the human investigators, once she explained the story to me," Kepelo said, her voice full and warm compared to the wateriness of Hazel's. "But they say there isn't much they can do."

Tonight, rather than embodying her full form as a twenty-foot-high drake, Kepelo was in human shape, albeit a tall human with gossamer red wings and shining scales in lieu of clothes.

"Much they can do about what?" Rafi asked.

"The korreds," Hazel said. "I was out for a walk on the footpath a few days ago. Or perhaps yesterday. Hard to say with the time difference. A korred came up to me."

Already Rafi felt sick with horror.

"He was very polite," Hazel continued. "He wanted me to come to his haunt for a bit, to tell stories. 'Like the ones you used to tell Rafi,' he said. 'He doesn't come around much anymore.'"

"Of course I don't. Not when they—" He made himself stop. "What did they do?"

"Naturally I wouldn't have gone. I know better. But I think he must have enchanted me, because I found I was walking into the woods with him. We went into his haunt, and all the korreds were there, gathered around. They were nice to me, Rafi, really. I don't want you to get the wrong idea."

He had no words. She was dead. There was no wrong idea to get.

"They sat me down and I told stories. Then I got tired and couldn't think of any more. They offered me tea. From the human realm, they promised. And, well, the tea may have been from the human realm. But the water they made it with probably wasn't. Neither was the wooden cup they served it in."

Rafi shut his eyes a moment.

"I had a stroke," she concluded. "It was fast. I don't remember much about it. Then I found myself like this, and they told me they were sorry for it, and they brought my body back to the path for people to find."

Rafi's lungs shuddered as he dragged air into them. He turned to his mother. "Tell me you've done something."

"Certainly," she said. "I wouldn't ignore the death of my mother through their influence, even if unintentional. I went to Brogyo's haunt and demanded recompense. He agreed, and one of his high-ranking folk volunteered to return to the elements."

"An ancient and bored one," Figo grumbled. "Who would have done so before long anyway."

"Even so," she said, "they've been reminded they cannot do such things to people close to me without losing one of their own."

"But that's not enough," Rafi said. "That's nowhere near enough."

"What would you prefer?" Kepelo asked. "What vengeance would you take that would improve things?"

"Not vengeance. A…stronger deal. Punishment if they enchant *any* mortals on the human side of the verge, ever. Even if the person survives."

"Impossible." Kepelo's calmness maddened him. Her being counted as fae, even with half-human ancestry, often made worlds of difference in her reactions to things that devastated Rafi. "The other fae already chafe at the deal that protects you," she said. "They would never agree to a deal reaching so far and covering so many."

"The one protecting you is the important one," Hazel added. "You're young yet, darling. You have so much time ahead of you."

Tears stung his eyes. After tonight he'd never again hear her call him "darling," nor anything else.

He swallowed. "The human government, the police—they should care. Lao Lao's a citizen."

Was, his mind corrected.

"It broke no laws of theirs," Kepelo said. "Fae actions are outside their control. They can't do anything, and trying to retaliate would be ill-advised."

Rafi knew that. He just desperately wished it were otherwise. "This isn't the first time. The things they've done…"

"We can't change what's happened," Kepelo said. "I'm grieved, too, Rafi. She was my mother."

Who you never lived with and hardly ever saw, Rafi thought. He'd spent more time with Hazel than Kepelo had. Kepelo's "grief" was nothing more than a traditional gesture of honor paid to one's forebears. Or perhaps he was just heartbroken and furious, and willing to think ungenerous things about everyone.

He wiped his eyes. "I'm going to them."

"No, dear," Hazel said. "Don't put yourself in danger."

"It won't do any good," Kepelo added.

"You think I could *not* go to them, after this? Do you think *Brogyo* would ignore it and say nothing if we took away someone important to him?"

"I hardly need point out," his mother said, "that your powers and Brogyo's are not equal."

He laughed, swift and bitter. "No. Because if they were…"

No point finishing that thought. *Not vengeance*, he had said.

But if he had his mother's powers, if he could become vast and made of flame rather than just flesh with a flamelike glow to it, if he had the loyalty of drakes and djinns to command…

Driving out the korreds and reducing their cool, redwood-shaded haunt to a stretch of smoking char wouldn't bring Hazel back to life. It *might* serve as a deterrent to other fae. Or it might only turn them all against him and spark dreadful retaliation.

All a fantasy anyway. He couldn't do it, and his mother wouldn't.

He turned to Hazel. "How long can you stay?"

"Until dawn." She spoke with calm certainty. Just something she knew now.

"Talk to me until then?"

Figo withdrew, leaving grandmother, mother, and son together. They sat in front of the cave, its majestic mouth open to the stars. Hazel spoke of things she had told them long ago, relating the details one last time. The brief affair in her youth with the drake in human form, whom she met at a festival, leaving her pregnant with Kepelo. Hazel's bitterness when she saw him later, at other festivals, kissing new lovers. Her greatest heartbreak, when her baby girl was born and the attending fae midwife assessed Kepelo and found she was counted fae—immortal and mighty—and therefore had to be given up to their realm. Hazel's healing over the ensuing years, both helped and slowed by the sporadic meetings with Kepelo.

"You were suddenly so grown up," Hazel said to Kepelo. "Your infancy, it just didn't happen."

"Of course I was an infant," Kepelo said, dignified. "I was an infant in the way that fae are."

"Which is nothing like a human infant, as you well know. Then you, Rafi. A new baby girl—or so we thought! Changing yourself over the years with your wonderful magic to show your true self. Kepelo, he's the finest gift you could have given me. Even if I only had him on the occasional visits."

"It's through my selfishness that you didn't have him more," Kepelo said. "I blame my human half for such unreasonable sentiment."

"By which you mean you blame me." Hazel laughed as she said it.

Finally Rafi asked his mother, "Could I talk to her alone?"

Rising, Kepelo nodded. "My heart is full with the gifts of reminiscence you have given me tonight, my mother." She extended her webbed red wings and bowed. "Through my child and me you shall be remembered, and through the elements and the Spirit you will live on."

Hazel rose, too, and bowed in response. "You are wondrous, my child. To have any part in the creation of such a being is more honor than most mortals will ever know." Though her tribute was fae-style in its wording, Hazel delivered it like a human, with sentimental pride.

Kepelo's wings carried her in an upward spiral into the night.

Dawn was seeping into the dark, black lightening to blue.

"Did you ever resent her for it?" Rafi asked Hazel. "Keeping me here, when I could have been with you all those years?"

"Oh, certainly. I was so bitter, Rafi! But by the time I even knew about you, you were already walking and talking."

"I've been thinking about it, now that I'm spending more time in town. And I can't believe she chose that. It's like she wasn't even thinking of you. Or of me. Just herself, and—and what entertainment I could provide."

"Keeping you did give her a unique appeal. Between that and her father's position, I expect it cemented her place as ruler when he returned to the elements. But *you're* unique, too, you know. Oh, of course, everyone is. You have opportunities, though, that you wouldn't if you'd grown up on the human side."

It was a complex enough subject to discuss for days. But they only had minutes, and it was a moot point. His childhood was long since over.

"I suppose it would have been a lot to ask," he said. "To take on a child by yourself."

"True. I was getting old. But I would have done it in a heartbeat, if she'd offered."

"I just wanted you to know I would have liked that. A calm town life, with you."

She reached out a transparent palm and cupped his face, cooling the tears that had spilled down his cheek. "Few lives are truly calm. And yours, Akurafi? You're made of fire, stone, and human passion. I think it would be going against your nature to hope for a calm life."

"I don't really know," he said, his voice broken, "what kind I'm supposed to have."

"You have reason for wanting vengeance. But don't let that guide you. Follow your love instead."

Who, or what, is my love, now that you're gone?, he wanted to ask. But his voice refused to work anymore, and she couldn't have told him anyway. Ghosts didn't know the future.

"And I," Hazel added, "have a path to follow." She gazed past him. He saw nothing but tumbled boulders awash with firelight. Only patches of her figure were visible now, shredding into ribbons.

His heart clutched. "Lao Lao."

"It's so lovely, Rafi. It's just how the footpath looked in spring, when I was a little girl. We'd go out at dawn on the first morning of Lady Festival. You could walk barefoot on the moss. It was so soft. Jasmine grew overhead, just like that. Ah, that sweet smell."

He saw no jasmine, and all he could smell was the mineral ash of the fae's flames and the tang of the tears clogging his nose. He tried to touch her shoulder, but his hand slipped through.

The joy on her face shone like starlight. "There's more yet, dear. For me and for you."

"Come see me again. Please, Lao Lao. Or—send a message. Whatever you can."

"The message will always be that I love you, and I want you to seek your happiness."

"I love you too. I won't say goodbye," he insisted. "Not if there's more for us both."

She kissed her fingers and held them to his face. "All your sides can play together in harmony. Remember."

She rose and floated toward the invisible path.

Tears blurred Rafi's vision. He blinked them away as the last wisp of blue daisy shawl swirled into nothing.

CHAPTER 2

"DO *not* GO TO THE KORREDS," KEPELO warned once more before he stormed out of her haunt.

He should have listened.

The border to the korreds' haunt was an impenetrable wall of boulders, tree trunks, and razor-thorned vines with one path through, which Mukut currently blocked. She was in the form that best served her for this purpose: a slab of rock ten feet wide and equally high. Mukut was a stone giant and easily kept intruders out just by blocking their path—or thumping her weight down on them if necessary. That was rare, though. Of all the earth fae who lived in Brogyo's haunt, she was one of the gentlest.

When Rafi approached, Mukut's three stone-shingle eyelids lifted with a scraping sound. She made a rumble, its tone suggesting sorrow.

"You heard, then," Rafi said wearily. "Let me in, please."

People who were counted as human—mortal, with limited abilities—weren't physically able to hear all the sounds in the fae language, let alone make them. So despite Rafi having grown up in the fae realm, he had only a partial understanding of the language. The speech of some fae, like Mukut, was almost entirely unintelligible to him. All he could glean was the general mood of it. He only knew Mukut's name because other fae had told him.

Four stone blocks elongated from the slab and reached for him, taking vaguely handlike shape. They settled on his arms.

"*No one* thinks I should go in. But they can't hurt me any more than they already have. I'll go over the top if I have to, but I'm tired, Mukut. Please don't make me."

In his draklike form he could skitter over her, too fast for her to catch. It had been a game when he was younger, one of the few things he had enjoyed doing in the korreds' haunt.

Mukut grumbled but retracted her stone arms. She slid aside.

"Thank you." He stepped onto the path.

Damp air bathed him, smelling of rock, vines, and decaying leaves. The light was greenish, seeping from glow-worms and luminescent fae in the forms of tree frogs, snakes, and banana-sized yellow slugs.

The cool air was one of the only other things he liked about his father's haunt. Kepelo's territory was always hot.

Rafi had long wished his father could have been just about any other type of earth fae, stone giants included. Dryads, hobs, gnomes, even hunters with their daunting antlers would all have been likelier to possess some modicum of kindness. Korreds, though, were folk of the mountain stones, cunning and tough, with about as much tenderness as any average rock.

When he reached the clearing, a dozen korreds converged around him, screeching his name in greeting. It had been many seasons since he was last here, but this was how they always behaved when he arrived. As was the next part.

"What do you bring?"

"Do you bring stories?"

"Do you bring pets?"

"Do you bring food?"

"Do you bring friends?"

Their hard hands pawed at him, clutched his sarong, tugged his hair. The korreds were shorter than him by a head, in their usual at-home form. But the strength of any one of them was like a tree and a gorilla combined.

He swatted them away, flaring his fire. It couldn't hurt them, but they pulled back, laughing.

"I bring you a warning," he said, "and that's it. Where are Sminu and Brogyo?"

"Here, stinky child."

He turned. Brogyo, ruler of the korred haunt, strode out from the darkness on his bandy legs. Sminu—Rafi's father and Brogyo's second-in-charge—walked a step behind.

Every korred was green-gray and looked like a human made of rocks and gnarled branches. Their bodies and faces were as mobile as any animal's, though, and both Brogyo and Sminu leered as they beheld Rafi.

"A warning?" Sminu said. "Do we hear the child correctly?"

Rafi stared at his father. "Was it you who brought Hazel here?"

"Not me. I wouldn't lower myself to such a menial errand."

Rafi surged forward, furious. An oak branch smacked him backward. It bruised his ribs and punched his breath out, then twisted up to its proper position in the tree again. On the ground, Rafi splayed a hand across his chest, channeling magic into opening his lungs so he could stop gasping like a landed fish.

Brogyo flicked his fingers, and the oak bumped Rafi's rear from beneath with one of its roots, then fell still. "I sent our folk out to find us some entertainment," he told Rafi. "It was merely good luck one of them encountered your grandmother taking her walk."

His voice was deep and resonant. Rafi had heard humans call it "sexy" when Brogyo took human form and crossed the verge to mingle with them. The remark always made him feel ill.

"Who?" Rafi asked, low. His breath still came short. "Who took her?"

"Oxlock." Brogyo nodded across the clearing. "Not that it matters. She would have interested any of ours."

Clambering to his feet, Rafi glared at Oxlock, one of the essentially interchangeable korreds who did Brogyo's bidding.

Oxlock stared back, impassive, then bared his teeth in a grin. "She told me herself! 'A korred,' she said. 'Then you know my grandson, Rafi.' We all remember your stories, Rafi, the ones she gave you. I knew Brogyo and everyone would love it if we could have her."

"You can't *have* her. And now she's gone—because you brought her here."

"We didn't mean to." Oxlock's voice became a whine. "We wanted her to live longer."

"People usually survive," Brogyo cajoled. "It isn't our fault some are so fragile. Besides, the stories, Akurafi. You know we loved those. We needed them again."

"The goat who climbs to the clouds and makes it rain milk!" someone chimed in.

"The merfolk who make the water rise up over Miryoku, and everyone grows gills, and it becomes a water town," another said.

"The trees who stretch their roots and branches all through the buildings so Miryoku becomes an earth fae town—ruled by us!" someone else said. That got the loudest cheers.

Rafi flinched. Those were all stories he, not Hazel, had made up, tales inspired by features he loved about the human side when visiting. The flavor of goat cheese. The footbridges and waterfront paths. The fragrant greenery woven among Miryoku's buildings and streets—"Jasmine Town," some called it.

"Stop going across and enchanting people." He separated the words clearly.

The korreds laughed. The fact that their laughter sounded more genial than malicious just added to the night's horror.

"You cannot set such a rule," Brogyo reminded him. "It's the fae's island. Humans live on it at our sufferance, because they amuse us."

"They would amuse you much more willingly if you didn't hurt them. Keep acting this way and no one will want to come near you."

"What does it matter if their cooperation is willing? We can *make* them willing."

Letting such remarks pass unchallenged had become a survival skill for Rafi. Years had spooled by, in fact, since the last time he'd stood his ground against them, let alone attacked back.

He'd already been knocked down by one tree branch tonight, and he was weaving on his feet from weariness. Turning around and walking out of the haunt would be the wise thing to do.

He nodded, smoothed his tangled hair out of his face, and lunged at Brogyo in a flash of fire.

It couldn't have been more than two minutes before they dumped him outside the haunt border.

"You're not beyond healing," Brogyo assured, crouching beside him. "No deals broken—just a few bones." He laughed, then his tone became earnest. "Rafi, listen. Once you're no longer angry, do bring someone back for us. At least some stories. We're family, after all. Right, Sminu?"

Sminu gave a sour smile. "Yet it would be so much better if he'd behave like a properly loyal child."

Rafi would have pointed out he was no longer any kind of child, but his mouth was full of blood and he was having trouble breathing. At least two teeth were loosened. They'd broken some ribs, too, and many of the bones in one foot. He didn't answer.

Brogyo thumped him on the shoulder, then strolled away. His korreds fell in step behind him.

Rafi lay on his side on the redwood needles. He tried sending self-healing to the worst bone breaks, but his energy was depleted.

A rumble vibrated in the earth. An expanse of stone, heavy but gentle, settled along his back. Magic zinged through him, making him shiver and sweat, but it left relief in its wake. His loosened teeth resecured themselves, and the broken bones eased from agony to mere ache. They'd take time to heal fully, but at least he could speak again.

"Thank you, Mukut." He planted a hand on the ground and raised himself, shaking. He spat out the blood and leaned back on her stone arm. She rumbled again. "Yeah," he agreed. "You were right. Shouldn't have gone in there."

His injured foot still hurt, but he limped to the creek and turned to make his way along it, back toward the verge.

Before he got more than a few steps, the water bubbled up in the center. The top of Tash's head emerged. She was in fish form, but as she shot to the bank in one graceful tail-flip, she transformed. She reached up with human arms to hoist herself onto the bank, and her tail divided into legs. She shook off the water and stood before him, green-haired and sequin-clad.

"Let me guess," she said. "You went after the korreds."

Rafi nodded, hand cradling his ribs. "You heard?"

"It's been three days out there. Jove and Izzy were getting all parental and worried, so I crossed the verge to ask around."

"Jove and Izzy, huh. Definitely not you."

"I care because we can use you for gigs. All right, idiot, this way." She wrapped an arm around his waist and steered him into the water. "Come see my people."

❦

"Where to?" Tash asked.

Rafi had awoken from the healing sleep induced by the shellycoats, Tash's people, and had eaten some food they'd brought—wild cress, snails, and the tart oranges that grew near the fire fae haunt. All of it had come from just outside the verge. Fae-realm food could hurt Rafi, but at least someone was likely to save him from the enchantment before he died. A courtesy not extended to his grandmother.

He pulled apart an orange numbly. "Where to," he echoed.

Most often he slept in Kepelo's haunt, in a hammock between boulders. It wasn't as comfortable or quiet as the couch in Hazel's house, where he had stayed as a child on his visits. But Hazel had sold that house years ago when she'd moved into the home for elders. Occasionally he'd spent nights in the korreds' haunt—out of their way, among the ancient trees near the border. He had even slept outdoors in the human realm now and then, nestled among driftwood at the seashore, or lying in a peaceful meadow near Miryoku.

None of those options appealed today. His mother's was the closest remaining thing to home—"home" was a notion he didn't ponder much and wasn't even sure he understood—but Kepelo's aloofness repelled him. He wanted to rage and grieve, and he wanted people who would rage and grieve along with him. But there wasn't anyone. Hazel's human friends were surely mourning her, but he barely knew them.

He had no place in the human realm, and the fae realm had killed Hazel. There was nowhere to go. He stared at the river, mute.

"Okay," Tash said. "You want to just sit here?"

He shook his head after a moment.

"Do you think you can still play music, at least?" she said, sounding a bit exasperated.

A glimmer of appeal tugged at the edge of his dark mood. Not that playing music solved the question of where to sleep for the next several nights, but since she asked, he nodded. At least it was something to do.

Tash pulled him to his feet. "Then come on."

Jove and Izzy did look parental in their worry, Rafi noted when they opened their door. Not that Rafi knew such concern from his own parents, but he'd seen that anxiety on Jove's and Izzy's faces when they fretted about their teenage daughter.

It had now been a week on the human side since he'd last seen the band.

It hadn't occurred to him that he could matter enough for them to worry.

"Shit, Rafi." Izzy hugged him. She smelled like sandalwood incense and bread dough.

Jove's large hand settled on Rafi's back. "Fucking awful. Such bullshit."

"At least I have the liuqin," Rafi said. "The one thing of hers I'd want. I'm just…not sure what to do now."

"Come in here." Izzy hooked him by the arm and led him into the practice room. Jove and Tash followed. The house was over a century old, passed down by Izzy's family, and this was one of four ground-floor rooms that faced the interior square courtyard. Aside from the practice room, the courtyard was the only other space in which Rafi had spent much time—the band sometimes practiced there on warm days.

Twenty-four songs were written in green marker on the room's whiteboard.

"How many of these do you know?" Izzy asked.

Rafi scanned the list. "Four, if you mean music and lyrics both. I could probably do the chords for…seven or eight others? I'd have to look up the rest."

"Then how about you stay here for the summer and learn them. And any other songs we need. Rent is free as long as you play gigs, but I'm warning you, there may be a lot of them. Summer's our busy season."

"I'd stay here?" Rafi's gaze moved to the olive-colored couch by the wall, then across the courtyard to rooms he'd never entered.

"Garden cottage, we were thinking," Jove said. "Give you more privacy. There's a room upstairs you could have if you prefer, but it's small and gets hot as Hades in the summer."

"Yes," Rafi said, stunned. "The cottage—of course, that'd be fine. Thank you. So, gigs, the whole summer?"

"Timing being funny like it is," Jove said, "Tom told us a couple days ago that he's taking that job in Amanecer. So that puts us out one mandolin player. Want to sub in for a while? Maybe long haul if it works out?"

Rafi's eyes welled with tears again. *Thank you, Lao Lao.*

He couldn't prove she had anything to do with this gift, but she had always liked to repeat the saying about how the Spirit moved unseen like groundwater, springing up as a fountain to replenish us in our thirst when we least expected it.

"Also," Izzy said, "for a little extra money, there are other jobs we sometimes take. We were thinking you'd be especially useful for them. If you're interested."

Rafi looked at Tash, who leaned on the wall like a long water-lily stem. He'd encountered her in the fae realm on occasion, asking oddly specific questions, tracking down items or animals or people, sometimes bringing a human along—a willing human, unlike those the korreds nabbed.

He'd assumed she'd taken on those deals herself. Seemed there was more to the story.

"Yeah," he said. "Tell me what I can do."

CHAPTER 3

THE THUMPING BASS LINE AND CATCHY CHO-rus of Pulp's "Common People" led Roxana Wei down the footpath toward the concert. Although it was a considerably more stripped-down version than the original, the song took her back to high school, when it had been new and popular.

Her daughter, Ester, likely wouldn't experience high school in Miryoku. The thought set off a tender pang in Roxana's chest. Gods, everything did lately. She had to stop looking at each sunrise, each take-out banh mi, each conversation with a neighbor, as if it was the last in her life. She and Ester were moving, not dying.

Gold and purple lights gleamed through the redwood branches. Moss and needles crunched under her sandals, their scents heavy in the humid air. The audience came into view, heads and arms bounding up and down as they shouted along with the words.

Entering the clearing, Roxana passed a bulletin board with a poster stapled to it, splashed with neon paint and black hand lettering.

Meloncollie, June 29, 8:30 p.m., Gusu Park. FREE. The '90s mangled lovingly, SWP style!

Eidolonia's southwest peninsula, or SWP, couldn't claim the music scene of Dasdemir, the capital; nor even of Port Baleia in the north; but it embraced what it had. Which included Meloncollie, Ester's favorite local group, a nineties cover band.

Whiffs of perfume, sweat, and weed met Roxana's nose as she sauntered around the crowd. She spotted her mother, Amaris, sitting on a blanket and talking to a neighbor. Ester was in the throng in front of the stage, bouncing as she chatted with two other kids. She waved at Roxana, then went on talking. Roxana waved back and continued to wander.

"Common People" ended, and the band swung into Soul Asylum's "Runaway Train."

Meloncollie had four musicians: two humans and two fae, according to Ester. Not that it was easy to tell the difference on sight. In tonight's heat, all of them wore sleeveless tops and sarong-style skirts.

The petite drummer with dreadlocks was Izzy Prior, a human citizen—Roxana knew her from around town. The bassist with long golden-green hair and a matching shimmery skirt was likely a faery. The guitarist in front, who looked like a cross between Lenny Kravitz and Prince, was Jove de Vera, Izzy's spouse. So the musician nearest Roxana, as she wandered toward the stage, was probably fae.

He had a black ponytail, and gold glitter surrounded his eyes. His bare arms and legs gleamed with scales, flashing red and gold. He wore a dark red vest, hanging open, and a black sarong patterned with silver moons and stars. His feet were bare, and he was playing a mandolin.

No—she studied it closer—not a mandolin. One of the Asian string instruments. A pipa, perhaps. She figured she ought to know, since, like many SWP folk, she possessed a fair amount of Asian ancestry. But in terms of personal music experience, she'd never gotten beyond a few ukulele chords herself.

The strings were metal, judging from their gleam. She moved closer, arms folded to keep her elbows from colliding with others. Instrument strings were often steel, but not if the musician was fae or even half-fae—they couldn't abide touching iron, and steel was mostly iron. Brass, then? Bronze? Nickel?

Engrossed, she stared at the strings for at least a full verse and chorus. Then she lifted her gaze, and a jolt shot through her. The musician's eyes were on her, dark and shining among the glitter. He smiled wryly.

Her face went hot. She smiled back, abashed, then spent the rest of the song casually wandering farther from the stage.

The concert ended around ten o'clock. The noise settled down to conversational babble, and folk began strolling home. Park attendants jumped on stage to help the band pack up.

Roxana's ears rang as she returned to the blanket where Ester now sat with Amaris.

"Ready?" Roxana said.

"Yes!" Ester leaped up.

Amaris rose, too, but then someone called, "Mayor Wei!"

"Hey, Hari," Amaris said.

Hari strolled up, wearing a tie-dyed T-shirt advertising his dessert café, Mochi Coco, its lettering barely visible under his bushy gray beard. "Listen, we got to talk about those pipevine fae. Twice this week I haven't been able to get my shop door open because they grew the vines so fast overnight. It's the same with the places next door, and the apartment windows upstairs."

Roxana linked her arm into her mother's. "I apologize, Hari, but I need to borrow my mom. We have to talk to the band about an event."

Amaris patted her hand and released it. "You and Ester go. I'll catch up."

Roxana glanced at Ester, who shrugged. "Okay," Roxana said. "Night, Hari."

"Night, folks!" Hari swung back to Amaris, lifting his hands into debate pose. "Now, we've tried the deals we talked about…"

Roxana and Ester crossed the trampled grass to the stage.

"Poor Nan," Ester said. "People are always doing that to her when we go out."

"She claims she likes it. *I* wouldn't want her job, myself."

"Me neither." Ester brightened as Izzy and Jove came out beside the stage, wiping their faces with towels. "There they are." She hauled Roxana forward.

Izzy greeted them with a smile that widened as she realized who she was talking to. "The mayor's daughter and granddaughter! Of course. I've seen you folks around."

They got onto the band's summer schedule within minutes. "Ester and Roxana Wei, going-away party, August thirty-first, eight p.m., Ti Falls Park." Izzy typed it in on her phone's calendar.

"We'll email you the paperwork as soon as we get home," Jove said.

"Thank you!" Ester gushed.

"Just sorry you're moving," Izzy said. "But Port Baleia's a cool city."

Roxana glanced toward the band's van. A park attendant was shutting its doors. She hadn't seen the mandolin—pipa?—player or the other fae musician. "So it'll be the four of you, like tonight?"

"Yep." Jove followed her glance. "Tash and Rafi are helping take things home. But they'll be there. Or if one of them happens to be out, we'll have a sub."

After saying goodnight to Izzy and Jove, Roxana turned toward home with her mother and daughter.

The air was finally cooling, a marine breeze blowing in. Crickets chirped and will-o'-the-wisps flickered in branches, mingling with the glow of shop signs. A floral scent clung in the air—sylph jasmine, a vigorous native vine, which had a way of climbing all over trees and buildings if one let it.

Roxana yawned. It had been a work day, and she'd been up since seven in the morning.

Ester still chattered, however, leaping between curb and sidewalk. "I'd never talked to her before, but I'd seen her at school. She's a grade above me."

"Ani, is that her name?" Amaris asked. "Jove and Izzy's daughter?"

"Oni," Ester corrected. "She says they live right next to the footpath, the one near the verge. In one of those old houses, the Chinese-style ones. I guess Izzy's ancestors built it. Oni says it's the gray one with the dragon pattern on the wall."

It had been a year or more since Roxana had ventured up there. So many beautiful paths, houses, views, that she took for granted. After August they'd be out of her reach.

"I should take a walk there tomorrow," she mused.

But Ester was already diving into her next flood of words, speculating which songs to request for their party and declaring she'd start a list and stick it on the fridge.

∽

The path was lusher than Roxana remembered. Likely she had last been here in autumn or winter, when the trees were bare. In late June, every bush, tree, vine, and ground cover teemed with growth. Petals from at least four different kinds of flowers carpeted the path.

The sun was setting. Thick forest ran along one side of the path, cool air flowing from its shade. The verge lay that direction, a minute's walk through the undergrowth. Even from here she could see one of the signs marking the border: *Warning! Respect the truce. Do not enter.*

She had never crossed the verge and had no plans to. Roxana respected danger signage.

On the other side of the path stood the old country houses, widely spaced with streams, garden walls, and paths between them. Downhill, the houses and shops grew closer together, Miryoku's rooftops tumbling down the slope before giving way to strawberry fields and tawny seaside grass. Beyond that gleamed the sea, cool blue dappled with sunset orange.

She would see the ocean all the time once they moved to Port Baleia. It sat right on the coast, rather than five miles inland like Miryoku. How often she had dreamed of that, looked forward to it. Tonight it seemed almost unsettling, living in the spray of the waves, barnacles at one's feet, rather than having a comforting buffer of grass and earth between oneself and the sea.

A flame glimmered in the twilight. A little figure hovered near her, at eye level.

"Friend, would you like a guide for walking in the dark?"

Smiling, Roxana shook her head. "No, thank you."

The will-o'-the-wisp bobbed along beside her. "The foxglove fae are dancing tonight. This side of the verge. I'll show you."

"Thank you, friend, but no." In the pocket of her capris, she hooked a finger into the ring of the slim iron chain she carried, just in case.

She had reached the stone wall with the dragon pattern. A dragon-like statue lay on the ground outside it, chin on its paws. No one else was in sight. But if Ester was correct, the gray house beyond this garden belonged to Izzy and Jove. A quick detour would bring her to their door if she truly needed help.

"Come, friend, come," the faery coaxed. "It's pretty tonight, so pretty."

A great flare of light exploded: a bright figure flickering in fire colors beside the stone wall.

Gasping, Roxana stumbled back.

It was a six-foot-tall drake—or at least, drake was her best guess—standing on their hind legs.

"She has declined," the drake said. "Leave her alone."

The will-o'-the-wisp responded with a spitting noise like a drop of water hitting a hot skillet. "But!"

"Go." The drake's voice had the timbre of a human's, with a hint of fiery crackle. "*We* let humans walk safely here, don't we."

The little faery circled a leaf, leaving singe marks on it, then grumbled, "Very well," and streaked away. Their light became one of many in the forest, winking on and off at a distance.

"That was kind of you. I appreciate it." Roxana retreated a few steps back the way she had come. "Have a good evening, friend."

"Wait." The drake's light flickered out, leaving behind a shadowy figure—who then rapidly changed.

The wings retracted, the front legs elongated to arms, the scales became skin, and the snout reshaped into a comely face. A naked person stood before her, nonchalantly dusting off his limbs—or at least, she guessed it to be a man, from the glimpse of anatomy she got before she looked away.

"It's you," he added. "From last night."

She recognized his smile then—and his hands, as he picked up a red silk robe that hung over the gate and put it on.

"The string player," she said.

"You were studying how I played." He took an elastic loop from the robe's pocket and swept his shoulder-length hair into a ponytail. "Something seemed to interest you."

She came forward, now that he was someone known, and someone dressed. "I was trying to figure out what your strings were made of. Nickel?"

He lifted his eyebrows. "They are. Very good."

She set her hand on the gate. "I get along best with metal. As a witch, I mean." The gate was iron, as nearly everyone's gates and fences were, especially those near the verge. He must have gotten adept at avoiding touching such things, if he regularly hung out on the human side. "What is your instrument? It looked like a mandolin, but not quite."

He leaned on the stone wall, arms folded. "Close. It's a liuqin." He pronounced it *lu-cheen*. "It's old and has its issues, but…it's my treasure." He looked across the path. "She wouldn't have done much to you. The will-o'-the-wisp. Would've led you into the sticky mud near the foxgloves, probably, just for laughs. But we shouldn't bother people, even in little ways like that."

"No worries. I wouldn't have gone. So *are* the foxglove fae dancing to-night?"

"Haven't checked. But she said it, so it must be true."

The gate's hinge felt clogged, slow. A focused shot of Roxana's magic, and the rust and dirt shivered off and fell in flakes to the ground.

His gaze tracked the motion, and his mouth curved up in acknowledgment.

"Did Izzy and Jove tell you?" Roxana asked. "You'll be playing for us at the end of August."

"Oh, that's you? The going-away party?"

"My daughter requested Meloncollie specially."

"The mayor's family. Quite an honor." He placed one hand on his heart. "My name is Rafi." He paused, then extended the hand to her.

"Roxana." She expected his skin to be hot, given he was by all appearances a fire faery, but his hand felt cool and dry. "What issues does your instrument have? Anything to do with metal?"

"Actually yes. It's the fine tuners, the little ones at the bottom. They—do you want to come see? Easier than describing. It's just right in here. No sticky mud or other dangers, I promise." He angled his head toward the gate.

A small stone house stood in the garden. Plum trees and jasmine vines interlaced so thickly they almost hid it, but a string of golden lights along the cottage's porch roof shone through to reveal its location.

A woman called something, and a younger voice—presumably Oni—answered from closer by, "I'm in the courtyard, Mom."

It was surely safe to step in, with the family so near, and besides, Roxana felt drawn to any small problem in metal she might be able to fix. She nodded to Rafi, who wrapped the robe's silk sleeve around his hand in a fluidly habitual motion, pulled open the gate, and led her in.

The path to the cottage was a tunnel through bushes and trees. The passage smelled rich and green for the few seconds she was in it, leaves brushing her shoulders and hips, then she emerged in a clearer space. The garden still burgeoned with vines, flowers, and knee-high grass, but now she could see across to the main house. Its windows and doors stood open in the warm night, light spilling out. The statues on the roof, of animals and fae, stood silhouetted against the twilight, giving the place the air of a stately manor.

The cottage in front of her, in contrast, had a covered porch so small it probably couldn't have even fit a chair. Rafi cleared the two wooden steps in one barefooted leap, told her, "Have a seat," and darted inside.

He was back out again seconds later as Roxana was settling onto the top step. He slid down opposite her, robe perilously close to flapping open. With typical fae nonchalance, he didn't seem to notice—though to be fair, it was a nonchalance shared with many humans, considering the number of nude-friendly beaches and naked festival performers on the Southwest Peninsula.

He swiveled the liuqin so its end faced her. "It's these two." He tapped the outermost screws, which secured two of the four strings. "They keep loosening, and I go flat."

"It's beautiful." The signature energy of nickel resonated when Roxana touched the strings. The soundboard was pale wood, its back painted shiny red, and four ornately carved pegs in a matching red protruded from the narrow neck.

"It is. I wish I could keep it in perfect condition."

It was odd, the things fae could and couldn't do. Compared to the magic of human witches, fae magic seemed nearly limitless when it came to manipulating the natural elements. But when faced with human inventions, they often found themselves stymied.

"Let's see." She touched the screws, sending in a thread of magic to feel out their shape and depth. They were brass, and loose, slipping too easily. "It's not so much a metal problem. It's the wood having worn away around them. I'm not as good with wood, but if it's just a tiny bit like this, and if I get the metal to cooperate too…"

She transferred her fingers to one screw and gave it another push of magic. The screw's threads swelled, biting into the wood, which expanded a little. The change wasn't even large enough to see from the outside, but now the screw held. She made the same adjustment to the other, then said, "Try that."

Rafi swung the liuqin into playing position and plucked the string. It sang out a clear, high note. He picked the string beside it to compare notes, adjusted the tuning screw, then danced his thumb between them in a tremolo. "Ha." In triumph, he tuned the other repaired string and finished with a frolic of picked notes. "It's perfect. You've made my night."

"Metal that sings." She cupped her chin in her palm, admiring the shine of the nickel in the soft porch lights. "I love it. I should work with musical instruments more often."

"You should. We need a luthier here in town. I've had other matter-witches do this, but the fix always wears off."

"So will this. But it ought to hold for, I don't know, a month? Maybe less, if you're playing a lot."

"I'll bring it right back to you when it needs redoing." Then his smile subsided into neutrality. "But I forgot. You're moving soon."

"Mm-hm. But not till the end of summer."

He strummed three chords in a cheerful progression. "In any case, I owe you. What might you want? Something from the fae realm?"

Roxana's nature itched to turn aside such offers, give without receiving whenever possible. But fae tended to get agitated if you tried to leave a deal lopsided. Setting her elbows on her knees, she pondered the indigo dark of the tree tunnel. "Would you be able to get fae-realm metals?"

"Of course. How much? Enough to make an enchanted knife? A helmet, perhaps?"

She smiled. "Nah, just small amounts, any kind. I hear there's copper and cobalt in the mountains."

"Tin and silver and iron too. Possibly others."

"I wouldn't ask you to get iron, of course. Any of those would be wonderful. Really, even tiny amounts, like the size of a grain of rice."

He laughed. "What could you do with so little?"

"Jewelry. I'm only good on the small scale, really. Those construction-worker matter-witches who can fling up walls? Not me. Never will be."

"Ah, but they're often less precise."

"That's the trade-off. I think of myself as a miniaturist."

"I see. If you add spells to this jewelry, fae-realm materials would hold them better."

"Yep. But the metals are hard to get hold of. Expensive. Which is why I only ask for a small amount."

"As it happens, I'm going across the verge tomorrow." He straightened his posture. "I grant you this deal."

The words were fae in custom, but he looked remarkably human tonight.

The gold eye glitter from the performance was gone—it could have been glamour or simple cosmetics—and his eyes were the same dark brown as the average Eidolonian human's, with charcoal-thick brows. Whether his arms were still covered in shining scales, she couldn't tell, as his robe hid them.

"It's gracious of you," she answered.

Rafi set aside the liuqin and stood. "Do Jove and Izzy have your number? I can text you when I'm back with your metals."

Roxana stood too. "They do."

"Can never tell how long I'll be, going across. The time variance."

"It's all right. No rush. Well—I should get home."

They walked back through the tunnel, and Rafi opened the gate. "I'll escort you, if you like. In case any other nuisances of my acquaintance appear."

"No need, I'm not going far."

"Then I'll see you when I return, Roxana Wei."

She nodded. "It was good to meet you."

Orange light flickered beneath the skin of his palm as he waved goodbye. Two stars twinkled above him. Roxana waved back, drew a breath of jasmine-drenched air, and walked home.

∽

After Roxana left, Rafi stood at the garden wall, resting his forearms on its top. The stone was still warm from baking in the sun all afternoon.

In the month since his grandmother's death, he'd spent several after-dark hours out here, placing himself on guard. He'd shooed away a grand total of three fae pestering humans, none particularly dangerous. No fair feasters or goblins. No korreds. Sinister fae could of course be elsewhere nearby, enchanting people into oblivion.

There were verge guards whose job it was to look out for trouble. A witch and a faery working together, in most cases; such a station stood at every mile-marker along the verge. But Izzy and Jove's house sat at the midway point between the two nearest guard posts, and a lot could happen in the space of half a mile, as Rafi well knew.

So though his presence wouldn't make much difference in the korreds' overall behavior, he kept watch. He felt restless if he didn't at least try.

He hadn't expected *her* to show up.

Audience members at gigs often gazed avidly at him and the rest of the band, but Roxana had been different—scrutinizing his liuqin, arms folded, seemingly not even trying to get his attention and not aware he noticed her. He'd grown curious: what captivated her? What did she want?

Then she had met his gaze, her mouth had untwisted into that meek smile, and she had ambled away, leaving him wondering.

Now the mystery was solved. He inhaled the night air, his mouth lifting at the corners. Sourcing fae-realm metals so she could make enspelled jewelry: what a particularly pleasant errand.

"Rafi?" Izzy's voice floated across the garden.

He turned as she came up, a silhouette against the lights of the house. "Hey," he said.

"Got everything you need for tomorrow?"

"Yep. Standard mail run, sounds like."

"Good." Izzy picked a clump of moss off the wall. "You know, if it gets lonely out here, you could move into the house. Or just come hang out more. We'd love to see you."

"It's fine," he said—probably too quickly, judging from the way her hand stilled. "It's a luxury, having my own place," he explained. "Not that it's mine. But a space without, you know, fae wandering through and making noise at all hours. I'm liking it."

"All right. We just want you to know you're welcome to come in. Don't want you to feel like a second-class citizen."

"Well, I am that," he said lightly. "But that's how I want it."

She nudged his arm. "Hey, Oni's going to start some vampire film in a few minutes. Come watch if you like. I'm making cheese popcorn. That seals the deal, right?"

"It does," he admitted. "I'll get dressed and come in."

She laughed, noticing the robe. "Good call. See you in a bit."

CHAPTER 4

A TEXT LIT UP ROXANA'S PHONE ON THE FOL-
lowing Saturday morning.

Hello Roxana, it's Rafi. I'm back and have things for you! Where shall I bring them?

Alone in the kitchen, in the house she and Ester shared with Roxana's parents, she beamed and set down her mug of green tea.

Hello! she typed. *I'm going into town in a bit. Would 11:00 this morning work? Could meet you at the Serpent Ave Bridge, near the amphitheater.*

His response appeared within a minute. *Yes that works. See you soon.*

He was waiting for her under the palm trees at the theater's entrance. Today he looked like any citizen in casual summer mode: blue T-shirt with Meloncollie's logo, baggy red drawstring trousers that ended below the knee, and clean setta sandals in hues of indigo and straw.

"Good morning," she greeted.

"Good morning." He swung a canvas bag off his shoulder and opened its flap. On the tan skin of his upper arms, scales glimmered in scarlet, gold, and black. He drew out a smaller cloth bag, dusty and stuffed full, and tugged loose its drawstring. "Hold out your hands."

He tipped the bag. Treasure spilled into her cupped palms.

To look at, they were nothing but chunks of rock. But power streamed from them in three, no, four different flavors, fizzing into her wrists and up to her shoulders.

Shaking the ore from palm to palm, she picked out the signature magic of each. "Oh my gods. Tin, cobalt, copper...silver! Rafi, this is amazing. This is way too much."

"Not at all. I know a friendly stone giant. Easy to get up into the mountains and smash some rocks loose, with help like that." His voice turned anxious. "Is it even enough to make anything from?"

"Are you kidding? This is worth—I don't know, probably thousands of lira, if I turned it all into jewelry." She closed her hands around the rocks and held them to her heart. "Bring me your liuqin anytime for the rest of my life if it needs fixing. I mean it. It's on me."

Eyes shining with pleasure, he gazed down at her. He was easily a foot taller than her. "I will, then." He held open the dusty cloth bag. "Here. To keep them in."

She carefully poured the rocks back in and took the bag.

"I suppose all the metal on the island used to be fae-realm metal," he remarked.

"Yep. All those amazing charms that witches like Rosamund Highvalley made, back in the 1700s, probably packed such a punch because they were mostly fae-realm material. But once the verge got moved back, and humans stayed on their own side and stopped crossing it so much—well. It may mean our natural resources are less saturated with power now, but it's probably for the best."

He nodded. His black hair slipped down to shadow half his face. "Less accidental enchantment. Less…death."

She tied the bag and tucked it into her straw shopping bag. "I already have ideas for what to make. I've been thinking about options."

Rafi focused on her again. "Does it matter which metal you use? I wasn't sure. That's why I got a few kinds."

"It can matter. The tin should be good for confidence and focus, though it's adaptable. Copper's good for things like love, creativity, harmony. And I could melt it with some of the tin and make bronze, which might hold a spell even stronger. Cobalt I've hardly ever worked with, so that'll be interesting. Silver—ah, silver's wonderful. Great for healing and calming."

"Is that why silver jewelry is so common?"

"It's why *magic* silver jewelry is so common. In the rest of the world, silver makes good jewelry because it's affordable, bendable, strong, and shiny." She stopped, her face warming. "Sorry. I get excited about metals."

"I like it. I haven't heard anyone talk about them quite like that." He tilted his head and lifted his fingers as if sketching an outline of her. "I wouldn't be surprised if you had earth fae ancestry, with that magic."

"Rumor has it my great-great-grandmother was a gnome." Roxana spread her arms at her sides. "Thus the physique: short and round. It's the family joke, anyway."

Rafi grinned. "What will you make first, then, metalsmith?"

The title pleased her. It carried genuine respect; he didn't seem to be teasing. "Well…sorry, you probably have somewhere to be? I don't mean to take up your whole morning."

"I have nowhere to be," he assured.

"Okay. I have errands in town. Want to walk along?"

They crossed the footbridge, a red wooden arch with Aria Creek rushing below. The rainbow scales of fish and water fae streaked past beneath the surface.

"First," Roxana said, "I'll make one piece each for Ester, my mom, and my dad. Also my best friend Satsuki. Her dad died recently. She could use a grief-soothing charm." They stepped out at the bridge's opposite end. Shops topped with apartments lined the street.

"This is your job? You make charms to help people?"

"Only my side job at the moment. I work in IT, fixing metal tech parts. But mental health jewelry *will* be my job in Port Baleia. I'll be working in a shop while studying at the art school to refine my skills. The shop owner is a friend of mine. She'll be ecstatic if we can sell fae-realm metal pieces there."

They strolled past the Chilean bakery. The smells of dulce de leche and empanadas wafted out. "No enchanted knives to dole out curses?" Rafi said.

She laughed. "Illegal. And I don't forge weapons. Though these metals would make potent ones."

"Witches can't make enspelled weapons? What about those iron bracelets, for prisoners?"

"Well, yes. The government makes those. Usually to block witches from accessing magic when they've used it to hurt people. There's also the empathy shackles, for people with sociopathic or narcissistic disorders, who've committed crimes."

"It gives them empathy?" he asked. "To make them understand what they've done?"

"Exactly. And do it less in future, ideally. Because with their disorders, they can't grasp otherwise why their behavior was cruel."

He hooked a tendril of vine around his finger. It uncurled as he pulled it, then sprang back into its spiral against the brick wall. "I know of fae who could use one of those."

"Well, different rules apply over there."

"Too few rules, I sometimes think." He flicked a scrap of leaf from his finger. "But you make nicer charms. To calm people who feel troubled. Things like that?"

"Things like that."

"Sounds useful. I'd like that. Sleeping better, taming my thoughts."

She allowed several paces before answering. "You're welcome to try them, but I don't know how well they'd work on fae. Although maybe with these metals…" She was under the impression fae didn't get all that anxious, however, and didn't need to sleep much, nor had trouble sleeping if they chose to.

He cast her a shy smile. "All right. You were good to my liuqin, therefore I trust you. Don't tell anyone, but I'm only half fae. I'm counted human."

Her mouth fell open. "But—I saw you—"

"Endo-witch. With what the legal folk call 'rare witch abilities.'"

"A form-changer." She kept her voice soft, more in wonder than discretion. Fae could change their forms easily, on the whole, but it was rare for humans to be able to do so to the degree of becoming an entirely different shape or size.

"It's simpler to pass as fae, since I'm not a citizen on the books. My upbringing was…atypical. The band knows, but most townsfolk don't. I'm sorry for the deception." He gave her a hesitant smile.

"But how are you…no, sorry, it's all right. I won't tell anyone. Thank you for trusting me."

He seemed to anticipate at least one of her questions. "I grew up in the fae realm. Both my parents are half human but counted fae. One's a drake, the other's a korred. I ended up counted human."

"A drake," she said. "That's what I assumed you were."

He turned his arm to show the scales. "These take no effort. Part of my default form. But I have to expend a lot of energy for proper fire form. Even then, I'm not really a drake—can't get as big as my mother, can't fly or set fire to things. I can just glow and move fast."

"I felt heat when you changed, on the footpath."

"Not enough to burn anything."

"Nothing from your korred side?"

"Can turn my skin to stone, become a statue essentially. You saw me like that on the path, before I flared up."

Puzzled, she thought back. "The dragon statue? Wait, that was you?"

He was grinning. "You'll notice it wasn't there when you left."

"I did not notice, in fact."

"It's my gargoyle form. That's what the band calls it. I end up looking kind of like a drake, but in stone."

She glanced up at the phoenix painted on the side of Starchime Music as they neared it. "Does your mother belong to Kepelo's haunt, then?"

"My mother *is* Kepelo."

Roxana's feet paused. "The mightiest fae leader around? Is your mother?"

"Around *here*," he said lightly. "She's hardly a Sia Fia, say. Or an Arlanuk."

Those were fae who ruled much larger haunts in the center of the island. They had held their territories since before humans had stumbled upon Eidolonia in the 1700s.

"Even so," Roxana began.

"Sorry, hang on. Delivery here." Rafi stopped at Starchime and swung his pack down. He got out a few thick turquoise cards, folded and tied shut with red elastic cords: chantagrams, the generic blank kind you could record magical video messages onto.

He selected one and stashed the others in his pack. "Shouldn't be long. Come in if you like." He entered the shop.

The iron-barred glass door was propped open, but to enter, you had to pass through a beaded curtain of tiny bronze bells. As Roxana slipped through, they stirred in a whispery jingle.

"Hey, Meg." Rafi strolled to the counter.

"Rafi! You made good time." The person behind the counter had wide jowls, a wider smile, and truly impressively wide hair, frizzy and bleached orange. Roxana knew them casually, mainly from the various times Ester had tried learning an instrument—rented from this shop—and then given up on it.

Rafi gave Meg the card. "All seemed well. She's looking forward to the next festival." He spoke gently.

Meg pressed their lips together and blinked rapidly as they took the card. "Thank you," they said to Rafi. "Really, thank you. I—I want to see this right away. I'll be in touch again, all right?"

"Of course."

Meg hurried off into the back room with the chantagram.

Rafi turned to Roxana. "We can go," he said quietly.

They slipped back out onto the street.

"I take jobs sometimes as a cross-verge message carrier," he explained, "since it's hard for humans to reach people in the fae realm safely. There's a faery Meg likes to stay in touch with."

Roxana nodded, still feeling tender from witnessing Meg's reaction. "Children, parents, friends, lovers. I've heard stories."

"I'd do it for free—and I have—but if people want to pay…well, turns out living on this side requires *money*. What's that about?" His voice had lightened again. "Speaking of which. You have errands?"

"Yes—the Bazaar. For groceries."

"I love the Bazaar." Liveliness quickened his step. "When I first saw it, as a kid, it seemed like a magical treasure house."

"Even to someone who lived in the fae realm? Which is literally magical?"

"The fae realm is dangerous-magical. I'd have been dead a hundred times over by now if it wasn't for Kepelo." He didn't say it breezily, but not grimly either. Just a fact of life.

Roxana shivered. "She must be a good mother."

"I'm not sure. I didn't see a lot of mothers to compare with, until later."

They turned down a brick-paved alley leading to the Bazaar. Chatter, music, and the scents of crepes and steamed buns flowed down the passageway.

"She didn't protect me in person," Rafi added. "Not much, anyway. It was a deal she put in place between her and all the other fae whose territories border hers. Kill Rafi, or hurt him irreparably, and she takes over your haunt."

"Is this deal still in force?"

"As long as I live. Which, to a fae point of view, seems like it won't be very long. Probably why they agreed to it."

Hard to know how to respond to that. This was easily the most unusual conversation she'd had all year.

She tilted her head toward the soapmaker's stall. "Here's where I get shampoo. Come help me pick some."

CHAPTER 5

YOU LIKE MINT? SOME FOLKS FIND IT TOO strong." The soapmaker, a man with a sleekly waxed mustache, held out a blue glass bottle with a green label.

Rafi sniffed it. A bright burst of peppermint hit his nose. "Mmm. I'd eat that."

Roxana and the soapmaker laughed. She sniffed the bottle too. "It is nice. But I'm still leaning toward the grapefruit."

While Roxana got out money to buy the grapefruit shampoo, Rafi glanced around the Bazaar. Though most of the stalls had changed since his childhood visits here with Hazel, it retained the same atmosphere: colorful awnings, music from a tiny corner stage—a solitary cello player today—and the smells of fruit, roasted meat, soap, incense, and sweets. Buildings with mural-covered walls enclosed it on all five sides, and a loose ceiling of leaves interlaced overhead, thanks to the plants on the green roofs. He even recognized many of the people now, from concerts or errands or—

His blood froze, then flashed hot.

Korreds. Two of them, Oxlock and another of Brogyo's idiots. They were in human form, all gleaming muscles and chiseled jaws, strutting through the Bazaar in one-shouldered black tunics that ended at mid-thigh.

Rafi stepped behind the stall, next to the soapmaker. The fragrant wares would mask Rafi's scent. Even so, he grasped his magic and changed his face, broadening and aging it, pushing a bit into his scalp to turn his hair gray.

Roxana and the soapmaker looked at him in surprise. "Please just let me stand here a moment," he said, soft enough that only the two of them could hear.

They followed his gaze and spotted the korreds, but still didn't understand—they looked at Rafi again.

His heart was pounding. "They can't be trusted."

"Korreds, right?" the soapmaker said, quieter too. "My best friend's had them come on to her pretty strong at events sometimes."

"They've done worse than that." Rafi watched them stroll through the market, tossing greetings and leers to people. If they lured someone away, even of the person's own free will, would Rafi's warning be enough to stop them? Or would he only make things worse?

The soapmaker gave Roxana her change. She tucked the bottle into her bag, then paused, waiting for Rafi.

A glimmer of green flitted through the crowd—two figures converging on the korreds. Shellycoats, Tash's people. They'd taken human forms similar to Tash's, with algae-green hair and clothes covered in rattling sequins.

They struck up a conversation with the korreds, got them laughing. A minute later, lured by whatever diversion the water folk offered, the korreds darted away with them. The ground shook faintly in their wake, and a mist blew through the Bazaar, smelling of river mud. The people in the market-place paused to look after them, then resumed their business.

Rafi unclenched the magic he'd been pumping into his appearance. It drained away, changing him back to his natural look and taking a fair amount of his energy with it.

"Thank you," he said to the soapmaker as he stepped out.

"Sure, friend, no problem." The man smiled uncertainly. Rafi had surely behaved like someone embroiled in an inter-fae feud, something no sane human wanted to get in the middle of.

Rafi moved back to Roxana's side. "Anything else to get?" he asked her.

"Produce and noodles to buy. Then lunch. Those steamed buns are calling to me. Want some? My treat."

The ache in his tired bones eased a little. "If you're sure," he said. "Thank you."

They bought their food, then snagged a tiny table along a wall.

"You said your father was a korred," Roxana finally said.

"Yeah." Holding the steamed bun in its paper wrapping, Rafi blew on it to cool it. The korreds' appearance had stolen his appetite, but he needed to replenish his energy and was working up to taking a bite. "I do not get along with his side of the family."

"They treated you badly?"

"They treat most humans badly. I've been avoiding them. But I also feel like I have to keep watch on them. They've…taken people, you know."

"I recall hearing such things about Brogyo, from long ago."

"He's the child of an early settler of Miryoku. From the eighteen-tens. My grandmother looked up the dates once. His mother was human, born of Japanese immigrants. Had a liaison with a korred when she was a teenager. The baby, Brogyo, was counted fae, so she did as she was supposed to and gave him over to them to be brought up." He took a small bite of the bun, tasting juicy spiced pork inside. "All he can tell is true stories, like most fae. He liked telling this one. I heard it a lot."

"Did he ever see his mother again? I don't remember the details."

"Oh yes. After some years, he went into Miryoku to find her and found out she'd had more children and was also a talented witch who'd crafted some of the city's buildings and bridges. Brogyo got obsessed. He demanded she give him and his korred friends one of the buildings for them to have, as their property. Of course she couldn't. They belonged to the city, people were using them. The way he puts it is, she hardened her heart against him and was ungenerous. When I got older, I could see, from the human point of view, that he was being incredibly unreasonable."

"And scary," Roxana said.

"Right. So—since his mother wouldn't give him attention, and neither would anyone else in town, he started to lurk and steal and cause trouble. Some of the other korreds didn't approve. It led to a rift. Brogyo and his friends formed their own haunt, and eventually Brogyo's antics led the townsfolk to judge all the korreds the same. To…what's that saying, about a brush?"

"Tar them with the same brush."

"That's it. The nicer korreds got tired of the drama and moved out to the mountains. They're still there. We hardly ever see them. So Brogyo took over the whole korred haunt along the verge, and he's been their leader ever since."

"Behaving badly for over two hundred years."

"Yeah." He stared at the bun in his hands, his appetite waning again. "A part of the story he especially loved telling was what happened later, when one of his mother's human daughters was grown up. His half-sister. Brogyo managed to get her alone one day and bring her back to the haunt." His fingers clenched in the crackling paper wrapper. "With the magic, she was barely conscious. They got her pregnant and kept her until she gave birth. The baby was counted fae, so they kept him and let her go. Her mind and body were wrecked. Her family was devastated. Apparently it took a massive diplomatic effort to keep the town from attacking the korred haunt in retribution—payments of fae-realm gold, threats, counterthreats, deals, everything."

"How have I forgotten this piece of history?" Roxana said, shocked.

"These things happen along the verge. One person now and then, it isn't uncommon. It doesn't change the course of the country." His mouth formed a bitter smile. "And guess who that fae-counted baby was? My father. Sminu."

She sucked in a soft breath. "Oh."

"It might mean Brogyo is my grandfather. But as he put it when telling the story, 'We don't really know whose it was. So many of us *had* her.' When I was a little kid and told this story to my grandmother, I remember I asked her was she an endo-witch, too, because otherwise how did she make her face turn so pale like that?" He huffed out a humorless laugh. "That's when I realized there must have been some things I hadn't quite understood about the story."

Roxana looked stricken, and guilt twisted his belly. Clearly he still had no idea how to pick appropriate subjects when talking to humans.

But she answered, "I'm so sorry you've had to deal with them. They haven't done similar things recently, have they?"

He lowered his eyes. He couldn't dump even more trauma into the conversation—his grandmother's death, his own beatings, the stories of any of the other victims. "They have," he merely said. "There's not much we can do. Which is why I'm on this side of the verge now."

"Playing liuqin with humans. When did you learn that? I'm guessing not with the korreds."

He laughed a little. "No. The liuqin belonged to my grandmother. Originally it was *her* grandparents', from China. Lao Lao—my grandma—said it came from there. An antique."

"No wonder it's so beautiful."

Roxana's eyes were on the amber side of brown. Gold lantern-shaped earrings gleamed under the waves of her black hair. Forged by her? Had she enchanted them with a spell to—what? What could someone so capable need?

A strange longing pulled at him: to stay with her all afternoon, learn to be as centered as she was, gift her with fae-realm metals or anything else that would make her light up in wonder the way she had when he'd tipped the rocks into her hands.

Rafi slid his glance aside. "I have a couple more chantagrams to deliver. Come along if you like, or…I guess you probably have to get home."

"I can spare half an hour." She stacked their lunch papers and swept them up. "I want to hear how a cross-verge kid ended up playing for Meloncollie."

Pulling Hazel by the hand, the liuqin's strap looped around his shoulder, Rafi raced to the stage in Heron Park. He'd grown as tall as Hazel lately, and his limbs were too long for the rest of him. His shoulders no longer fit into the two shirts he'd previously owned, so on this visit Hazel had given him three more. He wore one tonight, a blue-and-white plaid flannel, with a pair of khaki trousers cinched with a woven belt.

It was late January, Earth Festival, and she had insisted Rafi put on rain boots, too, even though he was used to going barefoot all year. Chilly toes were easily fixed by a warming boost of magic, in his experience. He had humored her and put on the boots.

Under a tent whose edges dripped drizzle, the local band Depeach Mode had just launched into "Take on Me." Rafi maneuvered himself and his laughing grandmother to the front of the crowd.

On the days he spent with Hazel, he frequently toyed with her radio. Memorizing lyrics to popular songs was both a pleasure and a useful skill, as he would later sing them to the fae if he needed to repay favors or simply offer entertainment.

With the liuqin lessons his grandmother had been giving him, he had figured out the chords for many of the songs too. He swung the instrument into his hands and began strumming along. The singer and guitarist—Jove de Vera, according to Hazel—caught Rafi's eye and winked.

"They do all eighties covers," Hazel said in Rafi's ear. "Bet you'll know some of these."

He knew nearly all of them, thanks to the radio. Strumming chords, he swung back and forth, happily lost in rhythm and harmony. Everyone in the crowd was moving to the same beat, singing the same words, and he was a part of it.

Then his elbow smacked someone. The man swiveled to scowl at him.

"Get your ukulele out of here," he told Rafi. The smell of alcohol permeated his breath. "You're not the act."

Plunged into an ice bath of humiliation, Rafi stopped playing. "It's a liuqin," he said, barely audible over the opening measures of the next song.

The man flicked his hand toward the street. "Go! You're in the way."

"Hold up a sec," an amplified voice said, and the music stopped.

Rafi turned to the stage, a few seconds after everyone else, and blinked to find Jove reaching toward him.

"You know the chords to this one?" Jove asked him—away from the mic, just one person speaking to another. "'Come On Eileen,' Dexys Midnight Runners?"

Rafi nodded, stunned.

"Well, climb on up here."

Rafi glanced at the other members of the band—bearded mandolinist, water-fae bassist, pregnant drummer. They were all smiling at him too. Well, the faery wasn't exactly, but shellycoats didn't smile often in general, and at least she didn't look hostile.

"Go on," Hazel whispered.

His heart thumped harder than the bass drum. Stone patches surfaced across his chest. But he could still move, so he took Jove's hand and climbed up, then turned to face the crowd—who, unaccountably, cheered. The drunk man smirked and looked away.

"This is not the Royal Opera House, in case you hadn't noticed," Jove said into the mic, though he was addressing Rafi. "We're pretty casual. Volunteers welcome. All right, from the top!"

They restarted "Come On Eileen." Rafi's trembling fingers somehow played the right chords, or close enough. It didn't matter much—his liuqin wasn't amplified like their instruments, so he doubted anyone except the nearest people could hear him. That helped him relax, and at Jove's invitation he stayed on stage through the rest of the set.

"What's your name?" Jove asked before the last song.

"Rafi. From Kepelo's realm." It was what Hazel had taught him to say. Not a lie, but enough of a misdirection to let people assume he was fae. The lawfolk got anxious about wanderers and would try to complicate his life.

Jove announced into the mic, "A special hand for our guest string player, Rafi!"

The cheers washed through him, lighting up a glow in his skin. Sure, it was only seventy or eighty people at a free concert in the park, and yes, his singing or storytelling performances in Kepelo's or Sminu's realms had met with adulation at times too. But these were humans. His own people, not that they knew it. This was new and precious, and now that he'd tasted it, he wasn't sure how he would live without it.

"Drop by anytime," said Izzy, the drummer, while packing up after the last song. "We really do welcome volunteers."

As the months and years wheeled past, he brought the liuqin to their concerts whenever he was in town at the right time. He grew up, Jove and Izzy's baby Oni was born, and Depeach Mode became Meloncollie as nineties nostalgia replaced eighties nostalgia.

The band learned early on that Rafi was a wanderer, not a faery, maybe getting the tipoff from Tash the shellycoat, who seemed to know everything about local fae and humans. None of them minded. Izzy shrugged and said, "Music is music."

Then one year when Tom the mandolinist was out of town more than usual, they asked Rafi if he was interested in stepping in as a temporary substitute.

It was love, of a sort—the beat thumping in his bones in tandem with his fellow humans, his voice soaring with theirs, and the infinite melodies that four little liuqin strings could make under his fingers. And even though that offer from the band had become, after Hazel's death, a long-term paid position complete with cottage lodging, a sizable portion of Rafi's identity was still that half-grown kid at Earth Festival: convinced he was a mere intruder, but too enraptured to step away.

∽

Roxana walked with Rafi while he delivered chantagrams. On the way he told her a short version of how he'd joined Meloncollie, and she found the follow-up questions spilling from her mouth as if she were interviewing him.

How old was he now?

He had no idea. Time spent on one side of the verge didn't add up to the same amount on the other, and he'd crossed back and forth a lot. But he guessed he was at least thirty—his Lao Lao had a picture of him as a little kid in the late nineties.

Had he seen his grandmother often, before she died? (Rafi hadn't said how she died, but Roxana didn't ask that.)

Not often enough. He cast his gaze down as he said it. She had opted against enlisting Cross-Verge Child Services to arrange meetings when he was a kid, to avoid their finding out he was a mortal and thus should be under the jurisdiction of the human realm. He and his grandmother tried setting their own times to meet, but the time variance between realms made it hard to keep appointments.

When did he learn to read, if he grew up in the fae realm? Was that from his grandmother too?

Yes, he said. She also taught him music and math and a scattering of other subjects.

He delivered his final chantagram, at the teal door of a townhouse. A few minutes later, at a quiet residential intersection, she stopped and nodded down the street. "My house is that way. This was fun. I'm excited to get started with these metals."

"It *was* fun," he agreed. "You're good at listening."

"It's all fascinating to me. I've never met a…human who grew up in the fae realm before." She avoided the common word that had almost come to her tongue.

"Wanderer." He smiled. "It's okay, you can say it."

"I've heard some people claim it's offensive. I wasn't sure."

The sound of flip-flops smacking the paving stones came up the street, accompanied by Ester calling, "Mom, Mom, Mom!"

Rafi looked over swiftly.

Roxana turned. "Hey, Ester. You know Rafi."

"Yes. You're amazing! Oh, and you live with Oni, who I was just texting."

"Well…" Rafi demurred, perhaps to dispute that he didn't exactly live *with* Oni's family, but Ester plunged onward.

"When we go to the beach, can Oni come?" she asked Roxana.

"Uh, sure. I don't know what day it'll be, but yes, if she wants."

"Yay!" Ester pivoted to Rafi again. "You should come too."

Awkwardness colored Roxana's laugh. "If you—I mean, if you don't have anything better to do, once we choose a day…"

"I love the beach," he said promptly.

"Great. I'll text you."

"I look forward to it. Thank you for your company today." The breeze sent a loose piece of his hair dancing across the corner of his mouth.

Strange thoughts floated through her mind: *If I weren't leaving, if I were one-tenth as adventurous as he is, if he were interested…*

She shook them off. None of those things were the case, so why ponder it?

"The pleasure was mine," she said, and meant it, which was somewhat astonishing. She often found new acquaintances more stressful than pleasant.

"See you then!" Ester told Rafi. "Mom, let's go pick a day, I want to tell Oni."

CHAPTER 6

NATURALLY RAFI WAS ONLY BEING NICE, Roxana kept thinking during the next two days. By now she had pulled all the fae-realm metal out of its surrounding pieces of rock and made several charms, but had held off on contacting him to share her progress. Surely he didn't really want to come play on the beach with two kids and a mom.

Rerouting her mind to her job, she watched her trainee, bent over a motherboard, restore damaged connector pins with a touch of magic. The tablet screen came to life with a glow. Her trainee pumped both hands in the air.

"Nice." Roxana smiled. "Guess this means I *can* take a day off like you all keep telling me."

And wouldn't inviting Rafi, after promising they would, be the least she could do?

She went to the office's deck, looking east over Miryoku. Heart beating, she texted him.

Hi! We're thinking of Wednesday afternoon to go to the beach. I'll be driving the girls, so if you want to come, you could ride along.

Band rehearsal, a trip into the fae realm—something would surely prevent him. Telling herself so, she watched gulls wheel around each other in the sky.

But in a couple of minutes he answered, *Yes thank you! I'd love that.*

Great! Will pick you both up at 1.

⚮

She actually invited him. The sentence repeated itself in dazzled disbelief in Rafi's mind.

He'd been castigating himself since their walk. She probably thought him eccentric at best, off-putting at worst. (*Pitiful mortal, what use are you?* His father's voice—or that of Brogyo, who used similar terms—had a way of surfacing in such moods.) It was a shame, because he had enjoyed talking with Roxana in a way he hadn't enjoyed anything in recent months except music.

In his younger years, while sporadically hanging out in Miryoku, he'd told a select few human lovers or friends about his fae-realm life, but telling them had never felt entirely good. They had rushed in with reactions, advice, judgments.

Roxana had just listened. Absorbed his strange jumble of information like a tranquil pond into which he could drop pebbles without it throwing them back at him. (There *were* such retaliatory ponds in the fae realm.) He had spent the days after their walk wishing he could talk to her again, learn more about her, while feeling fatalistically sure it wouldn't happen.

But on Wednesday she and Ester came to pick him and Oni up, and she was smiling brightly in sunglasses and a gauzy teal shirt that fluttered around her in the breeze.

Twenty minutes of cruising downhill between orchards, squash patches, and berry fields, and they arrived at Zamami Beach.

"Sand's easier without shoes," Roxana announced in the parking lot. Standing beside the car, she whisked off her sandals and deposited them in her straw bag alongside the towels and food.

"I'm used to barefoot anyway." Rafi stuffed his setta sandals through the passenger-side window of the car, which they'd left open a few inches. Then he ambled over and took the bag from her. "I'll carry that."

Ester and Oni had already ditched their shoes and pelted over the sand dune, each clutching a bundled-up kite.

Roxana and Rafi clambered over, too, feet sliding in the sand, beach grass scraping their ankles. At the top of the dune, a wind smelling of seaweed and ocean swept over them. The beach below was a huge, flat crescent. White-capped surf ruffled against turquoise water that shaded into darker blue as it stretched to the horizon. Slanting strata of green-topped black headlands framed the beach.

The girls set the kites by a log and waded into the fringes of the waves. From this distance, Oni was a slim, dancing figure with a cloud of frizzy curls, while Ester, short and round like Roxana, splashed with two feet at once, the wind riling her hair into spikes.

Rafi and Roxana floundered through the sand to a shelter of driftwood and flotsam. The boards of a rowboat, marked with script in some Asian language, made up one wall. Sun-whitened sticks formed the other two, with the front left open. The roof was a colorful, if dismaying, collection of plastic sea trash melded to ropes, nets, and branches.

Roxana spread towels for them inside the shelter. As she pulled snacks from the bag, Rafi picked up a broken shell and stared at its iridescent indigo hues while he plunged into the central thing he'd wanted to say for a few days.

"Did anyone in Oni's family tell you why I'm staying with them?"

"No," she said. "Haven't talked to them much."

He traced a spiral on his palm with the shell. "I mentioned my grandmother died, two months ago? Well, it was enchantment damage. After the korreds lured her across the verge."

Roxana sucked in a breath. "Hazel Gong?" she said, startling him into looking at her.

"You knew her?"

"A little. She taught music at Ester's school sometimes, and mine too when I was a kid." She pushed her sunglasses up into her hair, and her eyes rested on him with sympathy. "I had no idea. I saw the story in the paper. I don't remember it mentioning the korreds, or you."

"It didn't. She generally introduced me as her fae grandson, to keep anyone from pressuring me to get registered as a citizen."

He'd found the article online, too, after learning to use the browser on the phone Jove and Izzy had given him. It provided just the basics about her life and death, no accusations against any particular fae, and the tepid warning that citizens should "exercise caution near the verge."

"So her half-fae child was…Kepelo?" Roxana asked. "Because your father was born at least a hundred years ago. Hazel couldn't have been his mother."

"Right. The korreds weren't related to Lao Lao. They only knew her through me. I used to bring back stories she told me, to entertain them. Then, when I stopped hanging out there, they went out looking for entertainment themselves, and…found her."

"*Damn* them." The outrage in her voice gratified him. "To have your dad be responsible for that. Gods."

"To be fair, it was cronies of Brogyo, the haunt ruler. My father's his second-in-command. But neither of them stopped it. In fact, they encouraged it. And their non-apologies afterward…" He slid the shell's edge against the pad of his thumb. It stung, and a line of blood welled up. He flicked away the shell and curled his thumb into his palm, sending it a shot of self-healing magic.

"I expect they don't feel remorse the way we might," Roxana said. "With a lot of fae, the psychology's just different."

"Does that mean we have to forgive them? Let them off without punishment?"

"Were they not punished? I thought there was a fae code of honor. A balance kept."

He grimaced. "Kepelo did demand recompense. Hazel was her mother, after all. An old korred volunteered to return to the elements in exchange for her death, and with that, my mother considers it balanced. Case closed."

"But that's not enough for you."

He found a cream-and-purple clam shell that was all curves, no knife edges. "Maybe it'd be enough if that were the only damage they've ever done. But it very much isn't."

He wasn't going to tell her about the other victims he'd seen. No need to give her nightmares. Those had all been from years ago anyway; nothing to be done now.

"I wish we could make them understand why it's wrong," Roxana said. "Granted, I wish that for plenty of humans too."

"Can't we? With those—what are they? Empathy cuffs."

She lifted her eyebrows, tapping her fingers on her leg. "Right. They're iron, best metal for disciplinary spells. I haven't seen any in person. Forced empathy is not a fun experience, by all accounts. It's better than just locking people up, but it's traumatic, feeling the horror of what you've done."

A sickening thrill had come alive in his stomach. "Metal with a mood-changing spell. That's your specialty."

"Yes, but a cuff like that is essentially a weapon, so it's illegal to make unless the government commissions it. Anyway, I'm not sure it'd work on fae. The iron would cause them pain, but they'd probably only tear it off. Then you'd be in trouble."

"If it was regular iron."

"As opposed to? Oh. Fae-realm iron?"

"Yeah. Would that be different?" He loathed this line of thought. It was pointless even to ask. But his macabre curiosity, his beaten-down hopes for justice, craved the answer.

"I've never worked with it. The fae, obviously, don't feel like grabbing any and bringing it to us. But in theory it would be stronger."

"In the fae-realm mountains east of here, there's a cliff with lots of iron. The fae won't go near it. They call it the Unwanted Cliff." His heartbeat pulsed in his throat. This was merely theoretical. Roxana liked metals. She could be interested in seeing some, that was all. "I could get some. You could see what it's like."

"I still wouldn't make anything like that. Plus, how would you even put it *on* them? You think you'd survive?"

He looked down at the shell, flipping it between his fingers, his lurid hopes fading. "I'd survive, most likely. But I wouldn't enjoy it." His mind feebly conjured up ideas anyway—farfetched schemes of disguises, ways to get away with it. But even if it worked...

"It wouldn't bring your grandmother back," Roxana said gently, finishing his thought.

He nodded. "My best hope is that Brogyo will lose interest in charming humans and latch on to some other entertainment. Maybe if I stay away long enough, he'll forget about the tempting human arts I used to bring him."

"You're not responsible for what they do. You said yourself it goes back centuries, long before you were born."

He hummed in acknowledgment. But it was hard not to see the connection from where he sat, what with the korreds swarming him at every visit, clamoring for stories and human pets. How could he not entertain impossible thoughts of making it all *stop* so he could live in peace?

"What would you do if you could truly feel free of this responsibility?" Roxana's voice had become more upbeat. "Who would you be?"

He scooped up sand with the shell and let it shower out onto the edge of his towel. "I would be...a musician. An errand runner. Not much else."

"Member of the community," she suggested. "Friend to many. Or at least

I count you as a friend. We're hanging out at the beach together. That's the kind of thing friends do."

He smiled. "Guess I could be that."

"Yeah, try it awhile. See how it feels."

Their eyes caught, and he felt his life pause, swing around, and open up to show him a path he hadn't even known existed. For those lovely, suspended seconds, he thought he might even have the courage to step onto it.

Roxana picked up two bottles, one filled with something pink and the other with something orange. "Better choose drinks before the girls come back. Strawberry or mango?"

∽

The four of them flew the kites, shared snacks, and argued the merits of wasabi chips versus barbecue. They pointed to whale spouts and merfolk tails and the occasional air surrey or Eidolonian Coast Guard ship.

The sun sank, a laconic orange ball above the horizon. Oni and Ester, fueled by snacks, raced the waves and each other, then lingered by the water, dragging driftwood around and climbing onto rocks.

Roxana looked toward the girls, shading her eyes with her hand. "Does Oni know you're counted human?" she asked Rafi.

"No. Jove and Izzy say they haven't told her. Does Ester?"

"Of course not. You said 'Don't tell anyone,' so I haven't."

"Thank you." He hooked his arms around his knees, letting his gaze travel down the beach. "I had a date here once. Or at least, I came here with the person I was dating."

"When was that?"

"Years ago. I was a teenager—or so I'm guessing. My first human lover, a girl."

"Romantic place to bring someone."

"It didn't last," he admitted. "She had her life here. School, friends, family, job. I can't fit in with all that. I don't really live in the human world."

"Yet here you are, living in it." He didn't answer that, unsure of its truth, and she squinted toward the ocean. "I used to come here with Micah too. Ester's father. I remember walking all the way from that cliff to that one, eight months pregnant. It's good for you when you're pregnant, walking."

He listened to the wind drumming across the logs. "What happened with him?"

"He left us. Is the short version."

Rafi stared at her. "He what?"

"I'm not always great at choosing partners," she said wryly.

"He was just *dumb* if he left you two."

That made her laugh. "Thank you, but I'm over it. It's been ages. Ester was eighteen months old."

Rafi hadn't thought much about Ester's father, or whether Roxana was romantically linked with anyone. Having a child, in his experience, didn't necessarily correlate at all with being in a long-term relationship. But he found he must have assumed she had someone, for the revelation surprised him, and pleased him.

"Do you wish he'd stayed?" he asked.

"Not anymore. He did his part, legally—child support. That is, up until deciding he wanted to move crosswater a few years ago. Without taking along a memory charm." Eidolonians who left the island wouldn't remember it when abroad, unless they brought such a charm, created with the magic of witches and fae. Or so Rafi was told. He himself had never even left the southern half of the island, let alone the country. "Full desertion," Roxana concluded. "At least he told us before he left."

"What does Ester think?"

"She's okay with it, pretty much. He rarely saw us anyway. She never got too attached. I think there has to be some hurt under there, though, you know? It's inescapable."

Oni and Ester ran back a minute later, shuddering and exclaiming how cold the wind was.

Roxana used a spell to scatter the sand off everyone's feet before they bundled back into the car. She started the engine and switched on the radio. The first station was news.

"…Riquelme promises to limit the legally allowed magical actions by witches, place more guards along the verge against what he calls 'belligerent fae,' and even start negotiations for pushing back the verge and gaining more land for his constituents."

"A move," added the second voice on the station, "that's unlikely to get him anywhere, given no one's managed such things for two hundred years, and with good reason. The truce is popular, even in his province."

"Yet he's been elected governor, and he claims it's because the country is changing and his ideas are popular—do you agree with that, Alonzo?"

"Ugh." Roxana stabbed at the button to scan to the next station. "Let's not ruin our day by hearing about him."

"Who?" Rafi asked, mystified. He paid little attention to politics within Miryoku, and zero to politics outside it. Fae diplomacy was enough of a headache to keep track of.

"Akio Riquelme," Roxana said. "Governor of Costa Real."

"A province on the…east coast?" Rafi guessed. His geography knowledge beyond Miryoku wasn't the crispest either.

"Yep, northeast."

"My mom says he offends absolutely everyone," Oni contributed. "Fae, witches, non-witches."

"I'd say that's about right," Roxana said.

"He's an idiot," Ester added. "And a hypocrite. He says magic is dangerous, but he has witches working for him."

"Everyone has witches working for them in this country," Roxana said. "But it's true, he comes across very combative."

"Then why did they elect him?" Rafi asked. "Or did he just take over?" Takeovers by force were something the fae did often enough, and he was sure he'd heard of humans doing so too.

"The elections were fair, as far as I know," Roxana said. "I don't know why they voted him in, though. People believed his promises about how life would get better, I guess."

The twilight deepened. The berry patches they drove past were nothing but long rows of black shadow ending at silhouettes of trees.

People choosing to follow terrible leaders because they thought they'd benefit somehow: having lived alongside korreds, Rafi was familiar with the delusion.

Roxana parked at Izzy and Jove's house. Oni and Rafi got out. While Ester leaned out the car window to say ten or eleven last things to Oni, Roxana hopped out and opened the back to help retrieve Oni's and Rafi's items.

The front garden was lit with strings of lights. Izzy and Jove, lounging on the couch on the porch, called hello. Oni shouted a greeting back, then lingered at the car to keep talking to Ester.

Sandals in hand, Rafi smiled at Roxana as she shut the hatchback. "This was one of the most pleasant days I've had in a long time," he said. "Thank you."

The garden lights painted her with a glow. "Glad you came. I had fun."

He leaned down and kissed her on the cheek. It was what Jove did with his friends. Rafi had seen lots of people do it. It shouldn't have been anything other than easy and friendly.

But Jove's kisses tended to be hearty and precise, he realized, while this kiss was turning out softer and slower. Rafi breathed the sea-wind scent of her as his lips lingered on her skin. He lifted his face again.

She gazed at him. Her smile had turned mysterious, curious.

"Jove does that to everyone," Rafi said helplessly. "It's a band thing."

"Ah, band thing. Then I'll definitely have to come to the next gig."

"Yeah, do." He swung his sandals at his side, feeling sure he looked like a hyperactive child.

Izzy called something to Oni, who called back, "Coming!" Then after telling Ester, "Okay, bye, I'll text you!," she raced up the garden path.

Rafi and Roxana said goodnight. He walked up the path, feeling delightfully weightless.

❧

So your beach date yesterday went well?

Roxana read the message from her best friend Satsuki while alone in a storage room at work, surrounded by boxes of technology bits. The text was a welcome distraction.

It wasn't a date, haha! she typed. *But yes, good time had by all.*

Not a date, hmm. Is that why you've sent me three different pictures from it that are all practically begging for me to comment on how cute he is? Which he is btw.

Roxana pressed her lips together to suppress a grin. *How are things in Kagami?* she asked, in a blatant subject swerve.

Better. Mom and I are laughing more often and enjoying things. I should be able to come home in a few weeks.

I'm so glad. I miss you!

You too! Btw you should send Rafi these pictures if you haven't already. People like getting good pics of themselves. Another wink. Shameless woman.

After another mind-numbing half-hour of sorting tech scrap, Roxana grabbed her phone and texted Rafi.

Thought this one came out great. She attached one of the photos of him lounging on the beach with Oni and Ester.

He answered in a few minutes: *I like it! I should've taken one of you. Get any selfies?*

She reviewed her two selfies from yesterday and decided one was at least not horrible—backlit by bright ocean, mostly sunglasses and grin. She sent it.

Beautiful! he answered. *What are you up to today?*

Work. My replacement has taken over my desk, and I'm looking through old stuff to see what to keep and what to recycle before I leave.

Ah, stuff, he answered. *Stuff is a very human concern. When's your last day at work?*

Two weeks before we move. August 15.

A little more than a month away. The tedium of sorting her old career's detritus and coaching her replacement sank heavier onto her shoulders. Spending the rest of the summer wandering the Bazaar and beaches with Rafi sounded much more fun.

Still a long time, he answered, and she grunted in agreement. Then he added: *Izzy's cousin brought her all these boxes of strawberries from their farm. Izzy gave me one, but it's more than I can eat before they spoil. Can I share with you?*

Absolutely! I have lunch break in an hour and can come get them, if you're free?

❧

Roxana admitted, at the end of two hours, that she'd taken a longer lunch break than usual. "But they encouraged me to," she hastened to add.

Rafi had met her in town with a paper sack of strawberries, which she wanted to take to her house to refrigerate. She'd invited him to walk along. And somehow he had found himself in her family's small, sunny kitchen, sharing tea and a lunch of leftovers with Roxana, Ester, and Roxana's father Timo.

Ester pulled Rafi to the fridge to show him the list of songs she was compiling for their going-away party. He grinned at how long it already was. "This would take about eight hours," he told her.

"I know, I have to narrow it down. But they're all nineties songs. I checked!"

The latest on the list was written in a smoother hand: *Pogues, "Tuesday Morning."*

He touched it. "I don't know this one."

"I put that there," Roxana said, taking dishes to the sink. "It's one of my favorites."

"Then I'll learn it."

"How come you're never the lead singer?" Ester asked. "The other three all sing lead. And we know you *can* sing."

"You're very good in the harmonies," Roxana put in.

"Thanks. The answer is I'm too shy."

"You *should*," Ester urged.

"Only if you want." Roxana set a quelling hand on top of her daughter's head and smiled at Rafi. "But it's true, we'd love to hear it."

He walked Roxana back to work.

She stepped up and hugged him. "Thank you for the strawberries."

In his arms she was a rounded softness he wanted to sink into for the entire afternoon. He let his nose touch her hair, warm in the sun. "No problem. Thanks for inviting me."

With a sigh, she looked at the stairs leading into the building, then gave him a wry wave and went inside.

Outside his cottage, he sat in the grass in the shade and stuck in the earphones Jove had given him. Online on his phone, he found the Pogues' "Tuesday Morning." Catchy bass and drum began thumping in his ears, then came a plucked string riff—banjo or perhaps mandolin. That part would translate easily to liuqin.

The lyrics started, taking him lightly by the wrist and dancing him down a path, lilting and romantic. Each line fit Roxana more and more—or at least, so he fancied as the song charmed him into a three-and-a-half-minute daydream.

He listened to it three more times, then got his liuqin and worked out the notes and chords.

That evening at rehearsal, in the relative cool of the courtyard, Rafi fiddled with the liuqin's tuning pegs and said, "Hey, you know how you asked once if I wanted to try singing? Because I guess I could, maybe."

"Be our guest." Izzy waved a drumstick toward the front of the group.

"We've got nothing to lose but your dignity," Jove added.

Rafi smiled. "Okay. There's a song I want to try."

CHAPTER 7

AFTER REHEARSAL, RAFI LEANED ON THE stone wall bordering the footpath. His throat still buzzed from singing. Did Jove and Izzy mean it, he wondered, when they said he'd done great and could sing lead more often if he wanted, or were they just pitying him?

Oni's voice interrupted his musings. "Hi."

He turned, and she handed him a mug. "Iced lemon rooibos. My folks told me to bring it to you."

"Thank you." He took a swallow. It washed down his throat, soothing the buzz.

"You sounded really good, singing," she added.

He wrapped his fingers around the cold mug. "Roxana and Ester encouraged me. Thought I'd try."

She swung her arms, looking past him. "I'm glad you're staying out here. It's like someone's keeping watch. With the verge right there and everything."

"I try to keep watch. When I'm around."

"It's dumb, but I get nervous. From my window I can see fae lights in the woods. And I mean, it's really cool. But it's also dangerous, and sometimes I imagine things."

"It can be dangerous." He spoke carefully, aware it wasn't kind to scare children, while at the same time wishing to provide enough warning to keep her safe. "It's not all your imagination."

"It's not like I'm afraid of *all* fae. Obviously not Tash, or you, or the fae who hang out in town. But one time, when I was eight, I was out here playing." She brushed her shoe through the weeds along the wall, to indicate the spot. "And this faery jumped up on the other side, like 'Boo!' Just to freak me out."

Rafi's hand clenched the mug. "What kind of faery?"

"I'm not sure. Human form, but I think korred. They didn't climb over, probably because of the iron on the gate, but they tried to talk to me, asking me to sing songs or tell stories or something."

"Did you?"

"No way. I ran for the house. When I looked back, some other faery was buzzing them from the sky—a sprite or something—then they both left." She brushed her cheek against her shoulder. "I still get paranoid. Even though it's dumb."

"You did the right thing, getting away. Sounds like a korred. As their relative, I can tell you, they are horrible."

"Yeah, when I heard what they did to your grandma, even if they didn't mean to…well. I feel safer with you staying in the cottage."

He made himself smile again, though stress had throttled his chest. "You're safe with Ester as a friend too. She'd protect you."

"Ha. Yeah. She's not afraid of anything. She's like the exact opposite of me. Then my mind's like, 'wow, what if they go after her, though?'" Ducking her head, Oni gave a hollow laugh.

Rafi's fingers eased in their clench, sorrow softening his muscles. "Here's something my grandma told me once, when I was worried about losing people. She said, 'What are some things you love that you can't lose? Think of those.'"

Oni raised her gaze to him. "Like…the moon?" She sounded dubious.

"Sure, the moon. Closer to Earth, too, though. Things about being you in particular. For me it was music, and food, and using my magic. And seasons and festivals, and humans in general and all the cool things they do. I'll probably always have those, to some degree." He hadn't thought of Hazel's advice in years, actually. Funny that it took a conversation with a scared teenager to revive her words.

Oni nodded. "Music for me too. And dancing. And…the ocean, and wild animals. Art maybe. I think I'm getting *kind of* good at drawing. Anyway I like discovering other people's art." She grinned, her teeth a glimmer of white in the shadows.

"There you go. Plenty of things."

"Yeah. I like that." She swung a foot backward, toward the house. "Anyway. Mom says you can bring the mug back in whenever. Night, Rafi."

∽

It became compulsive for Roxana, finding reasons to contact Rafi. She would have desisted if he didn't comply so readily—if he wasn't, in fact, the one reaching out half the time. One day they ended up talking about books, and she met him again to lend him two novels: *Where the Mountain Meets the Moon*, a favorite of Ester's, and *Chocolat*, a favorite of her own.

"Are you coming to tomorrow's gig?" he asked, tucking the books against his chest.

"Sure, why not?"

"Good." His lips twitched up in a smile. "I think you should."

The gig was at Gusu Park again. Several fae from Kepelo's haunt happened to attend, filling the forest with flickering sparks. Each looked like an apple-sized star brought to Earth, scintillating in blue, red, green, yellow, and white.

A few songs in, Jove announced, "All right, friends, here's something new. Give all your love to Rafi, making his lead-singer debut with a song we haven't done in a while." As the crowd cheered, Jove added to Rafi, "No pressure, hon," then waved him to the mic.

Rafi stepped up, clutching the liuqin. He bent his head shyly, sequined vest sparkling in the lights. "This is for the lovely Wei family. I hope we do it justice."

Roxana's heart kicked hard, and when she recognized the opening notes of "Tuesday Morning," she folded both hands over her mouth. Ester grabbed her elbow and squealed. Rafi's gaze flicked to her as he performed a flaw-less job of plucking the banjo riff on liuqin. She let her hands melt into two thumbs-up. He smiled, then lifted his face, set his focus out past the crowd, and began singing.

Roxana beamed, unable to do anything else with her face. She swayed with the crowd, amazed her knees hadn't buckled. Rafi's voice was pure and honeyed, fae ethereality twined with modest humanity. He gained confi-dence, singing stronger with each line, and eventually tracked his gaze back to Roxana at the word "you" in the chorus.

Her face felt hot and dewy. *I am in so much trouble*, was all she could think.

At the end of the song, she applauded with hands above her head. Jove gave Rafi a kiss on each cheek, then Rafi stepped aside to begin strumming the next song. Roxana hardly registered what it was. Through the rest of the concert, she swayed on auto-pilot and let her thoughts cartwheel.

At the show's end, praying to the Lady (who comforted those aching in love and desire) that none of her turmoil showed, she hugged Rafi and gave him a kiss on the cheek. Not the way Jove had, but the way Rafi had kissed her recently, shy and gentle. He smelled of warm human skin and sparks on stone.

"That was magnificent," she said. "Thank you."

"Thank *you*," he echoed casually, but his gaze lingered on her as she stepped back, and fire flickered under his skin.

I'm loving Where the Mountain Meets the Moon, he texted the next evening. *It reminds me of the stories my grandmother told me. Some of them must have come from her Chinese ancestors.*

He was sitting on the cottage's porch. Humid clouds clung over the town, and lightning flickered among the mountains. It would rain before long, provided the air fae didn't sweep in and send the storm elsewhere.

She answered: *Plus you're related to actual dragons.*

Indeed, though drakes are somewhat different than the dragons in the book.

Did she make up stories about drakes?

Some. I remember one in particular.

Tell me, she said.

He set his fingers over the screen, hesitated, then tapped her name and selected Call.

She answered, sounding amused. "Hello."

"It'd be too long to type in texts," he said.

"All right." There were clinks like dishes behind her voice, and faint music. Domestic human-town sounds.

His resolve leached away. "It doesn't have to be now, if you're busy."

"No, tell me. I'm just tidying up the kitchen. My folks and Ester are off in other rooms, doing their own things."

"Okay. Well…" He straightened his spine and folded his legs on the step below. "She told it to me a few times when I was a kid. Once there was a woman who was fascinated with dragons and had always wanted to meet one. Then one day, at Fire Festival, she did.

"She danced with a man who was really a drake in human form. He took her on a ride, flying up in the sky with her. They darted around the fireworks and floated in the moonbeams. After the festival, he gave her a tiny red seed made of flame. She was frightened at first to take it, but it didn't burn her. It was warm and soft, and it glowed.

"Then he left, and while she waited for him to come back, she set the seed in a pot. It grew and grew over the months, forming a big round bud. She wondered what kind of flower it would be, and whether the drake would ever come back to see it. Sometimes the bud wriggled as it grew, especially when it was hungry. The woman put fresh persimmon juice in the soil for it—that was its favorite."

Roxana chuckled, a puff of air through the phone.

Thunder rolled through the fae-realm forest.

"When the bud finally opened," Rafi said, "a beautiful drake-child leaped out, who could be either human or drake, whichever she wished. And that day, the drake man finally returned. 'Thank you for tending this treasure,' he told the woman. 'You've raised a creature who will have drake strength and human kindness. She will be a link between our realms, making both worlds happier.' And he took the drake-child away with him to his home in the mountains."

Roxana made a dismayed sound. "Away from the woman? They just left her?"

"Well, the drake man and the child visited during festivals to take her on sky rides, and in between they sent fadas to clean her house and fire sprites to light up her garden at night. So she…lived a long and happy life." He couldn't quite say it with conviction.

Lightning lit the edges of the clouds, bright enough to cast shadows at his feet. The thunder cracked in its wake, a breath later.

"How long before you understood it was about her?" Roxana asked.

"Years. And when I finally asked her about it, she said the parts about the regular rides in the sky, and the fadas and sprites doing her chores, weren't exactly true. It happened a few times, early on, but tapered off eventually."

"Hm." The syllable was a sad sigh. "That figures."

"I never thought it was fair, even before I understood what it meant."

"Or," Roxana suggested, "*you* were the sprite lighting up her garden and making her life better."

A smile softened his mouth. "She did say something like that, when telling it. I think. It was a long time ago."

"It's a beautiful way to tell what happened. I hope it wasn't too sad for her."

"The fae like that story," he said. "Obviously Kepelo and the other fire fae do, since it's about them. But even the korreds liked it. They want a connection with humans. The problem is they have no social graces."

"We can't all be lovely lights, I suppose. Some of us have to be rocks."

"And some of us are both."

Roxana laughed. "So…did Hazel actually give birth to an egg?"

"Yep. Not nearly a small enough egg, she always made a point of saying."

"Oh wow. And—you? Did you hatch from an egg?"

"Of course."

Roxana laughed again. This time a streak of wild delight ran through it. "That's a first among my friends."

Raindrops pattered on the porch steps, wetting Rafi's bare feet. A branch of lightning arced across the sky, thunder cracking at the same moment.

"Yikes," Roxana said. "Did you hear that?"

"Yeah, I'm on my porch. It was right over me."

"Go inside, you maniac."

"You realize I've lived outside most of my life."

"You're a townie now," she chastised. "We go indoors during lightning storms."

"All right." Smiling, he scooted backward, pulling his legs under the cover of the porch roof. "Goodnight, Roxana."

∽

"This is what someone needs when they're reading *Chocolat*," Rafi said a few days later. They were walking on the footpath, and he held a paper bowl of mochi ice creams in assorted flavors. After he and Roxana had rhapsodized to each other about the descriptions of desserts in the novel, she had insisted they go to Mochi Coco, Hari's shop, for a Saturday afternoon treat.

She licked a sticky dot of filling off her fingertip. "One hundred percent." She picked another mochi—chocolate-orange—and sank her teeth into it.

"Is this what book clubs are like? Dessert and nice walks? If so, I'm understanding why people like them."

"This is nicer than most book clubs, in my opinion."

Rafi draped his arm around her shoulders. "Ah, why do you have to leave?"

The arm rested lightly, as if he wasn't sure of his welcome. She leaned into his side. *Yes. Welcome.* Their steps slowed. The trees whispered in the wind, sunlight sparkling through green leaves.

"It's a change I've wanted for so long." She heard the helplessness in her voice.

"I know. You've earned it."

"It's just now I…have more reasons to feel sad about leaving." One. One more reason, singular.

His fingers stroked her bare arm, sliding to her elbow and then back to her shoulder. Their gazes locked, and the world wobbled around her.

Then he turned his face forward, something wilting in his expression. Before she could read it, he smoothed it away with a neutral smile. "If I text you about books, or food, once you've moved away, will you still answer?"

She leaned her head against his shoulder. "Of course. Text me about anything."

He circled the bowl, rolling the mochi balls around. "Only two left. Which one do you want?"

With an unsteady hand, she picked up the white one and sniffed it. "Almond."

Rafi ate the last one, crumpled the paper bowl in his fist, and carried it along as they meandered forward.

Hold on to this, for later, she told herself. The weight of his arm around her. His body moving against her as they walked. The taste of almond mochi perfuming her mouth. Fae and kiryo birds caroling in the forest. Sun-spangled trees arching over the path as if enclosing the two of them in a bower.

Later would hurt. But at least she had this now.

⚬⚬

Rafi avoided thinking about Roxana's impending departure at the end of summer. Having lost Hazel forever, he knew it was important to savor the time he had with anyone, however long or short it might be. But it was impossible not to *want* more. He couldn't remember longing so deeply for anyone since adolescence, and that had been different—more hormones and general loneliness than true connection.

Obviously he wouldn't act on it. Much. They'd kissed on the cheek a few times and hugged a few more. Putting his arm around her during that walk had taken every scrap of his courage. It all should have maddened him. Instead it made him feel fantastically alive.

Meloncollie's next gig was a few days after their walk. The band would be one of four artists playing Goth Night at a dance club called Grotto Obscuro, which Rafi had never been to. Nor had he been familiar with their set of '90s goth songs, so he'd spent the week rehearsing them.

Shortly before the gig, Jove showed up at Rafi's cottage with his eyes ringed in black like Siouxsie Sioux's. He had painted his lips black, too, and wore all black clothes: a one-shouldered loose top, skintight leggings, and chunky boots.

Holding up an eyeliner pencil, Jove said, "Going to endo up your eyes or do you want me to do 'em for you?"

"I guess you can do them?"

"Good call. Saves energy. I know I've got to save all mine for hitting the high notes." Jove was an endo-witch too. Izzy, who wasn't a witch, liked to claim the other band members relied on magic in order to sound good while she alone used actual talent.

Rafi sat on the arm of his loveseat and tried not to let his eyelids twitch as Jove marked them up with the pencil. Finally he drew back and assessed Rafi. "Smoldering. Goth suits you."

Rafi stepped over to the tiny bathroom. In the mirror, his dramatically enhanced eyes stared back at him. Tan skin, black ponytail, black tank top, lightweight black kilt. The red glimmer of his scales was his only vivid color, and it struck him as vaguely sinister in this ensemble.

"I look like when raccoon fae take human form," he said. Jove whooped with laughter, and Rafi added, perplexed, "This is hot?", even as his brain added in silent hope, *Will Roxana think so?*

"You're always hot, Raf. Get your instrument. Let's go."

CHAPTER 8

ON THE WESTERN SIDE OF MIRYOKU STOOD an outcropping of rock ten feet high and as wide as a city block. A century ago, matter-witches—the construction-worker type—had sculpted the rock into a building, which was then named the Grotto: apartments on top, and the club Grotto Obscuro in the basement.

Carrying his liuqin case and Izzy's cymbal stands, Rafi followed his bandmates down stone steps into a cave throbbing with music. Vines and stalactites tangled across the ceiling—probably all artificial, but it was hard to tell in the shifting green and purple lights—and the stone walls glinted with crystals. Rafi felt like an insect inside a geode.

Excited voices rose behind him. He turned to find Oni getting pounced in an embrace by Ester, whose short hair was spiked out, adding three inches to her height.

"Doesn't she look great?" Oni said to him.

"It's vintage!" Ester opened her arms to display her cap-sleeved dress patterned with dark flowers.

"Very nineties-Goth," Izzy praised.

"Can you believe I fit into that once?" Roxana said.

Rafi turned with a start to find her at his side. His eyes, abandoning their manners entirely, traveled down her plum-colored mini-dress, opaque tights, and thick-soled shoes. "Wow," he heard himself say, a comment on her appearance rather than a response to her remark.

"But this is so cute!" Izzy stroked the shoulder of Roxana's dress. "Is it vintage too?"

"Yeah, but it's really stretchy, which is the only reason I can still wear it." Laughing, Roxana pulled out the fabric at one hip and let go. It snapped back.

Rafi jerked his gaze to her face. "You look great," he said, dazed.

"Thanks. But look at you! That eyeliner's amazing."

She had her curls tousled up more than usual and wore a black velvet ribbon around her throat, with a tiny yellow smiley face on it. Rafi tightened his fingers around the liuqin case to keep himself from reaching out to caress her neck.

Another pair of shadows swarmed out of the crowd and surrounded Oni: two adolescents he had seen at other concerts.

"There you are!" The girl had luminescent streaks in her hair that shifted from pale green to pink and back again—a matter-witch trick. "We haven't seen you in practically a month." She slung her arm around Oni's shoulders.

Oni murmured something about gigs.

"But you haven't been to the gigs *we* go to," said the other teen, who had a mischievous smile and bobbed hair. "Come *over* here." They grabbed Oni's hand, and within a breath the two had whisked Oni away into the dancing crowd.

Oni looked back with a crinkled brow at Ester, then people closed around her and erased her from sight. Ester's shoulders sagged, and she stalked to Roxana, grabbed her wrist, and started swinging it with ferocity. Roxana stroked her hand, calming the tempo.

Izzy beckoned Rafi to the stage. Once their set began, he kept trying to catch glimpses of Roxana. Ester, lips turned downward, stayed close to her. Roxana alternated between watching Rafi—with an intensity that sent a thrill through him—and talking to her daughter. Oni, meanwhile, had her back to the wall at a little side table, trapped by the two teens who had brought her there. They sat on either side of her, talking, drinking from glasses with glowing stir-sticks. Oni smiled and spoke in response, but her gaze frequently escaped to seek Ester or the band.

Three new shadows ambled forward, and a shock zapped through him.

Oxlock, who had enchanted Hazel and lured her across the verge. Unklag, one of Rafi's worst bullies. And Sminu, Rafi's father. They were in human form, their scanty black clothes happening to blend in well on Goth Night.

Rafi's fingers fumbled, hitting a wrong note.

The korreds hadn't even looked at him. They sniffed the air close behind people's necks in passing, as if choosing fruit at the market. Then Unklag looked up and saw Rafi, and her mouth gaped wide in a laugh. She smacked Sminu's arm and pointed. Oxlock noticed too. The three pushed through the crowd to within a few feet of the stage, where they stood looking up at Rafi, simply laughing.

His fingers slipped again. The discordant notes jarred the tune for two strums before he recovered. Jove shot him a frown. Rafi glanced at him, then back at the korreds.

Jove followed Rafi's stare, but he hadn't put it together, and Rafi couldn't tell him yet. The set had to go on, another seven and a half damn minutes.

Flee the stage. No, jump on them and fight. No, grab the mic and warn the audience. No, get down there and warn just Roxana. No, stand still, you can't do a thing, you're nothing, you're lucky you're even a musician, and if you fail at that, then what are you?

Sminu turned away, saying something probably dismissive and insulting, and they wandered back into the crowd to continue ogling citizens.

They didn't care about Rafi. He mattered that little. But his panic only slipped down a notch or two. This dimly lit crowd contained too many humans drunk or high enough to be easy marks for korreds.

Roxana had figured it out, though, Lord and Lady bless her. She was frowning at the korreds, who had paused to talk to someone a few paces away. Then she looked at Rafi and lifted her brows. He answered with a short nod. Roxana twined her arm around Ester's as if to secure her—not that Ester noticed. She was still eyeing Oni.

The song lurched along like a bad dream while the korreds prowled the crowd, taking their time in making a selection.

Tash finally saw them, toward the end of their second-to-last song. After scowling at Rafi when he mangled yet another chord, she noticed his intense stare and followed its direction. Her eyes went chilly as ice-melt. Then she gave Rafi a slight lift of her chin, which he took—uncertainly—as a promise to back him up if necessary.

One more song. Izzy's voice, behind him at the drum set, provided the brief introduction.

Jove stepped over to Rafi. "You okay?" he asked in Rafi's ear.

"Korreds in the audience," Rafi said quietly. "Three of them."

"Shit." Jove glanced outward. "Well. Lot of people here. They won't get near you."

"It's not me I'm worried about," Rafi said, but Jove was already stepping away, strumming the minor chord progression to the final song.

Four minutes. That was all they had left on stage. Yet a trio of korreds could walk past dozens of people in just one minute. Could approach the table by the wall—as they were doing—where Oni and the other two teens sat. Could cluster around them and charm Oni's acquaintances into conversation.

Rafi let his fingers fall still. It dropped an entire accompaniment line from the song, but by then the rest of the band was staring at the korreds too.

Oni looked petrified. Rafi could see the whites surrounding her irises as she looked to him, to her parents.

Rafi surged forward and jumped off stage, pushing between people, murmuring "Sorry" as he shoved through. He was vaguely aware of the music stopping as he reached the table.

Ester stomped up beside him, clenching a fist at her chest. Roxana followed, brows drawn together.

"Come with us and perform them, these songs," Oxlock, oblivious, was saying to the girl with the color-changing hair. "Have you ever been to a haunt before? Aren't you curious?"

Gazing at him, the girl answered something, Rafi couldn't hear what over the crowd's murmur. People were confused, hadn't yet figured out what the commotion was about.

"Do not go anywhere with them," Rafi told the teens.

"Oni, get out." Ester turned to the other teen and tugged their arm. "Let her out!"

"Bloody *Spirit*," the kid complained, but slid off the tall chair and edged out of the way.

Oni leaped off her chair and darted to stand between Roxana and Ester. Rafi moved close to help shield her.

Unklag smirked. "You must be so ashamed, Sminu. Having your only offspring be someone who wails like a monkey whenever he sees anyone having fun."

Sminu grunted and looked away.

Stone was spreading across Rafi's skin, trying to protect him, without his controlling it. He shouldn't care what they said. But knowing that and actually staying calm in the face of people who had terrorized him all his life were two very different prospects.

"Don't listen to them," Ester snapped to the girl, who still sat with her shoulder touching Oxlock's. "Get away from them. They're the ones who killed Hazel Gong."

"Oh, that I call a lie," Sminu said. "She died in our haunt, but we never intended it. We quite wanted her to live."

"And we can't lie," Oxlock said earnestly, nudging the girl.

"Stop touching her," Rafi said. The girl looked at him with a frown, her eyes glazed, and his stress level spiraled upward. "He's enchanting you. Don't let him touch you. Get away."

"It's what you did to Hazel," Ester shouted. "It's why she died!"

"Ester." Roxana set her hand on Ester's shoulder.

By now the crowd had formed a murmuring circle around them. Rafi glimpsed iron self-defense items being taken from pockets. Not particularly reassuring. A fight wouldn't benefit anyone.

The rest of the band picked their way through to stand beside him. Oni fled to Izzy, who hooked an arm around her and glared at the korreds.

Sminu laughed, tipping his head down for a moment in a way that made him look like an honest, self-deprecating man. "Friends." He clasped his hands at his chest. "We come to enjoy your arts, as has always been the tradition on this island since we, the fae, allowed humans to come ashore. This was the agreement, yes?"

"Enjoy," Tash said. "Not force from the unwilling."

"But we can *make* them willing," Oxlock said, sounding genuinely confused.

A mutter ran through the crowd. Iron blades and chains flicked open.

"Get away from her," Tash said, "and go home."

Sminu's eyes lit with an orange glow, and his cheekbones and jawline stiffened, becoming more rock-edged. "You speak to your fellow fae this way? Pathetic."

"Allow me to accompany you out," someone said. A drake stepped up beside Rafi, half again as tall as any human—Aulo, Kepelo's steadfast companion. She was not in full fae form, which in her case would have taken up a daunting amount of space, but looked more drake than human at the moment, with snout and clawed limbs and folded wings.

Aulo had been fairly aloof toward Rafi in his childhood, but never cruel to him. He was more relieved to see her now than he could ever recall being.

Ester flicked out the fist she'd been holding at her chest. "Get out!" A slender iron chain lashed from her hand and stung the nearest korred—Unklag—on the neck.

Rafi's heart seized in terror.

Unklag yelped, rounded on her, then eased into a smile. She reached out and caught Ester's wrist. "You're an entertaining one. Perhaps you'd like to come talk awhile. Might change your mind about us."

Roxana's sharp intake of breath was in sync with Rafi's own.

Ester's face softened, and her fingers dropped the chain. It hit the floor with a jingle.

Rafi and Roxana lunged forward, but so did everyone else.

Tash and Aulo got there first. In a flash of fire and a spray of water, Ester got flung back into Roxana's arms, and Tash and Aulo, along with several citizens wielding iron, rounded up all three korreds and escorted them toward the exit.

Sminu looked back, his smile sliding across the humans, lingering on Rafi a moment. "Until next time, friends," he called. "Lovely music."

CHAPTER 9

THE ADRENALINE KEPT COURSING THROUGH
Roxana, making her shake even as she assured Ester that everything
was fine, that she—Roxana—was all right. For of course the second Ester
had been released from the magic, she would have chased the korreds out the
door, whipping at them with the iron chain, if Roxana hadn't clasped her in
both arms and kept her still. Unconcerned for herself, Ester was furious at the
korreds for upsetting Roxana and Oni.

The rest of the clubgoers were laughing nervously, turning to their friends.
The next band was ushered on stage, and the MC was getting everyone back
into proper Goth Night spirits. The two kids who'd been hanging out with
Oni dashed off to join a group of other teens.

Roxana, Ester, Oni, and the members of Meloncollie—minus Tash,
who was helping escort the korreds home—stood in a stunned cluster. Rafi
looked shaken, his skin alternating between glowing scales and flinty rock.
The patches surfaced and disappeared all over him.

Ester hadn't stopped ranting. Roxana answered with reassurance, though
stress swarmed through her like her own version of flesh turning alternately to
fire and earth. Nothing in ages had scared her more than that moment when
a korred touched her daughter and infused her with magic that would have
had Ester following them across the verge to her doom, had no one else been
around.

But people *had* been around. Ester was undamaged. Everything was fine.
Everything is fine, she repeated to herself.

"Let's go home," Jove said, his arm around his daughter.

"Can you two handle bringing the equipment back?" Izzy asked Jove and
Rafi. Her voice was hard and clipped. "I intend to have a word with this venue
about their security."

Rafi recovered his focus. His skin resolved back to its characteristic scattering of scales. "Sure."

"Ester and I will help," Roxana said.

"It's okay, you don't have to," Jove said.

"Can Ester come over?" Oni cut in. "Please?"

Ester scooted to Oni's side and hugged her, getting Jove's arm in the middle of it without apology.

Jove's lips relaxed into a faint smile. "Of course. We'll have a mint party. Right?"

Twenty minutes later, after helping carry drum set pieces into Jove and Izzy's front room, Roxana asked Rafi, "What's a mint party?"

The two of them had wandered out through the back garden to his cottage.

He filled two glasses with water from the tap in his kitchen, set them on the counter, and turned to the mini-fridge. "A tea party with mint tea, I gather. And whatever else is around to eat."

"Ah." Roxana touched the potted vine growing on the kitchen windowsill. "That does sound soothing."

"My understanding is it's a way to make Oni feel better when she's stressed, or sick or something...here, we can use this in the water. Sorry, looks like I'm out of ice." He brought over a lemon, found a knife and sliced a couple of wedges off it, then plunked one into each glass.

"I can do the ice." Roxana picked up a glass, concentrated on where it touched her fingertips, and pushed the warmth out of it. The glass fogged, then a crust of ice formed around the surface of the water. She performed the same magic for the other glass and handed it to him.

"Thanks. Come sit."

"Place is cute," Roxana commented as she followed him into the main room. "No one lived here before you?"

"Not for decades. It was garden storage." Rafi sat on the loveseat, which was upholstered with faded orange velvet. "A gardener lived here once, early on. Worked for Izzy's ancestors."

There was no other seat besides the bed, which was across the room behind a standing screen. Since he had left space on the loveseat, she sat there. Their knees touched. "It's cozy."

The coffee table was an old wooden fruit box on its side. Another box by the window served as a shelf, holding a few books. The ceiling lamp, in the corner to their left, was a rattan basket housing a bulb. Of the bed, all she could see was the end of a mattress with a red blanket hanging off it, and one metal leg of a bed frame. The rest was hidden by a privacy screen—stained and faded to browns, but still beautiful, three panels painted with flowering branches and long-tailed birds.

"Jove and Izzy made it cozy," Rafi said. "I don't know a thing about decorating. They found all this stuff they weren't using, in their house or out here, and arranged it."

"Satsuki would approve. That's her job—upcycling. She hooks up matter-witches with used materials, to repair them or change them to something else, then she sells it. I like the plants too." She nodded to the potted orchids on either side of the window, blooming as vigorously as the vine in the kitchen.

"Tash made those grow. She says human homes feel like tombs if they don't have plants." He sipped his lemon water, then exhaled a long breath. She could hear the tremble in it.

She set her glass on the coffee table box, unhooked her silver gecko-shaped ear cuff, and turned to him. "Try a calming charm? You can wear this for a bit."

His gaze dropped to the charm. "Sure. Thanks."

Roxana closed her eyes to find the right energy, the feeling that hummed in tandem with a vision of tranquility in her mind, then let it flow from her body into the metal. Her breath quickened with the effort, and a light sweat broke out across her. "There. Let's fit it." She smoothed his hair out of the way and hooked it onto his ear.

He blinked, and his shoulders lowered a fraction. "Oh. That *is* nicer. How does it work, with a spell like that? What do you think of, or draw from?"

"By now it's just instinct. I think of how I want someone to feel when they touch the piece. The clearer I can picture it, and the more energy I have that day, the better it works."

"And the better the metal. Or type of metal."

"Yeah." She lingered sideways on the loveseat, one knee tucked up under her. "Does it need more?"

"No, it's good. I'm better. Thanks." Rafi took another deep breath, steadier this time. "It was like a nightmare come to life. Exactly what I've been worrying would happen."

"I know. To see one of them touch Ester…" She shivered. "But nothing did happen. People stopped it. See, it's not just down to you—everyone wanted them gone."

"Good thing it wasn't down to me. I did nothing. Tash and Aulo and the people armed with iron are the ones who got rid of them."

"Which is *good*. Others are on it. You can relax."

"Except I can't. It's not just my grandmother, or all the times they broke my bones or insulted me."

Her stomach dropped at the casual mention of breaking his bones, *all the times*, no less. She had gathered his childhood involved abuse, by a human definition at least, but she hadn't known the extent of it. He continued without pause:

"I've seen their victims, before Lao Lao. Three different times. I didn't even spend that much time in the korred haunt growing up, so I've always wondered, how many more did I not see?" He looked at her, eyes feral with urgency. "Your dad's a social worker, right? Have a lot of people gone missing over the years, or come back from across the verge with enchantment damage?"

"Not that many," she assured. "I mean, I don't have the stats on hand, and it's true that in Miryoku, per capita, there might be a higher number of people who get enchanted. Or die. Just because we're closer to the verge than most towns. Still, it's way better than, say, the eighteenth century, before the truce. But…you saw them?"

He looked down at his glass. "I was younger than Ester, the first time. Brogyo summoned me to their haunt to tell stories. After a couple days they got bored with me, and went out and brought back a young guy, some kind of performer. He seemed willing, did some theater, some dance. Then one of them said, 'Here, try being a korred,' and put a spell on him to turn his skin to rock, the way mine can. Except the way they did it, it hurt him. He started screaming. I remember huddling behind a tree, covering my ears…why didn't I help him?"

"You were a kid." Roxana touched the ear cuff, feeling his warmth through the metal, wishing she were an exo-witch who could stream calm straight into him from her hands. "You couldn't have stopped them."

"Then," he said, "they got annoyed because the fun was over. They took the spell off, did a half-assed job of healing him, and let him wander off. See, I should have followed. Made sure he got across the verge. I *thought* he went that way. But he was disoriented, I guess, because the next day I found him at the bottom of a cliff, next to the creek. It looked like he'd fallen. It was a long drop, a lot of rocks…" A shudder ran through him. "Some crows and vulture-fae had already gotten to him."

"That's horrible." Roxana fought the urge to put her face on his shoulder, to promise, *I'll stay, I'll heal you, as long as it takes.*

As if she could fix this.

"Some shellycoats showed up," he continued. "They took his body back across the verge. I ran to the fire haunt, and for a long time I refused to go back to the korreds. My mother humored me, told them I couldn't be spared when some earth-fae messenger showed up to ask for me. Sent me into town to stay with my grandmother more."

"But later they took others," she said.

"Yeah. I was a teenager the next time. I'd finally started going back once in a while, and things were…not okay, but at least there were no other captives. Then one night they showed up with this older guy, who had an accordion and was good at singing. They were smart enough not to turn his skin to stone. He even ended up sleeping with Unklag—one of the korreds at the club tonight—and seemed happy about it. He stayed awhile. Then one morning he just…didn't wake up. Enchantment again, probably. That time I volunteered to take his body back to the verge. Luckily Mukut helped me. It would've been hard to carry him myself the whole way."

"Gods, Rafi," she whispered.

"Then," he said, plowing on as if determined, "a couple years after that, they brought in a girl, a teenager. She was enspelled—that dazed look. And when she had trouble showing them whatever dances they wanted to see, they started seducing her. With more spells. I thought, no. Enough. I stopped them, I lied, I said I'd made a deal not to let this particular human come across the verge, and Kepelo would punish the whole korred haunt if she found out. They keep forgetting I can lie—it isn't easy, but I can manage it if I'm determined. I offered to get her out fast before anyone knew. She was already so damaged she could hardly walk, but I got her to town. After that I almost never went back to their haunt. Until my grandmother died." He drained the glass and set it beside hers on the box.

When he slumped back onto the loveseat, she asked, "Was the girl okay?"

"Not really. I asked my grandmother to find out. She heard the enchantment had altered her mind, and the family was moving to Dasdemir to be near healer specialists. I don't know what became of her."

Roxana let her head rest on the loveseat's cushion and gazed at the ceiling beams. "Why don't *you* get enchantment damage from being across the verge? Because you're half fae?"

"Probably, along with a lot of healing over the years. Lao Lao theorized it was like immunity, growing up among them, being saturated in the magic from birth. But I still need to be careful not to eat the food or drink the water from that side without using a purifying charm on it first. My mother learned that the hard way—had to heal me a lot."

"I'm glad she was there. And that you were resilient."

"It's also possible the damage will show up later. It does for some people."

That was too much worry to fit into her mind for one evening. "So. That was your father tonight."

"The one making the suave speeches. Yes. Apparently he and the rest still haven't found a new obsession. Still after humans to play with."

"And there's nothing we can do?"

"I keep thinking there has to be. That's what tortures me. How can I just accept this? When I think of some night in the future, when they'll approach some kid like Ester or Oni, or someone's grandparent, or *anyone*, how can I just shrug and say, 'It's part of life on Eidolonia'? Why does that, in particular, have to be?"

Nausca gripped her as she envisioned it: Ester, eyes dull and enchanted, being led into the forest. Lying dead in a creek. Carried out and dumped on the footpath by a casually sympathetic faery.

She pulled her spine upright, tucking both legs under herself. "You said you could get fae-realm iron?"

Rafi turned to meet her gaze. Deep in his eyes was the dangerous anger of a smoldering drake. "Yes. I think so."

"The shackle charm we talked about, to induce empathy. I could try making one."

His throat moved in a swallow. "Would it work?"

"I don't know. I've never made anything like it. I'd try, that's all. Do you think you could…get it onto one of them? Without endangering yourself? Gods, that's not even possible, there's no—"

"I could," he cut in. "I think. I have ideas so they wouldn't know it was me. But, the iron." He breathed out, spreading his hands down his thighs. "First I'd have to get that. See how it works."

"I don't approve of revenge," she cautioned. "That's not what I'm picturing. Just…defense. Justice, if anything else does happen. If no one else is going to do anything. Only then."

"I agree. It's not the kind of thing I'd use lightly. If it even works."

"If it even works." They sat silent, the air charged with this powerful new pact. "You said it came from some cliff?"

"The mountains in the middle of the peninsula. I've heard fae talk about it—the Unwanted Cliff. Mukut could take me there. I'd make a deal with her to not tell anyone. The korreds don't talk to her much anyway."

"What would she want in return?"

He smiled—a soft and genuine smile for the first time all evening. "Potato chips. Any flavor, but especially onion. She loves them. I'll promise her a whole crate."

Roxana smiled too. "And how long would it take to get up there and back? A day?"

"Probably an overnight trip at least. Maybe two nights in the fae realm. Out here, who knows, of course." He fluttered his fingers against his leg. "I could leave tomorrow morning. The band doesn't have any gigs for at least a week."

"I hope it's not longer than a couple days. I'd be kicking myself if I sent you on an errand that kept us apart for the rest of the summer."

His gaze flicked back to hers. "I'd hate that too."

They were inches apart, eyes locked. Now the charge in the air was almost tangible, thrumming through her. If it turned out she had to move to Port Baleia before he got back…

"Can I kiss you?" she asked.

His lips parted in a quiet, surprised laugh. "*Yes.* I was just about to ask that—yes—"

The word got caught between their mouths.

The taste of lemon. A hint of smoke and salt. Softer skin than she expected. A light touch, as if he was being careful, which she was too. *It's been so long since I kissed someone* and *Is this what he likes? Am I doing this right?* ambushed her mind in the first few seconds.

Then his calloused fingertips brushed her cheek and slipped into her hair, and he fitted their faces closer, dropping the delicacy. Her doubts melted away. A hum of pleasure escaped her mouth, and she kissed each part of his lips slowly, getting to know them. Her hand climbed his bicep, going against the grain of his scales, their ridges rounded like sequins. The skin over his collarbone was smooth, and when she dipped her head to kiss there, he groaned softly, and his flesh went hot against her mouth, a red glow kindling under the surface.

She lifted her face to admire it.

"Won't get hot enough to burn," he assured.

"It's so pretty." She splayed her fingers on his shoulder, watching the light roll and glimmer beneath. "Like coals. Or sea sparkle, except red."

"It means I like you. Not just physically. It's more about…connection." He stroked her hip, along the stretchy purple fabric of the dress. "Although physically…gods, you look incredible. Will you wear this again for me on some calmer occasion?"

She blushed warm enough that she surely glowed too, in her own human fashion. "Of course. You look distractingly hot yourself. The *eyeliner.*"

He scrunched his nose. "Wasn't sure when Jove put it on me. Raccoon, I was thinking."

She burst into a laugh, and he kissed her again. Heat flared from him, raising a sweat on her skin. She relished the little sounds he made when their tongues met or when her hand slid to the small of his back and found a gap of blazing skin between his top and his black kilt.

"Won't Ester come looking for you soon?" he whispered, lips at her cheek.

"Probably. How long does a mint party last?"

"No idea." His thumb grazed the side of her breast.

Feeling melted all over, she tilted her face as he trailed kisses down her neck. "I've wanted to kiss you for weeks," she said. "Just didn't have the nerve."

"If I'd known you wanted me to…" He pressed a kiss on the scoop neck of her dress.

"Do you…do this with friends and acquaintances often?" Roxana kept her tone mild. She meant no judgment. But she needed to know if this felt as momentous for him as it did for her, or if it was merely a typical evening for him, featuring the groupie of the week.

"Mm-mm." The sounds carried a negative cadence. He placed a slow, almost reverent, kiss on her cleavage. "Quite rare. Been a long time since I did this. Or felt like this."

"Same. I've dated a couple of people since Ester's dad, but…" But it was complicated, when you had a child whose life you would be impacting if you fell in love with a new person. It was frightening, taking that risk. It was difficult, finding anyone to connect with in the first place. "Not in a while," she said simply.

His mouth tipped into a smile, which she smothered with another kiss.

"I *really* hope your trip across the verge doesn't take long," she said after another minute.

"I'll try to be quick."

"I don't suppose your phone works over there…wait, do you have a glimpse mod?"

"No." He pulled back, gaze focusing in interest. "Though could you make one? It's a small piece of metal, right?"

"Alas no. I could fashion its shape, but that spell, to break through the fae-realm enchantment and send and receive signals, that's way beyond me. Apparently it takes huge energy, layers of spells, including some from fae."

"Damn. Then I'll just have to pray the Spirit cooperates on the time change."

They were immersed in another kiss when Ester yelled from outside, "Mom! Rafi!"

They disentangled. "Hi, Ester," Roxana called, shoving her hair into place, smoothing her skirt.

"Come on in," Rafi added, jumping up from the loveseat.

Roxana whispered at him, "Glowing!"

He sucked in a breath, squeezed his eyes shut, and shivered all over. The ember glow guttered and vanished, right as the cottage door swung open and Ester and Oni walked in.

"How was your mint party?" Roxana asked.

"Fine," Oni said. She smiled in her usual shy way, looking much calmer now than she had when surrounded by korreds.

"It's *eleven-thirty*, Mom," Ester pronounced. "We should go home. Is what *you* would say to me."

"Oh, how the tables have turned." Roxana picked up her glass and drank the rest of the lemon water. It had warmed to room temperature—she and Rafi had been sitting there for that long. Talking. Kissing.

She handed him the glass. "Thanks."

Their gazes held. "I'll let you know my plans," he said.

She turned to Ester. "Did you thank Jove and Izzy for letting you stay so late?"

"*Yes*," Ester said, exasperated.

Oni assured Roxana it was true.

Rafi stepped outside with them. They said goodnight, the girls blithely, Roxana and Rafi casually, trying not to make excessive eye contact and more or less failing.

She couldn't kiss him in front of the kids, not yet. And tomorrow he'd be off to the fae realm for an uncertain length of time. Torture.

Roxana allowed herself one look back. Rafi had stopped near the wall of the cottage. He had mussed-up hair and sparkling eyes, and he gave her a roguish smile.

Delicious torture.

∾∾

Rafi didn't let himself dwell yet on the dazzling turn the evening had taken. First, he went to inform Jove and Izzy he'd be leaving on an errand.

They were putting dishes away in the kitchen. The mint party seemed to have involved tea, strawberries, mint leaves, and a lot of brownies, to judge from the crumbs.

Rafi picked up the dustpan and crouched to sweep the floor. "Did you talk to the club about security?" he asked Izzy.

She snorted in derision. "Yeah. They said their policy is already to make no-harm deals with fae who want to come in, but not all the bouncers enforce it, because 'it's so rare' that anything happens."

"Things worked like they're supposed to." Jove sounded tired. "People stepped in, including other fae. Everyone was fine."

"I would think you'd want a little more action taken considering it's *your child* they were endangering," Izzy snapped.

"Izzy…" Jove sighed.

Rafi dumped the crumbs in the food waste bin. "I wanted to let you know," he interjected before they could drag him into the argument, "I'm going across the verge tomorrow. So I'll be out a little while. Any other business I should do over there?"

They both hit him with keen glances, as if suspecting his errand was related to tonight's events. But given that the right magic—from witches or from fae—could get a person to tell the truth, it was often best not to know too much. Izzy and Jove understood this precaution.

"Okay," Jove said neutrally. "Don't think we have any, no."

"You're not…putting yourself in harm's way?" Izzy asked.

Rafi could lie, unlike fae, and they knew it. But he hoped they trusted him as he laid his hand over his heart, fae-style, and said, "I truthfully intend this to be a peaceful visit, and I hope and plan not to see anyone except friends."

She answered with a wary nod.

"Careful over there, love," Jove said.

Rafi promised to be, then returned to his cottage.

Only then did he slump dreamily with his back against the closed door and pull up the sensory details he'd been saving. Her pliant mouth, sweet-scented skin, soft flesh under stretchy fabric, moans, fingers clenching in his hair. His fire flared back to life.

It was rare that he liked himself much, his own body. "Stinky child," Brogyo called him, a phrase many of the other korreds had picked up. It used to be true: Rafi had gradually realized he smelled in just about all the ways a human child could. It caused him to begin washing his clothes more often as well as bathing more, or at least using his magic to evaporate or expel the grime from his skin and hair. He learned to make sure he was not only clean but reasonably attractive, whenever possible. He had even changed his anatomy as he grew.

The fae viewed all genders equally and likely wouldn't have treated him any differently if he had left himself unaltered or taken some physical form other than this one. They were always changing themselves—their size or shape or temperature or texture—on a whim, easy as a snap of fingers. Rafi could never match their sheer magical power. But the ways he *could* change himself felt far more meaningful to him, even if the results mattered little to his fae family. Becoming his own creation was a precious project to which he devoted years, and his continuous physical evolution brought him closer to what he envisioned his true nature to be. Not a drop of that energy was wasted; he had never regretted it.

Still, though, they kept saying it, *stinky child, pitiful mortal.* It was impossible not to feel beaten down by the words sometimes, even if they might only have meant he smelled human rather than fae.

But this body apparently pleased Roxana, and for that, tonight, he did like it. He ran his hand down his chest, belly, and hips, letting the red glow flicker hot enough to turn his cottage into a sauna.

The next morning at dawn, after a short but deep sleep, he went to a grocery that opened early and bought as many onion potato chips as he could fit in his backpack, alongside the pickaxe he had found in the tool shed adjoining the cottage.

He texted Roxana, *Good morning, beautiful. I'll be as fast as I can and hope to see you soon.*

He expected her to still be asleep, but she answered before he reached the verge:

Be careful, lovely. I'll miss you. Will be waiting for you and thinking of you.

Very much same, he typed back. Then he strode across the verge before he could fritter the day away in sweet messages.

CHAPTER 10

"WHOO, YEAH." SATSUKI EXAMINED THE texts, then handed Roxana's phone back to her. "That's a person smitten with you. You lucky beauty."

Roxana propped her head on her hand. "I barely slept a wink. But I can get through the day just on those messages."

Satsuki had returned to town yesterday, and they had eagerly arranged to meet up for brunch at a riverside café.

"I remember when you used to look like that because of me." Satsuki's jest was gentle.

Roxana winced. "Sorry. I'll rein it in."

"Nah, it's sweet. We did not work as a couple, but I think we make awesome friends."

"We do." Roxana sipped her cold brew coffee. "I'm being a terrible friend, though. About to abandon you here, after everything you've been through. How's your mom doing?"

Satsuki shrugged, jingling her flower-shaped earrings. "Not bad. We both miss Dad, but she actually mentioned the possibility of dating again. And the new shop location is gorgeous—right on the lagoon."

"Bookshop on the sea. It's the dream."

"Yeah. So that part of my life might end up all right. But you moving to the frigid north?" Satsuki pointed at Roxana. Her finger was decorated with a tiny blue seahorse tattoo. "Harder to get over."

"I know. The timing on all this—you coming back, me meeting Rafi...I hate it. Maybe the gods are trying to tell me something."

"Maybe, but changing careers is clearly the right move for you. You're not the IT type."

"My schooling lasts two years, and if we don't like Port Baleia, I can move back here after that and still pursue the mental-health-charms career. But for those two years…gods, a long-distance relationship? I'm not sure I can do it."

"Doesn't have to be a relationship. It can be a summer romance for now, then a 'can we get together if I'm in town?' thing."

Roxana picked up her fork and poked at the half of the omelet she hadn't eaten yet. "After I've left, though, no guarantee he'll still be interested."

"If it's guarantees you want from life, it's not life you're looking for."

Roxana laughed. "Whoa. Deep."

Satsuki reached across to steal the orange slice from Roxana's plate. "So Rafi does Meloncollie's cross-verge services?"

"Mail runs, yeah. Saw him deliver some chantagrams in town."

"Probably the other errands too."

"What other errands?"

Satsuki's eyebrows slanted up. "Finding stolen things? Tourism? Hook-ups?"

Her brain scrambled to make sense of it. "I…have heard rumors, but…"

"Everyone knows." Satsuki's voice had the amused yet slightly concerned tone she used when Roxana was hopelessly out of the loop about something.

"Probably not my parents," Roxana said.

"Oh, they know. Ask them."

After dinner that evening, Ester dashed off to her computer, leaving Roxana and her parents at the kitchen table. The mild evening air drifted in, smelling of the moonflowers in the garden. Timo brewed decaf for the three of them.

"So, the band, Meloncollie." Roxana stirred cream into her coffee. "Have you heard of them arranging errands across the verge for people?"

"Of course," Amaris said.

"Never quite getting in enough trouble to be worth reporting," Timo remarked. "But Amaris and I have both warned them a few times to be careful."

"Then—they bring chantagrams or letters, but also look for things the fae took?" Roxana asked.

"I have no objection to that part," Amaris said. "Especially when it's pets."

"Honestly I don't even mind when it's family meet-ups," Timo said. "Our agency, and the others, can only do so much—*will* only do so much. If someone has a fae-counted kid and we haven't had success in setting up an official meeting, I can't blame people for trying another way."

Roxana looked from her father to her mother. "So they've been doing this for years? Jove and Izzy find human clients, and Tash and Rafi—or whoever they have as fae contacts—go across and do the errands?"

Amaris's eyes crinkled in a smile. "You're only just now hearing about this, honey?"

"What other services do they do?" Roxana said.

"Oh, you know, fae-realm goods," Timo said. "Those are worth something. The fae don't mind as long as the right deal is struck. Like those metals Rafi brought you—that's why I figured you knew. Really, you didn't know?"

Roxana tried not to look like a person who'd just sent Rafi back across the verge to get even more fae-realm metal. "Right, no, that makes sense."

"Missing persons," Amaris said. "Once all the human-side official channels have tried and failed, and the case is closed, loved ones usually still want someone to inquire further."

"I'd expect so." Roxana latched her fingertips around the mug. Those victims. *How many more did I not see?*, Rafi had said.

"Jobs," Timo piped up. "Fae willing to do magic for a deal, like fadas to clean stuff, dryads to make your garden flourish."

"Matchmaking," Amaris added. "Setting people up, if someone has a thing for certain fae types." She barked a laugh. "Exciting, but starts getting dangerous there."

"Tourism," Timo added before Roxana could process the matchmaking one. "Also dangerous."

"People pay for guided trips into the fae realm?" Roxana said.

"Yup," her dad said. "Not advisable. But I'll hand it to Jove and Izzy and their fae colleagues, so far I haven't heard of anyone getting hurt. Not much anyway."

"Their fae colleagues being Tash and Rafi," Roxana said, just to clarify.

"Those are the current ones," Amaris said. "They've had a few different quote-unquote 'band members' over the years, but fae don't always like to stick around."

"It's not a quote-unquote thing," Timo protested mildly. "They really do play music."

"You know what I mean." Amaris looked at Roxana. "Seems like Rafi's been around a lot. Is he thinking of becoming a townie?"

Roxana sipped her coffee. "I don't know. Maybe."

"That'd be nice." Amaris downed the rest of her coffee and clicked the mug on the table. "I always view it as a compliment to our town when a faery decides they want to live here."

Roxana murmured agreement. But her giddiness about kissing Rafi was tempered now, cooled by remembering all those moments he shrank from the idea of living in the human world, insisted he *didn't* live here despite the fact that in a basic and literal sense, he did.

Nor would she live here—in Miryoku—much longer.

She straightened her shoulders. She had five weeks yet. Plenty of time.

For what exactly, she didn't specify.

First Rafi had to wait for Mukut to be alone. He rubbed wild lemongrass all over himself to mask his scent—something he'd often done when he wanted to hide from the korreds—and lurked in a bush with his endo-witch chameleon powers on. It didn't take much energy, changing his skin and hair to a camouflage that matched the surrounding leaves and shadows. His magic couldn't change his clothes, but today he wore dark greens and grays that blended in well enough.

Finally, another stone giant took Mukut's place as the wall barring the korreds' haunt entrance. Mukut turned into her walking form and took slow, thunderous steps out toward the hills.

Rafi followed, then leaped up to grab her blocky wrist.

The deal they struck was swift and easy. "Don't tell anyone else I was here today," he said. "I'm only collecting some rocks, like before. I brought you these. Will you take me where I want to go? Deal?"

She accepted the potato chips with rumbles of delight, ate them all, and let him climb onto her shoulder.

First, as a smokescreen, he had her stop at some of the same places they'd gotten metals last time, where he dutifully chipped away small pieces to put in his pack. Likely Roxana would find a use for them. After that, he casually said, "Now the Unwanted Cliff."

Mukut made a low rumble with a rising pitch.

"Yes, really," he said. "You don't have to touch it. I'll take care of it."

She rippled her chunky shoulders in an approximate shrug—a deal was a deal—picked him back up, and set off uphill again, lichen-covered feet scraping and thumping along the landscape.

Even with Mukut's tireless steps, the walk took the better part of the day. The Unwanted Cliff stood in the air fae territory touching the eastern edge of Kepelo's haunt. Sylphs swooped over Rafi and Mukut, blue and indifferent, and bird fae of a hundred varieties screeched at them, but no one attacked. After a teetering walk along the side of a vertiginous scree-covered slope, which Mukut negotiated with the placid surefootedness of a mountain goat, they entered a valley between towering hills. Across from them stood the cliff.

Though unwanted by fae, the cliff was plenty wanted by ordinary birds. Hundreds of gulls had made it their home, along with a few eagles near the top, keeping an eye out for gull eggs to snatch. The gulls consequently spent a lot of time swirling and shrieking to keep the eagles away and were happy to target anyone else who got near.

Rafi stood at the bottom of the cliff, a safe distance from bird-dropping splatter. He'd never been this close to the cliff before and hadn't anticipated the avian chaos. "Hmm," he said.

Lurking behind him, Mukut echoed the sound dubiously.

He approached—the cliff's base was bird-free, at least—and touched a stripe of mineral, silvery-black with reddish glints. It stung his fingertips like a nettle. Definitely iron.

He set down his pack, took out the pickaxe, and got to work.

But the vein of iron in that section was tiny; he only ended up with a few crumbles. Squinting up at the mess of feathers and flapping wings, he told Mukut, "Nothing for it." He stripped down, turned himself to fire form, took the pickaxe between his elongated teeth, and backed up on all fours to get a running start.

He tore forward and scrambled up the cliff, his clawed feet catching where his human hands couldn't have. Scattering gulls on the way, he propelled himself up until reaching a vertical crevice. It was just big enough to jam a foot into to hold himself in place. From there—while ear-splittingly loud birds dive-bombed him—he struck the pickaxe over and over against a vein of iron above the crevice. Chunks of rock tumbled to the ground; he dodged them to keep from being stung, and below, Mukut stepped back to get out of the way.

When his body started to shake from the double exertion of mining rock and holding on to his drake form, he leaped down and retreated. He gathered the rocks he'd chipped off. They might not be enough. The sun was setting, and he was resigned to one full night in this realm, though hopefully no longer.

He turned to Mukut. "Help me find a safe place to sleep? I'll finish tomorrow morning, then we'll go back. Okay?"

He had never spent a night in this air haunt, and doing so alone wasn't wise. Ghoul-sylphs sometimes floated out at night in air-fae regions, seeking fear in living things to amplify and drink in. He'd met one once, and that was enough.

Mukut lumbered across the floor of the valley to a quieter rock face. She stretched herself into a wall, curving into place until she had created a stone hut with a gap big enough for Rafi to weasel into. He thanked her and crawled inside. It was dark, but that was no trouble to an endo-witch: he lit up his hands with a glow while he got out his camping lantern. After eating the food he had brought, he spread out a thin blanket and fell asleep, exhausted.

He jolted awake after a nightmare involving Sminu strangling him. The powdery light of dawn sifted through the doorway crack. He blinked, getting his bearings as he shook off the dream. Then he remembered he would see Roxana again today and leaped up, revived.

One more flight up the cliff, hammering among angry gulls, and he had enough rock specimens that they filled his pack to an almost unliftable weight. He hauled it onto his shoulders, then turned to Mukut. "To the verge, please."

CHAPTER 11

ON THE FIRST MORNING AFTER RAFI'S DE-
parture, Roxana awoke early, anticipation fluttering in her chest. No
messages. She left him one just in case.

*Suppose you won't get this till you're back. Just checking in. See you soon, I
hope!*

She was a tangle of nerves all day, busying herself with tasks—completing
forms for her art school classes, emailing Ester's school in Port Baleia to verify
her spot there, cleaning out a drawer.

Would she kiss Rafi again if he did return in time? Longing to wasn't a
good enough reason. She was about to move away; was this really a good time
to date someone?

It was best he still wasn't back by that evening. She hadn't decided a thing.

On the second day, she considered the notion of a summer romance. Satsuki had thought it normal enough, even for Roxana. If Rafi wanted it…well,
they could at least talk about it.

But he wasn't back that day either.

On the third day, Roxana decided she would at least kiss him in greeting.
See what happened. Except he still hadn't returned.

On the fourth day, Roxana texted Tash, whose number she'd gotten from
Izzy.

Rafi's been across the verge for four days. Do you think he's okay?

Probably, Tash answered after many hours. *He grew up there. He knows
how to be safe.*

True. Would you hear if anything had gone wrong, though?

I hear sometimes, Tash said. *I did last time.*

The indifferent messages cowed Roxana into responding merely *OK,
thanks.* She was fretting too much. Typical. She cleaned out another few
drawers.

On the fifth day, she admitted to herself she ached to make out with him again, not just a greeting kiss.

As to the iron charm, she hadn't given it further thought. Its success would depend on the quality and amount of metal he brought back. Besides, she didn't *have* to make it. Or would he be disappointed if she didn't? Great, another thing to stress about.

On the sixth day, her dad brought home a stack of cardboard boxes so she could start packing. She sat alone staring at the boxes. Her tizzy of indecision settled to the bottom of her soul, becoming an inert sludge. The boxes made it real. This was happening. She was moving away.

By nightfall she knew she would scream internally at herself for the rest of the year, perhaps the rest of her life, if she didn't invite Rafi into a proper, full-blown, sweaty summer fling.

On the seventh, eighth, and ninth days, she sorted her possessions, dealt with more emails, pined for him, worried about him, and burned with desire.

On the tenth day, in the morning, a lazy but drenching storm rolled up from the tropics and settled itself over Miryoku. The rain hissed on the garden pavers and flooded the birdbaths till they spilled over. Thunder rolled around the edges of town.

Her job hours had dwindled to the point of allowing her to work from home. She was archiving emails and sipping a midmorning cup of tea at the kitchen table when the text message bloomed bright on her phone.

Hello! I'm back. Want to come see a bunch of rocks?

Everything in Roxana leaped into the air and came down scattered. She couldn't catch her breath. She began typing an impulsive reply.

Rafi added another line before she could send it.

I'm sorry it was so long. I started swearing when I saw it had been ten days since I left.

Roxana laughed giddily, alone in the kitchen.

TEN DAYS, she responded. *I was about to say! Ten days you left me hanging. Yes, I will come right over. So glad you're back.*

Perfect, he said. *I'll be in the cottage.*

If she acted fast enough, filled the minutes with enough tasks, she wouldn't have time to lose her nerve. Mug in the sink. Computer logged out. Old T-shirt and shorts stripped off, fast shower taken even though she'd showered a few hours ago, and dress put on—dark blue linen, short-sleeved with buttons up the front. Casual enough for a rainy summer day, cute enough for a date. Teeth brushed. A pause at Ester's bedroom to tell her she was going out for a bit, and that Timo would be home soon. (Ester waved goodbye, involved, it appeared, in making up a silly dance for some song and trying to film herself doing it on her phone.)

Roxana put on sandals, grabbed an umbrella, and went out.

By the time she reached Rafi's gate, she was drenched from the knees down, her shins and feet spattered with flecks of grass. The hem of her skirt clung to her legs. Why had she bothered with another shower? Or for that matter the umbrella?, she thought, in manic humor.

Then she was unlatching the gate, folding her umbrella, and entering the dripping tunnel of greenery.

Rafi was already on his porch, sitting cross-legged under the roof. He jumped to his feet when she arrived, a smile blooming on his face. He was barefoot and wore a one-shouldered sarong, black with silver moons and stars, the one he'd worn when she'd first seen him on stage.

She hurried to the steps, and he drew her up under the shelter. "Oh my gods, it's pouring," he said. His hands lingered on her arms.

"Yeah." Roxana shook back a curl stuck to her cheek and looked up at him, giddy with the smell of him, rich and close in the humid air. She took a lock of his hair between her fingers, finding it damp. "You get caught in the rain too?"

"No—well, I did, but now I'm wet from showering. Grimy trip."

"Right." She was breathing fast, though the walk hadn't taken much exertion. "Ten days. Missed you."

"I missed you even though it was only two days for me." He slid his hand beneath her hair, against the back of her neck, and lowered his face toward hers.

Roxana rose on tiptoes and sealed their mouths together. Her umbrella sloshed to the porch boards. She wrapped her arms around his neck, and he lifted her around the waist. A few stumbled steps to cross the threshold into his cottage, and he shut the door.

"Do, um," he said between kisses, "do you want to see the iron?" He made no move to untangle himself, his back against the door as he held her.

"In a bit." She tilted her face, dipping her tongue into his mouth, and felt the vibration of his moan. Heat flared against her body everywhere they touched. The glow flickered under his skin, and she spread her palm on his bare chest. Instead of hairs, tiny scales like flecks of mica were scattered there, the thickest grouping of them massed in a line down the center of his rib cage.

She traced the trail with her finger until meeting the diagonal sweep of his sarong. *How far down do these go?*, she would have asked if she were a bolder style of seducer. But coming here today and touching him like this was essentially the boldest Roxana Wei ever got.

He swallowed, a click of his throat. He touched the collar of her dress and circled his finger on the iridescent shell surface of the top button. Roxana unfastened it. His skin glowed hotter. With a crooked smile, he let his fingers drop to the next button and unfastened that too.

"I never got," he said, his voice husky, "why humans wore clothes in summer. Till I realized how thrilling it could be when they're taken off."

She slid her hand under his sarong, stroking his bare hip. "Yeah, I think Hari and other business owners also don't consider it hygienic for naked people to sit in their cafés, or something. Weird."

He nuzzled her nose. "You better guide me," he said softly. "I don't always understand humans. I don't want to do anything wrong, especially with you."

"You're human too."

"Yes, but…"

"Want to undo the rest of these?"

He made a sound like a whimper and nodded.

Her dress and his sarong were soon draped over the arm of the loveseat. They'd both skimped on undergarments this morning, Roxana wearing no bra, only hip-hugging briefs, and Rafi wearing none at all. Roxana left her sandals at the door and drew Rafi across to his bed.

She let her briefs stay on a little while. "Because then it's more exciting when they get taken off," she reminded him.

In a windowless corner shielded by the antique screen, his bed was a lush cave lit by the diffused daylight from the main room and the ember glow of

Rafi's body. The twin mattress had yellow paisley sheets faded to softness, a red blanket they quickly shoved to the floor, and a tendency to creak with each shift of their position. The air smelled of his skin and hair and of old garden tools. She could hear rain pattering off the eaves on the other side of the wooden wall.

"Gods," she said fervently into his neck. "I love this."

"Even with the rain, and in a garden shed…"

"Yes, honestly, I love it. I feel…wild. Doing this in here, with you."

"Wild. Huh. You make me feel domesticated." When she laughed at the word, he clarified, "Safe." He cupped her cheek. "Cared for."

A minute later, he helped her peel off her underwear, which his hands had been entirely inside anyway. She wrapped herself, uninhibited, around him.

She guided him, as requested, showing him what she wanted. He guided her, too, begging for more of certain touches or movements, assuring her that nothing in him of fire or stone could hurt her, not just by accident or proximity, anyway.

"I never thought it would," she assured, then dug her fingers tighter into his shoulder blades, asking for *more* and *again*.

As he brought her to the crest, and as all of him blazed heat when he followed a few seconds behind her, she kept her limbs wrapped as tight around him as a jasmine vine.

I almost decided not to do this, she thought in wonder. *I never would have known what this was like.* What a travesty that would have been, what a lost treasure. She held him, listening to the thunder and the dripping rain and the birdsong, and soaked up every spark, every summer raindrop, to store for the cold seasons.

❧

"Guess what." Roxana lazily caressed his thigh. "It's actually Tuesday morning."

Rafi pulled his dazzled thoughts back to mundane matters such as the calendar. "Is it? That's appropriate."

"The night you sang that for me, I probably would have had sex with you then if you'd asked."

"Which is what we always ask when we play a request. Standard payment."

She gave him a fingernail flick, dangerously close to the groin.

He yelped, then turned his face toward hers, on the pillow. "I was already imagining sex with you when I was learning the song," he confessed.

She shifted onto her side. "I want us to do this while we can. But I still have to move at the beginning of September."

Somberness flitted across his mood, a ghoul-sylph darkening the stars. "I know."

"And you have a life here—your mother, the band, the errands. Hooking people up with fae lovers and all that." She smiled.

"I've hardly ever done *that*. Messages, stolen property, bit of tourism—that's usually all."

"Apparently everyone knew about that but me. I finally asked around. But it's good, it's something you're uniquely qualified for. You're needed here."

"You have family here too. Friends." He tried not to sound like he was pleading.

"Definitely. I'll still visit. So…we can do this for the summer, part ways amicably, then see what we feel like when we meet up again?"

That *part ways amicably*, that was the ghoul in the darkness. He averted his mind from it. "Okay."

"For now I'd also prefer we keep it from Ester. Which probably means keeping it from most people, since she has a way of talking to everyone, and someone might tell her."

"Whatever you think is best."

"It's only that she's still young." Roxana sounded helpless. "I'm not sure she'd understand. It'd confuse her, and could make her more upset that we're leaving…"

"You're her parent. I defer to you. I don't know what's normal for a kid in these situations." He smoothed his hand across her curls. "Secret lovers for the month of August and maybe beyond? I don't hate this idea."

"I do want to keep 'beyond' open."

"Maybe if I can figure out trains or whatever, I can even visit you in Port Baleia."

"Yes. I can help with trains and logistics. You should."

Rafi brushed a kiss, soft as a petal, on her lips. "I grant you this deal."

She breathed a quiet laugh.

"So *now* do you want to see the iron?" he asked.

CHAPTER 12

H OW DID YOU CARRY THIS?" WEARING HER mostly buttoned dress again, Roxana tugged on the top loop of his backpack. She couldn't even budge it off the floor.

"Not saying it was easy." Rafi rubbed one of his shoulders.

She crouched and took out a grapefruit-sized chunk of rock with dark silver and rusty red veins running through it. Its sober energy radiated into her hand. "Hematite," she said. "Common iron ore. But, whoa, *strong*."

"Will it work?" He sounded anxious.

"Sure. That is, you got more than enough." She set down the rock and slid her hands into the pack, feeling the iron energy thrumming down among the specimens. "Should be able to make a wrist cuff of some kind. As to whether it'll work the way we want, no guarantees. But…" She settled cross-legged on the floor and drew the rock onto her lap. "May as well smelt it here so I can bring it home and try making something. I'll never be able to carry all those rocks."

She focused on the iron: austere, cold, reminding her of a school headmaster in old British stories, or a prison guard on American TV. After a deep breath to fortify herself, she pulled at the iron, coaxing it to soften and emerge. It resisted at first, clinging within the rock, then seemed to break, and moved in one flowing mass into her palm. The surrounding rock crumbled, bits bouncing off her knee to land on the floorboards.

The lump of iron was the size of one of Hari's mochi balls. Roxana squeezed it with a bit of magic to morph it into egg shape, then lifted it to admire its dark sheen. The red rust had shivered off. She brought it to her nose and sniffed the bloodlike whiff of iron. The smell would surely cling to her palms after this.

Rafi settled to sit in front of her, watching.

"There we go." She held up the egg. "Pure fae-realm iron."

"That was incredible." He looked entranced. "You did it so gracefully. The korreds extract metals from rocks sometimes, but their way involves a lot of bashing. You do it like a gnome."

Gratified, she tossed the egg back and forth between her hands. "That would make sense, if my ancestry rumor is accurate. I don't actually know any gnomes. Not well, at least."

"There's an earth fae haunt of mostly gnomes, in the foothills. Mukut's taken me there a couple of times. They keep to themselves, but they trust Mukut, so they let me see some of the ways they shape stone and metal. You'd love it. It's beautiful."

Affection sped through her. She smiled at him, then set down the iron egg and took out a new chunk of rock. "All right. Next."

She broke into a sweat and her heart thumped steadily as she worked. After setting down the fourth lump of smelted iron and wiping her brow, she looked up to find Rafi handing her a pale green drink in a glass fogged with condensation.

She thanked him and gulped it down—chilled green tea. "Whew. I'm going to sleep well tonight, after all the day's exertions."

One of his eyebrows lifted, and he sank lithely to all fours and advanced upon her.

Soon they had to move back to the bed, as certain activities just weren't suited to a wood floor strewn with rocks.

⚮

It took Roxana three days to smelt all the iron.

"Such a shame, having to spend so much time here," she said on the third day, as Rafi molded himself to her side on the loveseat and mouthed her neck, interrupting her work with the rocks.

It was odd how little her family seemed to suspect. Her parents were busy with their own work. Ester was often talking online to Oni or meeting up with her, or brainstorming details for their going-away party. Roxana tried to have as little as possible to do with that, not wishing to think about disentangling herself from Rafi's arms and leaving him two hundred miles behind.

No one even noticed the fae-realm iron eggs she brought back, a few in her pocket at a time. She stashed them in the back of a workroom drawer filled with rings, charms, and other metal pieces. In her household, only her father, from whom the earth-fae ancestry came, would have a chance at sensing what the iron was, and then only if he went poking into the drawer, which he had no reason to do. Like hers, his matter-witch powers manifested most strongly in the earth element, but his tended toward stone, on a broader and less miniature scale. He mainly used his magic for mending garden pavers and making birdbaths and the like. Ester and Amaris, like roughly half the human population of Eidolonia, hadn't inherited any witch abilities.

Thus, undetected in her workroom, Roxana fashioned a cuff of fae-realm iron. Rafi had gauged that Brogyo's forearms were about the circumference of Rafi's upper arms, so she worked from that measurement. The final cuff was some three inches across and a quarter-inch thick. She gave it a hinge in the middle and magnetized the ends of the cuff so it could be easily clapped shut. For Rafi to be able to carry it without undergoing pain from the iron, or torment from the spell, she gave it an enamel exterior of glossy midnight blue. Atop the enamel she added a thin silver vine, ending in two halves of a jasmine blossom that came together into a whole when the cuff was closed. It looked respectable when done, like a funky fashion piece rather than a disciplinary tool.

Into the silver vine she infused a spell to steady and calm the mind, as Rafi would be touching the exterior and might need such a spell if he ever did intend to use the cuff on someone.

Finally it was time to create the spell on the interior. She pulled the cuff onto her lap and rested both hands inside it, against the cool iron.

Hazel, lured away and struck down by enchantment. The people Rafi had seen, dead or damaged. The missing citizens he hadn't seen, forever unaccounted for. Oni, surrounded and petrified at the club table. Ester, her belligerent spirit drained out of her at the grasp of a korred's hand.

Others in this world were cruel, too, lacking remorse for what they'd inflicted. There was Micah when he'd left Ester and Roxana—*be honest*, she told herself, *you'd have used it on him*. Or those who abused children or animals or others in their power. Even politicians like the hypocritical, greedy Akio Riquelme, the recently elected governor of Costa Real—it would only do the country a favor to slap an empathy shackle onto him for ten minutes. The dictators of the world in general: who would protest such a treatment being forced on them?

Rafi and Roxana, along with countless others, were evidence of the harmonious fae/human mixing that blossomed all over the island. But human extremists, along with certain fae like Brogyo and his korreds, were a different case. They had twisted and grown in a disruptive direction, like ivy wrapping around a tree to the point of suffocating it. They couldn't see their own error; their nature wouldn't allow it. Someone had to retrain them to grow a different way. The dose of empathy would be painful, but better in the long run, by far, than allowing them to go on hurting and killing as they were.

She gathered that weighty conclusion, with all its complications, to the forefront of her mind and began feeding it into the iron cuff.

Four nights later, she brought it to Rafi. It was after dinner, and the air smelled of smoke. The sunset had been blood-red with it, and now a crimson glow glimmered above the eastern hills.

"Kepelo's fae doing one of their burns?" she asked when she got to his porch.

He nodded. "Smells like it. Right time of year for it too."

She shivered. "I know it's natural, and good for the woods, but it always unnerves me. The thought that they're burning the forest, not far away."

"Only a piece of it, and they control it well." His gaze was focused on the small bundle wrapped in silk she had taken out of her shoulder bag. Forest fires, evidently, didn't faze him; they had been part of the nicer side of his upbringing. But this cuff was another matter.

She sat on the loveseat, and he perched on the coffee table box, their knees touching. She unfolded the silk. The cuff's enamel gleamed dark blue, while the dull black inside seemed to suck away the lamplight. "I've never layered a spell so many times into one charm," she said. "It just has so much more metal than my usual pieces. And this iron holds a lot."

"It looks nicer than I pictured." His voice was quiet. "More civilized." He reached out a finger to stroke its exterior.

"Don't touch the inside," she warned.

He carefully took the cuff from her, cupping his hands under the silk. "How did you manage? You had to touch it while making it."

Her hands felt light without the cuff's weight. She clasped them on her elbows. "I can block my own spells on items, even other people's spells if they're not too strong. Most matter-witches can. Just takes extra coordination, blocking a spell with part of my mind while layering in more magic with another."

"Layering in…guilt? Do you have to make yourself feel it?"

"Empathy was the idea, but·yes, guilt too. Ordinarily I don't need to feel an emotion too strongly to put it in a charm. It doesn't take much. It's like how a little pill can trigger enough of a brain chemistry shift to change someone's mood. But those were always nicer moods I put into charms before. I had to look up how they do this one for the criminal shackles."

Rafi lifted his eyes to her. "Was it awful?"

"Less pleasant than usual. And no one had precise instructions, of course, so I can't even be sure it's right."

"Yeah, I guess it…hasn't been tested."

She swallowed and looked down. "No, I did test it. Earlier today, when I finished it. Just for a second."

A whole minute, actually. She had timed it. Made herself endure it.

"You—" He cut off the word, his voice sounding strangled.

"It's okay," she quickly said. "I'm not fae, or even half fae, so the iron itself doesn't hurt me. I could only feel the spell. Really, it's all right."

His gaze dropped back to the cuff.

"It just," she added, "made me remember things I don't like to think about. Things I hadn't thought of in years. Funny that a spell I cast myself can do that to me."

"You couldn't have done anything that awful. Not compared to the people this is meant for."

"Well, it finds the things I *have* done. Times I lost my temper with Ester or my parents or Micah, said things I shouldn't have. Gods, one time was with Satsuki way back in high school, when I snapped at her to get over a crush she had on a water faery. Such a dumb teenage thing. But under this spell I felt such raw guilt, like I had just said it ten minutes ago." She squeezed one hand with the other, wishing she could wring out the sensation. "So—yes, it's been tested. Just not on a faery."

He searched her face before looking down at the cuff again. His features resolved into determination. "Then it at least needs a test on a half-fae."

And before she could say more than "No!", he snapped the cuff around his wrist.

⌒⌒

Roxana's words of alarm came through as background noise to the storm. White sparks pinpricked his vision. A dull roar filled his ears. He could feel her grab the cuff and try to take it off him.

He yanked his arm away, stumbling back, dimly aware of the box he'd been sitting on falling over and banging his foot. Panting, he held his cuffed wrist behind himself. "No. No. If I'm…going to put it on anyone else…then I should know what it's like."

Though agony etched lines in her face, she let her hands sink. "Just for a minute. No more than that."

His wrist felt like biting ants were crawling all over it. And that wasn't even the worst. A clawing remorse had seized the core of him, nauseating him and making him feel as if he had just flung someone off a cliff and was staring down at their body. Still…

"Fifteen minutes," he said.

"No."

"Time it. Please."

"Rafi…"

He sank to his knees, eyes closed, forcing himself to examine each harrowingly clear memory that surfaced. The offense and embarrassment he had caused his fae families through being clueless or emotional or helpless. The people in town he had frightened, deliberately, as a youth roaming in the company of mischievous fae, desperately wanting to fit in as a powerful faery. The desolate, cruel words he had hurled at his first human lover when she had broken up with him. The heartache he had caused Hazel every time he chose to return to the fae realm after visiting her, even though he knew, *he knew*, she wanted him to stay.

The physical pain, meanwhile, was stiffening his hands into claws, his body trying to protect itself by hardening his skin to stone. Not that it helped—the iron's power didn't seem diminished at all. Given how rigid his hands had become, he wasn't sure he *could* take the cuff off. It was for the best, maybe: falling unconscious and staying that way forever was what he deserved.

Except…a spark stayed alive in his chest, and it whispered to him that Roxana was here, that he must come back for her, and that also he must go on living so as to make amends and become a nobler soul.

He found he had his forehead on the floor. He was in stone-drake form, still racked with misery, but he forced his face and neck to soften and turned his head toward Roxana.

She was sitting on the floor, too, knees pulled up, face cradled in her palms.

"Has it been fifteen minutes?" he croaked.

She lifted her face. Rather than being tear-streaked, as he somewhat expected, it was ashen, her lips tight and eyes bleak. "Close enough," she said.

She rolled forward on her knees to come to him, but he murmured, "Let me," and wrapped his hand around the cuff.

He focused all his strength on tugging at it. Over and over he tried. But he was too weak, and the iron held its magnetic grip. Panting, he let his shaking arm fall to the floor.

Roxana scrambled over. With both hands, she yanked the cuff off. It clattered to the floorboards and lay there open, a dark black-and-blue numeral 3.

Rafi's cheek stayed on the cool wood. The physical torment dropped, leaving only the ache from the storm of inflammation. The mood stayed, a sensation of having done irrevocable wrong.

Roxana took his hand. "Find the goodness under it. The love. The reason you don't want to hurt anyone. I found it helped when I focused on that."

Follow your love. Rafi shut his eyes. Tears filled them, creeping along the closed seams of his eyelids.

A few deep breaths and the steady grip of Roxana's hand returned enough strength to him that he was able to shove up to a sitting position. He wiped his face and tried to straighten his clothing. Jove's cast-off T-shirt and shorts, despite being too big for Rafi, had ripped in a few places in his transformation to stone.

"Promise me something." Roxana still held his hand. "Promise me you won't ever put it on again, no matter what you think you've done."

"I'm not in any hurry to."

"Never again." She looked him in the eyes. "You're kind and conscientious, and you already blame yourself too much. That"—she spat the word toward the cuff—"is not for you."

"You tested it too. It isn't for you either."

"I have to test all my pieces. It's my work. Besides, the iron doesn't add extra pain for me. You promise?"

He hated that he wavered. But a promise was something to hold on to, and he needed as many anchors as he could get. "I promise."

She took something from her pocket, silver in the shape of a round citrus slice, bigger than Eidolonia's two-lira coin. She pressed it into his hand. Soothing calm spread into him. "Hold that," she said. "I'll get you a drink of water. Then let's go get some fresh air, if we can find any in all this smoke."

As they walked downhill, an ocean wind swept in, tempering the burning smell with cool marine air.

"Maybe I should just destroy it," Roxana said as they wandered into a cul-de-sac.

"*No.* And have you and I be the only ones to ever wear it? That's ridiculous."

"It's too strong. I never thought I could make anything that strong, and I hate that I did."

"But it would have to be strong to work on the fae. Is it strong *enough*, is what I'm wondering."

She looked at him in disbelief. "After what it did to you?"

"The korreds are stronger than me by far. It might just make them angry." Rafi shrugged, tired. "Who knows."

"The more important question is, will it work the way we hope, psychologically? I've always designed my charms from the human point of view. Fae psychology is quite different. To the degree we know anything about it."

A small park was tucked into the neighborhood. Rafi veered into the grass and sat under a tree. Roxana joined him, her face gold-washed in the setting sun. "It is different," he admitted. "But not as different as humans usually imagine. Look at all the fae who adapt to human-side life. And even the ones who don't want to live on this side can accept the terms of deals. They can adapt their mindset that far."

"The cuff could hardly be called a deal."

"Could be leverage for one. A deterrent. Stop hurting humans or get this pain again."

"Again," she repeated. "Meaning you'd have to get it on them once in the first place and live to tell the tale."

"Ideally they wouldn't recognize me or catch me. What good are form-changing powers if I can't pull off a convincing disguise?"

Roxana puffed out a sigh. "Even so…"

"Assuming I ever do it, which possibly I never will, I do think it might affect them the way we hope. Most fae, like most humans, can be reasoned with and wouldn't even need this cuff. But Brogyo and my father and the others are like…what did you call them?"

"Sociopaths? Narcissists?"

"Right, those. They need their view shaken open so they can grasp what it means to hurt other people. Wearing it was awful, but it also left me wanting to do less harm. Stopping them is one way of reducing the amount of harm done in the world."

"You do see the irony in wanting to do less harm via clapping an instrument of pain on someone."

He squinted up into the tree. "I do. Although it makes no less sense to me than a lot of things in human society."

"Fair." She threaded her fingers around the wrist where he had worn the cuff. "I still hate that you were hurt by something I made."

He stroked her palm, finding tiny calluses from her years of handling metal. "I hate that I made you use your wonderful magic for that."

"It will not be a part of my career portfolio, I can say that for sure."

"If we're extracting promises from each other, you have to promise to stick only to charms that heal, after this."

"That's an easy one. I accept." She kissed his forehead. "I know something that'll make us feel better. Come here. Let's see if they're out."

"If what's out?" he asked.

She got up. "Come." She led him into an alley. At its end, the neighborhood turned into fields. She stopped at the last fence—interlocking spirals of iron—and beamed through the bars. "Hello, sweeties."

Rafi smelled hay and warm furry animal. His mouth fell open when he saw them. "What are they?"

"Mini alpacas." Roxana crouched, picked a dandelion leaf, and held it through the fence. "My mom's best friend owns this house. The mama just had the little one a month ago." She looked up toward the house and waved. Someone in a window waved back.

Two brown animals ambled on woolly legs to the fence. A littler one, its fur lighter brown, frolicked up behind them. One of the adult alpacas lowered its long neck and gobbled the dandelion from Roxana's fingers.

Rafi crouched too, transfixed. "I've never seen anything with so much fur on its face." Roxana had reached through to pet the nose of the large alpaca, so Rafi slipped a forefinger past the iron—careful not to touch it—and stroked the forehead of the little one, who had jammed its nose up against the fence.

"The fur is why she keeps them," Roxana said. "She shears them and makes yarn. People pay good money for it. Aren't they cute?"

"They look like they're smiling." Rafi found it was impossible not to smile back.

"The baby's name is Osgood."

"Hi, Osgood." The baby lipped his fingers, then made a pensive humming sound. His parents echoed the sound in a deeper pitch. "They kind of remind me of a deer I made friends with once. Except woollier. Plus apparently they hum."

"The sounds crack me up." Roxana picked more dandelions.

"I hope the korreds never find these."

"Did they do something to your deer?"

He fed a dandelion stem to one of the parent alpacas. "They ate her."

Her head drooped. "Ah."

"I tried to make a deal so they'd spare her. But they'd already caught her and were hungry, and were setting a price impossible for me to meet—five mountain stags by that night. As if I had any way to get even one, ever. They ran out of patience, and…" He sat back on his knees, shrugged, and let the baby nibble at his hand again.

"Yeah." Roxana's voice hardened. "You go ahead and keep that cuff."

CHAPTER 13

THE FOREST FIRE SMOKE CLEARED. THE BAND had a lull in performance dates, and Rafi had a lull in cross-verge errands. Roxana attended her last day of work, complete with a lunch party at a Vietnamese restaurant. She felt guilty for not paying enough attention to her kind coworkers and daydreaming instead about all the steamy days she'd have with Rafi for the next two weeks. Ester kept busy, going out with Oni or Timo or Amaris. The korreds didn't show up in town, as far as anyone heard. The cuff stayed wrapped in silk, hidden behind a book in Rafi's cottage.

On her first morning as a woman between jobs, Roxana visited a shrine to the Lady. It stood near a footpath beside Aria Creek, tucked under a big rhododendron: a plinth supporting a small stone statue of a woman with a globelike belly and leafy hair, sitting in cross-legged position. On the statue's base were the carved initials *TB*. Roxana's father, Timo Bartolo, had fashioned plinth and statue as a festival gift to the town, years ago. At the Lady's feet was a copper bowl with the moon phases etched around its sides. Roxana had made that. The bowl had turned green with age and was filled with pebbles, coins, flowers, folded notes, and other offerings. Incense ash dusted the ground. Roxana wiped off the statue with a cloth dipped in the creek, then got out the fresh incense stick she had brought and stuck it in the bowl. She lit it, and sweet sandalwood infused the air.

"Lady, a thousand thank yous for Rafi and the time we have together. Please help me enjoy it and use it well." She let her fingers rest on the round belly, smoke bathing her wrist, before wandering away and texting Rafi to arrange their next rendezvous.

An hour later, she whipped the sand out of her underwear and wriggled back into it while Rafi did the same with his shorts. She leaned over on their beach towel and kissed the scales on his arm. "That was as daring as I've ever gotten."

He glanced up the cliff behind them. "Think those seagulls saw us. They might tell the merfolk."

They were at the same beach where they'd flown the kites. Near the south cliff they'd found another driftwood shelter, dragged a few logs over to add to it, then declared it a good enough privacy screen and spread their towel behind it.

She tugged her sundress back down and leaned against him in happy exhaustion. "Have I mentioned I appreciate how you can make your hands move extra fast?"

"I've gathered you like that. I enjoy it myself." Resting back on a log, he wrapped his arm around her. "Could use my magic other ways, too, if you want. Would you like any shape or size adjustments? Color maybe?" He swept his fingers playfully across his torso. "Make my skin cheetah print?"

Laughing, she caught his hand and held it against his chest. "Don't waste energy on that. You're perfect as is." She tilted her head up to admire his profile. "Although *is* any of this self-engineered? Whatever you did, I approve in advance."

"Thank you. There's a fair amount, actually. If I hadn't changed things, my anatomy would probably lean a lot more female—or at least that was everyone's best guess when I was a baby."

"Impressive! I imagine that took tons of energy for it to stick."

"It did. I started before I even reached puberty. Just felt like it fit me better. Poured magic into changing myself for as many hours a day as I could, until basically passing out from exhaustion, for…I don't know, months. Maybe a year."

"Human parents usually wouldn't allow that route. Children's magic isn't very refined—the outcome is not always what's intended." She pondered Ester's childhood for a moment and added, "Plus they'd miss a lot of school."

"But I didn't have school, of course. Or any other obligations. I was lucky in having my mother and other fae around, too, to help me heal and adjust the magic. Anyway, eventually the change started sticking, and it got easier."

"Morph your face like that and it'll stay that way. Is what parents say to their endo-witch kids."

Rafi laughed. "It's true! But it probably only stuck because I was still growing and developing."

"Also because you have incredible powers." She nuzzled his neck. "You did a beautiful job."

He slid his hand down her hip. "What about your powers? Could you make a lust charm?"

"Like we need one."

"But they exist, right?"

"Sure. And I can. But I don't give those out, since there's the potential consent issue."

"Right, good thinking. But…you've made them?"

She smiled. Her face heated, not that it would show in all this afterglow. "Occasionally. For trusted friends. Or myself."

"Oh?" The syllable rose in pitch, a sound of interest.

"Of course." She tipped her face up, seeking a kiss.

He brushed his lips across hers. "Bring one tomorrow."

"We might get a little out of control."

"But in such a fun way." He pushed down a strap of her dress and cupped her breast in an overflowing handful. "What do you think?"

"Okay," she murmured against his lips. "Tomorrow."

The days of August peeled away, one slip of paper after another, filled with packing, errands, and party preparations. The sorrow that threatened to swamp her at every task was kept at bay by the intoxication of her affair. Every kiss, every touch, might never have happened in the first place, she reminded herself. It was windfall from the gods. Doing anything less than delighting in it was ungrateful. She was grateful, too, for the relative peace. The korreds stayed absent, and if the news reported obnoxious remarks from politicians, she was free to change the station.

But her heart grew heavier as the month advanced, and she felt the sadness in the cling of Rafi's embraces too. By tacit agreement, they spoke of it as little as possible, and with false casualness—*It'll be fun to be in a completely new place. I can come visit. Yeah, we'll make plans. We'll both be busy, though, it's cool, whatever works.*

Then it was August thirty-first.

She went to his house in the morning, since they'd be occupied with the party that night. *Our last time*, her heart wept inside her, through every sweet and heated second of it.

For now, her mind retorted.

After, they stayed wrapped in each other's arms. Tears leaked out of the corners of her eyes. She pressed her face to his arm, feeling the scratchy, satiny touch of his scales and skin.

He swallowed, and when she lifted her face, tears shone in his eyes too. But he smiled—the same wry smile he had given her, as a stranger, from the stage at Gusu Park in June—and kissed her wet cheekbone. "We'll make tonight fun, yeah?"

"Yeah," she creaked. After all, no point making it miserable.

∽

If Roxana alone had been left to the planning of a going-away party, it would have been a dinner in her parents' back garden with a half-dozen friends and family. But in the hands of Ester with her unlimited ambition, and Timo and Amaris, who knew everyone in town, Ti Falls Park was teeming with guests and decked out as if for a festival.

The falls, a section of Dragonfish River, were only ten feet high and not much wider, but spilled prettily from their small cliff. Lush vegetation, including ti plants with palmlike fronds, surrounded the falls and river and enclosed a long oval lawn. Every tree and bush sparkled with lights, and lanterns floated in the waterfall's pool. Tables of catered food stood alongside the grass, smelling resplendently of their three chosen restaurants.

The stage at the end of the lawn had a banner over it, reading "We'll miss you, Ester and Roxana!"

Roxana couldn't look at it without tears filling her eyes. She and Rafi would never even have met if it weren't for this party, and the need to approach the band back in June to book them for it.

When Meloncollie arrived, she could hardly look at them either. Rafi seemed to be following the same discipline: whenever she glanced his way, he kept his gaze on the liuqin's tuning pins. She'd tightened them with a touch of magic one last time this morning.

Feeling bruised under the ribs, she sought out Satsuki, who looked breezy and delightful in a loose turquoise off-the-shoulder dress. They hugged.

"Oh, honey," Satsuki said.

"I know." Roxana laughed hopelessly and pulled back.

Satsuki knew by now. Roxana had confessed the affair to her not long after it started. "This part sucks," Satsuki commiserated. "But the rest was worth it, right?"

"Can't say it wasn't."

She doubted herself, though, as the evening advanced, and song after song played, and person after person took their turn at the mic to say love-ly and affectionately teasing things about Roxana and Ester. Why leave the warmth of this community? Why put everyone to all this trouble?

Such regrets came too late. The moving van had already gone north with their possessions. Their apartment awaited, the key already on her keyring, enspelled with a sense of welcome whenever she touched it.

She pictured herself in her new bedroom, ignoring the view of the sea in favor of watching videos of Meloncollie's performances, aching for Rafi and Miryoku. In twenty-four hours, that was likely what she'd be doing.

At least the party was staying peaceful, she conceded, grasping at straws of consolation.

Then a will-o'-the-wisp flashed onto the stage in the middle of a song and spoke in Rafi's ear. Rafi's gaze shot across the party, out into the surrounding darkness of the paths and trees. And Roxana knew the peace was over.

∽

As soon as Figo zipped onstage, Rafi knew, even before hearing the words.

"You know how you wanted me to warn you if they were coming?" Figo said. "Well, they're here. Sorry. Little late to be of use, I suppose, but..."

The shapes emerged: korreds in human form, blocky and strong, strolling in. Perhaps fifteen of them this time, infiltrating from three sides.

His fingers went still on the strings. Tash's bass line ceased, then Jove's voice and guitar, then finally Izzy's drumbeat. Murmurs rippled through the party. *Korreds*, he heard, and *what happened at the Grotto.* They hadn't appeared in town since that night, as far as he knew.

Brogyo was among them. Flanked by four others, including Sminu, he sauntered up and grinned at the band. His large, square teeth looked like white rocks ready to grind things down. "Why stop the lovely music?" His deep voice carried across the party. "We came to hear it."

Rafi didn't trust himself to speak. His skin was changing in defense again, cycling between stone and scale and flesh. Itch, burn, tingle.

Jove said into the mic, "We want to make sure listening to the music is *all* you're here to do, friends."

"May we not eat?" Brogyo said, sounding both sly and hurt. "May we not speak to people?"

The other two clusters of korreds were already trying to engage guests in conversation. To little luck, it appeared: people were pulling away, forming huddles.

Tash stepped forward, hand curled around the neck of her bass. "Will you take any humans away from here with you?"

Brogyo turned to Sminu. "They give us not even one whole song before attacking with such questions."

"Answer." Tash's voice was louder now, reverberating with the sonorous thunder of rainfall. "Do you promise none of you will take anyone away from here?"

"Can these people not go where they wish?" Brogyo returned. "If they want to come to our haunt, why should we forbid them?"

"Answer her," shouted someone in the crowd.

"Yeah, will you make a deal?" someone else called. "To not take anyone, not enchant anyone?"

Brogyo huffed and didn't answer, instead moving his gaze to the crowd and sending people sultry smiles.

Sminu spoke up. "If your people greet us with such hostility, how do you expect us to respond? May we not enjoy the music, as at any festival?"

"This isn't a festival," Jove said. "It's a private party. If you're going to be peaceful and leave everyone unharmed, then maybe you can stay. If not..." He nodded toward the forest. "Best return to your haunt."

Rafi spotted Roxana near one of the food tables. Their eyes met, hers wide with alarm. They'd spoken of this possibility, of course. She, Ester, and Oni all wore charms she'd made, providing a boost of resistance against enchantment, along with charms for clear thinking. But they knew these were pitiful defenses that wouldn't stand up to any direct dose of fae magic for long.

Rafi hadn't brought the iron cuff. That was also something they'd agreed on. If he ever used it, it would be in secret. Such an attack in public would be escalation beyond anyone's wishes.

Please make them leave, he begged the gods. *It's bad enough having them here, the night I have to say goodbye to her. What have we done to merit being punished like this?*

While he stood paralyzed, Brogyo, Sminu, Jove, Tash, and people in the crowd continued bandying challenges. The other korreds wandered, trying to charm their way into humans' good graces. Rafi tried to keep an eye on them, but there were too many, the shadows and the people kept shifting, the stage lights were too bright in his eyes.

Someone shouted. A few people moved abruptly, one tugging, another stumbling.

"Don't touch him!"

"Leave him alone!"

An arm lashed out. A korred yelped. Another growled and charged.

Between one breath and the next, humans were confronting korreds, whipping iron chains, shouting. The korreds were dropping their alluring appearances, snarling, grabbing, and shoving.

"Stop!" Rafi yelled, one of a chorus of voices saying it. But the party had become a melee.

He yanked the liuqin off and leaped from the stage to try to get to Roxana and Ester. The rest of the band jumped down too—he saw Jove and Izzy breaking up fights, Tash lashing korreds with whips of water. Magic tingled his skin as fae and witches attacked or defended or separated combatants. Someone's elbow punched his ribs by accident on his way past. The end of an iron chain stung his ear.

When he caught up with Ester and Roxana, they were with several others surrounding Timo, who stood with his hands splayed on his head, looking confused.

"Papa! Are you okay?" Ester shrieked.

"Dad!" Roxana said. "Dad, what happened?"

Rafi spotted Oxlock strolling away, offhandedly baring his teeth now and then at anyone who tried to come at him.

"Enough. Enough!" The voice roared through the mic.

Everyone looked to the stage. Amaris stood there, the anger on her face incongruous with her Hawaiian-print jacket and trousers. She awaited everyone's attention with the dignity of not merely a mayor but a royal, her gaze sweeping the party.

The korreds collected into one group, the last few chased there by armed citizens or fae allies. Divided by a stride's span of grass, korreds and party guests glared at each other like opposing armies in a war film.

"Korred haunt leader Brogyo," Amaris said.

He turned with nonchalance. "Human town leader Amaris Wei." He put his hand on his heart in greeting.

"You were asked to agree to a deal not to harm any humans. You refused, and now your folk have done harm."

"We received harm first," he said. "Your folk hurt us. Naturally we hurt them back."

People started shouting again.

"Quiet." The word snapped through the speakers. "We wish no more violence, friends." Amaris addressed the words to Brogyo. "Can we make a deal now on that front?"

"Very well. I am content to count us even for tonight. Hurts are taken on both sides, and a gallant fight it was too." He smiled at the humans as if complimenting them.

"Then will you return now to your haunt, with all your folk, and leave us to our festivities?"

"It's a pity we couldn't stay. We will have to return another time. For tonight, we will go, leaving none of us here and taking none of you with us. A fair balance."

"And you won't return till next festival," Rafi said. The strength of his own voice, and that he'd spoken at all, surprised him. Many people murmured in agreement.

Sminu scoffed loudly enough that Rafi heard the sound from fifty feet away. Rafi tried to stare his father down, but Sminu looked away in disinterest, as if Rafi were just a pointlessly squawking bird.

"Then someone must summon us for the festival," Brogyo said, "so we do not miss it."

"I will," a shellycoat said, grudgingly.

"Lovely. We shall see you then, friends." Brogyo pivoted, managing to give off an air of triumph, and led his korreds away.

No one bade them farewell. Everyone watched in silence—aside from those whispering and a few crying softly—while the korred troop walked into the shadows. They made the ground shake in their wake, an unsubtle reminder of their power. A handful of other fae followed to ensure their retreat.

The next festival was autumn equinox in September—a few weeks of reprieve. Rafi would worry about that later. With a breath he expelled some of the tension in his chest, then turned back to Roxana and the others surrounding Timo.

"I'm fine, really," Timo assured Roxana. "He only touched me for a second. It was a little sensation through my head, that's all, but it's gone now."

From other sectors of the party, voices were rising in alarm, calling for assistance. The korreds must have enspelled several people. Rafi's legs shook as he imagined the countless ways even one hostile touch could affect someone.

"What day is it?" Ester demanded of her grandfather.

"August thirty-first, of course," Timo said. "Last day you two are in town."

"Name the days of the week."

He rattled them off.

"Can you walk?" Roxana asked. "Use all your limbs?"

"Of course, honey, look." Timo moved around in a circle for them, flexing his fingers.

Amaris had gotten off stage and come to join them. "What happened?"

"One of them hit him," Ester said. "When he asked them to leave Oni and me alone." Her voice trembled with anger.

"Touched me, that's all," Timo demurred.

"We're doing a damage check," Roxana said. "Spell your name."

Timo opened his mouth, then paused. A furrow appeared between his brows.

"What's your name, Papa?" Ester urged.

"I…well, that's odd."

"What's *my* name?" she added, louder.

Timo reached out and stroked her hair. "You're…heck, you're my grand-kid, you're…" He looked from one friend or relative to another, landing on Roxana, who stood mute and pale. "But I know everyone's names in town," he said, puzzled.

Amaris took his arm. "Let's find a healer. Everyone, please make sure all the rest of the people affected tonight get to healers, too, as soon as possible."

Rafi stepped toward Roxana, but she stalled him, lifting a hand. "I'm sorry. I need to go with him. Can you…help do what she says, and find out who needs healing? Please?"

Rafi swallowed. "Yeah. Of course."

"Thank you. I'll check in soon."

Ester, Roxana, and Amaris led Timo away—despite the man's gentle protests that he was fine; he was sure it would wear off.

Oni seized Rafi's arm. "Oh my gods." Her voice was a high-pitched whisper. "It's my fault. Timo was defending me."

"No, no." Rafi took her hand, keeping his touch gentle despite his panic. "We defend each other. That's what we do. It's *not* your fault, not ever."

Her eyes fastened on his, wide and glistening in the torchlight.

"Let's help your parents organize some healers," he added.

She nodded, and he led her back to Jove and Izzy.

As he and Oni reconvened with the band, a man approached, guiding a friend who was gasping in pain. "You two are fae, right?" the first begged, his gaze shooting between Rafi and Tash. "Can you heal him? Please?"

Shit. Everyone thought Rafi was counted fae and thus had magic to heal others. When in truth, as an endo-witch, the sole living thing he could heal was himself, and then only to a limited degree.

Tash volunteered, saving Rafi for the time being.

Rafi locked gazes with Jove, then Izzy. "How do I help?" he asked.

Izzy's lips parted, but she said nothing, at a loss.

"I think this party's done," Jove said. "Want to take charge of packing up?

And keep an eye out for any more trouble. We'll cover for you if anyone asks."

Rafi trudged to the stage to dismantle their gear.

The enchantment damage, it turned out, involved seven people, each hit by a korred in the brief fight. Some of the spell injuries were physical, and some mental, like Timo's. Fae and exo-witch healers were doing what they could, though everyone knew the prognosis in such matters was unpredictable.

Back at the house, after unloading the gear, Rafi retrieved the iron cuff and went out to prowl the footpath.

No one showed, of course. The korreds had made a deal not to come back until the autumn equinox. It was stupid to waste his time out here when he could be with Roxana, while their last few hours in the same town spilled away into the void. But he wouldn't force his company on her while she was taking care of her father—who was injured thanks to Rafi's extended family attacking him.

What had he brought upon her?

He pressed his forehead against a banyan trunk along the path and squeezed the cuff in his hand, its exterior silver charm spreading sweet calm into him. Despite Roxana's skill, it only took the sharpest edge off his despair. If he hadn't promised her not to, he might have clapped the thing on his wrist again. Surely the korreds wouldn't have been so determined to come to this party if they hadn't been hounding *him*, if he hadn't provoked them at the Grotto and so many times before that.

With a deep breath, he lifted his head.

His phone said it was 11:30 p.m. Earlier, he and Roxana had arranged to meet at midnight for their final goodbyes. It would look odd if he came to see her off tomorrow morning; she'd have only her family and closest friends there, and their affair was to stay secret. Now he suspected she'd be too busy to keep that midnight meeting.

Or maybe she wouldn't leave town after all. Maybe she'd put it off, stay and care for her father awhile.

Conversely, maybe she wouldn't want to see Rafi again, ever.

She'd texted him an hour ago—*Dad seems all right except for not being able to remember anyone's name. But that's still bad, given his work, and who knows if more damage will surface. Have you heard of others?*

Rafi had expressed his concern for Timo and given a brief list of the six other people, and what he knew of their conditions. She'd thanked him, and the thread had gone silent.

Now, thumbs heavy with reluctance, he typed: *Do you still want to meet at midnight?*

Bracing himself for a rejection, he waited. Crickets trilled. The hypnotic rise and fall of the magnolia fae's song floated from near the verge.

His phone buzzed.

Yes. Everyone's going to bed. Nothing more to do tonight. I'll meet you there. All right, see you soon.

A better answer than he hoped. But given this would be goodbye for the gods only knew how long, he couldn't feel any real gladness. He stashed the cuff back in its hiding place in the cottage, guessing she wouldn't want to sense it anywhere near her, then set off.

CHAPTER 14

"I SHOULD STAY," ROXANA HAD INSISTED, ALONE with Amaris in the kitchen.

The healers had left—a faery and an exo-witch—promising to come again tomorrow to check on her father. Timo was in bed, Ester curled beside him on top of the covers like she used to do as a little kid, and they were both drifting to sleep.

"You should go," Amaris countered. "Stick to your plan."

"You and Dad need me. I can spare another week or two. Nelleke will understand, and my classes don't start till—"

"Roxana." Amaris caught Roxana's swinging hand and held it still. "You've worked for this. You've set everything up. We'll be okay. And you'll just be a six-hour drive away, not at the other end of the world. If we need you, we'll call."

Timo had already told her the same, in his usual blithe manner. As if getting hit with a fae curse that made him forget all names including his own was just an ordinary weeknight occurrence. If Roxana didn't know him so well, she wouldn't have detected the spark of panic under his smile lines. How could she leave?

But wasn't she perhaps using this selfless reason as a cover for her more selfish motive to stay? Hang around a couple more weeks in Miryoku, help her parents, sneak out every day for a rendezvous with Rafi—that had its appeal.

Which was exactly why her mother was right. Roxana had veered far enough off track already. This attachment to Rafi, which she'd hoped would be a breezy, short-term indulgence, had led to far more heartache than she was prepared to cope with.

Roxana had lowered her face, kissed her mother's knuckles, and nodded.

Shortly before midnight, Roxana slipped out. The street was silent except for the crickets and a couple of owls fluting at each other in the tall camphor tree on the corner.

She approached the stone wall beneath the tree. Rafi was nowhere to be seen. Then suddenly he was there, melting out of the shadowed stone, in black tank top and kilt. She startled.

"Sorry," he said softly. "Chameleon spell. Didn't want to look suspicious, lurking around."

She nodded. They wandered down the street, keeping to the shadows.

"Do they think he'll be okay?" Rafi asked.

"Hard to tell. The healers will keep coming back to monitor and treat him. Mom's been getting updates from other victims. Sounds like no two cases are alike."

"Yeah. The korreds do whatever strikes their fancy in the moment."

As Rafi well knew. Roxana reminded herself that no matter how much her world had been rattled tonight, the incident shook Rafi far deeper, cracking open hurt after hurt from his past.

"The deal they made," she said. "To stay away till Spirit Festival. Will they honor it?"

"Yes. It's a deal. I worry what they'll do at the festival, though."

"It's still three weeks away. My mom and the city council will be planning for it."

"And the cuff…I'm not sure what to do, now."

"Nothing. Tonight, don't decide anything. We're all too shaken up."

"Then when?" he said.

"I don't know. Part of me hopes never. Can you talk to Kepelo, see what she thinks about how to deal with them? Without mentioning the cuff."

"I'll try." His voice sounded flat, no particular hope in it.

One owl swooped across the street, a blur of pale gray and a whisper of wings, then vanished.

"What will you do?" Rafi asked.

The other owl left the tree, soaring the opposite direction.

"Keep to the plan. Leave tomorrow. I offered to stay and help, but Mom says they'll be all right and I should go."

"You have everything prepared in Port Baleia," he said, barely any louder than the owls' wings.

"Yeah. Most of our stuff's already there."

They stopped under a lacework of honeysuckle vines strung over the street.

Roxana turned to face him. "I hate this. I really do. But it was our agreement, and it'll be better in the long run if we keep to it."

He lowered his face, all shadow, no passionate glow lighting him now. "I knew I'd hate tonight. I just didn't know they'd give me a reason to hate it even more."

Her heart ached like an ember under her ribs. *Don't drag this out*, she told herself. *It isn't mercy to string him along. Say what you need to say.* But it was hard labor to bring out the words. "I'll check in a lot. But I'll be busy. We'll be settling into our new lives. I have to give that as much attention as I can, otherwise…" She folded her arms miserably, seeking a different way to explain. "I'm not the kind of person whose mind can be half in one place and half in another. I'd be unhappy, and I'd make you unhappy too."

Rafi kept his head bowed. "No, you're right. We'll be in touch. Checking in. We'll manage."

She wanted to wilt against him, let him wrap her in his arms, stop time and stay there. But a deal was a deal, and her life awaited.

"This past month," she said, "was one of the loveliest things that's ever happened to me. I don't know what the future will bring. But I always want to be your friend, at least."

"Friends only, or friends who…if we're in the same town…"

"Maybe that. But in the meantime we both have to be free to live our lives, and everything right now is—ugh. I don't know. No one in this town should make decisions tonight."

The breeze stirred. A honeysuckle blossom fell at Roxana's feet.

"True," Rafi said. "That's what we agreed."

Roxana twisted her bangle bracelet around her wrist. She'd put it on before coming out here, but its calm-and-focus charm wasn't having as much effect as she needed. Or perhaps it was. Maybe she'd have been in tears by now if not for the spell. "Well. Long day tomorrow, and it's been a long one already today. I should try to sleep."

"Goodbye, then. For now."

Roxana stepped forward and hugged him.

Embracing her, he sighed, a gust against the top of her head. "Same for me," he murmured. "This past month was the loveliest ever."

She swallowed against tears. She couldn't have tired eyes for a six-hour drive tomorrow.

The words to break things off as agreed on had been agony to produce, but the words *I love you* wanted so badly to emerge that she had to block them with clenched teeth. She couldn't love him. They'd dated for one month and only known each other for two. Some people could fall in love in such a short time, but she couldn't. Or so she'd always believed. Besides, look what had happened with Micah: she had clung too tightly, tried too hard to force the relationship to work, and he had only ended up running as far away as he could. She had to give people their freedom, or ultimately they'd want nothing to do with her.

They stepped apart. Said goodnight and "have a safe trip" and "good luck" and other phrases that didn't really matter.

Then Roxana walked away from Rafi, her feet firm, her path resolute. She only looked back once, at the corner, to wave goodbye. In the darkness where he stood, it was hard to tell the difference between his answering wave and the moving shadows of branches.

She returned to her stripped-down room, where luggage leaned against the walls, and mechanically got ready for bed, trying all the while not to be hurt by the fact that *he* hadn't said "I love you" either.

❧

Rafi trudged a winding path back toward Izzy and Jove's house, hardly aware of the route he took. All was the same anyway: darkness with patches of streetlight, the sounds of night fae and insects as the town slept, the smell of late-summer jasmine starting to ripen into oversweetness. Such would be tomorrow night, and the next, and on and on until the weather cooled and it became autumn rain and falling leaves, then foggy winter hush, while he stayed the same, hurting, wandering.

Roxana had ended the affair, neatly, decisively, keeping to their agreement. She hadn't entreated him to come north with her, nor suggested plans to meet again soon. A tepid "maybe," a diplomatic "I don't know," that was all he got. He had longed to say more—offer to come see her (never mind how, when he'd never traveled anywhere in the human realm by himself), even tell her he loved her. But what did he know of love? Who was he to thrust himself into her carefully planned life?

Entering the cottage, he looked around at the space that was his to stay in, thanks to the generosity of Jove and Izzy. At least they would keep giving him work, the pleasure of music, tasks to distract him and make him feel useful.

But they had lives beyond the band and the errands—a daughter, a house, other jobs. Jove was a part-time lifeguard and swim instructor, Izzy did accounting for her fruit-growing family, Oni would undoubtedly grow up to become many things to many people. How long before they, too, tired of him hanging on their sleeves and dismissed him? What would he do then?

He'd go back to his mother's haunt, he supposed. Roam the ravines and forests, eat wild cherries and bracken and drake-fire-roasted rabbit. Just existing. Like the tolerated oddity he was.

He retrieved the cuff and sat on the floor with it, turning it in his fingertips, a hair's breadth from touching the iron interior. Perhaps this was the one other thing he could be: an instrument of revenge. Justice, rather—but truthfully, he didn't quite see the difference. Fae and humans rarely seemed to agree on what counted as a fair reckoning, even in quarrels within their own haunt or city or family.

"How am I supposed to know what to do?" he asked softly, staring at the cuff.

It didn't answer, nor did any ghosts or gods.

⁂

All along the Great Eidolonian Highway, beneath a clear sky, green meadows tumbled down to a cobalt sea. Ester was uncommonly silent, staring at the scenery, face averted. Roxana didn't feel much like speaking either, but to keep up morale, she pointed out the occasional landmarks.

"Timber plantation up there. I hear the fae have helped grow the trees extra tall this year."

"There's the exit to Kagami, where Satsuki's mom lives. Remember the lagoon, and the canals? We should take a vacation there."

"Amizade Bridge. Longest and highest in the country."

"I know," Ester said at the bridge remark, with a hint of irritability. But as they crossed it, she lifted her phone to snap a picture of the tree-fringed ravine that plunged beneath them.

Easy enough, Roxana found as the miles passed, to keep from feeling too lonely, given the balm of constantly changing beauty and the to-do list that awaited her in their new city. When her forlorn mind whispered, *But I won't see Rafi today or tomorrow or likely all month,* she answered firmly, *Because that's done for now, as you planned. Instead you get to move into a bedroom with an ocean view, shop for dinner at a new market, pick a café tomorrow morning for breakfast, see Nelleke, set up your items at the shop.* All the dazzling novelties she'd been stockpiling in her head for the past year, all the reasons to move.

But a lump closed her throat when she saw assorted mochi in the shop where she and Ester stopped for lunch. The memory flooded her: the sunlit footpath, Rafi's warm arm around her, his husky voice close to her ear, the mochi melting between her teeth, the magnetism between them that would soon topple all their inhibitions. She blinked away the tears and grabbed Ester's favorite chocolate bar to add to their purchases.

A couple of hours later, they rolled into Port Baleia. Ester perked up, craning her neck to look around. While most of Miryoku's architecture and cuisine reflected the predominantly Asian origins of its early settlers, Port Baleia was a larger city with districts styled on different global regions. Ester and Roxana's apartment, as well as Nelleke's shop, was in Little Europe. When visiting Nelleke and apartment-hunting months ago, Roxana and Ester had been delighted by the black-and-white-striped café awnings, the balconies with wrought-iron railings, the temple with a Gothic spire and rose window, and Portugal Avenue with its buildings painted in citrus colors.

It still lifted her spirits to see it all now, but she also thought *I want to show Rafi this.* "Like a magical treasure house," he had said regarding his childhood impression of Miryoku. He'd been to Dasdemir a time or two with the band and seemed equally dazzled. Perhaps if she could lure him north to visit…

Such thoughts would only keep her stuck in longing. The lure of greater independence had brought her here, and that was the guiding light she had to follow.

They found their parking spot under the apartment building—underground parking was a feature Miryoku didn't have and which struck Ester as thrillingly urban. An elevator took them to the seventh floor, a height also exceeding any building's in Miryoku. The corridor was quiet, its floor gleaming hardwood with a carpet runner of red medallions on black leading them nearly all the way to the end, where Roxana handed the key to Ester and let her unlock their door.

After their single-story greenery-embraced house in Miryoku, shared with Timo and Amaris and the occasional cockatoo, the airiness and light struck her, enhanced by the space still being mostly unfurnished except for the new couch and the many boxes the movers had set near the walls. Roxana and Ester drifted across to the living room windows, still naked of blinds or curtains, and gazed out at the view that had sold them on the place. Across a span of rooftops stood a rocky black clifftop, and beyond that stretched the ocean, near enough that they could see a red channel buoy rising and plunging in the waves. Sea stacks studded the ocean, wild and treacherous and swirling with birds. Roxana slid the window open. Cool air poured through the screen, smelling of brine.

They both breathed it in. Even Ester said nothing, her hungry senses perhaps sated for once by such a flood of novelty.

Roxana slipped an arm around her and kissed her head. "Shall we make it ours?"

CHAPTER 15

THE REQUESTS FOR REVENGE STARTED COMing in almost immediately.

Three separate people approached Jove and Izzy in the four days following the farewell party.

"He was like, 'I know none of *us* can fight them,'" Jove related to Tash and Rafi after one such conversation, "'but if you get me in there and hook me up with some fae who don't mind helping out, maybe they can do something, you know? It's my brother. Someone's got to do something.'"

"Which one was this? The brother?" Rafi asked, leaning against the wall of their kitchen.

"Guy who can't see anything anymore except green. Like he's stuck inside a bush. Feels it too—leaves and branches against his skin all the time."

Rafi nodded. He recognized the case, though didn't know the person. These past four days, the part of his brain that wasn't consumed with missing Roxana had filled itself with the details of the damage sustained by the seven stricken individuals.

"Anyway." Jove lifted his hands from the kitchen table, then dropped them with a thud. "I told him no. Same as the others. We feel you, we're angry too, but we don't do revenge. Recommended he look for more fae healers instead. Maybe fae-realm plants for medicine."

"Is Kepelo going to lean on Brogyo for recompense?" Tash asked Rafi.

He shrugged, a slight movement of one shoulder. "I'll talk to her. But I doubt it. With Hazel, that was her mother. These people aren't connected to her, and they did attack the korreds with iron and spells. Obviously not a balanced fight, but she'll still see it as the humans asking for it. She already has the deal in place to keep me safe from other fae. Doesn't want to overstep and get called too soft on humans."

Tash just nodded as if that made sense. Izzy scowled, and Jove looked depressed.

"Well, the mayor's sure to say something about it," Izzy said. "Her own spouse got struck."

"But what can she do?" Jove said. "Send an army of witches against the korreds? Sounds like a seriously fucking bad idea."

"Not an army," Izzy shot back. "Deals. There must be deals they can make to keep things peaceable and get these people healed."

"The guy who wants to help his brother," Rafi interjected, hoping to head off a lengthy debate. "Did he end up arranging an errand with us?"

"Yeah." Jove sighed. "Seeking out someone across the verge who might be able to fix the spell or get plants or whatever—he's looking for that. You want to take that on, Raf?"

Rafi shifted his shoulder blades against the hard wall. Crossing the verge meant being out of touch for an untold number of days, missing Roxana's check-in texts.

Not that there'd been many of those, nor had the texts been particularly personal. People needed Rafi here. This was something he could do.

"Sure," he said. "I'll take it."

Those vengeance requests got him thinking, of course. The cuff might do exactly what those victims' friends and family members wanted. Rafi wasn't interested in their money, nor could he have openly accepted the job anyway. The cuff had to stay secret, or else the korreds would almost certainly go after the people Rafi cared about—and they'd also break Rafi to the extreme boundary of what magical healing could fix. But if Rafi could pull it off, if a mysterious pain were to befall Brogyo and force him to rethink his entire reigning philosophy…that could potentially save hundreds of people from suffering in the future. Prevention, not revenge. But how to manage it?

The next morning, he texted Roxana, *I'm going across to look for a cure for one of the victims from the party. If such a thing exists. Not sure how long I'll be out of touch. Hope all's well with you and Ester.*

She responded, *Be safe, and I hope you're successful. No worries on timing, I have so much to do these days. Kind of going crazy, ha.*

He felt it like a bite from a fly. New life in Port Baleia. Too busy to talk. You live your life and I'll live mine.

I miss you so much, he typed before he could reconsider. *Things feel so dismal here. I just have to do something to try to help.*

He added the heart symbol, an emoji she liked to use and receive—or at least, she had liked it back in August. Then he stuffed his phone into his pack and walked across the verge before she had a chance to answer.

⌒∞⌒

Tears stung Roxana's eyes as she read Rafi's message. She blinked rapidly to keep them from spilling. She was in the shop, at the till. Nelleke was near, humming along with the radio as she arranged jewelry on a shelf. Two customers browsed and chatted. This was no time to get emotional over texts with her summer fling.

But neither Rafi nor Roxana had dared say anything so raw yet in their messages. She'd *felt* sad, of course, drenching at least one hankie in quiet weeping every night so far, and she guessed he felt the same. But they'd kept their texts polite: sympathetic friends checking in, not pining lovers. Until now.

His words so closely expressed her own feelings that it felt like a stab from a shiny steel pin.

I miss you too, she typed back. *So much. But yeah, we just have to do what we can, where we are, and eventually it'll get better.*

She sniffled, nudged her shoulder against each eye to blot the tears with her shirt, and lifted her face with a bland smile. Cashier and jewelry creator, ready to greet customers. Her heart raced, fearing his answer while craving it too.

The customers came up to coo over her jewelry pieces, freshly unpacked and sparkling in disarray across the glass countertop. Roxana explained the materials and charms for each; consulted with Nelleke, who danced over to suggest prices far higher than Roxana would ever have set; and sold one at the asking price, to her amazement.

Rafi still hadn't answered by the time the door swung shut after the customers.

Nelleke caught Roxana sighing when she checked her phone. "News from home?"

Nelleke knew about the fiasco at the going-away party—minus the part about Rafi being Roxana's lover. Roxana was still working up to talking about the romantic side of the tangle. Nothing to discuss there anyway. Nothing that wouldn't fade in time.

"Not really," Roxana said. "Sounds like things are about the same."

Nelleke tossed a lock of her wavy hair over her shoulder and scrutinized Roxana, full lips turned downward. They'd met at university in Dasdemir a decade and a half ago. She was two years older than Roxana but looked barely thirty, one of those people who exuded effortless style. Probably helped, Roxana thought, that Nelleke had spent the last twelve years staying mostly single and building her business rather than raising a kid by herself. But now Roxana and Ester got to benefit from Nelleke's enterprising spirit, at least.

"No improvement on his name recognition?" Nelleke asked.

It took Roxana a moment to realize she was referring to Timo. "Not yet. I'm going to mail a few more charms, just to see." Not that the ones she'd tried so far, made of fae-realm metal, had fixed the problem.

Nelleke was nice enough not to mention that. "There's nothing you could do if you were there," she said gently.

Roxana slid a copper coin bracelet with blue beads along the countertop to reunite it with a matching one with green beads. "I know."

Rafi hadn't answered by bedtime either. Likely he'd already crossed the verge.

She had enough to keep her busy in the meantime. The school year was starting for Ester, and the first few days of that involved plenty of confusion, novelty, and information overload for them both.

At the end of the week, Roxana allowed herself to text Rafi, *Are you back yet? I worry after everything lately. Hope you're safe.* He didn't respond. He was safe, she told herself. Just inaccessible. A thin wire of stress still ran along the edge of her awareness. He had the cuff and he had written that he needed to "do something." It wasn't hard to imagine him bringing it into the fae realm, lying in wait for Brogyo, and possibly accomplishing nothing except getting himself hurt.

The next week, Roxana's classes started at the arts college, and her life became a rotation of taking a streetcar to campus and back, meeting Ester in the afternoon, working shifts at Nelleke's shop, studying, making pieces for her classes, and trying to relax in her off-hours by exploring Port Baleia with her daughter. The wheels were turning, propelling her life forward, whether or not she felt ready. She had no choice but to adapt.

Spirit Festival was coming up, spanning a few days around the autumn equinox, and Port Baleia was setting up for it. Roxana and Nelleke made jewelry to give to the fae, as well as pieces to sell to humans, but Roxana's mind kept flitting to Miryoku, where the deadline awaited with the korreds.

Mayor Wei was on top of it. Roxana learned, on the phone with Amaris, that the citizens of Miryoku were preparing for a grimmer Spirit Festival than usual, everyone aware they should not only create extra gifts but carry iron and self-defense charms. "Not to be used," Amaris said sternly, "unless actually attacked. We don't want any human going on the offensive. We're crystal clear on that."

On a more hopeful note, Amaris had pulled together the funds to book the traveling Quicksand Theatre Company in Miryoku for the whole of the festival. "They'll come up with fun things the korreds haven't seen," Amaris said. "That'll satisfy them for this festival at least, Lord and Lady willing."

"Spirit willing," Roxana corrected, half wryly, half in sincere prayer. "But after that? Next festival?"

"*Aiyo*, child," Amaris said, reverting to an exasperated phrase she'd often used in Roxana's youth. "We'll worry about that next month."

When Spirit Festival was five days away, Roxana risked bothering Tash again by texting to ask if she'd heard from Rafi. Tash responded: *I have not. He knows the terrain. I'm not concerned for him.*

Chilly, Roxana thought with irritation. But Tash had defended humans against the korreds more than once. She was an ally. Roxana thanked her and got on with her life.

Five days later, she allowed another text to Rafi.

Today's the start of Spirit Festival. Please just tell me you're all right.

He didn't answer that day, nor the next.

I'm not built for this, Roxana thought in misery as she gave jewelry and polite smiles to people at the shop's street fair booth. *I'm not made for long distance. For feeling this way about someone across the verge, where anything might happen and I'd never know.*

Paper lanterns in the colors of autumn chrysanthemums swung above the street in the evening breeze. The scent of the sea, eternal and aloof, stole in under the smells of cooking smoke and incense. *True, you aren't*, the wind seemed to answer. *You knew that. It's why you planned to wrap it up when August ended. Now it's the start of autumn, and you're still pining.*

Roxana tore a scrap of red crepe paper from the edge of the table décor. She lifted it to chest level, waited for the next gust of wind, then let go. It sailed away.

She sent Rafi one more text:

I can't be this worried for someone far away, who I can't reach. Let me know you're all right, please, but like we talked about, know that I have to do my best to pull most of my focus here. For now.

People traded festival gifts for the next three days, thanked the fae for allowing humans to share their magical island, wrote prayers to the Spirit on slips of paper for well-being in the darker half of the year, and burned them with sparklers or buried them among the roots of new plantings.

Rafi sent no answer.

∞

Rafi began with his mother's haunt. Might as well start with the most influential faery around, despite having already predicted her response.

Kepelo, indeed, remained as impartial as the black-robed judges on TV shows.

"The humans struck, the korreds struck back," she said. "Of course the korreds struck too hard. But they didn't take anyone to their haunt, and it's true they're entitled to entertainment as much as any faery. This is one of those temporary feuds groups get into. It's best to let them burn out on their own, which they do before long."

Rafi walked with her through the ashen remains of the latest forest burn as she fluttered from one scorched stump to another. Sometimes she paused to torch a remaining twig or to send up a shoot of green fireweed by tapping a claw against the earth.

"But Brogyo has this greed," Rafi said. "He *wants* humans, and entertainment, more badly than most. Doesn't he? Am I wrong?"

"You aren't wrong. They're the covetous branch of the korreds. Remember there are more peaceable ones deep in the mountains, who leave humans alone. Those who hunger for humans and their arts are naturally drawn to the verge. When Brogyo took over—longer ago than even my father could remember—the calmer ones found his avidity distasteful and broke off to live far away."

"It sounds like he's only gotten worse since then. Like he's losing perspective."

"Assuredly," Kepelo said. "He's quite old. As fae age, they often want to cling and fight and acquire more, because they're wearier of everything."

"They seek novelty?"

"Yes. Then one day they break and give up and return to the elements. Every ancient tree must eventually reach its greatest size and then topple."

Rafi clambered over the singed log of one such ancient tree. It left black ash on his hands. "How long before Brogyo breaks?"

Kepelo swiveled a wing in the air in a figure-8 movement. "A few years? Ten, twenty? Surely not much more than that."

"Ten or twenty years is not a short time from the human perspective, Mother."

"It *could* be sooner."

"And you're going to do nothing meanwhile?"

"Spark of mine, I've already assisted and still will. Aulo was there at this Grotto, helping avert the korreds' aggression, was she not?"

"Yes…"

"And Figo assisted at the party. Neither did so against my wishes. You know very well I won't miss Brogyo once he does decide to be reborn. Mind you, that would place Sminu in charge. Your father. But he would at least be different."

"Would he be any better?" Rafi said sourly.

"I'm never sure what you mean by 'better.' You tend to tell me I've misunderstood."

"I mean would he attack humans less? Because I doubt it."

"Hard to predict. I have no fondness for him anymore either, but he would be interesting."

The fae placed a lot of importance on *interesting*.

Rafi had asked before, in his youth, why she and Sminu ever had a romance in the first place, liked each other well enough to have a child. Novelty, once again, seemed to be the answer. Neither of them had met many half-human fae, and they'd gotten it into their heads to wonder what a child of theirs might turn out like.

Rafi gathered most humans put a little more serious thought into the decision to have offspring.

"Any ideas on a cure for the green-vision spell, or the others from that night?" he asked.

Kepelo rose into the air and clutched the trunk of an island redwood with her hind claws. The bark was scorched, but the tree had survived the fire. She cocked her head, looking like a giant bird in thought. "Whoever casts a spell is of course the best one to undo it, if it can be undone. But the korreds probably wouldn't agree to do so."

Rafi dropped to sit on the carpet of fallen redwood needles. "Yeah. Wasn't going to ask them."

"I expect they'd hurt you if you did," she agreed, reasonably. "Besides, korred spells on humans are like smashing a dove's wing with a rock. The dove may live, but will never fly the same again. Still—there are approaches you can try."

He followed her recommendations. First he scoured the less-recently-burned parts of her haunt and collected plants, though he would have to consult a human healer to make sure they were safe to use.

Then he hit up the rest of the nearby regions: The water fae of the rivers and creeks. The smaller, plant-dwelling earth fae of the forests. The air fae who lived in the treetops or were visiting with the east wind that day. Some fae agreed to go into town and attempt healing (for recompense of gifts), with the caveat that they doubted they could accomplish much. They kept pointing Rafi onward. More materials, more fae to consult.

He ended up spending two nights in the fae realm. Tromping back toward the verge with his pack of assorted fae-realm plants and streamed crystals, he was stopped by an iridescent blue sylph who swept up to him.

"Going to the festival?" they asked. "It's almost over. Hurry if you want to enjoy it!"

"Which festival?" he said.

"Autumn equinox. Spirit Festival. Today's the last day." The sylph held up an arm draped in beaded chains and colorful woven fabrics, which Rafi presumed were festival gifts, then shot away in a swoosh of cool air.

"*Fuck*," Rafi hissed, and broke into a run.

He dashed across the verge into the cloudy, mild air of a September afternoon. He kept running till reaching the footpath, then stopped to catch his breath. His phone, in a side pocket of his pack, vibrated over and over, loading up some three weeks' worth of text messages. Panting, he got it out and did a quick scroll—some from Roxana, some from Jove, one from Tash, but no words like "emergency" or "ASAP" jumping out at him. Could he spare a minute to read Roxana's as he ached to, or should he race out to learn what the korreds had done in his absence?

One minute wouldn't make a difference. He tapped her name. The messages spilled forth, spaced several days apart.

I miss you too. So much. But yeah, we just have to do what we can, where we are, and eventually it'll get better.

Are you back yet? I worry after everything lately. Hope you're safe.

Today's the start of Spirit Festival. Please just tell me you're all right.

I can't be this worried for someone far away, who I can't reach. Let me know you're all right, please, but like we talked about, know that I have to do my best to pull most of my focus here. For now.

The breath punched out of him, and he leaned his shoulder on the nearest tree.

This shouldn't hurt. She'd said the same thing when they parted in that joyless midnight meeting.

Do you get it now, Rafi?, he thought.

He slowly tapped in:

I'm all right. Two nights away added up to three weeks out here…anyway I get it. You're right. That's probably healthiest, for now.

He echoed her last two words as both understanding and hope. Maybe there'd be a later, beyond "for now"? But hope wasn't what he felt as he hustled to Jove and Izzy's house and got directed by Izzy—who was home with Oni—

down to Gusu Park, where the Quicksand Theatre Company was performing their last evening. It was the likeliest place to find the korreds. He thanked Izzy, apologized for his prolonged absence, didn't dare ask yet whether they'd already replaced him as a band member or what (he couldn't handle *more* profound rejection in the space of five minutes), and left her with the bag of fae-realm materials.

No, it wasn't hope at all. His tired legs carried him down the hill and through the town's streets on a tide of bitterness.

Roxana had had almost three weeks to mull it over. She knew her mind. Her message proved what he'd already dreaded: he couldn't be enough for her. She wanted a real human, someone who existed on public record, someone steady and respectable who could gracefully handle issues like careers, ballots, renting houses, driving cars, and attending colleges. Not someone who roved back and forth over the verge and didn't count as a proper denizen of either realm.

His phone vibrated again, and he had to look despite his dread.

Roxana answered: *Oh thank goodness you're okay. Sounds like Miryoku's holding together too, according to my parents. Onward then, I guess. Be well, Rafi.*

Kindhearted. But the message still read, to his eyes, like a goodbye. It asked nothing and invited no response. A thin layer of stone hardened the skin across his chest. He closed the text without answering and moved along to the park.

At least twenty korreds were watching the performance, commandeering the front of the crowd, Brogyo and Sminu in the center. The rest of the audience, fae and human alike, gave them an arm's span of space, and even as they watched the performance and laughed, their gazes kept flicking to the korreds. Rafi stood apart and observed the audience activity, not the performance, which apparently had something to do with history but incorporated tumbling and physical comedy and ridiculous hats.

As festival crowds went, this was an odd vibe, as humans said. A few citizens wore iron chainmail gloves, or iron chains in artful but menacing loops on their belts. When he meandered behind them, he picked up tingles of magic: protection charms, most likely. It wasn't the mood in which festivals were supposed to be conducted. All seven of the yearly festivals, in addition to having certain prayer focuses for the religious, were meant to reinforce the harmony between fae and humans, mainly via humans providing fae with arts and entertainment. Generally the humans loved it just as much as the fae did.

At the performance's end, the actors bowed, and Rafi morphed his appearance into something the korreds wouldn't readily recognize: smoothing away his scales, shrinking his nose and lips, lightening the color of his eyes. Just a random human.

While the crowd dispersed, the korreds stayed to chat up the performers. A few of the Quicksand troupe were willing, cajoling and teasing and making the korreds erupt with laughter. A scattering of Miryoku citizens kept watch, Rafi among them.

Most of the performers were tidying up the venue and loading their costumes and props into colorful, battered buses and caravans at the curb behind the stage. Standing near them were Roxana's parents. Rafi studied Timo, but couldn't tell from this distance if he still suffered from his curse. He wore his usual placid expression, and Amaris wore her usual stern one.

On stage, the last remaining performer, a man with a garishly painted face and (for reasons Rafi couldn't recall) a bodysuit covered in orange fringe, was executing a cartwheel for the korreds, back and legs bending in rubbery fluidity. Then, as he bowed, Unklag shouted, "Come back with me!"

"Yes, come to our haunt," said another.

Deftly leaping out of reach, the actor wrung his hands at his chest. "Ah! Good friends, I long to, but I cannot. I have made a deal, a most sacred deal, with these maladroit oafs and foozlers I travel with. Dreadful though they are, I must stay with them a great while yet. Deals are deals. You understand."

"When will you come back to us?" Unklag shouted.

"As soon as I can, friends. When my captors next deem me worthy of being brought here, or when I valiantly escape. I swear I shall someday return to fair Jasmine Town, where my heart shall forevermore reside."

While they grunted in appreciation of his poetic speechifying, he blew them kisses and then handsprung his way to the safety of his troupe.

"Town leader Amaris Wei," Brogyo called.

Amaris walked up the short set of backstage steps and crossed the empty stage to stand under the bright lights. Arms folded, she gazed down at the korreds. "Happy festival to you, haunt ruler Brogyo."

Timo came up too. Even he with his inherent affability wouldn't muster up a smile for the korreds.

"We enjoyed it," Brogyo said. "Though we grieve that not a one will come back to our haunt with us and entertain us further. Don't you know we only wish to have a town of humans of our own, as charming as yours, but ours to govern?"

"You're welcome to keep visiting ours or keep trying to expand your own," she said. "As long as your efforts don't involve enspelling humans. Our free will is of the greatest importance to us, you see."

"Strange, but so it does seem," Brogyo conceded.

For one tender moment, Rafi dared hope he was watching successful diplomacy in action, that this was the beginning of the de-escalation, that he could finally start to relax.

Then Brogyo added, "Next festival, we will come back, and we expect just as good as this or better. Such enjoyment is of the greatest importance to *us*."

Around Rafi, the remaining citizens ran iron chainwork through their hands.

"We always do our best for our fae friends," Amaris said. "I promise to send someone to summon you on the festival's first day."

They exchanged nods, and Amaris turned and walked away with Timo, ignoring the entreaties from Brogyo's underlings:

"What about tonight?"

"Who will come with us?"

"More gifts!"

"Look at you, covered in gifts," Brogyo retorted to one, who was festooned in necklaces and gripped a paper sack overflowing with trinkets. "One would think you're a bower-bird rather than a noble korred. Come. We'll take these little treasures home, then return next festival for better ones still."

CHAPTER 16

RAFI WAS ALL RIGHT, AND ROXANA COULD breathe again. His response seemed unemotional, hard to interpret. It hurt to think he might honestly not mind moving on. It equally hurt to think he was suffering and putting a neutral face on it.

But interpreting his message wasn't her job. So many things *were* her job now. Ester was among the most challenging: she hadn't made friends at school yet, felt judged by her fashionable urban classmates, and, fast approaching thirteen, was brimming with moody hormones. There had been one instance so far of "I hate it here!" followed by a slammed bedroom door, but two hours later she had come out for dinner and suggested going to the Czech bakery on their block to get dessert pastries. So that was a constant situation to monitor, but it could be worse.

Then there were Roxana's classes. The college taught magic in the arts, all its students witches. She met other miniaturists and metal specialists, as well as witches whose talents lay in water or oils, making them adept with paints; earth, giving them an edge in clay sculpture and pottery; or plant materials, which they explored as weavers, woodcarvers, or textile artists. Never before had she been among such an assemblage of people so like herself, and never had she felt less special in her abilities. It was both humbling and inspiring.

Nelleke provided Roxana not only wages but companionship. She introduced Roxana to neighbors and shop regulars—some of them single, she mentioned. "I'll let you know when I'm ready for that," Roxana said, with as realistic a laugh as she could fake.

Because as to that…what was wrong with her? It was like a chronic condition. Some days she was fully in the present, enjoying a jewelry project, pastries, or a conversation with another student, and she barely gave Rafi a thought. Then a nineties song would drift over the speakers in a grocery store and she'd find herself blankly holding a bag of rice while in her memory she locked eyes with Rafi on a stage and he smiled at her in a *Yes, we'll ravish each other after this gig* type of way. And for the rest of the day she'd feel bereft, distracted.

It wasn't always sadness. Once she walked by a couple making out on a bench on campus, and something—the slant of the sealed-tight kiss, the way one woman's hand slid into the black hair of the other—knocked her into a state of breathless lust. Not for the couple, but for Rafi. On that occasion she brought up his name in her texts and came dangerously close to asking if he'd be up for sexting, just as a thing between friends. Luckily she returned to her senses, said nothing, and stuffed her phone back into her pocket, appalled.

She wasn't used to her new situation yet, that was all. She had to adjust and leave him in peace.

∽

The next few weeks were a continued cycle of failing, in terms of Rafi's attempts to acquire cures for the Ti Falls Seven, as people had begun calling them. Half the plants he'd brought back from the fae realm had to be discarded, as healers declared them too strong or unpredictable or just too little known in terms of their effects. The other plants brought only temporary reprieves from the curses, which then rushed back into place as soon as each dose wore off. Town fae were the best bet, people like Tash who could administer hands-on healing, but those cures wore off too. Timo and the others were left with the hassle of seeking daily treatment or else simply putting up with their curses.

Timo, Rafi heard, mostly chose the latter. He hired an intern whose sole job was to keep track of names for him, then stubbornly went about his social work, the intern hustling along at his side.

At least Rafi didn't lose his job in the band. When he'd dejectedly come to Jove and Izzy, that final night of Spirit Festival, saying he understood if they'd replaced him by now, and he could move out if they wanted, Jove had responded, "Do you *want* to quit the band and move out?"

"No, but if you want me to, it's fine and I get it."

"Hon, we aren't kicking you out. You were gone on an errand for *us*. Lord and Lady, this boy. Go dust off your liuqin, we're rehearsing tonight."

But gigs weren't as gratifying anymore, with the days ticking down toward Lord Festival and rumors flying about what the korreds might try. The
national news wasn't helping either. Miryoku had been in the spotlight, reporters visiting often. That governor in the northeast, Akio Riquelme, had
picked up the Ti Falls Seven story and was blaring it in his speeches, using it
as an example of why his "Humanist Party" aimed to do a better job protecting innocent Eidolonian humans from dangerous fae and witches. Rafi, too,
naturally wanted to protect people from such threats, but Riquelme's way of
talking about it seemed oddly repulsive. He offended everyone, like Oni had
said—yet despite such offense, he seemed to get endless broadcast time.

Truly, Rafi did not understand human politics.

He paced the footpath, cuff in his pocket in case any hostile korreds
showed. None did. The October days slid by. Red leaves fell to cover the path.
The rain turned chilly.

One evening, when it was pouring too hard for him to bother patrolling
anymore, he slogged into the practice room to get some sheet music. Oni
wandered in and brought her phone to him. "Look."

It was a social media app, showing a picture of Ester and Roxana in tall
hats and gleaming carnival masks. His heart twisted into a giddy, sad knot.
He drank it in—her full lower lip in a saucy pout, the way her hair had gotten longer and coiled on her shoulder—then read the caption by one ester.
duchess.of.cheese: *Happy birthday to meeee! Making our Lord Festival costumes.*
@roxana.x.wei

"It's Ester's birthday?" Rafi said.

"Yeah, now that she's thirteen, her mom's letting her have an account. She
texted me to add her." Oni flopped to sit on the green couch. "I miss her."

Rafi sank onto the couch's arm. "I miss them too. You have those other
friends, though, right?"

The two kids who had been accosted at the Grotto had sometimes shown
up at the house to hang out with Oni.

She shrugged. "They're okay. I don't know. It's like…they're two years
older than Ester, but I think Ester's actually smarter. It's easier to talk to her."

Rafi nodded. They sat morosely a minute, Oni scrolling and Rafi staring
at the sheet music. Then he said, "Can you show me how to use that app?"

∽

Maybe it wasn't a good idea, installing the app. He found Meloncollie's account, which included pictures and video clips with him in them. When he realized Roxana followed it and had "liked" several posts in the past, a rush of hope swept him. But her own feed betrayed nothing of him, not even when he went back to her August posts, during the thick of her affair with him, not even in a subtle way that only he would get. Jewelry pieces, a lunch with co-workers, summer scenery, all with matter-of-fact captions, that was it. Well, of course: she'd stipulated secrecy. She wouldn't break that clause herself. Still, it discouraged him that not one glimmer of that shared joy came through on this record she kept, as if their dalliance hadn't mattered to her.

The new posts, cropping up every other day or so, depressed him even more. Roxana beaming with two exceptionally good-looking fellow art students pressed up on either side of her face. Her pieces made for classes, with captions about how much more refined her spells were getting under Professor Such-and-Such's tutelage. The ocean beyond the Port Baleia rooftops with caption *Still not tired of this view.*

He closed the app, flopped on his back on the loveseat, and let his skin turn to stone all over.

She couldn't have meant, with those posts, to set herself farther out of his reach, but they accomplished exactly that. Which shouldn't have happened. He was supposed to have stopped caring by now.

He didn't dare add her on the app, nor Ester. He added no one and posted nothing; he just checked Roxana's feed and the band's and occasionally ones linked by them or suggested by the app. He wouldn't even have uploaded a profile picture, except Oni told him it would make him look like a "bot" if he didn't. So he snapped a picture of one of his porch lightbulbs glowing in the dusk with overgrown greenery behind it, and that stood in for the profile pic of sparkstonestrings.

As Lord Festival approached, Mayor Wei urged everyone to remain civil above all else. But the rest of the town, Rafi definitely included, worried that in the merry chaos of Lord Festival—which encompassed Halloween and involved several nights of costumes, masks, and running amok outdoors in the dark—there was ample potential for someone to get whisked away by a korred.

The band got approached with requests for fae bodyguards, or fae willing to layer on extra-strong spells on self-defense items. They had to turn those down. Those were getting into combative and legally dicey territory that Jove and Izzy wanted no part of. There were already town fae happy to defend humans, they suggested—make friends with those. And no, Tash and Rafi couldn't do it; they'd be playing gigs those evenings.

Even if no new attacks happened, the Ti Falls Seven continued suffering, and their loved ones got ever more upset. A few came to the band asking for *anything* that would help. "Take me to the korreds," they said. "I'll ask them for a deal myself. Whatever they want, as long as they fix it."

The band members staved off those requests, telling such folk that entering the korreds' haunt would assuredly only increase their suffering. Rafi suspected it was only a matter of time before one of them walked straight across the verge themselves, without a safe escort, to try it.

He prepared in secret. Alone in his cottage, he rehearsed moving and speaking differently. A matter-witch at Spirit Festival had been handing out lozenges that changed one's voice for a few hours—the raspberry-flavored ones made it higher, the anise ones lower, the lemon ones smoother, the blackcurrant raspier. Rafi had an assorted tin of them and used one sometimes to practice an alternate voice. He was creating his own Lord Festival costume, one he didn't particularly want to put on but felt ever more certain he would.

The first day of the festival, the thirtieth of October, he went about with each heartbeat a tiny shock, every movement in his peripheral vision making him twitch. He was entirely on edge by nightfall, relying on muscle memory to play the familiar songs at the gig, his gaze jumping from one disguised figure to another. He had asked Figo to keep his ears open for rumors of what the korreds would do, but hadn't heard from him yet.

When the gig ended, he raced up to the footpath and patrolled for a couple of hours. No korreds.

Leaning on the chilly wall outside his cottage, he checked Roxana's online feed, as if she might have posted some supportive coded message for him. Instead he found two pictures not an hour old. In one she wore her mask and top hat, agleam with metal gears and cut-out stars, and she was playfully holding a toy knife to the throat of an attractive woman with a nose piercing, who wore red twisted horns and a stuck-on goatee. In the other picture, the goat-costume woman kissed the beaming Roxana on the cheek. The caption said *Happy Lord Festival! Shenanigans in Port Baleia.*

He made a sound like the whimper of a wounded fox.

Such shenanigans were indeed common at Lord Festival, between friends or even strangers. But other people got to be with her, and he wasn't, and that constituted deep torture.

Halloween arrived. While the rest of the town carried out their odd blend of gleeful revelry and defensive stance, he got through the cloudy day, the twilight, and the windy evening. Meloncollie played at a street party that night, all wearing animal costume pieces. Rafi humorlessly donned a jacket resembling a mountain cat's spotted coat and a headband with fuzzy ears.

At the end of their set Figo appeared, his glowing form weaving through the sea of costumes.

"I hear the korreds spent last night scaring people outside a haunted house," he told Rafi. "A fake haunted house, I mean, not one with *real* ghosts. And then eating some vendor's entire supply of candied hawthorns. No great harm done. But tonight there seems to be a party at Okeu Park up at the verge, and your stone giant friend told me the korreds were planning to crash it."

"Thank you." Rafi handed him a color-changing starfish hat someone had thrown onto the stage. "For you."

He took his liuqin back to the cottage, discarded his costume, and slimmed his body down to his human disguise: a bit shorter, narrower in the shoulders, hair and eyes lightened to tawny brown, gender indeterminate. He put on the clothes he'd gotten for the purpose—black jeans, high-top sneakers, green flannel button-down shirt, long black raincoat, and knit cap. He spritzed himself all over with the free sample vial of Spice of Autumn Leaf by Mirage Isle Perfumes, another festival gift. Finally he got the iron cuff, put it in his coat pocket next to the tin of voice-changing lozenges, and went out.

CHAPTER 17

T HE CHAOS WAS ALREADY BEGINNING.
Rafi halted behind a bushy tree and peered between branches.

There were about ten partygoers, all of them probably teenagers. To judge from the drink cans, snacks, and orange lanterns on the picnic table in the wooden pavilion, they had started their celebration there. But now all of them had backed up to the footpath, exclaiming and laughing in half-offended and fully-intoxicated shock. Korreds swarmed the pavilion, eating the food, climbing the pillars, tugging at the animal statues on the roof. Brogyo and Unklag stood near the youths, trying to coax them back in.

"No, look," one teen said, "we just wanted to see if you'd show up. Like, to dare ourselves, 'cause it's Halloween and we knew your haunt was right on the other side of here. We didn't plan to hang around if you came, though. Seriously, take the snacks, it's cool."

"But *snacks* aren't interesting enough," Brogyo said, his voice a deep purr. "We want you to stay. We want your appreciation, your delicate bodies, your arts."

"Holy shit," one of the other teens said, yanking a friend's arm. "Let's *go*."

"Stay!" Unklag cried.

But the youths fled—to Rafi's relief—sprinting down the footpath so fast he could feel the reverberations of their heels in the packed dirt. Their scared laughter diminished into the wind.

"This art will have to do, then," called a korred on the roof, rocking a statue back and forth until it broke off. "I like it! I'm keeping it."

"I like the whole thing," another said. "It's just two hops from our haunt. Why should we not take it? Join it to ours."

Rafi blinked in astonishment. Despite the many instances of fae luring away humans, he'd never heard of any violating the truce of the verge and taking territory.

Taking it *back*, his mind amended. But that had been the point of establishing the verge: humans having their place to live in relative safety, while providing regular gifts and entertainment to thank the fae for their generosity.

Brogyo eyed the pavilion. "I do hear talk of some loathsome human leader wanting to take fae territory—push back the verge or build roads across it. As if they could."

That would be Akio Riquelme. Rafi had heard similar things. He couldn't argue with the "loathsome" label, but surely the fae knew that most humans didn't agree with Riquelme?

"Then we should show them how easy it is," Sminu said, "for us to take some of theirs."

Unklag bounded onto a boulder. "Yes! Like Akurafi's story of the forest growing through the streets, and Miryoku becoming our own earth fae town."

The way she said the words was almost wistful. At the mention of his name, Rafi's skin went wild with alarm, stone snaking out across it.

"No, no, no," he mumbled.

This needed to stop. Now.

He slipped a raspberry lozenge into his mouth, breathed deeply, and sent his magic out to settle his skin back into its disguise. Then he walked into view, his gait careful and slow.

Unklag, on the boulder, spotted him first. "Why, hello," she called. "Have you stayed for the party?"

In his higher-pitched voice, he said, "I have. My friends ran away, but I'm still curious."

More korreds popped into view, in and atop the pavilion. "Come in, then," they called.

Rafi ducked his head, hands in his pockets, tracing his shoe on the dirt in the habit he'd seen in human youths. "I have…kind of a crush, though. What if there's just one of you I want to hang out with?"

His half-fae nature let him speak the lie without too much effort, as it was at least partly true. He hoped the rest of the statements he needed to say tonight could be similarly categorized, or his ruse might fall apart.

While a few korreds protested, "No, come with all of us," the majority asked, "Who? Who is it?" They couldn't resist a juicy secret.

Rafi glanced at Brogyo and Sminu, who had sauntered closer. "Haunt ruler Brogyo," he said, "would you go for a walk with me?"

A ripple of delighted laughs ran through the group.

"This human aims high!" Unklag said. "I respect them."

"Lovely friend, I'm flattered." Brogyo strolled toward him.

Sminu examined Rafi. "What if they mean you harm, Ruler?"

"What harm could they do *me*?" Brogyo extended a hand to Rafi.

Rafi took it and tamped down a shudder. The fingers that closed around his were cold, tough, and scratchy like sandstone. He already knew they would be. What made him sick was the realization that Brogyo had never touched him so gently in all Rafi's life. All the other occasions, those that had made him familiar with the texture of korred skin, had been grabs, shoves, hits, wrenches.

"Where shall we walk?" Brogyo asked.

"This way?" Rafi tilted his head to the footpath.

The korreds sent up a thrilled cacophony.

"Enjoy, Brogyo!"

"Bring them back to us soon!"

"Tell us everything, share the stories!"

Brogyo chuckled as they walked away. "They're envious. But it's right that you chose me. Is it indeed stories you wish to tell?"

"I can think of some." Rafi cleared his dry throat and nodded toward the ancient trees silhouetted ahead. "Will you take me in there? Into your forest? I've always wanted to see those trees. They're magnificent."

"Those old things? They merely stand there and serve as a border for our haunt. We spend very little time among them."

Rafi knew. That was why he chose them.

"So you're saying no one will disturb us if we hang out in there?" He sent Brogyo a coy glance.

"Excellent observation." Brogyo laced his fingers tighter into Rafi's, a sensation like twigs wrapping around his hand. Rafi tried not to cringe.

They left the path, waded through the strip of forest on the human side, and crossed the verge. The air crackled around Rafi's skin, and he remembered to shiver and giggle as if unfamiliar with the sensation, a naïve human who'd never entered the fae realm before.

Brogyo pulled him along. Their feet sank in decaying leaves, and they had to climb over a fallen tree, its wood crumbling under their hands, before landing in a small clearing where the roots of four trees met and tangled: two cottonwoods and two banyans, each with a trunk wider than Rafi's cottage. Their bulk, along with the tangle of branches overhead, would have consigned the clearing to complete darkness but for thousands of glowing mushrooms, along with several glow-worms, that speckled the ground and the fallen log, bathing the space in pale green light.

Again, Rafi behaved as if he'd never seen this place before, hadn't spent hundreds of nights sleeping here to avoid the korreds. "It's so beautiful," he said, taking the opportunity to pull his hand out of Brogyo's as he looked around.

"Do you think so? It's hardly the most interesting spot in our realm. Ah, the places I would like to show you."

Rafi had said similar things to Roxana, in August. Charmed her with descriptions of the fae realm, daydreamed of bringing her here. She would have loved this spot, tranquil and glowing and hidden.

He slid the cuff from his pocket, holding it by the outside, and opened its hinge. The calming spell of the silver flowed up his arm, a soft thread that soothed his stomach. He fancied he could feel Roxana in the essence of her magic. Even so, he sweated and his ears were ringing.

"I brought you a gift," he said. "A festival bracelet."

Brogyo stepped forward, muscling into Rafi's space. "How generous. I shall give you a kiss in return."

Rafi willed his smile to stay in place. "First…may I put it on you?"

Brogyo gamely held out his arm, an arm that could crush Rafi's skull with one blow.

It was too easy, really.

Rafi snapped the cuff shut around Brogyo's wrist. Brogyo's face contorted and he emitted a choked cry.

Flaring his fire magic for strength, Rafi scrambled up into the nearest banyan tree, preparing to flee at top speed in case Brogyo managed to tear the cuff off.

But though Brogyo scrabbled at the cuff with his other hand, then dropped to the ground to try with both feet, like a rabbit kicking at a wolf's jaws, he couldn't knock it loose.

While Rafi crouched eight feet overhead on a branch, trembling, Brogyo twisted and grunted on the ground.

"Iron," Brogyo managed to rasp. "Why?"

Rafi swallowed. His voice remained at higher timbre even as his tone turned cruel. "Can't you guess? What does it make you feel?"

Brogyo kept making guttural sounds, writhing in the dead leaves. "No," he said, then repeated it in the fae tongue, along with unintelligible words.

Rafi's fury swept back in, shoving out the fear. He leaped to the ground and prowled in a circle around Brogyo, spitting the words at him. "I'll tell you what it's *supposed* to do. It's supposed to make you remember all the times you've hurt others. Make you understand their pain, feel it yourself. Is that even a concept you know?"

Brogyo kept twitching, but with less vigor. Either the iron was draining his strength or he was distracted by the memories flooding his mind. Or both.

Perhaps it didn't work the same on someone counted fae. This was the first real test. Rafi had no interest in inflicting mere physical torture—empathy was the point.

Frustrated, he went on, "Is that what you're feeling? All right, if you need help thinking of what you've done: Long ago, your half-sister, Sminu's mother—it's unforgivable what you did to her. Recently too. The people at Ti Falls Park, none of them have recovered. You've terrified and abused and injured humans, some of them children. You've brought people into your haunt. A performer—he died within a day. Another man, Unklag's lover. He died too. A girl, enchanted into coming here. She got out but was never the same again. A kind old woman." Rafi's voice throttled. "She told you stories, then you let her die. Are you remembering? Are you feeling what they and their families felt? *Are you?*"

He shoved Brogyo with his foot on the question.

Brogyo curled up until he looked like a boulder in the leaf litter. "Yes," he hissed.

A tiny flame of hope leaped in Rafi's chest.

Korreds couldn't lie. It was working.

"All right," Rafi said. "All right, then listen. You want this pain to never happen again? The way you're doing things, the ruler you are—*stop*. No one respects you this way, no one but the fae in your haunt, and they're horrible, they're stupid and cruel. They just love that you let them get away with hurting everyone. Is that what you want to be known for? You've driven away better korreds—they live way the fuck out in the mountains just to keep away from you. The rest of the fae around here, they're disgusted with you too. And humans? Sure, they fear you, which I guess you're into, but they also hate you. You want to go on like this, being the haunt ruler no one respects?"

Another kick to Brogyo's stony shoulder.

Brogyo didn't speak, only twitched his fingers upward in a way that might have been acquiescence. He stayed in a ball, quivering. It sent the tiniest shake through the earth, but only within a close radius.

Roxana would have phrased all that more kindly, some piece of Rafi's mind admitted. He was so unmoored without her around to consult. But then, maybe harshness was the only tone Brogyo would respond to.

Rafi exhaled carefully. He shivered as the heat of his fury evaporated and left his skin cold.

"We're going to wait," he told Brogyo. "You're going to wear that and go through all those memories. Lord knows you must have a lot of them. Then, when…when the moon's overhead, I'll take it off you. And you'll start making some changes. Or else this all happens again. Deal?"

Brogyo's fingers twitched once more.

Rafi took it as acceptance and climbed back into the banyan tree. He settled into the mossy cup, shut his eyes, and sank into his stone form. He needed to recuperate while waiting this terrible night out, and retreating into stone was the best way. He'd only chosen the position of the moon arbitrarily; he had no idea what the most effective length of time would be. But he guessed taking off the cuff too soon was a greater risk than leaving it on too long. Ideally he would only do this once.

It was probably about midnight, and the moon would take a few more hours to get overhead. Though who knew, time being the chimera it was in the fae realm.

The wind made branches creak and sent dead leaves spiraling down. He tried to rest, waiting out the hours of Brogyo's torment. His stone skin sedated him, as it usually did, rendering his body sluggish and slowing his thoughts. But those thoughts were a bad dream now, circling relentlessly around the atrocity he had enmeshed himself in.

As time passed, it almost began to seem he was trapped in the cuff himself, for all he could think about were his own regrets and mistakes and cruelties—tonight's in particular. On the many occasions he had imagined retaliating against Brogyo, he had never pictured how much he himself would suffer in committing the act. He felt no relief nor even a sense of grim justice, only horror.

He unsealed his stone and opened his eyes a crack. Silver light gleamed among the clouds: the moon had risen. It wasn't overhead yet, but he was sick of this exercise. It had lasted long enough.

He stretched his stiff limbs. Below, Brogyo still huddled, stationary now. Rafi ensured his disguise was in place and prepared the speech he would give, the deal he would insist on—along with planning the escape route he would take at full speed if Brogyo happened to revert instantly to strength and fury.

Then Brogyo's shape crumbled in on itself. Rafi squinted. In the pale mushroom light, Brogyo had become flatter, shapeless, like a heap of dark sand. The glowing lights of the foxfire and worms blinked out, one by one. Something whispered in the fae tongue, and something whispered back.

Fear crackled through him. In the darkness, Rafi leaped out of the tree and lit up his palm as he crouched on the ground.

Sand. Earth. It ran through his fingers as he touched it. Brogyo had been right here, yet...

"Brogyo has returned to the elements."

The whisper, in the fae tongue, slipped out into the woods. Rafi couldn't hear all the sounds, but he picked up enough of the audible parts to recognize the phrase. One of the little faeries in the trees had spoken.

Other fae repeated it, in croaks and songs, echoing outward through the forest. The glowing mushrooms and worms began to wink back on, and more lights fluttered in—fae from elsewhere, landing in the branches to exchange the news. Already some were cocking their heads at Rafi, trying to identify him and his part in this.

Panic thundered through his veins. He held tight to his disguise and extinguished his glow.

The cuff's enamel shone through the heap of earth that had been Brogyo. Rafi seized it, vaulted over the fallen log, and ran.

He crossed the verge in a sizzle of electricity and shifted to his fire form. No time to strip first. He let his clothes stretch and tear as he sprinted down the path, away from his cottage, away from town. One shoe's sole ripped loose in a meadow, tripping him. He rolled into long, scratchy grass, yanked off both shoes and threw them aside, then leaped back up without ever fully coming to a stop.

He ran until his lungs and heart felt on fire, and still kept going. The wind blasted him, strong with the smell of the ocean. The moon regarded him between clouds, lighting his way even as she condemned him.

I'm sorry, he thought to the moon, the Lady, the Lord, Roxana, Brogyo, Hazel, the elements. He had no breath to speak it aloud, but it spiraled through his mind, his only coherent thought other than the need to escape. *Forgive me. Please don't cast me out. I'm sorry, I'm sorry, I'm sorry.*

CHAPTER 18

RAFI HUDDLED IN A NICHE IN A CLIFF FACE overlooking the ocean. The hollow was just tall enough for him to sit in with his knees pulled up, and wide enough that he wasn't about to topple off. The sun had risen—it stayed behind a thick blanket of clouds rather than being warm or golden or healing—and he had a clear view of the waves slamming against the rocks fifty feet below. The cliff was part of a headland perhaps two miles south of the beach where he'd spent a couple of idyllic afternoons with Roxana, in some other lifetime.

He'd run out of energy for his disguise. He looked like his miserable default human self again. Any hour now, one of these bird fae or sylphs swooping by would recognize him and report his whereabouts to the fae across the verge, and then…

His imagination offered many possibilities, none of them pleasant. He didn't actually know if there was precedent for it—a human, or indeed anyone, forcing a faery into regeneration. He could only assume it came with vicious consequences.

The time hadn't shifted much at all in this trip back and forth across the verge. His phone said it was the morning of November 1 here in the human realm, as if nothing of consequence had happened overnight, as if his whole world hadn't fractured.

A little after 11:00 a.m., Jove texted him: *Hey, you good? Can't find you. We have the afternoon gig remember.*

Rafi read it via the notification without opening the message. He couldn't answer, couldn't fake an excuse, couldn't show up in person only to be outed before their eyes as a killer by the fae who would come for him.

Another message, from Oni this time: *Hi, are you ok? I'm worried. I hope you're just across the verge after a fun Halloween but let me know ok?*

He ached to reassure her but couldn't do that either. He put away the phone and pulled his freezing bare feet closer to himself, hugging his knees.

Then, a bit later, Tash: *Just got word Brogyo has returned to the elements. Where are you?*

He stared at the notification. His thumb crept to it and tapped it open. *Is that all they said about it?* he typed.

Yes. He walked off with some human as a last celebration, then gave up this life. Are you coming to the gig or do we need to get Meg to fill in for you?

Rafi bit his chapped lower lip. It tasted of salt spray.

Just "some human." If no one had mentioned Rafi, maybe no one knew he was involved. His disguise might have worked. The thread of hope dangled before him.

I need you to come talk to me first, he responded. *Please.*

Tash sent a wave speeding up the cliff, carrying herself inside it in fish form. She leaped neatly onto the shelf beside Rafi, scattering seawater all over him as the wave broke, then shifted into human form.

"Interesting location," she said.

He turned sideways to face her, as much as he could in the little alcove. "I have to tell you something. But I need to make a deal with you first: you cannot tell anyone, not without my permission. What do you ask in exchange?"

Her eyes with their fish-scale sheen traveled up and down him, and she lifted her nose as if sniffing him. "Nothing beyond that. Now all I want is to know the secret."

"Thank you," he said sincerely. "I know you don't like sentiment, but you're honestly a really great friend, Tash—"

"Yes, yes. Tell me."

Rafi drew the cuff from his pocket and unfolded the cloth to show her. "Don't touch the inside."

She sniffed it and reared back. "Oh."

"The iron's from the fae realm, and it has a spell on it to make the wearer feel guilt. Empathy, rather. The guilt they *should* feel, for the hurt they've caused."

"Roxana Wei made you such a thing?" Tash's voice was hushed, and she seemed shocked—an emotion he couldn't say he'd ever seen on her before.

"I…never said that."

"Clearly she did. It's her style of metal art, and you two were lovers."

Rafi scooped the cloth back over the cuff. "I didn't—that's—"

"The two of you were not invisible, you know, traipsing around town together. Not to mention I could smell her on you lots of times."

He cast his gaze out toward the horizon. "Right. Does everyone know?"

"Some fae do, but we don't care about humans' sex lives. Jove and Izzy suspected and asked me. I said you hadn't told me anything about it."

"Okay. Doesn't matter. So yes, she made this, but only because I asked her to. And last night I used it."

He described everything, from the korreds' crashing the party to Rafi's fleeing the ancient grove in panic.

"I murdered him," he finished in a rasp. "I didn't mean to, but that doesn't excuse it."

Tash scoffed. "What's happened to your brain? You can't *murder* fae."

"But forcing someone to reincarnate—"

"Is not the same thing. We choose to regenerate. That's the only way it happens. No one can make us do it."

"But no one's had *this* before, have they." Rafi held up the wrapped cuff.

"Well, no, and I'd go on keeping it a secret if I were you. No point inviting trouble. Still, we all knew he'd return to the elements one of these days. It wasn't murder, and it wasn't suicide. It wasn't even really death. Why are you thinking in human terms about it?"

"Because! I am human!"

"Half. And also half fae. What you did was attack a faery, which other fae do all the time. You had good reason. And sometimes a faery decides being bested in a fight is a sign that it's time to start over. Fine, you found a new way to attack, but the result is the same. Relax."

Rafi slumped against the side of the alcove, resting his head on the dank rock. "But won't they come after me? Where can I possibly go?"

"I haven't heard anyone mention you. All they're saying is Brogyo's gone. I'm sure they'd be talking about you if you'd been recognized."

"But the mysterious human he walked off with…"

"What could a human do to Brogyo? They figure that person was his last indulgence. And if the human disappeared afterward, never to be seen again—well, you tell me, would the korreds care about that?"

A flicker of his anger returned. "No. They would not."

"If any fae did recognize you, my intuition is they'd stay quiet. They'd be on your side. They wouldn't condemn what you did. Let's be honest: no one's going to miss that fucker."

Rafi swallowed, exhausted now that his panic was receding. "The other korreds might."

"Not even them. I bet right now they're too busy fighting over how Sminu's rule is going to go. Oh yeah, you'll have to congratulate your father on his promotion."

Rafi had thought of that, without any real feeling, over the course of the night. "At least he'll be something different," he said, echoing Kepelo.

"He's a fucker too," she said thoughtfully. "But yes, different."

"So no one will come after me? Are we sure?"

"Even if they did, wouldn't Kepelo protect you?"

"I don't know. I hope she doesn't have to find out. I hope no one does." Part of his mind began insisting *No, that's not true*—he wanted to come clean—but he couldn't cope with the possibility that it might make everyone shun him.

"I think no one finding out is a reasonable thing to expect." Tash got out her phone. "I hate to sound like a human and care what time it is, but we do have a gig at two. If you aren't coming, tell me now so I can get Meg to sub in."

If he didn't come, it would look suspicious. If he meant to continue on as if all was normal, he'd have to show. "I can come. I think. What will I tell Izzy and Jove?"

"You could say you were out late, fell asleep somewhere, and your phone died." Tash rose to a crouch. "It's quite annoying that I have to think up your lies for you when I can't even lie myself. Can we leave?"

∽

It was a tumultuous town Rafi returned to, people simultaneously relieved that Brogyo was gone and worried what the next korred haunt leader would do. Rafi's own disquiet went unnoticed. He played the gig, crashed into sleep that night, and slogged about the next day with his head, throat, and joints aching. A cold, he recognized: he'd caught a cold. It was the kind of thing easily treated with magic, especially for an endo-witch, but he abstained. He accepted the pain as his punishment. It made him feel the tiniest bit better to view it like that.

His cottage had been growing colder as the season turned, but he didn't seek any way to change that either. While he was used to warm conditions in Kepelo's territory, he had spent plenty of chilly nights in the ancient grove or elsewhere. Not having to be near the korreds was good enough for him, whatever the temperature.

On the last night of Lord Festival, he drank a cup of licorice tea to soothe his cough while the wind howled outside and slithered through the crack under his door. His phone buzzed. The sight of Roxana's name on the text made his beleaguered lungs squeeze tight.

I just heard about Brogyo from my mom. Oh my gods. Maybe a good thing though?

He considered his answer before typing it in.

I hope it is. I haven't heard from anyone in the korred haunt yet.

A few minutes went by. Then she answered:

Can I call you? There's something I have to ask. I'm not sure I should write it.

Yes, he typed. Though he dreaded her inevitable question, he grabbed at the chance to hear her voice again, even if only in the role of stern confessor.

She called. "Hey, how are you?"

The living tones of her voice walloped him with sweet poignancy. He shut his eyes. Sitting on his loveseat, he curled his knees up to his chest. "Hey," he said. "Fine. You?"

"Things are all right. So…you probably know what I want to ask. With Brogyo. The cuff. Was that…what happened?"

He hesitated. "I used it. I didn't think it would make him do that. Not just without a word like that. I've…kind of been freaking out about it."

"Oh. Gods. Does anyone else know?"

"Tash. Because she had to talk me down from freaking out. No one else, I don't think. If they knew, someone would have come after me by now."

Her voice was soft and scared. "Just instantly, he...gave up?"

"Not instantly. It was on him awhile. I mean, you and I, we both wore it awhile, so I thought...for him, he should at least...it doesn't matter, I'm a horrible person. I feel like a torturer. An executioner. Tash tells me it's not like that with fae, and I know it's not, I grew up with them, but how can I not think it?"

"Oh, Rafi." Now she sounded warm, compassionate. He frowned, not sure he was interpreting her voice right. "Sweetheart. You're not a horrible person. I'm the one who made it, who layered in all those spells. How could you be worse than me, just because you delivered what I created? Gods, I'm so sorry. You shouldn't have to carry this alone."

Tears flooded his eyes. Stupid cold, making him emotional. "You wouldn't have delivered it. You wouldn't have acted the way I did."

"I don't think that means you're a bad person and I'm a good person. It's not that simple."

"If I could believe I really made things better, that would be one thing. But it's too early to tell. Everyone's still upset—because of the Ti Falls Seven, the politicians..." He broke off to cough.

"Are you okay?"

"Just a cold. From stress, not sleeping."

"And you're not fixing it? You're just suffering?"

"This is how it should be."

"Rafi. Heal yourself. Or get someone else to. How does it make the world any better if you suffer?"

The tears trickled down his face, hot streaks in the chilly air. *I miss you*, he wanted to say, but he'd already said that in texts and she hadn't wanted to hear it. "How does it make it any better if I heal?"

"You'll make me worry less."

He sniffled, hoping it sounded like regular congestion. "All right. I'll try."

"Did..." She paused, long enough he began to wonder if the connection had dropped. "Did Brogyo hurt you? The night you used it? Did anyone?"

"No. He didn't even know it was me. At least I don't think he knew. If I hadn't put it on him, I expect he would have done something to me. Sexual, probably. Thinking I was just some innocent, curious human."

"See." She sounded bitter. "How can you think you're horrible, when that's how it would have gone?"

"I did kind of entrap him."

"I'm just relieved you weren't hurt." She sighed. "I had to know, when I heard about him. Thank you for telling me."

He wiped his eyes on his sweatshirt sleeve. "Thanks for calling. I've missed…being able to talk to someone."

"Get some rest, all right? And healing. I mean it."

"Roxana?"

"Yes?"

"Do you…forgive me? For using the cuff?"

"Of *course*. I mean, probably it's best if you don't use it again, if this is what it does, and how it makes you feel. But maybe by using it you've stopped things from getting worse. Think of it like that."

"I hope."

"Do you forgive me for making it?" she asked quietly.

"What? There's nothing to forgive. I got the metal for you, I asked you to do it."

"I feel guilty too, though. We share this blame. All right?"

He drew in a breath. "I guess."

"Then you forgive me too?"

"Yeah. Of course I forgive you."

"Thank you," she said. "We'll let everything settle. It'll get better."

"Better," he echoed. Then he added, without even quite knowing what he meant, "It'll be summer again someday."

"Exactly," she answered, as if he had said something that made actual sense.

∽

After the call, Roxana curled up on her bed. The sound of the TV show Ester was watching squawked through the closed bedroom door. Rain pattered on her window.

His voice. She shut her eyes, hearing it again, intimate and raw.

He wasn't all right, and they were both complicit. The act was done, irreversible—her making the weapon and his using it. How did heroes in shows, like the one Ester was watching right now, slay the villains and feel righteous instead of stained? She and Rafi hadn't even meant to *slay* Brogyo, just shake him into changing course.

It wasn't murder, she reminded herself, as Tash had told Rafi. Brogyo had made the choice and was on his way to some new incarnation now—hopefully a more peaceable one. But Rafi was right too: it was impossible for a human not to think of it like murder.

She made herself wait twenty-four hours before texting him again, and then only to say, *How's your cold? Making you keep your promise to get some healing.*

He responded, *I asked Izzy and she gave me some spell teas. They're helping.*

Good. The band needs your lungs in shape so you can sing again.

Ha, I suppose, he said.

A pang shot through her at the memory of him singing "Tuesday Morning," his glance darting to hers, rich with romantic intent. She could not bring up such reminiscences with him. Not when she'd been the one saying they had to move on. He'd been good about it, too, not reaching out.

Take care, then, was all she dared say.

I will. He said nothing more either.

CHAPTER 19

IT WASN'T A FESTIVAL DAY, NOR EVEN A BAND gig, when Rafi's father showed up in Miryoku.

It was a foggy mid-November evening, and Rafi had gone to the Bazaar to buy groceries. He felt low and hoped the cheerful space would lift his spirits. He also harbored thoughts of using the visit as an excuse to text Roxana again, since he hadn't heard from her in two weeks. *Was at the Bazaar tonight,* he could say. *They have a new flavor of steamed bun.* Whatever turned out to be even partially true.

Rafi stopped at the soapmaker's stall to get some grapefruit shampoo, thinking the smell would remind him of her.

"Someone told me you were Sminu's kid," the man said. "I'd always heard you were Kepelo's."

The more people Rafi did errands for, the more tidbits of information about him got around. "I'm both," he said, unfolding lira bills to pay for his purchase. "They're my parents."

"Huh. Unusual, a faery being a cross of two elements. But it happens. I met one, years ago, who was half merfolk and half tropicbird sylph." He counted out Rafi's change with dreamy languidity. "Really beautiful, that mix."

It didn't occur to people, much as it hadn't occurred to Rafi's parents, that the offspring of two half-human fae parents could end up counted human. He continued letting them make the wrong assumption. It was easier.

As he put away his change, a voice announced, "Good evening."

Rafi's stomach cramped. He pivoted, ready to change into disguise, but the korreds—a party of perhaps ten—were only a few paces away, and Sminu had already spotted him. He merely ran his gaze up and down Rafi, then returned his attention to the citizens, all of whom had paused in their errands.

The korreds were in human form, looking wrong for the chilly weather in their one-shouldered black tunics and bare feet. Sminu raised both hands, smiling. "Friends! I am not my predecessor. I hope for more harmony between my folk and yours. Let us put the past behind us."

"Will you heal the Ti Falls Seven?" someone called. "The people your korreds cursed at the Weis' party?"

"Oh, you mean those who attacked us." Sminu waved a hand, as if forgiving that detail. "No matter. Of course, we will try, although it does seem humans are delicate things and cannot always be healed. Nevertheless, I vow we will do our utmost."

Murmurs of hope, and annoyance too, ran through the crowd. Even if the victims could be healed, and even if the korreds did try to do so, Rafi did not trust Sminu's motivation in extending the offer.

"I hope you see my rule will be a happier one," Sminu added, "and that we might be friends."

"Will you promote your son?" the soapmaker called out sardonically. "He seems like a nice person."

Rafi opened his mouth to deny any interest in such a position, but dozens of eyes turned to look at him, and he couldn't speak.

"My son? Who, *that?*" Sminu laughed. "Of course not. He doesn't live with us. He's not even counted fae."

Rafi's world fell from his grip and broke into pieces. He reminded himself to breathe, to stand still like a reputable person, not attack, not drop to the ground and become a gargoyle.

Confused voices piped up:

"Isn't he?"

"Yes he is, he's counted fae."

"I've seen him in fire form. Haven't I?"

Rafi knew he should speak, confess it himself. But once again his father overrode him. With a tongue-click of impatience, Sminu strode forward and grabbed Rafi's arm. Before Rafi could do more than stumble, a hot streak of pain crossed his hand.

Sminu held up Rafi's arm, showing the bleeding gash he'd made across Rafi's palm with his stone fingernail. "See?" Sminu said. "Human. I bring you the truth. Shouldn't it be me you trust, rather than those who deceive you?"

He let go of Rafi on the word *deceive*, shoving him so Rafi tripped and landed on his knees on the cobblestones.

He stayed there, cradling his bleeding hand and keeping his gaze on the cut rather than meeting the eyes of his fellow citizens.

Not fellow citizens. He wasn't one of them, had been hiding his humanity to keep them at a distance. The truth would have come out eventually, but to have Sminu be the one to announce it—Sminu, who had only been promoted because of an action Rafi had taken…

Everything was backward, seen in a warped mirror. His lungs hurt, as if his cold had come back.

"My brother was cursed at that party," someone called out warily. "If I bring him now, you're saying you'll heal him?"

"By all means." Sminu seemed to have already forgotten Rafi. "Play us some songs—you two, do start playing again! We shall enjoy the music while these folk bring their wounded."

The keyboard and sax duo on the corner stage, who had stopped playing when the korreds arrived, started up again hesitantly with a wintertime folk song.

Someone knelt beside Rafi, squirted milky goop on his cut that made the pain vanish, then wrapped his hand in a strip of gauze. The soapmaker.

"Sorry, friend," he muttered to Rafi. "I need to learn to keep my smart-ass remarks to myself."

"It's all right," Rafi said.

Someone took hold of Rafi's elbow and helped him to his feet—a hob, an earth faery living on the human side of the verge, who had been a friend of Hazel's. He'd only met her a couple of times, years ago. She patted his arm. "You'll be fine," she said.

Someone else, a teenager he didn't even know, picked up Rafi's shopping bag, which he'd dropped, and handed it to him. At the teen's shoulder stood Oni, gazing at him with sorrowful eyes.

He said, "Thanks," still numb and in mirror-world. "Sorry," he added, to Oni.

She shrugged, a smile ghosting across her lips.

It moved him that even these few would help, after what they'd heard.

That Oni might not hate him.

But when he looked past them, at the rest...

Most had turned their attention back to the spectacle of the korreds promising to heal the Ti Falls Seven. Deals were being made and publicly witnessed; some people were running out of the Bazaar to summon others, while others were running in after hearing the news. A few, though, murmured with their heads close together, gazes darting to Rafi. He saw the wariness. The hostility.

Wanderer, he heard in the middle of someone's sentence, emitted from their mouth like an unwanted morsel of food.

"I need to go," he said. "Thanks. Thank you." He sent the words vaguely to either side, to the soapmaker and the hob and the teen and Oni, and fled.

They stepped aside and let him escape. No one stopped him.

"My father says being counted human means I'll die," Rafi said. "My mother says it's true."

He felt calm about it, mostly. He just wanted to see if Sminu and Kepelo had been right about this notion, or if Hazel had different information. Rafi was still young, much smaller than Hazel, and viewed her as being a great deal wiser than nearly everyone. Wiser even than Kepelo, perhaps.

To his surprise, his grandmother's features pinched in what looked like pain, then she swooped in, sitting next to him on the rug in her house, and hugged him so tightly he squeaked. "Has this been worrying you?" she asked, her voice gentle in comparison to the hug.

"No," he said. "Or, not a lot. Sometimes. Is it always true? Does it ever change?"

Hazel let go of him and ran her finger back and forth across the slightly pointed tip of his ear. "It can't be changed. And so far, it's always true. Humans are mortal, fae aren't."

"Fae don't die, they regenerate." He recited the words Kepelo and his other fae family had given him many a time in answer. "They choose to start over with a new life, when they want to. They can't be killed."

"Precisely. That's the difference, and it's rather a big difference! They don't age like we do. They only get wearier in mind, more tired of life, or that's what we hear, anyway. Regeneration fixes that."

"How can they tell when someone like me is born? Someone who's part human and part fae—how do they know which one they're counted as?"

"Certain witches can do tests to find out," Hazel said. "But the fae just know. They can smell it on you." She said it with a playful wrinkle of her nose and pretended to sniff him, which made him deduce that the test didn't involve literal smelling. Or maybe it did, but it didn't matter.

"They 'just know' a lot of things I don't," he conceded.

"Indubitably. But you will also know things they don't. I bet you already do. After all, you know what it's like to be a mortal living in the fae realm. A wanderer. That's something they'll never really understand."

"Is being a wanderer also something you can't change?"

Hazel smoothed her daisy-patterned shawl down her ribs. "It *can* be changed. Being a wanderer just means the human lawfolk haven't written your name down yet and made you start paying taxes. But you're in no hurry to do that, are you?" Her dark eyes crinkled with amusement.

"No. I don't have any money," Rafi said, alarmed. "Any at all."

Hazel laughed and kissed him on the head. "Then there you are. No rush." She assessed him with a longer look. "Have you had to stay at your father's haunt more often lately?"

Rafi looked down, stroking the two fingers that Unklag had broken on his last visit, careless in hauling him to the haunt when he didn't want to go. Mukut had healed him. He hadn't told Hazel. "Some. They've started being more interested in me, now that I can tell stories and sing songs. They didn't care about me when I was a baby—or at least that's what my mother says. I can't remember."

Hazel caught his hand and latched their fingers together. "Most of us can't remember being babies. Your father…seems like he might not be as pleasant to stay with."

Rafi shrugged, still gazing at his small healed hand in her soothing grip. He was thinking of the first few times he'd been summoned to stay there, torn from the familiarity and pretty fires of Kepelo's haunt and thrust into the shadowy, thorny den of korreds, all of them demanding entertainment. Hurting him when he cried instead. He didn't want to tell her that either.

After several seconds of silence, she thumped their joined hands lightly against his leg. "Shall we go to the Bazaar and pick something for lunch?"

⁓

Sminu showed up in the Bazaar when I was there. Told everyone I'm counted human. So everyone knows I've been lying. I talked to Jove and Izzy, and we agreed I should take some time off. Therefore I'm taking more errands across the verge, will be away awhile. I mention it in case you try to get in touch and I don't answer.

Roxana found the text waiting for her when she woke up, the sky still black at 6:00 a.m. He'd sent it half an hour earlier—either a very early morning for him or a sleepless night. Given the news, she suspected the latter. Wincing, she turned on her bedside lamp.

Oh no. I'm sorry, she typed. *Are you okay? I really think everyone will get over it soon.*

The people in town trusted me, he answered. *And now they see I wasn't being honest. I hate it, but I've decided it's my punishment.*

For...what we talked about?

Yes. Elemental balance maybe. Who knows. But I'm glad you always knew, at least.

Of course, she typed. *It's not a crime to be a wanderer. And it's not your fault.*

At first it wasn't. Now...well, too late. Be well, Roxana.

It's never too late, she thumbed in. *Text me when you settle back in, all right?*

I will. If I do.

She wanted to demand *What do you mean "if"?*, but he was having a bad enough day without her challenging him. He needed to lick his wounds awhile.

I've got your back, she said instead. It was what she'd want a friend to say.

Thank you, he responded, and went silent.

⁓

This was admittedly easier, he thought, lounging in his hammock in the fire haunt. The fae expected little of him here, generally left him alone, didn't much care whether he told the truth since they didn't ask him many things to begin with. The drakes and other fire fae didn't hound him for human arts and stories to anywhere near the same extent the korreds did. If they wanted such entertainment, they were adept at going to Miryoku and getting it themselves without causing incidents.

Given this would be his fifth night in a row here, it could be December by now on the human side of the verge. For once, he sort of hoped so, hoped time over there was spooling by quickly, people forgetting him and his humiliation.

A certain few people, however, were the reason he couldn't just give up and stay here, go full wanderer again. He had made commitments—to return eventually, to get back in touch, to resume playing with the band. Besides, he did care what happened to them. Why else would he be lying here wondering whether Oni had joined that school play she'd been talking about, or what obscure nineties songs Jove and Izzy were scrounging up to add to Meloncollie's rotation, or whether Tash was keeping the cottage's houseplants alive in his absence, or what Roxana was studying and whether she ever thought about him anymore?

Not to mention his other reasons to go back: the errands he was fulfilling, the few cold cases he had solved. For some clients he'd bring good news; for others, sad. A stolen ring found; a fae offspring located and a promise secured to come to the next festival; a fae ex-lover tracked down but found to be totally uninterested in reuniting; a chipped red bell that had been worn by a cat who had defected from the human realm two years ago and had since died, but at least whose final months could be reported as full of fish meals in a riverside fae haunt.

He could send all those findings back with Figo or someone else. But he knew he'd bring them in person himself, probably tomorrow.

Then there was the benefit that on the fae side, it was easier to hear rumors of what his father was up to.

He'd snuck up to Mukut on wall duty today, bringing Figo to translate.

"The korreds fought awhile when Brogyo left," Figo related after conversing with her. "Some didn't want Sminu in charge, favored others instead. But Sminu convinced them he'd be best at getting humans to like them. Said he had plans." Figo waved in apology toward Mukut. "She didn't hear all the de-tails. She was out here at the border and pieced it together later."

As if that notion of "plans" wasn't alarming enough, Rafi had then run into Sminu a short time later. Rafi was walking alone, upstream along the river, and Sminu and three other korreds were coming down it.

"Hiding in here, are you?" Sminu greeted. They stopped a few steps apart. "People asked after you in town. We stayed an extra day, you see, to do the good work of healing for whoever wanted it. I supposed you must have fled."

Rafi stared at the murky rush of the river. "Were they healed?"

"We did our best. You know how delicate humans are, though. Like mag-nolia petals. And you're no better. Look at you. Sulking, hiding, because I told them something you should have told them from the start? You make no sense."

"It's complicated." Rafi shut his mouth, regretting having said even that much. Sminu was the last person he wished to discuss this with.

But his father sounded thoughtful. "Well, that's true. It *was* interesting, what they said about you. Many feel sorry for you and still trust you—which I truly can't understand. You'll have to tell me how you charm them so. But others? Well. I heard them talking. They said it just goes to show that the 'Hu-manist Party' is right and that fae, half-fae, wanderers, and rare witches like form-changers can't be trusted. Not that I know or care what this Humanist Party is, but it sounds ridiculous."

That was Akio Riquelme's new political party. While Rafi agreed it was ridiculous, he didn't answer, too disheartened by that revelation that there were people in Miryoku, people who knew him, who could think of him so disparagingly and take the side of someone like Riquelme.

"I hope it's true what you said," Rafi answered. "That your rule will be kinder."

"I hope they view it as such," Sminu said. "People are welcome to visit and get to know us."

Rafi walked off without another word.

That was the central reason he had to keep an eye on both the fae and the hu-man side of the verge, if he continued to have any compassion at all: the korreds could keep enchanting and killing people. Just in newer and sneakier ways.

"You could just, you know, join us," Izzy had said before Rafi departed for the fae realm. "Get on the record as a citizen—if you're ready. People would welcome you."

He had mumbled something about how he wasn't sure, and he'd think about it.

Roxana had suggested it once too. After he'd successfully performed some bit of town interaction—friendly banter with a shop clerk while buying a pair of sandals—she'd tucked her arm into his, walking down the street, and said, "See, it isn't so hard being a human. You could do it officially and full-time, I bet."

His wave of anxiety at that remark had nearly shut down his lungs. He'd said, "Most of it's not that easy."

"Sure it is. It's just a bunch of little pieces like that, one after another."

"About a *million* little pieces that never stop coming. You only think it's easy because you grew up with it." He sounded defensive, though he hadn't meant to.

He hadn't deserved her forgiving demeanor—the way she leaned her head on his arm as they walked, and gently said, "That's true." They'd dropped the subject. It was one of the only times they'd had anything like a disagreement.

When Rafi thought of the hurdles, the obligations, the thousand complications involved in legally joining the human realm, panic squeezed him. It felt like he was being strapped to the ground by fast-growing vines that pinned his limbs and crawled over his face—a punishment the korreds had literally inflicted on him more than once in his younger years. He would fail if he tried being fully human—lose all the money he managed to make, say all the wrong things, socially ostracize himself, disappoint everyone who had believed in him. He'd only end up crawling back here.

Couldn't join the human realm, and simultaneously couldn't keep away from it. What a conundrum.

All your sides can play together in harmony, his grandmother had said.

He had figured she meant the kind of life he led already: moving between the two realms, not being tightly tethered to either, using his freedom to do good wherever he saw the opportunity.

Tonight, listless in his hammock, he had to admit that "free" was not at all how he felt.

CHAPTER 20

ROXANA DIDN'T TEXT RAFI THIS TIME, RE-
specting his word that he would get in touch when he returned. She
didn't ask Tash about him, nor did she ask her parents if they'd seen him. (Her
father usually understood who was being referred to when he heard a name;
he just couldn't come up with names on his own. Despite Amaris's strong
objections, he had gone to the korreds for healing when they were in town,
and had received it. But the effect was weak and soon faded back to the curse's
original level of total personal-name aphasia.) She did ask Ester, twice, if Oni
had seen Rafi, since the girls stayed in touch. Evidently she hadn't, thus he was
still across the verge.

Roxana had bad dreams sometimes, as the nights grew longer. Often she
was in the fae realm looking for Rafi, surrounded by darkness full of eerie
laughs and screams; or walking on ground that broke like a fragile twig under her feet every few steps, with an ocean surging beneath, which she barely
managed not to fall into; or rambling as a one-person funeral procession for
her mother or father or Ester, for whom she sobbed as she searched for Rafi.

Roxana had never crossed the verge, not even on an impulse or a childhood dare like most humans had. In August, she'd had Rafi describe fae
haunts he'd visited. He was her own taste of that magic, a piece of it she could
hold and caress.

"I could take you across," he'd told her once. "I've done it for people before, the paying tourists. I can keep you safe. I know the places to go."

"I'm not brave enough." She hid her face on his bare shoulder. It was a
sweltering day and they had just taken a cool shower together in his cottage.
They stood in the tiny bathroom draped in nothing but a towel each.

He stroked her wet hair. "Just across and back, in Kepelo's haunt. You can
smell the flowers and see the flames. Just for ten minutes."

"But it might not *be* ten minutes. It might be hours—or the next day."

She lifted her face. "How would I explain that to Ester and my parents?"

"You could tell them ahead of time. It doesn't have to be a secret."

She shook her head, fear gluing her feet to the bathroom floor. "They'd worry. Plus I don't want to risk losing any more days with you." Which made for a good excuse.

But the shame of her fearfulness had stuck with her, as had the disappointment that flickered in his face before he'd replaced it with a gentle smile. Gods, she was a coward. Her romance with him was the bravest thing she'd ever done, and she couldn't even take that as far as visiting his mother's home.

Not until late November did a text from him finally arrive.

I'm back, at least for a little while. How are you?

She caught her breath as she read the message on the swaying streetcar, clutching the phone so she wouldn't drop it. *Hi!* she typed back. *I'm all right, busy with term projects. How about you? Errands successful?*

Some were. Town's in a weird mood. Grumpy.

It's the whole country, politics have been vicious. Ignore it if you can. Play some music. I like seeing the clips the band posts.

I will, he wrote. *I don't trust my father though, so I can't ignore that. Might be tense until we see what he's going to be like as a ruler.*

My mom thinks the offer of healing was just to get on everyone's good side so they can charm more people across the verge, she said.

Exactly what I think. I'll keep watch.

Her stop arrived. She tucked away her phone. It was raining, the sideways, slashing, frigid rain Port Baleia apparently got from November through April. She hustled home in raincoat and wool cloche.

There were too many things she wanted to ask—*What did Kepelo say? How are people treating you now? I keep having dreams about you; do you ever dream about me? Do you think it's worth having a phone conversation to talk about everything? Because things feel so unsettled with you and I want to hear your voice again*—but texting was an unsatisfying medium for such questions.

Yes, she finally typed, resigned, rain dripping from her coat onto the floor of her apartment hallway. *I guess it all just needs more time.*

∽

A couple of weeks into December, Rafi sent another text letting Roxana know he'd be going on errands across the verge again. *Hopefully I won't miss Fire Festival,* he added, *but you never know with the timing.*

The band surely needs you during festivals! she protested.

Their original mandolinist Tom will be visiting, so he'll step in if needed. Proper band reunion.

It insulted her on his behalf, the notion that this Tom was a "proper" Meloncollie member while Rafi was just some sort of understudy.

Mandolin? Whatever, she wrote. *Liuqin is where it's at.*

Ha, he answered, with a smile emoji.

She viewed it as a minor triumph—he hardly ever used smile emojis.

Then he was, presumably, gone across the verge. And she was faced with the question of whether she and Ester would return to Miryoku for Fire Festival.

She hadn't planned to originally. Back in summer, Amaris and Timo had spoken of coming to Port Baleia for it. But now Timo had his curse problem, and Amaris was busier than anticipated, with the increased number of agitated citizens worrying about the fae.

"I hate to say it," she told Roxana over the phone, "but I might need to be here to steer the town through the festival and keep a lid on things."

"Mom, it's not all down to you," Roxana chided. "But…we could come there. Port Baleia's cold and wet in winter anyway. Would be nicer for you two to visit here in summer."

She already knew, even before asking Ester, that Ester would leap at the chance to visit Miryoku. Indeed, Ester literally jumped off the sofa and hugged Roxana, clamoring, "Yes yes yes!"

Oni was the main allure, Roxana figured, more than Ester's grandparents and the rest of Miryoku put together, but no matter the reason, it saddened Roxana that Ester was still so unattached to their new home and so ready to return to their old one.

Having made that offer, she had to commit to it. So…she could see Rafi, if he was back.

She put off informing him of their visit, reasoning he probably wasn't back yet, and when he did return, he'd hear about it from Oni. Or, she realized as the date grew closer, maybe he had returned and heard about it, but didn't want to meet up, so wasn't saying anything.

Finally, the day before they drove down, Roxana texted him. *Hey! Just letting you know, in case you're back, Ester and I will be in Miryoku from the 20th to the 24th, visiting my parents. Hope I can treat you to coffee if you're in town.*

Hands shaking, she sent it off and packed her bag.

∽

Rafi drifted out of the fae realm and shivered at the burst of frosty air after the warmth of Kepelo's haunt. A djinn had darted in today to let them know Fire Festival had begun.

But according to his phone calendar, it was now December 24, already four days into the festival, and his text messages piled up on the screen—several from Roxana.

In the first, she let him know—his breath punched out of him—she would be in Miryoku. Until the twenty-fourth. Today.

Madly he scrolled through the rest.

December 20: *Arrived! I gather you're still across the verge. Hope you get back soon.*

December 21: *I guess just let me know as soon as you're back on this side. That is, if you want to meet up.*

December 23: *If by chance you've returned but don't want to meet up, it's all right and I understand. We can talk if you want. Or just give it space.*

December 24, 10:04 a.m.: *Oni says you're still in the fae realm. Shoot. We're taking off at 11:00, so unless you're back by then...I guess see you next time. Happy Fire Festival.*

It was now 3:51 p.m., his phone clock said.

He roared through clenched teeth.

Noooo, he texted back, though she was probably driving and nearly to Port Baleia by now. *I can't believe I missed you. I wish I'd known. I hate this so much.*

After sending that, he added another: *I wasn't avoiding you. I would have met up in a heartbeat.*

It would not fix anything to smash his fist against the nearest tree, appeal-

172

ing though the idea was. He stomped to his cottage. He deposited his pack of fae-realm materials in a corner, sat on the coffee table box, and stared at his phone. Nothing happened. Right, fine, she was driving.

He took a shower. A message was waiting for him after.

Argh!!! This is my fault. I should have given you more advance notice. I will next time. But I'm glad you weren't avoiding me.

Never, he typed. *Yes, next time hopefully.*

Next time, next time, next time. His whole life seemed to be flitting by in increments of "next time" without his having accomplished anything useful.

He could propose to visit her. Figure out the trains, somehow. But then where would he stay? Sleeping in her apartment was too great an imposition. Awkward as well, with Ester there. Hotels? They cost a lot, people said? He couldn't just dash across the verge and travel on that side, nor sleep on that side, not in the north. He didn't know the fae in any other region of the island. The ones bordering Miryoku were the only ones complying with Kepelo's deal to not harm him. Once he got beyond a few miles of here, he'd be in just as much danger as any other human. He was stuck on the human side if he wanted to travel, a side on which he had little idea what he was doing, especially outside Miryoku.

But even if he did learn how, she might not want him to come. She hadn't proposed it since moving there.

A message came in from her, as if reading his thoughts.

If the band ever comes up here for music festivals or anything, let me know!

So those were the conditions she was all right with: the band bringing him. A respectable excuse.

I will, he answered. He allowed a moment to quietly shut away the idea of figuring out how to travel on his own. Just as well. He would have messed up uncountable steps.

He dragged himself out to see if he still in fact had a job with the band or whether they'd rehired Tom and were cutting Rafi loose.

⌒〜⌒

Oni showed me your feed and I saw the liuqin charm you made. I love it. Charge a thousand lira for it, it's worth it.

Roxana beamed at Rafi's message. It was early January, and she was taking a break from sweeping up bits of drywall.

What other shape for her new charm could she have chosen, tormented as she was by their missed meetup? She had captioned the post, *The liuqin, a Chinese mandolin. In honor of a good friend back home. Fae-realm bronze, super powerful! Soon to go on sale at the shop with your choice of spell. Inquire to reserve it!*

You did see it! she typed back. *I'm glad. Do you have a login there?*

Yes, I don't really post though.

I'll add you anyway. What's the handle?

A minute's pause, then Rafi responded, *I'm the one who just liked that post. I think you'll guess.*

She switched to the social app and found a notification informing her of a like from sparkstonestrings. *Ha,* she texted. *Perfect. There, added you.*

Adding you back. Looks like you and Nelleke are busy.

She glanced around the space, cleared of everything but the floorboards, the built-in shelves, and one mural of a sperm whale and a squid that they'd deemed too cool to paint over. She had posted a picture of it yesterday.

Yep. She finally got a chance to buy the place next door, so we're expanding the shop. It's all renovation all the time. How about you? Still doing gigs, looks like.

Yes, those are fine. Town mood is still weird though. Especially with the news about Riquelme, ugh.

Ugh is right, she responded.

A few days ago, Akio Riquelme had announced he was running for prime minister of Eidolonia. The election would be in October. The country was thus in for ten months of obnoxious campaigning.

There's no way he could win, right? Rafi wrote. *I don't know much, but I can't see why people would choose that.*

Eidolonians get island fever sometimes and want a change, and stupidity can happen. But I still think it's unlikely he'd win. It'll just be a headache to hear about in the meantime.

Sminu, Riquelme, which one's worse? Hard to say.

Good question.

She was about to ask what he'd heard of his father lately, but then the door opened, bumped in by Nelleke's hip, and she entered carrying a rain-spattered box. "Tiles!" she announced.

"Let me help you." Roxana typed, *Got to go, Nelleke just got back with floor tiles. Stay in touch!*

Good luck, I will.

"You're smiling," Nelleke teased, singsonging the words. "Texting your cutie fellow student with the nose piercing?"

"Oh. No, a friend from Miryoku." With guilt, Roxana glanced at the texts she'd left unread so far today, from said fellow student. The woman was indeed dazzlingly cute, had bestowed cheek kisses on Roxana at Lord Festival, and often slid over to her table in class to compliment Roxana's projects. She was probably ten years younger than Roxana and seemed to have dozens of friends. Why she wanted Roxana among them, or possibly as more than a friend, Roxana couldn't fathom.

"No wonder you wanted to go home for Fire Festival," Nelleke said.

Roxana knelt to open the box. "He wasn't there. Our timing didn't work out."

"Ahh. Missed connections. Heartbreaking."

Roxana picked up a burgundy tile and turned it in the rainy daylight, examining the hue. "We had a thing over the summer. Would've been nice to see him again, at least."

"Gotcha. You've been more than just homesick! I wondered." Nelleke nudged Roxana as she crouched beside her. "So now you're sending steamy texts to each other, or…?"

Roxana laughed. "Nah. Just checking in." She set down the tile. "You know what's a good remedy for frustration, though, is tiling a floor."

☙

Rafi was glad, in a grim sort of way, he wasn't present when his father visited Miryoku again in mid-January and strolled around telling people that he and his korreds stood ready to protect them against hostile fae.

"I know you've heard of such folk," he had apparently said. "We in the fae realm hear even more. The things some fae say they would do to humans! No, no, I don't want to worry you. I mention it only to assure you we will keep watch and intervene to protect you. Please don't be concerned."

Meg of Starchime Music had been on the street where Sminu had addressed the impromptu crowd. They had related it to Rafi the next day when he stopped by the shop.

"You know what pisses me off, Rafi," Meg said, thumping their finger on the checkout counter, "is how some of the people listening were actually *grateful*. After what Sminu did to you at the Bazaar! For that alone, I can never get behind him."

"Thanks."

Oni had said the same recently: "I hate him for what he did to you." Those words in her soft voice had moved him, and he had apologized to her—for about the third time—for the secret he'd kept. To that she had shrugged and said, "I don't care. People get to keep things private. Anyway, it doesn't change anything."

But of course not everyone was so reasonable. Even after witnessing, or hearing about, Sminu's public outing of Rafi, many townsfolk considered Sminu someone worth giving a chance. Or even viewed him as the revealer of truth, and Rafi as a swindler.

Rafi slipped Meg's chantagram, addressed to their loved one in the fae realm, into his bag. "People want to be safe. They want to believe things will get better, he'll protect them, he's not the threat."

"No different than the people going all Humanist Party lately." Meg scowled. "People I've known my whole life, some of them. Feh."

Rafi brought the cuff on his errands sometimes. It wasn't exactly that he intended to use it. He certainly didn't want to—Halloween still haunted him in nightmares or sleepless hours. There was no guarantee it would make every faery regenerate; it might do only what they'd hoped in the first place and instill empathy. Which would be excellent. But since he couldn't be sure, mostly he carried the cuff as a last resort, in case he happened upon something truly awful being done.

He wasn't present when, in March, a giant spider-crab faery surged from the surf and cornered a pair of human beachgoers against a cliff. With timing not nearly enough people found suspicious, Sminu popped up with two other korreds and intervened. The two korreds, at Sminu's command, drove back the spider-crab faery, and Sminu ushered the humans out of the way to safety. Exactly as he had promised! Such an honest friend.

They made some kind of deal with the crab fae, he texted Roxana. *It's 100% fucking clear.*

I'd put money on it. Can anyone get to the crab faery and ask? she responded.

That's the beauty of it. Those crab fae don't speak human tongues. They probably could I mean, but they don't, because they have no interest. And finding them would not be easy in the first place, considering they live on the sea floor.

He's clever, your father, Roxana wrote. *I'll give the asshole that.*

In town, many agreed with Rafi and Roxana—Jove, Izzy, and Tash among them—but he also heard statements like "Now we can stop worrying about the korreds, but we have to worry about crab fae." Or "Maybe Sminu's been telling the truth and he's nothing like Brogyo. It's worth giving him a chance." Or "Look, I'm not his biggest fan, but I'd rather have him on our side than against us."

It was enough to drive a many-times-battered child of Sminu's mad.

He did his work and played liuqin. Tried now and then to learn a human-world task, such as bargaining with a matter-witch to fix a leak in his cottage's roof. Tried to keep his emotions level when Roxana posted pics of what looked suspiciously like dates with the woman from Lord Festival.

He prided himself on his patience when, in April, after a few weeks without any such posts, he texted, *Have you had any more dates with your friend? She looks nice.*

Roxana answered, *Not lately. We sort of tried dating, but I just wasn't feeling it. Luckily she's all right with just being friends.*

His chest expanding with elation, he typed, *Well, you're worth being friends with. She must be smart to have seen that.*

So the next time Rafi met up with Roxana…?, he wondered, though didn't dare ask. She obviously had a successful life going on in Port Baleia, not to mention another whole year of her college program. Any "next time" could be only a limited visit.

That said, he had to suck in a sharp breath and sit down on the nearest park bench when he got the message from her in late May:

OK, giving you proper notice this time: we're coming to Miryoku on July 1 to spend a few days with my folks. They want to celebrate my finishing my first year of classes. Would love to see you!

She added three smiling emojis. Three!

Rafi gazed in stunned joy at the flowering jacaranda and dogwood around him in Heron Park. Birds sang, children laughed on the playground, a French bulldog licked Rafi's ankle as it walked past with its owner. A glorious day.

I will ABSOLUTELY be here, he typed back, and added three heart emojis.

Perfect! she said.

Then someone said, "Hey *wanderer*. When you going to get justice for the Ti Falls Seven for what your father did?"

Shock splashed through his body. The source of the voice was a man with a bald head and a beard, walking with a woman with downturned lips who narrowed her eyes at Rafi.

"I'm trying," he answered automatically. It sounded feeble and defensive to his own ears. "I'm looking for ways, but I don't...have fae powers..." As his father had announced to everyone. As had become common knowledge.

His pulse was tapping in his ribs, his fingertips. Others slowed to watch, concerned, suspicious.

The man huffed. "Useless freeloader." He and the woman walked on.

Rafi got to his feet, restored his equilibrium with a glance at Roxana's message, and hastened toward home.

These things happened sometimes, these days. He could sit in the garden by the cottage if he wanted to enjoy sun and flowers and think about Roxana. It would be fine.

CHAPTER 21

I *need you to tell me two things,* ROXANA TEXTED to Satsuki during the last week of June. *First, tell me to take a deep breath.*

OK. Take a deep breath.

Thank you. Second, tell me whether I should sleep with Rafi when I visit Miryoku.

Lol! Uh. Do you want to?

I don't know? Yes? But it might be a bad idea. I don't even know if he's interested.

Given he caught up to me on the street the other day to ask details about your visit, I would say his interest is solid.

Did he? Aww.

I know you half regret hooking up last summer, but it seems like that's because you liked it too much. Right?

Yes…sigh.

So no harm if you want to do it again.

I don't know. It might make things worse.

True or false: you worry that about basically everything.

True. True.

See how you feel once you're in his presence. That's all I will advise.

∽

These drives to and from Miryoku, were they ever *not* going to be fraught?

Even having answered "Will I see him?" and "Does he want to see me?", the greater questions of "What will we do?" and "How will it go?" loomed over Roxana.

Ester, oblivious, probably thought she was contributing to a positive mood by gushing, "I'm so glad I'm done with the school year. That was the hardest one ever. I cannot wait to see Oni and Nana and Papa." All it did was make Roxana shrivel with guilt for having dragged her child into exile from all that she loved, apparently.

The humidity of the Southwest Peninsula rolled into their open windows as they crossed the Amizade Bridge. The smell worked its own natural magic, soothing Roxana with its familiarity: flowers, forest, beaches. Even before they reached the Miryoku exit, the scent of jasmine wound its way into the car. As if reeling them in on a line, it pulled them up the hill and into town.

Her heart began drumming in happy nervousness. The last time she'd been surrounded by this air, this scent, she'd been falling in love with Rafi.

That word again. It kept sneaking in, refusing to give up and transmute into "infatuation" or "lust." But now she had to turn her attention to a different kind of love, as they were arriving at her parents' house, and Amaris and Timo were on the front walk, waving in greeting.

The afternoon tumbled by in merry disorder. They had iced tea, strolled in the back garden to see what was blooming, cooked dinner, and had Satsuki over for the meal. Roxana showed everyone some of her new metal charms, and they passed them around and lauded them.

"I can get the spells to last longer now, even on human-realm metal," she said. "I'm getting better at detecting my own spells on things from a distance—though not much of a distance, maybe twenty feet or less. And I've improved at layering different spells, too, to take effect in sequence or all at once, whichever you prefer. When they give you some of the expert work to hold and study, you can feel how it's done and then practice till you can do it."

"And so pretty!" Satsuki spread out a necklace of multicolored sea-glass petals, each petal wrapped in a gold bezel. "The gold is divine with these colors."

"Vermeil technically." Roxana propped her chin on her fist. "Gold over silver."

"Whatever! Your artisanship has leveled up, lady. This is gorgeous."

"It's yours. I'll put a spell on it if you like."

While Satsuki exclaimed in delighted protest, Timo told Roxana, "And thank you for sending those charms over the months. They really just keep getting better."

Roxana grimaced. "Except they don't do the one thing they're supposed to."

"Aw, honey, none of us can turn around a korred curse—not even a korred, apparently. The charms do make me feel more clearheaded, though! They give me a good attitude."

"Dad, I think that's just your natural temperament."

Timo turned to Ester. "Listen to how your mom refuses to take compliments. Are you hearing this?"

Ester nodded sagely.

Though Roxana laughed along with the rest of them, it still made her heart twinge to know that all these advanced skills, all these charms, couldn't fix Timo's curse or indeed that of any of the Ti Falls Seven. She had mailed one box after another to her parents, full of charms for Timo and the rest of the victims, to no avail. Rafi had consoled her, in text, when she'd told him about those failures a couple of months ago. He'd had the same experience, sourcing plants and rocks and actual fae from the fae realm to try to help, but he had essentially given up by now too.

"Oni's coming over soon," Ester announced. "She just texted." She leaped up in a squawk of scooted chair legs.

Roxana got up to take plates to the sink and grabbed the chance to look at her phone. As she hoped, a message from Rafi had just come in:

I'll be walking Oni over. If you happen to be around and can come say hi now…see you soon!

A starburst of nervous anticipation bloomed inside her.

Satsuki came up, carrying more dishes.

"So," Roxana said. She showed Satsuki the text.

Satsuki elbowed her. "I'm on it." Then she raised her voice so Amaris and Timo could hear. "Rox, can I steal you to walk back with me?"

"You kids go ahead." Amaris lifted her wine glass. "We'll hang out and make sure these teenagers don't burn the house down."

"Thanks, Mom." Wiping her hands on a tea towel, Roxana darted over to kiss her mother's forehead. "Give me just a minute, Satsuki." She draped the towel over a chair and hurried out of the kitchen.

I am around! she texted Rafi. *See you soon!*

As they left the house a few minutes later, Satsuki remarked, "You made yourself look *so nice* to take a walk with me. It's really sweet."

"Hush," Roxana said under her breath.

She had thrown together what she could in the five minutes available: quick change into the stretchy purple dress from the Goth Night gig, this time with bare legs and flip-flops, deodorant touch-up, teeth brushed, hair tidied, and a swipe of tangerine lip balm.

"Honestly," Satsuki said as they pushed open the gate, "you look beautiful. He'll be dazzled."

Ester was already outside, balancing on the curb while awaiting Oni. She yelled in greeting and ran to meet the two figures who came into view around the corner, beneath the street lamp.

Roxana's breath stopped. The lope of his stride, the angle of shadow under his jaw, the way his eyes tracked to her and locked there even from half a block away—how often she'd tried to remember all those details, thought she *had* accurately remembered them. But it turned out her memory couldn't possibly catalog all the three-dimensional features of Rafi, living and present.

Satsuki plucked at her arm. They moved forward. Ester had already hugged Oni, then Rafi, then Oni again. Pulled into a hug with the two girls, Roxana marveled aloud that Oni, like Ester, had somehow gotten taller than Roxana within the past year.

Then before she could make the moment strange and full of staring, she turned and transferred her embrace straight to Rafi. His arms wrapped around her, hands spreading warm on her back. He bent his head and said, "Hello."

At the softness of the word and the intimate smell of his skin, tears pricked her eyes. She stepped back a second later, still keeping up appearances—just a hug between friends. "Hey," she said casually.

Not that Oni and Ester noticed, as they were pitching each other ideas for the evening. Ester said, "Come on!", and they launched toward the house.

"Oni, text me when it's time to walk you back," Rafi called.

"I will!" she shouted.

The girls flung open the gate and went in.

"Well!" Satsuki clapped her hands. "I'm off. Have fun, you two." She squeezed Roxana's hand, then crossed the street.

"We can walk you home," Roxana protested feebly.

"Nah, I'm biking." Satsuki wheeled her bike out from where she'd propped it against the fence and switched on its headlight. "Catch up tomorrow. Night, Rafi!"

Rafi and Roxana called goodnight. Satsuki pedaled off amid the chirps of crickets.

Roxana finally looked at him. His mouth hitched up on one side.

"Ten months," she said.

"To the day."

So he had the dates burned into his memory too. They hadn't seen each other from just after midnight on September 1 until tonight, July 1.

"Your hair's shorter," she noted. Easily the least important thing to discuss. "Looks great."

He ruffled a hand through it—just above his shoulders and in shaggy layers. "Thanks. Something we were trying so I could look more grunge."

"Did you cut it with your magic? Same way you shave?"

"Yeah, but Jove had to fix it afterward with scissors, since I made a hash of it." He smiled. "Yours has gotten longer. I like it."

"Thank you. Ester and I are growing ours so we can do braids and things."

"Do you—should we walk? Do you have time?"

"Yeah, let's. Grunge, huh?"

As they ambled down the street, he explained there'd been a grunge theme for one of their Air Festival gigs. She remembered now. She'd seen the video clips. Great PJ Harvey impression he'd done. Not as good as Jove's Eddie Vedder, Rafi demurred. He asked about her classes and what next year's would be like. More of the same but harder, she predicted.

"How are things really?" she asked as they wandered under the palms beside the amphitheater. "How are people treating you?"

"A mix. Some are nicer than ever. Some more hostile. But they're also being hostile to each other, so maybe that's just the vibe this year."

"As evidenced by that shit." She pointed her chin toward a sign in a window, advertising a Humanist Party rally. *Riquelme 2019* took up the bottom half in an aggressive typeface.

"On days they have those, I've learned to stay home and shove earbuds in," he said.

"One of them's running against my mom for mayor. Some beach resort owner guy. Barely even lives *in* Miryoku."

"He doesn't have a chance, according to Izzy. Amaris is well-loved."

"Mom doesn't seem concerned. But he's been spouting nasty rhetoric about her, which makes me and Dad angry."

"Me too. I can't wait for October so the elections can be over."

Roxana mentioned the Humanist Party rallies she'd seen in Port Baleia, and the slogans on their picket signs. More Land for Humans: The Verge Is Ancient History! was the most dangerous, in their opinions.

"We should probably talk about the cuff," she finally said.

"Yes. But not out here."

"Tomorrow or the next day. We'll make time."

They reached the path along the river where the shrine to the Lady stood. A magic cool-burning torch cast a violet glow behind the statue. Small solar bulbs on the ground marked the path. The river burbled, black in the night.

Even in the midst of talking about Nelleke's shop, Roxana's mind drifted to the incense she had lit here, the thanks she had given for the gift of Rafi.

When their knuckles touched as they walked, she grasped his hand, sliding her palm to seek the liuqin-string calluses on his fingers, a movement that felt habitual even though ten months had passed since last time she'd done it.

Rafi's voice trailed off. He sank his fingers between hers, interlacing them.

Her heart thumped a rapid tempo. "Do you remember how we said if we met up again, and if we were interested…I mean, are you seeing anyone, or…"

Rafi hooked his arm around her waist, lifted her, and seated her on the low wall bordering the path. His body melted against hers and he kissed her neck slowly. Then he paused, a glow dancing under his skin. "I hope this was what you meant. Otherwise this is awkward."

Laughing, she nudged her nose against his. She had both arms around his neck. Her body and soul had burst to life in shooting stars, raining petals, singing sprites. "Yes. It is what I meant."

"Good. I'm not seeing anyone, no." He kissed her mouth, lingering and rich.

"Me neither." She clung to him, teasing his tongue with hers, mindful not to lean back too far and topple both of them into the river. The image made her laugh again.

His mouth stretched in a smile. "This might not be the *best* spot." After a few more kisses, he drew back and beckoned her up the path.

A short distance upstream was a riverside beach, a small half-circle of silty earth with logs framing a firepit. It was often in use on summer nights, but by some stroke of luck (perhaps another gift from the Lady), the firepit was cold tonight, no one around. No one, that is, except some tiny pink lights weaving around one another at the riverbank among sedges and wildflowers.

"The foxglove fae are dancing tonight," Rafi said in her ear as he helped her down the tree-root steps from the path to the beach.

She grinned, recognizing the offer she had turned down from a will-o'-the-wisp a year ago, when Rafi had stepped in to protect her. "So they are," she said.

As Rafi and Roxana drew nearer, the pink lights resolved into the bell shapes of foxglove blossoms, with whisker-thin limbs that caught at each other as the fae whirled in their dance. They sang as they twirled, a reeling whistle of a few hypnotic notes.

Roxana found a spot to sit, behind a log, on short grass with sedge screening them on all sides. "They're beautiful," she said, admiring the fae's twinkling lights.

Rafi settled beside her. "Harmless too. As long as you don't eat the foxglove, of course."

"Poisonous," she agreed. She kissed him again. "Will they tell tales of what they saw people doing here?"

"Down here? Nah. They've seen it all."

"Right. This is one of the nude-friendly beaches."

He flipped the hem of his black kilt up to his hip, exposing a thigh.

Matching his rakish gesture, she tugged up her dress to the hem of her underwear.

His gaze dropped there. He stroked her side, over her ribs. "This dress."

"I remembered you liked it."

"I've missed it." His lips brushed her neck. "And you."

She swung a leg over his lap and landed with their mouths locked in a kiss, her bare knees sinking into silty earth on each side of him. His hands plunged into her hair. Their tongues twined, first in her mouth and then in his, a dance fiercer than the foxglove fae's.

No one had made her feel like this the whole of the last ten months—this wild joy and desire sheeting through her. He kissed her above the dress's low neckline, a tantalizing touch that was soon not enough. She pushed the stretchy fabric down to free one breast. He gathered its heaviness in his hand; his mouth rolled against the soft flesh, massaging with his lips, pulling her nipple in against his tongue. Roxana leaned into him, melting him back against the log, her hips sinking to latch against him and rock there slowly through their rumpled skirt hems.

Rafi's hand slid up the back of her thigh, then along the lace edge he found there. "Ah, at least one of us has underwear on."

Roxana tugged at his kilt until getting it out from beneath her. "You and your clothing-optional ways." She dragged three fingers up between his legs in the way she remembered he liked to be touched.

He tipped his head back. His body glimmered so coal-fire bright that he cast shadows around them. She pressed herself closer to the heat, relishing it.

Rafi's hands spread around her rear, holding her against him in their rhythm. After a couple of minutes, she paused to wriggle out of her underwear. Skin to skin, they writhed together, Rafi's ember glow flaring and fluctuating. The foxglove fae kept circling, aloof, at the riverbank.

Most days, this would not have been a position that could get Roxana all the way there. But tonight it was easy—even with her knees in the dirt and her mind scandalized that she, humble and predictable person in her late thirties, would be doing this in a public spot in a town where everyone knew her.

Instead of hindering her, it drove her higher, the way Rafi had every time they met last summer. She shook apart in his lap and drew him soon after to follow, the pair of them wrapped in arms and mouths and glow. Catching her breath, she felt enfolded in the elements, part of them rather than a scandalous interloper. Singing foxglove fae, river-scented air, decaying log, twinkling stars, entwined lovers.

"How did I get through the past year without this?" she said.

He snagged her underwear from the log and offered it to her. "This?" he said lightly, as if referring to outdoor sex in general.

She set the underwear on her knee, then framed his face in both hands. "This."

He looked up at her with such yearning that she anticipated some declaration, a *Let's make this real, how do we do that?*, and her breathing went shallow from both wanting it and not being ready to answer it. But all he did was kiss her again, his lips softened to perfection from their tryst.

Rafi's arm twitched under her, and he looked down as he got his phone out. "Ah. Oni says, 'I'm supposed to be back at eleven. If you're not nearby, Timo says he can walk me.' It's ten forty."

Roxana shimmied back into her underwear. "Let's go back. We don't have to send my dad out."

He typed *I'll walk you, be there soon*, and they climbed back to the path.

"I used to walk alone at night in Miryoku when I was a teenager," she said. "It was safe as long as you carried some iron, and you almost never had to use it. Are Jove and Izzy extra cautious?"

"No, it's how things have gotten since…Ti Falls Park basically." He kicked at a dandelion stem. "Then incidents like the spider-crab fae—people are scared. I don't blame Jove and Izzy. The korreds probably view Oni as someone close to me, so I wouldn't doubt if they'd mess with her to get at me. I'd be keeping a close eye on her even if her parents weren't worried."

"Why is the world going mad lately?" Roxana said.

Not that he or anyone else could explain that. He didn't try. He only sighed and took her hand to hold for the last few blocks of their walk.

Rafi felt weightless with bliss. She did still want him. She'd been so sweet and tender.

Then other thoughts crackled in like static. What about the rest of their lives? Was a few days per year, even a few weeks per year, truly enough to live on? And what was she going to say about the cuff?

She visited him at the cottage the next day and paused to look around after stepping inside. "Wow. Being back here. Time warp." She touched the lavish purple bloom of a potted orchid, then turned to him. "So. The cuff:

here's what I'm thinking."

He stayed by the opposite wall, four paces away. Dread gathered itself hard in his stomach.

"I can take it back, if you want," she said. While he blinked in surprise, she went on, "Strip off the spells. Destroy it. Then you wouldn't have the burden of keeping it and having to decide whether to use it again."

He made an indecisive note of a sound.

"You sounded so agonized after Halloween," she added. She folded her arms, clutching her elbows. "I couldn't stop thinking about it. I'm just as guilty."

He found his voice. "No. No, of course you aren't."

"When someone makes a weapon and hands it to someone else knowing exactly what they'll do with it, yes, they're complicit. I *want* to share the burden with you. I hate that I dumped it on you, left you alone with it."

The knot inside him softened. "I still don't think you would've acted the way I did that night."

"Probably not, because I wasn't raised with them. Maybe how you acted was more in line with justice, though. Regardless, it's done, we can't change it. The question is, are you willing to get rid of it?"

He paced along the wall and back again. "I've thought about it. If I brought it to my mother, or any drake, they could melt it."

"Yeah, drake fire ought to do it."

"But they'd realize what it was. They'd sense the magic. They can't lie, once they know something, so then that info would be out there, and we probably don't want that. Besides…do I even want to destroy it? I'm not so sure."

"You still don't trust Sminu."

"Of course I don't. If I can catch the korreds in some moment that proves they're out to hurt people, and I can stop it, then I want to. Even if it's my own father. *Especially* him."

"Or Akio Riquelme. Should you get the chance."

"Well, I don't doubt he deserves it. But his bodyguards are probably too good."

"Yeah. Only a joke. If I got the chance with Riquelme, would I?" She let her arms swing loose. "I'd probably get put in jail, and that wouldn't be good for Ester's life, so. Perhaps not."

"Honestly I don't think I could do it to someone I didn't personally know. My own father, though, is another story."

"You have the right, with him."

"I'm not sure if that's true, but…I hate the idea of being defenseless against him. Having no recourse if he does some new terrible thing."

"Okay. Then hang on to it a bit. But be careful, understand?"

He nodded and reached out when she walked over to hug him.

Outside the cottage's thin walls, the birds sang and the breeze rustled the leaves, as if it were any unremarkable summer day.

Roxana's few days in Miryoku sped by too swiftly. There were so many people to see and places her parents wanted to take her. Stealing thirty to sixty minutes each day to see Rafi alone was all she could manage.

At the cottage on her last morning, he gave her a small purple box with a silver ribbon, shyly saying, "Satsuki *may* have let me know your birthday was last week."

The box contained raw chunks of crystal: clear, pale pink, amber, cranberry red, and translucent white shot through with purple. While she crooned in delight, he added, "It's not metal, but they're still from the fae realm, and since you and Nelleke specialize in jewelry…"

She kissed him and assured him of *course* they could use them.

"This time," she added, "let's be better about staying in touch."

"Yeah?" Arms looped around her, he nuzzled her hairline. "Think we can manage?"

"I think it could hardly hurt less than not talking to each other, like last year."

He tipped up her face and kissed her. "Going to send you *so* many annoying messages."

This time she felt not only heartache as she and Ester set off north but irritation at this confounding disarray of where people lived and where they wished they lived instead.

"We should have stayed longer," Ester said. "That wasn't enough time."

Though Roxana agreed, her prickliness answered instead, "Some of us have jobs."

Ester swung her feet, letting her sandaled toes kick the underside of the dash repeatedly. Roxana planted a hand on her knee to stop her.

The road curved toward Kagami. The sea flashed in the sun like a million crystals. Roxana's heart eased a little, recalling the crystals he'd given her. New loveliness to work with, something to look forward to.

"Is it true if Riquelme wins, Rafi will have to either move back to the fae realm or go to jail?" Ester asked.

The words hit Roxana like a belly cramp. "Riquelme talks nonsense. And he won't win."

"But he was saying he'd have everyone with rare witch abilities reported to the law, and wanderers too, and Rafi's both."

"He can't lock people up just for existing. Having those abilities, or being born a wanderer, isn't a crime. And Riquelme would have a hard road if he tried to make it one."

Ester slouched in her seat so her hair bunched up behind her head. "Oni's worried about it."

"I don't think it'll happen. Don't borrow next month's trouble."

"The election's in October, not next month."

"It's a *saying*."

But the political news was inescapable as the summer dragged forward. Even the satisfying hours of work Roxana and Nelleke put into the shop expansion couldn't keep the latest outrage of the day from leaking onto her radar.

Roxana and Rafi vented to each other via text most evenings, and occasionally via video calls, his latest step in becoming tech-savvy. Satsuki and Nelleke teased her when they learned about those, but despite her friends' innuendoes, the conversations had not, so far, turned lascivious.

But there were *moments*. Mentions of a riverside log or the cottage in a rainstorm. Lingering gazes, studying the screen with a smile. A tone of voice that dipped into suggestiveness. She reveled in the connection, even while aching at being so far away.

Neither of them got brave enough to say it out loud: "So what is this between us? What are we to each other? What do we do about it?"

Why ask it when there wasn't a lot they *could* do, without upending their lives?

Onward they muddled. Rafi fumed about the korreds' latest win: several humans had taken them up on their invitation to visit the haunt and had made it back without apparent damage, raving about how much fun they'd had. The korreds had offered jaunts around the nearby regions of the fae realm, riding on the shoulders of Mukut (who submitted because at least then she would be able to help keep them safe) while delighting the korreds with stories or songs. Apparently the korreds had been wise enough, or lucky enough, not to give their guests any food or drink, nor enchant them to any dangerous degree.

Those who came had been an odd cross-section of human political profiles. Some cherished the fae, abhorred Akio Riquelme, and wanted to cultivate a new era of harmony between the two sides of the verge. Others were proud Humanist Party members who saw it as an opportunity to do as Riquelme promised and forge inroads into the fae realm by making allies there. None of it made Rafi nor Roxana feel optimistic about the future.

September arrived. Ester returned to school, scowling about being far from Oni for the second academic year in a row, and Roxana returned to college.

On Election Day in October, voters nationwide cast ballots for positions from prime minister down to city officials. The results came back late that night.

Amaris Wei, to her friends' and family's relief, retained her post as mayor of Miryoku.

And Akio Riquelme had been elected prime minister of Eidolonia.

CHAPTER 22

IN THE WEEK AFTER THE ELECTION, RAFI tried harder than ever to understand human politics. He made zero headway. For what it was worth, everyone else seemed appalled too—except the members of the Humanist Party, who were crowing and lording their victory over the rest of the populace.

Some people marched in protest. Others rallied in celebration. Talking about each new horror with Roxana was the only bright spot in his life, aside from the moments of being absorbed in the rhythm of a song, and even during those, he saw in the audience members' eyes the same disbelief, frustration, and anger that he felt.

Riquelme took office a week after the election. One of his first orders of business was to present a law requiring all who were counted human to be registered as citizens and taxpayers, along with fae who had jobs or residences on the human side of the verge. Further, all witches with rare witch abilities would be checked up on regularly, and penalties for unauthorized use of said abilities were to be drastically increased. The nation exploded with more protests.

As both a wanderer and someone with rare witch abilities, Rafi was screwed twice over, as Jove sympathetically put it.

I'm sickened, Roxana texted the night of the announcement. *For you and so many people. Here I've been telling you it'd be fine to come on over to the human side. Now I have to eat my words.*

You aren't responsible, he assured. *It's not what you wanted.*

It's completely antithetical to what I wanted, she said. *I'm thinking of you and I've got your back.*

He thanked her, but he knew their power was minuscule against such a rising tide.

Legal matters took a long time to put into practice, however, especially when so many people planned to be noncompliant, so no one showed up to demand his documentation during the next few weeks. He dragged through his daily tasks, stunned, asking himself if he'd been fighting the wrong enemy all this time. Was the human government actually a greater threat than the korreds?

But that had become more confusing too: the fae in general were, naturally, offended by Humanist Party rhetoric and the imposition of what they saw as a one-sided deal they had never agreed to. Even friendly fae became disgruntled. Sminu, in the one appearance in town Rafi heard about during October, assured humans that he himself held no ill will and hoped to continue this new friendship his haunt had formed with the town.

Nothing about such words rang any more true than they ever had for Rafi, but somehow Sminu had become only the second- or third-most disturbing of his problems.

Rafi encountered Amaris one blustery October day, as she came out of the town hall on Dragon Street. He nodded to her, ducking his head, preparing to walk past.

She stepped into his path. "Rafi."

He looked up, a dread of all things human-law-related washing over him.

"In case you hadn't heard," she said, "I'm resisting the national investigation order. Lots of mayors around the country are, and the majority of the city council is behind me. We're not out to get you. Or anyone else this law affects."

"Oh. Well—I don't want to be any trouble. I can just go across the verge…"

She held up her hand in such an imperious manner that he instantly stopped talking. "I like you," she said, "but this isn't any kind of personal favor. This is me doing whatever I can to block a shitty piece of legislation. Understood?"

He smiled a little. "Yeah. Thank you."

She began to move along, then paused. "Are the rumors true about you and Roxana? Ahh." She swatted her hand in the air. "Never mind. Don't answer. She'll tell me if she wants to."

While Rafi stood with his mouth hanging open, Mayor Wei strode off down the street, raincoat swirling behind her.

∞

One exceptionally joyful event did occur that autumn: Meloncollie came north for two days to play at Port Baleia's Halloween music festival, bringing Oni along. Ester and Roxana were jubilant.

The band booked two hotel rooms for their overnight stay, Izzy's family taking one, Tash and Rafi the other.

"Tash figured out about you and me last year," Rafi told Roxana after the show, as they strolled through the city amid costumed revelers. "Tonight she told me, 'Yeah, I know, you're going to be out awhile, now go.'"

Roxana laughed, her arm linked in his. "And my mom's guessed too? Damn, maybe the secrecy thing is getting a little silly."

He looked down at her, his face gorgeous in a makeup job involving not only pigments but dozens of glued-on jewels that gave him the look of a seductive drake. The band was showing solidarity with the fae through wearing fae costumes this year and had gotten a local makeup artist to do them all up before the show.

He leaned down and kissed her, there on the street in Little Europe. "Who needs secrecy?" he agreed.

They strolled on, enjoying the décor in shop windows and the spooky glowing creatures of matter-witch magic soaring back and forth between rooftops.

"Will you tell Ester, then?" he asked.

"She's really the only reason it was secret in the first place." Roxana sighed. "I can't decide."

"I leave it in your hands."

The assurance reminded her of their first time, when he'd said much the same thing. She leaned her head on his shoulder, a vague despair spiraling down inside her. Had she made no progress at all in courage, in a year and a quarter, when it came to him?

She slowed under a black-and-white awning and nodded to the window, through which a throng of people were visible, eating pastries and laughing, their colorful costume hems spilling over the edges of their chairs. "One of my favorite cafés," she said. "French-themed. They have musicians come play here. Sometimes when I'm taking a croissant break and listening to them, I picture it being you instead. Playing solo liuqin and singing French café jazz."

"Would I have to sing *in* French? Because I don't know a word of it." He sounded uneasy.

"Nah. They do English versions often enough."

They entered her building. The babble and music fell to a muted hum as the door shut behind them.

"Ester's out?" Rafi asked as they climbed the stairs.

"Yeah. She and Oni are going to a play, then roaming around with Izzy to enjoy the festival."

Roxana unlocked her apartment, nervousness running like threads of magic up her limbs. They'd never done this, been alone in *her* home rather than his or the nearest convenient outdoor space. She found she deeply wanted him to like her apartment, to feel comfortable there.

They stepped in, and after a glance around, Rafi went to the window and looked out at the bright city lights. "So much bigger than Miryoku. Almost like Dasdemir."

She hung up their coats and joined him. "Not as big as that. But yeah, a different world from the Southwest Peninsula."

"It's strange. That people can just move somewhere else and get used to it."

"You did it. You moved to the cottage."

His gaze stayed out among the streetlights. "That move was about a quarter of a mile."

Roxana gave him a side hug, tucking herself under his arm. "I bet you could handle more. I'd love it if you lived up here, you know that."

"That quarter-mile move was huge for me. I still haven't adapted. And *more* of the human world, now, with this government?"

"No. Right." She kissed his shoulder, chastising herself. She was doing it again, trying to drag others into her comfort zone, regardless of their wishes. Wouldn't she balk just as hard if he proposed she move into the fae realm, even if—somehow—she could do so without enchantment dangers? What good would come of pressuring him, especially now?

"Not to sound cheesy," she said, "but would you like to see the bedroom?"

He looked at her and accepted with a warm smile.

Some time later, she was drifting in half-sleep on top of him, trying not to let it become full sleep, each of them wearing no more than one or two bits of clothing. The sound of the front door lock snapped down the hallway. Rafi and Roxana scrambled upright.

The door closed with a whump. "Hi, Mom," Ester yelled.

"Oh! Hi," Roxana called back, while she and Rafi grabbed clothes and put them on in a rush.

"The play was super funny." Ester's shoes hit the floor beside the door, then her sock-covered feet thumped down the hall, and she was pushing open the not-quite-shut door and standing in the doorway.

Not even Rafi's endo-witch speed had been fast enough. He was still buttoning his shirt. Roxana fared worse, caught in the midst of swiveling her skirt around to face the right way, her torso only clad in her camisole. Her sweater and tights lay on the floor between her and Ester like signed confessions of guilt.

Roxana smoothed her hair and smiled at her daughter. "Oh, good. Oni had fun?"

Ester took in the sight of them, her face unusually blank. "Yeah. Hi, Rafi."

"Hey," he said, amiable if unsteady. "Happy Halloween."

"You too." Ester swiveled away and went back down the hall. "Wind was cold on the walk back. I'm going to make some hot chocolate."

Roxana and Rafi locked eyes. Roxana cringed.

Rafi finished buttoning his shirt, picked up her sweater, and handed it to her. "So much for secrecy."

She hid her face in the sweater. "Right. Here goes."

"I'll head out. You two can talk."

She saw him to the door. "We'll meet up in the morning before you leave."

"Night, Rafi," Ester called from the kitchen. Ordinary voice, no weirdness. A promising sign.

"Night, Ester." He smiled at Roxana but didn't kiss her, then slipped out.

Roxana padded into the kitchen. Ester had just taken a mug of milk out of the microwave and was testing its temperature by dipping a fingertip in.

Roxana got out another mug. "Hot chocolate sounds good. I'll make some too."

Ester slid the mug back into the microwave and punched in another thirty seconds. "Is Rafi your joyfriend?"

Roxana laughed, startled. "That's a fun term. Seems to be catching on lately."

Ester didn't answer, just watched the tray rotate.

Roxana bowed her head over the empty mug. "I guess. Yeah. We liked each other last year, but didn't think it could go anywhere. We were moving away, it would've been complicated…but we stayed in touch, and it turns out we still like each other." She poured milk into the mug. "I'm sorry I haven't told you. I planned to."

Ester got out her mug and stirred the ground chocolate into it, spoon clinking. "I kind of knew. Or like, Oni and I guessed."

"Really? When?"

"That summer. The way you two acted around each other. But yeah, we were moving, so."

Roxana wrapped her hands around her own mug and channeled heat magic into it until steam began to swirl from the surface. "It's okay if it's weird for you. Me dating someone. You can ask me anything—or not talk about it if you don't want to."

Ester got a bag of marshmallows from a cupboard and plunked a large pale blue one into her mug. "It's the same with me and Oni."

"What is?"

Ester slurped some of her drink and mumbled, "Joyfriends."

Roxana stared at her. *No, it isn't the same, you're fourteen*, she wanted to say—then reminded herself how well it usually went over when one told adolescents such things. Herself included, at that age. "Oh, that's cool," she said instead, in an encouraging tone.

"It blows. Being far apart."

"It does. I'm sorry. I know how that feels." Roxana stirred chocolate into her hot milk, watching the drink darken. "So if it's…romantic, you and Oni,

I want to make sure you have…anything you need, healthwise…"

"Oh my gods." Ester sounded mortified. "Yes, it's romantic, but I'm *four-teen*. I'm not doing—whatever you think I'm doing."

"I'm not thinking anything," Roxana said, too quickly.

"You and Rafi, though."

"Well, we *aren't* fourteen."

They sipped their chocolate, then both sputtered with a laugh.

Roxana stepped over and kissed Ester on the forehead—and her chest twinged at how these days she had to lean *up* a few inches for that. "If you were with anyone else, I'd worry. But Oni is basically the gentlest and most considerate person in the country."

Ester rolled her eyes with a despairing sort of smile. "She's too good for me."

"Nonsense. I'm happy for you both."

Ester picked up another marshmallow. "Rafi's cool. Sucks what Riquelme's trying to do to people like him."

"Yeah." Feeling hollow after all the surges of emotion, Roxana leaned on the counter and sipped her hot chocolate. "It's pretty horrible."

❧

Rafi got a text from Roxana that night assuring him all was well with Ester. *Guess we can officially ditch the secrecy*, she added.

You get to tell your parents, he said. *I'm not doing that part.*

Lol, I will. They'll be fine with it.

They met in the French café the next morning for breakfast. Rafi examined the morning's musician, an bass clarinetist playing songs mellow enough for morning-after-Halloween revelers to take, and tried imagining it. Being a regular here, in this café where he mispronounced half of the menu items because they were in French. In this northern city where he knew no one but Roxana and Ester. Among a vast network of streets he couldn't navigate without his phone—a phone that in the first place had been a long-term loan from Jove and Izzy.

He'd probably have to get his own phone if he moved here. (First splash of anxiety.) He'd also have to find his own jobs, all in the human realm since he had no fae-realm protection up here. (Anxiety went up a notch, floodwaters rising.) If he wasn't in a band anymore and didn't have cross-verge errands via which to do good, Roxana would surely no longer find him half so impressive. The relationship, on shaky legs all its life already, would threaten to collapse. (He put down his croissant as his throat constricted and his limbs turned weird temperatures.)

"I'm glad Ester took it so well," Roxana said. She was focusing on her tea strainer, removing it to set on a saucer. "Surprised about her and Oni, though."

At that, Rafi managed to smile a little. "Are you? I suspected ages ago."

"You never told me."

"Well, I figured I could be wrong."

She squinted. "You okay? You look pale."

"Yeah. Just. Strange being in another city. Shakes my nerves. And going home might not be any better, with…" He flicked his fingers toward the street, to indicate essentially everything.

She nodded, then reached over to unhook his ear cuff—a cat-shaped one she had made him. "Ah, as I thought. Needs a recharge."

When she finished boosting the anti-anxiety spell and put it back on him, a fresh feeling of calm washed over him. He could think objectively again, as well as eat again, and he thanked her with a kiss on her hand.

But not everything he feared was irrational. He relied on Roxana for an awful lot of his functionality, which in itself probably wasn't healthy. And it was not his imagination that if he stayed in the human realm and if Akio Riquelme remained in power, someone was going to bring down major trouble on Rafi sooner or later. That was an inescapable fact.

CHAPTER 23

I'M JUST SAYING," ESTER EXPLAINED ONE morning before school, "if the person you're dating is there, and the person *I'm* dating is there, we should consider moving back."

Roxana wasn't sure whether to laugh at her daughter's persistence or screech in frustration. "And I'm just saying I can't make promises yet. To you or to anyone. I have the rest of this school year to finish, and I have to do that here."

"But after that..."

"We'll keep it a possibility."

Ester's smile was big enough to brighten the gray November day.

Roxana pointed the apartment key at her. "*Just* a possibility. Everything's a possibility. Moving to Hawaii or Mongolia or Botswana are also possibilities. Technically."

"We should buy a vacation place in Hawaii." Ester zipped up her puffy winter coat.

"Oh, yes, of course. Do you have three million lira? No? Weird, me neither."

But even as she mulled over the idea of moving home again, everyone she talked to in Miryoku kept reporting that lately it was not the idyllic jasmine-wreathed southern town she used to know and love.

"Things are definitely interesting," her mother said.

"People need some time to get used to the change, now that...what's his name is in office," her father said.

"Everyone sucks lately," Satsuki said.

"I don't know who to trust," Rafi said. "I never really did, I guess. But now people know what *I* am, but I don't know what they are. Whose side they're on. Whether they're going to betray me."

Because that was starting to happen, nationally. A government webpage was set up, along with a hotline, where everyone was encouraged to voluntarily submit their own details for the new registry, but could also report on fellow islanders. Wanderers, fae working or living in the human realm, people with rare witch abilities—all were fair game.

Noncompliance was rampant, of course. Riquelme's government poured money into an abyss, paying workers to follow up on reports and go door to door among citizens, and getting a lot of fake information or flat-out refusals for their attempts.

A chipper young man showed up in Nelleke's shop one day in mid-November with an electronic tablet. He wore a green sash, indicating he was a matter-witch working in an official capacity. On the tablet he already had both Nelleke's and Roxana's names, addresses, and educational histories, including their abilities as matter-witches. "Just here to verify." Smiling, he tapped his sash, looking around. "I'm a matter-witch myself. Beautiful pieces."

"It doesn't bother you?" Nelleke glowered at him with a force that should have terrified any sensible person. "Working for someone who might slap legal restrictions on witches any old day now, just to control as many people as he can?"

"Aw, why would we want to shut down a nice place like this? You folks can rest easy." He swiveled the tablet to show them. "This all look accurate? Any rare witch abilities to add?"

We had to verify it all, Roxana typed to Rafi that afternoon. Her fingers still vibrated with impotent fury. *They could yank Nelleke's business license if we refused to cooperate. Anyway, they already knew everything, including my specialty with metal and small work. They didn't learn anything useful. Still. I'm so fucking angry.*

I'm angry too. I hate that they're doing this to you. Or anyone.

They came to Ester's school too, to hand out forms to fill out. Ester said some of the teachers were yelling at the officials. Others were crying.

Arrrgh, he typed. *Same happened at Oni's school.*

Ester apparently checked the "non witch" box, threw it back at the official, and yelled, "There, I'm not a witch, but if I were, you would know it, because I'd curse you first." Which, you know, not the best idea.

Ha, but I love her for it.

Me too, she admitted. *Apparently there were a lot of, uh, creative answers on the forms turned in by other teens.* "Rare witch ability: can charm your mom," *and so forth.*

I have new hope for the future, with these kids.

Same. I'm still mad though. Wish there was more I could do.

I could mail a certain thing up for you to use if another such person shows up? he offered.

Better not. I might actually use it.

It wasn't even a joke. All that evening and the next day she caught herself fantasizing about clapping the iron cuff around the wrist of that young man who had entered the shop; watching his shiny, clean face contort with horror; lecturing him about the harm he was doing by carrying out Riquelme's orders; making it sink into his brain and change his actions.

No. She should not be trusted with such a weapon. Rafi's restraint in having used it only once was wondrously admirable, all details considered.

∽

Rafi came back to the cottage one evening in early December to find a woman waiting for him at the footpath gate. She wore a fitted gray wool overcoat with a yellow sash, had hair lightened to blond with dark streaks stylishly left in, and carried an electronic tablet. He stopped a few steps shy of the gate.

"Akurafi?" she said. "Hi! I'm Kylie. I'm following up on information about local citizens so we have accurate records. It's a pleasure to meet you."

He said nothing.

Her tablet lit up as she tapped it. "We've had a report that you're a wanderer. Is that correct?"

Izzy and Roxana had both instructed him that he didn't have any legal obligation to say anything at this stage.

Kylie must have been used to noncompliance. She still sounded cheerful. "And an endo-witch with rare witch abilities. Correct?"

Stone crept across Rafi's skin while his heart beat like a trapped bird's. He stared at her, showing no emotion, hoping she'd get creeped out enough to flee.

"Form-changing," she said, reading his electronic file. "That's a great one all right! And you've been living on this property for more than half of the past year, we're told?"

Now *that* would get Jove and Izzy in trouble. He shook his head minutely and looked away. "More time across the verge."

"But you have a job here, so even fae would need to be registered in that case. Naturally a wanderer would. It sounds like you do not dispute the other descriptions, then. Correct?"

"I have nothing to say." He turned and walked toward the verge.

"Friend," she called after him.

He looked back. She was holding out a slip of paper.

"Your official record of our visit. You have ten days to verify the information on our webpage before we visit again. Please keep in mind it is now against the law in Eidolonia to be an unregistered wanderer or an unregistered holder of rare witch abilities. Thank you for your time and cooperation! I wish you a good evening."

In a boost of fire speed, he flashed toward her. It gratified him to see the startled widening of her eyes, the crack in her happy facade. He snatched the paper from her and whisked himself away into the dark woods.

⸛

Well, Rafi texted Izzy, from under a gnarled tree near the verge. He attached a picture of the notice the woman had given him.

UGHHHH, she answered. *That little worm knocked on our door too. Rafi don't worry. No one's cooperating, including us. Come back. They got their hands full and won't bug you again for a while.*

I'll come back for rehearsal tonight. But soon you should get someone to replace me. I'll probably have to stay away more.

Don't say that, she wrote. *We are going to help you. Besides, I know they're shitheads but all they're technically asking is that you verify your name and abilities.*

To do what to us eventually?

Well, pay taxes, which sucks. Beyond that no one's sure yet. What else could they really do?

The next day they had their answer, or the beginning of it. He had cautiously come back for rehearsal, then slept (albeit little) in his cottage, and woke up to Tash banging on his door.

She held up her phone to show him a news article. "You and I have some choices to make."

He skimmed it, slowing to take in the most consequential points:

Three different fae have reported being offered deals to avoid punishment for noncompliance in exchange for providing greater human access to fae territory. In other words, to push back the verge and grant humans more land. All have refused and retreated to the fae realm. Reports are pouring in of expensive fines levied against witches using rare abilities without being "authorized" to do so, including in contexts such as a swimmer with the ability to form gills on their body, and a matter-witch able to conjure fire who sent up festival fireworks for her community. A source says that the government has iron charms ready to use to convince fae where possible, as well as to use against noncompliant witches.

"Holy shit," he said.

"The idiot's actually trying to do it," Tash said. "Get more fae land. This will go *very* badly for him. But it'll also go badly for us, in the meantime."

"What are you going to do?"

"I turned their official notice into dripping pulp in front of their eyes yesterday," she said calmly. "They're likely aware I'm not going to cooperate. My plan is to be uncatchable and keep doing good for people, around the edges. Like always, but a bit more sneaky."

Rafi leaned on the wall, exhaling, tasting the staleness of his mortal pre-breakfast mouth. As a human, he had fewer options than she did, and greater chances of getting hurt.

"Why did you start working with Jove and Izzy?" he found himself asking.

They had never discussed it. He had assumed it was the same as with most fae who hung out on the human side: she liked the novelty.

She was quiet a moment, staring at the orchid in the window. "I sometimes think I'm too much like the korreds," she said. "Fascinated with humans. Wanting them to like me. Wanting to charm them. I sometimes think that although I help them, the reason I'm doing it is because of that. I don't like it."

"Everyone wants other people to like them. That doesn't make you a korred. You're nothing like them."

"Then also," she added, ignoring the consolation, "I love music. Rivers and oceans keep a beat, it comes naturally to us water folk. Of course I couldn't make up my own songs, but I could imitate perfectly. A cover band was ideal."

Fae adored, and sometimes envied, human arts precisely because they themselves had a limited ability to innovate. Even the absurd little tunes Rafi had made up as a child had delighted his fae families, helped keep him fed and sheltered. Literally singing for his supper.

"You're a flawless bassist," Rafi said. "I hope you don't leave. They'd have a hard time replacing you."

Tash disregarded the comment with a hand motion reminiscent of a fish tail-flip. "You're being sentimental. Doesn't help. What are *you* going to do?"

⌒∾⌒

What are you going to do? Roxana texted to him. She had waited until lunchtime to ask, wanting to give him a calm morning after the notice he had gotten last night—he had told her about it, despair coming through even in his brief texts.

He took almost half an hour to answer.

I'm talking to Jove and Izzy. Need to figure it out.

We want you safe and free and happy, she wrote. *Whatever that takes.*

That night he requested a video call. Stress and worry had stolen her appetite, and she'd hardly eaten any dinner. Sitting cross-legged on her bed with her laptop open, she watched his image blink into place with a mellow chime.

He looked tired, the skin darker under his eyes. He was sitting on his cottage's floor, the orange loveseat behind his shoulders.

"I talked with Izzy and Jove," he said. "I…can't endanger them. They'd be facing legal action if they went on sheltering and employing me, and they have a kid to worry about."

"Plus I don't want you to get arrested," Roxana said. "Normally I'm the one who's all for following rules, but this—this scares me. I've heard rumors involving prison. Iron shackles."

"And I wouldn't be doing my friends any good if I were locked up and neutralized."

She was afraid to put the question into words, to hear the answer.

He looked down. His shaggy black hair fell around his cheeks. "I'm going back across the verge. To stay. Not forever, I'll still step over to check messages, visit. Do what I can."

Her insides were sinking, folding in on themselves in grief.

"But I…have left the band," he went on. The words came out stilted. "I can't be seen having a job on the human side. Especially one on stage, at scheduled times. It'd be too easy for them to find me."

"Them," spoken with that haunted tone, used to mean the korreds. Now it was the government. Reckless, misguided humans. Her own people.

She cleared her throat to speak past the lump there. "I hate this. It's all wrong."

"I was always a wanderer. I'd just gotten more involved in the human side lately. All I'm doing is going back to how it used to be." He put a thin optimism in his voice.

"You'll be away more. The time difference."

"Can't be helped."

"What if we found another way to shelter you on this side? We all want that, right? Didn't Jove and Izzy argue against you leaving?"

"Yes, but…you all have lives. I don't want any of you getting in trouble on my behalf."

"You're *part* of our lives. You—" She expelled a shaky breath, realizing by her pounding heart that she was really about to say this, unprepared, tonight. "You're one of the most important parts of my life. When I think of a life without you in it, I get panicky, depressed."

He lifted his face, his eyes solemn. Since he didn't speak, she went on:

"I never would have guessed when I met you on the footpath and fixed your strings. I had no idea how important you'd become to me, that before long I would fall in love with you."

His shoulders lifted with a breath. It seemed he *might* speak, but she plowed on regardless:

"So don't go claiming we shouldn't bother on your behalf, because that's how much you matter, do you understand?"

"Yes," he said, hardly above a whisper. Then, stronger, "Yes. Roxana, I love you. I've wanted to say it, I've been so careful *not* to say it in case it was too much."

Tears had filled her eyes and spilled over in the scant time it took him to speak. She wiped them off her cheeks. "Ugh. It's so unfair we're not together for this conversation."

"We will be, eventually. It'll just be like the other times I've been away."

"I hated those," she pointed out.

"I did too. But…meet up when we're in the same town? Our original agreement?"

She winced. "That agreement sucked. I admit that now."

"But you had to put it in place, for your life and the people counting on you. I understood. Now this is what I have to do for mine."

"But." She shut her mouth. Imagined him being clapped into neutralizer shackles in a prison, then perhaps returned to society some months later, with all his old traumas torn open and fresh ones carved into his soul.

She looked down to conceal the new tears filling her eyes. "Less time together is all right as long as you're free," she said, her voice almost steady.

It wasn't. It wasn't all right. It was only better than the alternative.

⁓

She loved him. That, at least, kept him afloat, made him determined to do *something* around the fringes of the human realm even when he could no longer do most of the things he used to.

Funny how accustomed he had become to those. Now, from his hammock in Kepelo's haunt or some perch in a tree, his mind kept reaching toward an idea, only to remember he couldn't follow through.

The next band gig—no, he didn't belong to the band anymore.

Asking for errands to take on—no, someone could use the meet-up to entrap him.

The next festival—not safe to attend. Officials would probably be in the crowd, looking for anyone on their watchlist.

Visiting Jove, Izzy, and Oni—same problem.

Merely strolling the streets of Miryoku, hanging out in a park, buying something from a shop—each came with a calculated risk. He would have to be ready at all times to drop everything, put on fire speed, and escape.

His life had slowed to a limited handful of activities. Sleep. Eat. Use solar charger to juice up his phone. Slip back into a hidden place in the human realm to see what the date was and exchange messages with Roxana and others.

Then a concern had occurred to him. What if their text messages got hacked by the government? He wasn't sure if they could do that, barely knew how phones worked at all, but he asked Roxana about precautions.

Oh don't worry about that at least, she had typed. *Remember my IT background and my metal tricks. I have long since added a teeny mod to my phone to enchant against hackers.*

What about mine though? he asked.

Yours already has one. I talked to Izzy about it once. Naturally they protected their phones and the ones they give their fae liaisons, with the errands they arrange.

A minor consolation there. It still left him with little to do.

Though Rafi himself couldn't go into town without a disguise, he received reports from friends in Miryoku: Jove, Izzy, Oni, Satsuki, Meg. The korreds showed up in town often, winning themselves paper lanterns, bahn mi, dances with willing humans, and front-row seats to plays, in exchange for healing or fae-realm goods or excursions across the verge.

Rafi prowled near the earth haunt, watching for any tourists. Finally one day, there they were: two humans stumbling out through the ancient grove, their blue jeans and muddy winter coats looking forlorn in the riotous wild of the fae forest. Unklag was escorting them, an arm around each.

"There, you see, the verge!" she said. "All will be well, just as we promised."

Rafi strode forward, boots crashing through the undergrowth. "What happened?" He directed the question at the two humans.

One was a small woman, perhaps sixty, with dark gray hair in an unraveling bun. "There was a ghoul-sylph!" She lifted a shaking hand to point back toward the wilderness. "Gods, it was the most terrifying thing that's ever happened to me."

"Only for a moment," Unklag reassured. "We rescued you. Didn't we?"

Rafi ignored her. "You went into the air haunt?"

The other human nodded—a burly, short-haired man about Roxana's age. Rafi had seen him selling kebabs at the Bazaar a few times. "The korreds gave us a tour. It was super pretty. Got to ride on this stone giant. But then as we were leaving, and it was getting dark, *swoop*. This ghoul-sylph was suddenly right in front of us."

"It—it—hovered around us like a dark curtain, and it made me feel this—this terror," the woman stammered. "Like I was about to die. There was a time when I was twenty and I got caught in a sneaker wave at the beach and almost drowned, and I felt like it was happening all over again. I honestly thought I was going to die."

"One time my leg got run over by a car," the man told Rafi, with earnest entreaty, "and it's like I was suddenly in that moment, feeling that pain and being scared I was going to get killed or never walk again, but also like—like I was watching everyone I knew have the same thing happen to them. Like they were all screaming and I couldn't do anything." His face was grayish and shiny with sweat.

"But then?" Unklag said, hugging them to her on each side. "Then what?"

The woman's eyes brightened. "Sminu was there. And Unklag. They chased away the ghoul-sylph and got us back safely."

Rafi locked eyes with Unklag. "Of course they did."

"And you both wished to go home," Unklag added, "so that is where we're taking you. As promised."

"I'd stay on the human side if I were you," Rafi told them. "And warn other humans to do the same. Tell them what happened."

"Indeed, share your story," Unklag said. "Remind your townfolk that it's dangerous to venture into most of the fae realm, but *we* welcome you in our haunt and can protect you."

He's strategizing, Rafi texted to Roxana, after ensuring the humans got home safely. *He's showing humans why they shouldn't try Riquelme's idea of taking more fae territory, while at the same time trying to make people come to his haunt so he can keep them as pets.*

Clever I suppose, she said. *Can you prove it to people, though? His deal with the ghoul-sylphs?*

Going to try.

⚬⚬

It turned out to be fairly easy. Ghoul-sylphs weren't the type of fae a human should approach on their own, for the reasons demonstrated by the tourists. But friendlier fae also lived in the air haunt. As it bordered Kepelo's, Rafi was even protected there. A day's worth of asking turned up a fruit-bat faery who, in exchange for half a pineapple (which on Eidolonia grew only in human-realm hothouses and thus were a special treat), ascertained to Rafi that they had witnessed Sminu making the deal with a ghoul-sylph. Ghoul-sylphs hated the noise and light of the human realm and thus rarely left the fae realm, but they did love tasting the rich, complex fear within humans. To bring them a pair to sample, even just for a minute, was payment enough on their end. They didn't mind letting Sminu play hero after that if he wanted.

Promising the other half of the pineapple as well as a banana, he led the fruit-bat faery back to Kepelo's haunt and had them tell her the account.

She nodded, listening. Then, while the bat faery devoured the banana in Rafi's hand, Kepelo asked Rafi, "Do I guess correctly that you want me to take action of some kind?"

"Please tell the mayor—Amaris Wei. I would do it, but people know that you can't lie, whereas I can."

"I'm not sure I see the point in meddling. Humans who enter the fae realm must already know they take great risks."

"Sminu's bringing harm to them intentionally, and it's piling on to the mistrust the humans are already feeling toward fae. Please. It's important to me."

She swiveled her wing. "Very well. Sminu *has* said disrespectful things about me, I've been told. I'm not averse to reminding him which of us has greater power."

She followed through that same day, which turned out to be the second-to-last day of December on the human side. Rafi didn't go with her, but heard later that she caused rather a stir, striding through town in her red-and-gold scales and gleaming wings, even with her form toned down to a mere seven feet tall and wearing a human face.

Amaris naturally found time to greet the region's most powerful haunt leader. The next day she made an announcement, posted on bulletin boards and circulated on news and social media, reporting what Kepelo had learned about Sminu.

I wish to reiterate that our town is in no way aligned with the anti-fae sentiments currently endorsed by our nation's central government, she added. *Our peaceful alliance with Kepelo and her haunt shows the value our community places on both its humans and its fae. It is vital, however, that I issue warnings to our citizens about any existing dangers I learn of, and entering the fae realm is such a danger—especially under the invitation of someone hiding their true intentions. Please be exceedingly careful in your deals and your actions, and honor the truce by keeping to this side of the verge.*

Sminu raged about it, Rafi heard. It felt like a win. But then it turned out it only convinced *most* of the population. Riquelme's fans remained determined to ignore reason.

I'm trying to warn people who still cross the verge that the korreds view them as easy marks, he texted to Roxana in early January of 2020. *But they don't listen. They view me as "witch cult" and therefore nothing I say is true.*

It's maddening, she answered. *Contrarians, all of them.*

Am I misunderstanding what "cult" means or are they not using the word right? Because I would have said their side is more like a cult.

No, you are correct. They are the cult. Part of their contrariness involves using words in a way contrary to their meaning.

Do you know who I saw partying with the korreds on New Year's? he added. *Hari. Of the mochi café. He was at a Riquelme rally too. I can't believe it.*

Same with one of my favorite high school teachers, according to my mom.

Also Izzy's parents, Rafi said. *She's been fuming and sad about it. The fae are saying it hasn't felt like this before in their experience. They say it almost seems like before the truce, when Ula Kana was stirring everyone up.*

Do you know fae old enough to remember that??

Ha no, but they pass down the history to each other.

Ah, right, she said. *With accuracy, no less. Anyway, better topic: Satsuki is offering some dates for our February meetup. Shall we plan?*

Much better topic. Let's.

CHAPTER 24

LATE IN JANUARY, EARTH FESTIVAL BEGAN, with Hunter's Night at the close of the first day. Rafi was accustomed to spending it in the fae realm, but last year he had spent it with Izzy's family, and once, when he was half grown, he had stayed that night with Hazel. Humans stayed indoors from sundown to sunup and lit all sorts of lights. Not that the fae or wild animals were actually any more dangerous that night— not since settlers' days, at least. But humans deemed it wise to respect the dangers of the wilderness at the end of winter, the hungry times.

Those two particular Hunter's Nights in his past had been surprisingly convivial, singing and playing games and making warm spiced drinks in the glow of hundreds of lanterns and candles. He would have liked all his nights to be like that.

But this year, back in the fae realm, he had nothing planned. He had dared venture out in disguise to see part of Meloncollie's set at the amphitheater during the day, in a chilly drizzle. Meg filled in lately for Rafi, playing pipa, and a college-student bass player filled in for Tash. It hurt, seeing the group go right on without them, under the same band name, same nineties songs, two string players swapped for two others. The belonging he had once felt had been torn out from under him. Jove, Oni, and Izzy missed him—they said so in messages and when they met him in person—but he lived apart from them now. The cottage was empty, dark, and cold, and surely gaining resident mice in his absence.

From Port Baleia, Roxana sent pictures of the lanterns and treats and queued-up films she and Ester had prepared. He only ached more, gazing at those while huddled under cedar boughs a few feet from the verge—the only relatively dry outdoor place around, aside from Kepelo's realm.

He put his phone away, tugged his wool socks higher to cover his knees under his thick wrap skirt and coat, and got up. The sun had set a mere couple of hours ago. A long night lay ahead. Any humans who did break tradition and venture out would be easy pickings for his father's haunt.

It didn't surprise him to encounter Sminu and a pair of younger korreds on the footpath.

"Yes, go, bang on some windows," Sminu told the other two genially. "I wish to speak to my sad-looking offspring here."

In his coat pocket, Rafi's gloved hand splayed around the iron cuff. He carried it often these days. But using it anonymously was already impossible tonight, since his father had spotted and recognized him. Irritating. He said nothing as Sminu strolled up.

"I saw the most delightful performance today," Sminu said. "That Quicksand Theatre Company was in town again, did you know? They presented a play about the long-ago days of Ula Kana's campaign of terror. That was what they called it. I quite liked that phrase."

"Course you did," Rafi said.

"Given it's Hunter's Night, they gave the focus to Arlanuk, the hunter. Earth faery, like me. He still rules his haunt to this day, did you know?"

"I did, yes."

"The actor's costume to portray Arlanuk's antlers was quite funny. They used paper tubes with lights dangling from them."

Rafi glanced aside, watching the other two korreds creep across someone's roof. "You know if they damage anyone's house or garden, that's not going to do favors to your haunt's reputation."

"Yes, and they know too. They're only out to tap on windows and add some delicious scare to the night. Arlanuk, though," Sminu said, swinging back to the previous topic without pause, "he is complex. He did disappoint me somewhat, partnering with the humans to capture Ula Kana—a fellow faery, and an impressive one."

Given Ula Kana, in the late 1700s, had flown around torching humans, destroying buildings, and using a rare power she had to sway other fae into wreaking havoc, Rafi found the word "impressive" a bit disturbing.

"Then again," Sminu went on, "there are fellow fae I wouldn't mind removing from my life. And Arlanuk did gain a human mate, who loved him and bore him children. That I think I would like."

"I hear he didn't even have to enchant her," Rafi said dryly. "They say she consented willingly. Imagine that."

Sminu ignored the remark. "Ula Kana isn't gone, you know. She sleeps, under guard in Arlanuk's realm, like that prince fellow in the humans' palace. Ah, if only I were Arlanuk. I would free her and encourage her to do as she wished."

"Please go say that to your human friends. See what they think of your fantasy."

"Oh, I have! With a human I spoke to in the audience just today. They said, 'As long as she burns the witch-cult neighborhoods, I'm for it.'"

Naturally. Riquelme fans. Sick with anger, Rafi looked away, finding the silhouettes of the other two korreds between houses now, reaching out with a stick to tap at a window. When people screamed from inside, they cackled and scampered to another house.

Rafi blew out a sigh. "Why are we speaking? Did you want something or can I go?"

"Such hostility. I know our past encounters were not always to your liking, but things have changed. Brogyo is gone—speaking of one faery who I do not mind having out of my way—and I wish for cooperation between us now."

"I'm prepared to laugh at what your idea of cooperation is."

Sminu sauntered in a circle around Rafi, leaning in to sniff at him. Rafi twitched. "You carry iron," Sminu said. "I'm not concerned—what could *you* do to me, even armed? And doesn't it hurt you to touch it as well?"

Rafi tensed. He drew out the *other* piece he carried, in his opposite pocket: iron knuckles. Through the weapon's holes, he wiggled his fingers in their sheathing of thin wool. "Gloves."

"Clever! I must acquire such garments. But never mind, you won't have to use your meager weapon on me. In fact, I want to talk to you about iron." Sminu poked at a blackberry vine on the nearest garden wall. "The night Brogyo regenerated—have you heard about the young person who was with him and disappeared? The scent of iron, the trace of witch magic, which some of the nearby fae are sure they detected?"

Rafi's mouth went dry. He kept the iron knuckles on, letting them hang at his side. "I've heard. So?"

"Everyone's dismissed the idea that such details could have *caused* Brogyo's departure. A human, a bit of iron! Laughable. But I cannot help thinking—and perhaps this is just the imaginative human part of me—that maybe such things did influence him. Sway him. The way Ula Kana could sway fellow fae into doing what she wished, although surely not as powerful as that."

"I imagine we'd hear about it if someone around here had those powers." Rafi did his best to continue sounding bored.

"Precisely. Even so, I'm curious. I want to find this person, this weapon." He pressed his knobby fingertip on the blackberry vine. From its winter-brown stalk, green sprouts erupted and curled upward, spreading thorn all over the wall. "It was likely something enspelled by witches. Or even fae. Or both."

Rafi willed his breath to slow as he stared at the vine. His body remembered being wrapped by similar vines, pinned to the ground by thorns while the korreds laughed, his father among them. "Are you asking if I know who was with Brogyo that night?"

"You? Hardly." Sminu let the blackberry alone once it had made a complete tangle of the wall. He broke off a length of it and wrapped it around his wrist like a bracelet, his stony skin not taking any hurt from the thorns. "A person who did such a thing would have to be someone of courage, of purpose. Therefore I knew it could not be you."

"Thanks," Rafi said, hollowly.

A short distance away, someone opened a window and began singing a playful festival song, the one that began, "Oh, Hunter's Night, the dark, the fright, enspell the doors, my dear!"

The other two korreds, just below the window, hooted in appreciation.

Sminu kept his focus on Rafi. "But I hear you have skill at finding things and individuals. You could assist me."

"You want me to find out who the person was?"

"I shall make a deal with you for it."

Rafi let out a sharp laugh. The refusal was lined up on his tongue. No matter what Sminu offered, Rafi wasn't interested in pretending to search, and sure as hell wasn't going to tell his father the truth. But refusing would mean

Sminu would just ask someone else, and possibly get answers. If Rafi accepted, he could at least stall the investigation for a while. Not forever, though. And he loathed the idea of checking in to tell lies, to act cooperative, to have to see his father at all.

"The trail's probably gone cold," Rafi said.

Sminu would someday lose interest. Or Rafi would have the chance to snap the cuff on him and reroute his life first. He had to hope for one of those outcomes.

"Ah, but I have ideas," Sminu said. "Among the fae, I've already made inquiries. It's among the humans where you can help. Some don't trust you, but those who do are the sector who do not trust me. So they are likely the ones with the information I need."

"I'm not interested, and I don't know where I'd even start."

"That Wei family," Sminu said, casually as ever, but fear speared Rafi's heart. "Their party at Ti Falls Park was what started so much of this tension between us and humans."

"That—no. You hurt people before, lots of them, for years—"

"But *this* phase of the tension, I mean. Shut your useless mouth and listen. The Wei family has a youth, and there were youths near the verge the night Brogyo departed. He went away with one. Perhaps it was the Wei child in disguise."

"No." Rafi's lips refused to hold back the words. "She'd moved away by then. They were nowhere near."

"Shut up, I said." Sminu didn't even sound angry. "Then it could have been one of her friends. Also! Her mother, that Roxana Wei—she specialized in metal charms. I recall festival gifts she made in the past."

Rafi's hands squeezed into fists, stone scabbing over his skin, stretching the gloves. He itched to smash the iron knuckles into Sminu's face. But his father would only fight back, and even if Rafi dared use the cuff, those other two twits would be back in a flash when they heard the scuffle, and then he'd be getting savaged by three korreds rather than one.

"That charm could have been her work, could it not?" Sminu went on, toying with his bramble bracelet. "I've asked, of course, but no one seems to recall anything of use. Either that or they aren't willing to speak to me."

"From what I know of her," Rafi said, "she would have hated the idea of making such a thing." Not a lie. Despair sank him. He had dragged her into this, pulled her this low.

"I suppose you would know. You were friends. Lovers? I heard something of the sort. In any case, she left you here, so it couldn't have meant much. I don't really care."

Much as that stung, it was another bit of luck in its way. Sminu honestly didn't know or care if Rafi and Roxana were close. He would forever underestimate human love. That was for the best.

"I don't think there's anything to find out about this person or this item," Rafi said. "I did ask. I listened to rumors too. I have nothing to tell."

"So you'll simply give up? Aren't you curious? Don't you want to know?"

"I want you to leave humans alone. Come to the festivals if you like, but don't invite people across, don't enchant them, don't make any more deals arranging for ghoul-sylphs or spider-crab fae to attack them—just *stop* all this. Live your life and let us live ours."

He faintly registered that by the end of his appeal he had switched from "them" to "us" in referencing humans, but rage and fear were roaring in his ears, drowning out such semantic nuances.

"Why should I be required to leave them alone?" Sminu said, finally sounding offended. "I *am* half human."

"Maybe that's what went wrong with you. Brogyo too. You inherited the worst type of humanity, the Riquelme type."

Sminu bared his square teeth. "You compare me to that weak, lying—"

"You're just like him. You want to control people. Want them to worship you, view you as their savior. It drives you insane when they have their own lives and don't want you in them."

A blackberry vine whipped off the wall and raked across Rafi's face, thorns lacerating his cheekbone, eyelid, lip. He stumbled and fell.

He had expected the attack, in some form, yet had hoped maybe it wouldn't happen. Hoped Sminu had truly begun to understand how to get along with humans. Test failed.

His father loomed over him. "I approached you, you ingrate, because I *wished* for more cooperation between you and me. Between humans and fae."

"No." Rafi tasted blood, dripping from the gash in his lip. "You want to know if there's a weapon you don't have yet, magic you can use for yourself."

"But I invited you to help. I would have appreciated it." Sminu rather undermined the intent of his words by kicking Rafi in the hip, with a foot like a sledgehammer.

Rafi's breath left him again, pain stealing everything but a gasp.

"Fine," Sminu said. "If you won't help, I'll ask the Wei family myself. The woman and her daughter, next time they visit, or even her parents in the meantime. A little enchantment gets people telling their secrets quite swiftly."

Rafi's hip muscle had been mashed, his bone cracked. He numbed it with a flash of magic and lunged at Sminu. The iron knuckles collided with his father's belly, knocking him back. But Sminu only grunted, glared, and surged forward again, and then things became a blur of agony for Rafi. Amid the kicks, thorn-stabs, and rock-fisted blows, Rafi scrabbled for the cuff, reckoning he should at least try smacking it onto his father before he blacked out, risk be damned.

But the other two korreds arrived then, excited at the spectacle, and joined in. He abandoned the effort to get the cuff and folded his bleeding arms over his head instead.

The ground shook, several heavy beats, each increasing in strength. Then the blows against his body stopped and the korreds wailed in protest. Rafi peeked up. In his weaving vision stood a stone wall where one hadn't been before. It had four blocky arms, and three of them held the korreds high above the ground, their bodies encased in stone.

Mukut grumbled something urgent at Rafi, then lumbered away with the korreds in her grasp, even while Sminu shouted a torrent of abuse at her in the fae tongue.

Rafi tried to crawl away, but toppled over on his first try and threw up into the gravel.

All right. Rest a bit first.

Hunter's Night. No humans out anyway. No one to be horrified at his condition if they stumbled across him. No one to turn him in to the government.

No one to tell Roxana either. That was good. Didn't want to upset her.

Therefore he couldn't crawl down the path to Jove and Izzy's door for help. Even if he asked them not to tell her, one of them would anyway.

He lay shivering, drifting in and out of delirium. It started raining, a steady shower that felt brutally cold on most of him but soothing on his throbbing bruises.

A spark looped out of the forest and swung down to hover near him. "Akurafi. You provoked him. Unwise."

Whether or not the will-o'-the-wisp was a dream, he mumbled in agreement, "I was asking for it."

He let his eyes close, but the spark's light flashed back and forth beyond his eyelids. A warmth touched his hip, the one Sminu had kicked first, and the pain eased there. Then the will-o'-the-wisp squeaked something involving "Kepelo" and left.

He still wasn't sure if the encounter had been a dream. But just as he was trying to get up again, a swarm of sparks poured down the footpath and surrounded him. A hundred little limbs took hold of him, lifted him into the air. Everywhere they touched, the agony receded.

He relaxed into half-consciousness, but registered the milestones toward safety as he passed them. The winter air breezing across his body. The crackle of static as they crossed the verge. The warmth and smoky smell of Kepelo's haunt. His mother's voice, murmuring in the fae tongue and then the human, telling him serenely that yes, he had asked for it, before wrapping him in a spell that sent him into a placid sleep.

When he awoke, he was in his hammock. It was still night—or perhaps night again—and he had been stripped of his clothes and wrapped in a patchwork blanket Hazel had given him years ago. The air was warm, flickering with orange light from the midair flames that in his childhood he had called Kepelo's streetlights, once he'd been to the human realm and learned what streetlights were. When he shifted, swaying the hammock, his body twinged in about twenty different places, but with the dull ache of healing, not the stab of acute injury.

His mother was in her mostly human form, reclining on a rock ledge nearby, her legs stretched out and crossed at the ankles. Her toenails were, at the moment, shining gold claws. Then his bleary gaze caught the shimmer of dark blue in her hand, and he sat up, wide awake.

She was examining the iron cuff, holding it by its enamel casing. "It was in your coat pocket," she said, without taking her gaze from it. "I'm surprised your father didn't take it from you."

"He would have, if he'd known it was on me."

"I'm also surprised you didn't use it on him."

"I would have if I hadn't been too hurt to move," he said, more quietly.

"That's what I guessed." She didn't sound as stricken as the human parents in his life would at hearing of their child's injuries, but she did sound gentle. "It makes the wearer feel…sad. For the pain they've caused."

"You touched it? The iron?"

"I put it on." She lifted one leg to flourish an ankle. He took it to mean she'd worn it there rather than her wrist.

He winced. "Mother. It isn't meant for someone like you. I'm sorry. I should have told you about it."

Kepelo finally looked at him, her amber-orange eyes clear. She cocked her head, puzzled. "It certainly wasn't pleasant, but at least it was enlightening. I am well."

"That's…a relief. How long did you wear it?"

"Not long. The moon was still in the span when I put it on and when I took it off." She tilted her chin toward the narrow gap of sky between clifftop and forest. Celestial movements were the only things resembling clocks here. Not that they were reliable measures either, given the way time broke all its rules between one side of the verge and the other.

"And you took it off under your own power?" he asked.

"Of course." She frowned, rotating the cuff. "It was more difficult than I thought it would be. The iron hurt a great deal and weakened me. Made me smaller. But I was still able to remove it. Have others been unable?"

"They…first, did anybody else see it?"

"Not yet. I asked the will-o'-the-wisps to leave you with me so you could rest."

"Good. Well…" Rafi settled his gaze on the violet-blossom pattern of one of the patchwork squares and spilled the story. The cuff being made, and what Rafi had used it for on Halloween night, a year and a quarter ago.

When his words ran out, his mother sat in silence. Now she wouldn't like Roxana, he thought, miserably stroking a fingertip on the frayed edge of the violet square.

"And you plan to use it again?" she asked.

"I figure you'd say that was an abhorrent idea."

"Why? This charm shows the truth and evokes empathy. It disturbs as it does so, yes, and we fae are never going to be fond of touching iron. But it is quite a remarkable piece of human art. Isn't that what all human art aims to do? Evoke empathy, whether pleasantly or violently?"

"I suppose." Rafi studied her. "I thought you'd condemn us for making it. Let alone deploying it."

Her brow wrinkled in what looked strikingly like human wryness. "You and I do keep having trouble understanding one another. I feel…sorry about that." Her gaze dropped to the cuff again. "It's one of the things I felt most strongly when wearing this. The ways I've hurt you by not understanding."

Maybe it was because of his weakened state, but tears rose in his eyes. Unusual when it came to his mother: she inspired calm, was never anything *but* calm. He had always believed she loved him, but only now did he feel it as truth.

"Compared to my other parent," he promised, "you have not hurt me much at all. Thank you for being my safe haven."

Kepelo smiled again, and this time he fancied her eyes had an extra glassy sheen in them. The fae could weep, uncommon though it was. She rose, kissed him on the forehead in a blaze of warmth, and set the cuff on his lap. "Given it's a human invention, I leave it to you humans to decide its fate."

He covered it with a fold of the blanket. "I think I only want to use it once more, if at all."

He didn't have to say for whom. She merely nodded. "To protect you and Roxana and her family," she said, "I suppose it's best if I don't speak of this item to anyone."

"Right. Please don't."

"The other regret it inspired in me." She wandered a few steps away, looking up at the stars. Her folded wings shimmered red and yellow in the torch-light. "Not doing enough to protect humans. And yet, when is it helping and when is it meddling? I've never wanted to do the latter. Push other fae into acting as I wish, and lord my will over humans, simply because I have the power to do so. That would be the behavior of the *worst* fire faery."

"Ula Kana? Funny, I was just talking about her with Sminu."

"He admires her. We spoke of it before you were born. I hoped he was just being naive in his enthusiasm about her." Kepelo flicked one hand upward to send a streak of sparks into the air, as if throwing away the memory of Sminu. "At least he gave me you. There can be no other reason the Lady lured us together."

Rafi edged his stiff legs off the hammock and dropped to the ground. Holding the blanket around himself, he shuffled forward and kissed her on the cheek. In her current form, they were almost exactly the same height.

Then he noticed the dawn lightening the sky. "Shit. How long did I sleep? I have somewhere important to be in February."

CHAPTER 25

KAGAMI LAGOON'S SURFACE WAS A THOUSAND facets of turquoise and sapphire, changing constantly under the winter wind. On the boardwalk, Roxana hunched her shoulders inside her coat. "I remembered it being smooth as glass," she told Rafi. "And warmer. Guess I usually only came here in summer."

He wrapped his arm around her. "It's gorgeous. I've never seen anything like it."

Two jetties of black rock curved out almost a mile into the ocean, encasing the lagoon. Even from here she could see the crashing foam of the gray breakers hitting the rocks. The boom of the surf rolled inland on the wind that whipped against them, smelling of cold seawater.

"I can't imagine it," Rafi said. "Crossing that."

"The lagoon or the ocean?"

"The ocean. Though in this weather, either, I suppose."

His tone was somber. So far, this getaway hadn't felt as amorously delectable as Roxana had hoped. It was the first time they'd seen each other since his Lord Festival visit to Port Baleia, and it had been weeks in the planning. Ester was away at a school arts camp for a few days, and Satsuki's mother was gone for the month, traveling with her new boyfriend (joyfriend, if one preferred), leaving her Kagami apartment vacant. Satsuki had offered it to Rafi and Roxana and had even given Rafi a ride up here. From the moment of their greeting embrace, though, he had seemed weary.

"You never want to get off this island?" Roxana said. "Even with everything going on lately?"

He kept his eyes on the cloudy horizon. "The rest of the world has problems too. Besides, if I'm clueless in the human realm here, how much worse would it be in a country I've never been to?"

"But if I went with you? If we were newcomers together?"

"Maybe." He kept gazing outward, as if he didn't trust the ocean to be left unwatched.

His hairline was a dull gray, not gray hairs but tiny flecks of stone. They dappled the backs of his hands too. They were new since she'd last seen him, and had been there since the two of them reunited an hour ago. His stone-skin phases usually faded more quickly. She took his hand and ran her thumb over the hard grains. "Feels defensive to be in a new place?"

"I guess. And everything with my father, and Mukut…"

"You warned my parents, that's all you can do. They won't let a korred get close. Anyway, they don't know about the cuff. There's nothing they could say if they *were* enchanted."

A couple of weeks ago, after an absence of several days, he had told her he'd had a run-in with Sminu, who suspected the existence of a witch-en-spelled iron weapon used against Brogyo. Mukut had intervened to let Rafi escape, a favor that had cost her dear: Rafi later heard Sminu had banished her from his haunt. She had retreated to the hills, and he didn't know where she was now.

Meanwhile, Rafi had come clean to Kepelo about the cuff—her response was to remain as hands-off as before—and then returned to the human realm to seek Amaris and Timo. To them he hadn't spoken of the cuff or Roxana's in-volvement. He had said only that Sminu was convinced there was something to be learned about the night Brogyo returned to the elements, and that he suspected the Wei family because of the Ti Falls Park party. "I know you don't have any information for him," he had assured Roxana's parents. "But I still don't want him to enspell you. Please be on guard."

Amaris had assured him they were always on their guard these days and that she wasn't afraid. Roxana was doing her best not to worry either. But Rafi seemed shaken, and she suspected the encounter with his father had been more damaging than he let on. Mentally and possibly physically. The trouble with endo-witches, especially ones with powerful fae friends to heal them, was that evidence like bruises or broken bones could get whisked away before loved ones could see.

When she'd asked in texts if he was all right, he had answered only, *Yes. It's other people I'm concerned for.*

So he didn't want to talk about it. That hurt, in terms of the openness of their communication, but then, the subject wasn't ideal conversation material for a romantic getaway.

She clasped his hand and took him on a walk. Down the lagoonfront with its long curve of shops, apartments, and restaurants; inward along the canals, beside the boats that served as vehicles in most of Kagami; around the boardwalk trails through the swamps and rivers on the inland side.

They had a dinner of takeout wraps and bought some eggs and pastries so they could have breakfast by themselves in the apartment the next morning. Satsuki's mother's apartment was above the bookshop, on the lagoonfront, a cozy high-ceilinged space with excess book storage filling half the rooms. Roxana got the gas fireplace going as night fell. Rain lashed the windowpanes, and wind juddered around the stone building. They reclined on the couch after dinner, cuddling, then moved to the bedroom.

Staying in his arms for the night was a piece of heaven, but a poignant one, given they could only do this the once, until who knew when. The hours progressed and she couldn't quite stay asleep, as the wind shrieked outside and the rain crashed across the metal chimney cap.

When she shifted and saw the gleam of Rafi's open eyes, she murmured, "The ocean fae wouldn't send a tsunami as punishment for Riquelme being an ass, would they?"

"Never know," he said. Neither ominous nor humorous. Just a fact of life: you never knew what the forces of nature might do.

She turned onto her side, pulling his arm with her so that he spooned her. In that position she must have eventually fallen asleep, because she opened her eyes to daylight.

Rafi was asleep at her back. When she gently lifted his arm to slip out from under it, his eyes snapped open and he grasped her wrist. Light sleeper. And one who often couldn't trust those around him.

It sparked an ache in her chest. She took his hand lightly. "Hi."

He relaxed, sinking back. "Hi." Flecks of stone still dappled the back of his hand. His gaze trailed to the window, screened by a gauze curtain. "Storm over?"

"I think so." It was quiet now, just the faint songs of gulls and selkies filtering in from the lagoon. She kissed his hand and pulled away. "I'll get breakfast started."

⚬⚬⚬

Rafi held his fork with care, as if unused to utensils—which was probably the case lately, she supposed—and his gaze roved around the kitchen as he ate his eggs and sliced pears.

"Cute place," Roxana ventured. "I like the tiles."

"Been a while since I've had a meal in a house." He said it casually, with no self-pity.

She set down her coffee mug with a *thunk* solid enough to make him look at her, startled.

"I hate it," she said. "I hate that you don't get to be in the cottage anymore, that you never got to live with your grandmother in her house, that you can't or won't just come move in with us."

He looked at her, stunned. "I'm safe at Kepelo's. It's warm, I have shelter. I'm fed."

"I know, but…" Roxana pressed a napkin against the drop of coffee that had splashed onto the table. "I want to talk about where we're going. How to make things better."

Rafi lowered his eyes. "Okay."

Gods, she was doing it again. Plowing in with what she wanted, grabbing the steering wheel. But they were both tired, and her restraint was too weak this morning to resist spilling all her pent-up words. "The way I see it, we have two main options if we want to stay together. Breaking up would be a third, but…I don't want that. Do you?"

"No." He sounded hesitant. "But I want whatever's best for you. Even if it's that."

"Why are you saying that? Don't you care? You get to care, you get to have preferences."

"Well, I would *prefer* that the laws were different and that my father would cease to exist, but I can't do much about the first and haven't had a good shot yet at the second, so…"

"Fine. Fair. But given the way things are, one of our two options is to keep on going like this. Long-distance, meeting up when we can, you spending a lot of time in the fae realm and being out of reach."

Rafi retracted his fingers from the fork and sank back, setting his hands in his lap. "You're not happy with that option. Obviously."

"I *miss* you. I worry. I hate that you're not getting to play with the band anymore, because you loved that, and I'm frustrated we aren't trying harder to be together. Because what is life for otherwise?"

"What is the other option, though?" he said quietly. "I renounce being a wanderer, come across the verge, sign on as a citizen, follow the rules?"

"Not necessarily, but at least come to this side to stay. Because—"

"And get found out by the neighbors before long? Get reported, get checked up on by the authorities? Get targeted by Riquelme fans everywhere I go? Get arrested if I use my 'rare witch ability'—which I don't even entirely control?" He held up one hand, rotating it to show the stone encrusting the back of it—more than there had been since before she'd shoved him into this conversation.

"Those laws won't last forever. Riquelme will get removed. People are already trying to arrange a referendum to vote him out; there's all kinds of scandal coming out around him. But yes, the other option is you come back to live near Ester and me. Even *with* us."

"I want to," he said. "But why not wait till they get rid of him, till things change so we don't have so many risks?"

"Because we don't know how long that will *be*. Law and government can take years. Meanwhile our lives are passing us by."

"But I'm out of my depth in Port Baleia—look at me, I couldn't even take a train here, to Kagami, because of authorities watching the stations, not to mention my cluelessness on how transit works. I had to get a ride from Satsuki, and—"

"It doesn't have to be Port Baleia. Ester and I could—move back to Miryoku." She pulled the damp napkin to her lap and twisted it. "I haven't promised anything. But she loves the idea, and once I'm done with my schooling in June, why not?"

Hope kindled in Rafi's eyes. Then it guttered and went out. "You can't. Not till my father's gone. If you were in Miryoku, he'd find you eventually and get the truth out of you. I feel sick just thinking of it."

"We're going to let his *existence* stop us from being together? Really?"

"Well," he defended, "I'm trying to end his current existence. So as soon as that's done…"

"Oh my gods. Stop that. Why are you sitting here matter-of-factly talking about murdering your father?"

"It's not *murder*." Finally he sounded almost as irate as she did. "You can't murder fae. My mother tried the cuff on, and it did no more to her than it did to you or me. Sminu has to *change* for me to have any peace, and if the cuff does that, even if the change is as drastic as Brogyo's, I'm going to try it. I just need a chance to get at him. Then we're done with it. I swear."

Anger and hurt tumbled inside her, stormy as the ocean. "That's the only way out you can see? You'd rather do that, keeping us apart for however long it takes, than move to another town? Like here—Kagami. What if we moved here? It's smaller than Port Baleia, and—"

"And the laws! They're still the same. I'm still a wanderer and a form-changer. And while I'm here, what is Sminu doing to people back in Miryoku?"

"It's not your job to stop him," she yelled. "I've said this a thousand times. Gods, I wish I'd never made the cuff. I hate that it exists, I hate that I had anything to do with it. Will you give it back to me? Please? I'll strip off the spells, pull the whole thing apart."

Rafi stared at her as if she'd gone insane. "He's threatening *Ester*. He'd go after her, too, if she was back in town. You think I could live with that?"

Fear wrapped around her throat, strangled her. She tried to come up with a retort but couldn't form words.

"And even if we destroyed it," he added, "he'd just demand you make a new one. Or some other piece that suited his whims. He'll find out who made it by enchanting one of us, eventually, and dragging the truth out of us, and then you'll be his new obsession."

"He might find some other obsession." Her voice felt ragged. "There are lots of people he's interested in lately. You've said so yourself."

"Yeah, maybe. But considering just a couple weeks ago he was still fascinated by this idea of the person with Brogyo, and the iron they used, and it's been more than a year since that happened—can you see why I'm begging you to give it more time before coming back to Miryoku?"

Roxana tossed the napkin onto the table. "And can you see why it might be a good idea for you to *leave* Miryoku?"

Rafi gave a sideways tilt of his chin and didn't answer.

"Kagami's nice, right?" she tried once more. "And closer to home. I'd be able to visit my parents more often than I can now."

"I want you to be able to visit them safely, for as long as you want, whenever you want. I want my father to *stand down completely*." He said the words softly but in separate, emphasized beats. "And other than letting lots of time pass or using the cuff, I don't know how he ever will."

They sat in stillness, their gazes slumped among the half-eaten eggs and the coffee mugs, the room silent except for the distant sounds of boats in the canals and the *tick-tick-tick* of a wall clock.

Roxana stacked her plate on top of his and picked them up. "I still have three months of classes." She took the plates to the sink. "We don't have to decide today. I would just feel better if we had a plan. If I knew what we were going *toward*."

The chair scraped, then Rafi brought over his mug and a handful of utensils. "Plans. I was never very good at those."

The self-conscious smallness of his voice crushed her. She despised herself for flinging demands at him on a morning when neither of them were in their usual element and hadn't slept well. Hands in the soapy water, she tipped her head to touch it to his shoulder. "Wasn't really part of how you were raised. The fae don't make a lot of plans."

"Rudimentary ones. Go to the festival when invited. Agree on a deal and see it through. Enchant people to make them adore you at any cost—if you're my father."

"It's a stupid human habit really," she said. "Trying to detail what our future will look like, when we can't actually control it. Causes a lot of stress. I'm not sure why we keep doing it."

Rafi started drying a plate with a tea towel. "Plans can lead to cities. Art. Concerts. The things we love about humans. But I'm…" The wet plate slipped out of his grip and shattered on the floor tiles. "…still not sure I'm any good at being human," he finished, his voice as wrecked as the plate.

They both crouched to pick up the shards.

"It's all right," she said.

The backs of his hands were almost completely stone, clumsy as he tried to grip bits of broken ceramic. "I'll apologize to Satsuki," he said, miserable. "I'll get her something in exchange."

"It's okay. It's just a plate. Really. We've all done it."

He looked at the fragments in his hands and let out a hopeless sigh.

They had only the rest of the morning together. They went out for another walk, all the way to the end of the south jetty. The wind blew more gently today, and weak sunbeams streamed through the thin clouds. The waves crashed against the rocks, occasionally showering Roxana and Rafi with salt spray. Flat patches of rock housed tide pools full of purple starfish, orange anemones, and red sea slugs—some of which turned out to be fae, unfolding little faces that blinked at them.

At the jetty's end, they gazed out. "We're looking straight toward Japan from here," Roxana said. "Next piece of land across this water."

Rafi hummed in acknowledgment.

She wasn't going to say it. She clamped her lips shut just to make sure.

But he did say it, rather to her surprise.

"I suppose that's one other option. Leave the country. Together."

"Yes," she admitted. "Though probably the hardest."

"No magic. Except what we can bring in charms."

"That part's difficult. When I visited China and Europe, years ago, I felt powerless, not being able to manipulate materials the way I can here."

"I wouldn't be able to heal myself. Or change form. It'd be strange."

"We'd also have to find a place in a new culture, while not being able to talk about where we came from."

Rafi glanced down at her. "Would you choose to remember Eidolonia? Bring a memory charm?"

"Of course. Would you?"

His gaze floated back out. "Some days, it seems like heaven, getting to forget almost everything up till the present and start over."

She huddled closer to him. The wish sounded so bleak, the mark of a sad life.

Or possibly just a frustrating day, or year. Which it certainly had been.

"In any case," she said, "Ester would pitch a fit if I proposed moving crosswater, when she's so in love with Oni. And my parents are here, and Sat-suki, and my livelihood—I'd have to learn to do something else entirely with my life, and so would you. So I guess I'm not super fond of that option."

"No," he agreed, sounding forlorn. "In another country I'd be...adrift."

She found his hand within the folds of his coat and tucked her cold fingers into it. "We'll take troublesome fae and our terrible government over the unfamiliarity of another country with only humans in it. Strange, aren't we?"

"Better the devil you know." He squinted back at the island before facing the sea again.

Before parting that afternoon, they agreed to revisit the conversation in another month, around Water Festival in March.

They didn't end up fulfilling that goal.

The world came crashing down instead.

CHAPTER 26

FOR RAFI THE MONTH HAD GONE DREARILY, his fears and hatred about his father weighed down even further by his insecurities about Roxana. He reached out in text to Izzy—as the only human mother in a stable relationship he knew well—to ask what she thought Roxana wanted. Her answer was:

She wants you. She wants you safe and happy and involved in things you love. She wants you there where she can see you and talk to you and hug you at night if either of you can't sleep. She wants you to help with her day-to-day life and she wants to help with yours. She's not getting much of any of that right now, so she's unhappy.

They were sweet words and would have made for good romantic ballad lyrics. But they only twisted him up tighter in inadequacy. How could he be all of that? Rafi the wanderer, the shabby relative of the fae, denizen of no particular realm or town or country or even any one element?

He prowled around after Sminu, failing to get a chance to snap the cuff on him, and doubting whether he should anyway after Roxana's revulsion at the idea. He checked in with her in text, speaking of weather and news and her classes. He slept, badly, in his mother's realm and sometimes lost several days at once on the human side.

Then on a night in mid-March, on the first day of Water Festival, a commotion exploded.

Voices trilled and crackled in the fae tongue. He jumped out of his hammock and followed them around to the clearing in front of his mother's cave. Seemingly everyone from the haunt was gathered around Kepelo and a bird faery he didn't know. Kepelo, in drake form, was speaking urgently to the faery, who was in the form of a spotted hawk some four feet tall.

Rafi maneuvered closer and grabbed Aulo's arm. "What's happened?"

She looked down at him. "Ula Kana has awakened. This hawk faery comes from Arlanuk's realm to inform every haunt leader in our region."

The words rang unreal. Ula Kana was a name from history books, someone put into a forever sleep in a mighty tree fortress deep in the fae realm. She couldn't be awake, free, an actual threat. "Arlanuk freed her?" he said in disbelief.

"No. She awakened, none know how, and broke free. She swayed some of Arlanuk's guards in order to assist her escape. Now she flies loose, collecting fae for her forces."

"Maybe other fae arranged it? As an uprising, because they're angry about Riquelme and his people?"

"Maybe." Aulo sounded doubtful. "But no one's heard of such a plan. She and the human prince were to stay asleep, their enchantments linked. If one's spell was broken, so would be the other. Thus we can rest assured the prince has awoken, too, though we don't know which side the breaking occurred on or why."

Prince Larkin from the year 1799 being awake would have been a delightfully fascinating prospect if it weren't for the much huger problem of Ula Kana being free.

Rafi's hands and feet had gone cold in fear. "What will she do with these forces she's collecting?"

"No one's certain. It seems she hasn't bothered speaking much yet. But in the past her aim was to drive all humans off the island, or kill them if they wouldn't leave. She was extreme in her views on the matter."

Roxana, he thought. Ester. The band. The sweet, vulnerable humans he loved. He was trembling; stone encased his limbs. "Then—we need to warn people."

"We will," Aulo assured.

What could anyone, though, even with modern technology or a fae-realm-iron cuff, do against Ula Kana? And what horrific retaliation would occur when people tried anyway?

"Where is she now?"

"We don't know. From Arlanuk's realm she flew to the great volcano where she once lived, and it was hoped she might stay there. But later she was seen soaring away, with others she enticed into following her."

The hawk faery exchanged bows with Kepelo, then shot into the air and wheeled south. To the water fae, Rafi supposed, Tash's people, the next realm over. Then after that the messenger would go to Sminu and share the news.

Rafi didn't have time to dwell on Sminu's delight at hearing it or the red carpet he would roll out to welcome Ula Kana, should she come this way. He wriggled forward through the sunshine-hot crowd of fire fae to get to his mother's inner circle.

She was giving orders. Though she used the fae tongue, he understood the basic idea: several small fae, mostly sprites and will-o'-the-wisps, were sent off in multiple directions to take up watch at the edges of her territory. They were to bring back word immediately if they saw Ula Kana approaching.

Then she named Aulo and five others, the largest and strongest of the drakes and djinns. She glanced at Rafi and switched to English in addressing them. "We six must keep hidden. With our powers, we are the ones who pose the most danger to everyone around us—especially humans—if Ula Kana catches us and sways us to her side. The smaller fae can do harm, too, of course, but in our case the disaster would be ferocious and swift."

Indeed. Sheets of fire blasting from half a dozen gigantic flying fae, along with Ula Kana and whoever she brought along, would reduce Miryoku and its inhabitants to ash in minutes.

Rafi found his knees were shaking, the stone on his skin clacking like river rocks.

The others retreated into the cave behind her, whose tunnels reached deep enough into the hill that no one would spot them in a fly-over. Kepelo strode into the cave as well, shrinking her form with each step so that she fit neatly beneath the ceiling. Then she turned to Rafi.

"I'll go to the town," he said. "Warn them."

"Find out what they've heard. Bring back any news we should know."

"What can they do against her? What should I tell them?"

"Tell them to hide." She looked more somber than he had seen her since Hazel's death—more even than that night. She touched his cheek, the scales on her hand sleek and warm. "Tell them we must all band together. That's the only way she was ever defeated before. Fighting her as any one individual, or even as a whole town, is a hopeless notion."

He twisted his mouth into a humorless smile. "Not the cuff, then."

"Don't you dare get close enough to try. She is of Pitchstone Mountain, its fury and its lava. She would feel the pain for but a moment, then would melt the thing in the next second and kill you in the one after that."

While he absorbed that, she pulled him in for a hug. He found himself clasped against the smoothness of her shining red drake skin in a fervent embrace.

"Stay out of her way, spark of mine," she whispered. "I beg you. If I must keep hidden, so must you."

He nodded, his arms twining up behind her shoulders, unable to reach all the way around her huge wings. "I'll warn people. I'll keep as many safe as I can."

But when he tumbled across the verge a short time later, night wheeled instantly to a bright midday, his phone telling him a day and a half had passed since what he would have called "last night." And to judge from the text messages and national emergency alerts piling onto his screen, the humans of Eidolonia already knew.

❧

Roxana first heard through people on the streetcar, remarking while reading their phones with concern. Three surveyors had been killed on Pitchstone Mountain, in the fae realm. They'd been there to study the volcano. The attack was led by a fire faery.

"Awful," someone said.

"Terrible idea in the first place," their friend said. "Going that deep into the fae realm, sent by Riquelme's government. Sure, it was for science, and they had fae guides, but there's going to be other fae who see it as an invasion."

"Especially the way *some people* have been talking about the fae lately," the first friend agreed.

Roxana had to get to class. She didn't have time to read the news, beyond the troubling headline.

Then in the middle of class, everyone's phones started buzzing with an alert. The professor paused, and all the students, Roxana included, looked at their screens.

!! NATIONWIDE ALERT !! Central Dasdemir is being attacked by band of fae. Take cover immediately. Keep alert for further updates and emergency instructions.

Murmurs filled the room. Though usually the most rule-abiding student in any classroom, Roxana swiped open her screen and found the live coverage. A chill lanced through her. Floriana Palace, with its gold-capped towers and pristine blue-and-red national flags, was wreathed in black smoke. One tower was entirely gone. The camera swung down to show the heap of rubble, rescuers running in and out.

For some reason she thought of Rafi. He had only been to the palace once, he'd told her. Just stood outside it, hadn't even seen its interior. *It's the most beautiful building I've ever seen in person,* he said.

The professor held up her hand for attention, reading her own screen. "I'm getting further instructions from the college. The prime minister will give an address at two-thirty. So far there is currently no known threat to our county or to the north of the island in general, but if anyone needs to leave, you're free to go."

Though deeply distracted, Roxana stuck it out for the rest of class. She was grateful to get a text from Ester almost at once, who assured her everything was fine at school but expressed concern about the capital.

Roxana texted Rafi too, a message on top of the one she'd sent yesterday. That one had merely said, *Happy Water Festival! Going to any events?*—which she had hoped would spur him into acknowledging that it was time to revisit that conversation about their future. Now, with a palace tower incinerated, and disturbing rumors of Ula Kana spreading, such a concern seemed petty.

Oh wow the news, she texted. *How are things there? Have you heard anything?*

Satsuki sent a message, verifying that Miryoku, just one peninsula and one bay away from Dasdemir, was bracing itself, and that Roxana's mother was sure to have a busy day ahead.

Roxana sent her mother *Hang in there Mom. We're thinking of you.* She expected no reply from a mayor in emergency mode, and indeed got none by the time she left campus.

After arriving home, she set her computer on the kitchen counter and brought up the live feed of the prime minister's press conference. Ester was still at school, where Roxana expected they'd be pausing classes to report anything urgent from the broadcast.

Akio Riquelme stood at the podium on the sunny steps outside Parliament. He wore an overwrought purple-and-black robe of office, and the breeze made his graying hair stand on end from one side. Roxana grimaced at the sight of him, but forced herself to watch and listen.

"This morning's news, from both our survey team and from Floriana Palace, has been bad indeed," he began. "The fae who attacked the palace a short time ago were indeed led by the fire faery known as Ula Kana." While Roxana's mouth dropped open with a squeak, he went on, "Not only did many present at the palace have visual confirmation, including one faery who was alive at the time of the Civil War and recognized her, but Ula Kana herself spoke. We're reviewing footage captured on the phone of a witness and are not yet ready to release it, but I can tell you she said: 'Your people have invited severe vengeance for what you've done to me and my land. I am furious to find that during my captivity you've turned my island fouler still, smearing your ugliness and noise and light everywhere. You've loitered too long, and I shall burn you all to ash.'"

Roxana was swaying. She gripped the edge of the counter, her knuckles white.

"Given these threats," Riquelme continued, "we feel sure that the murder of the three surveyors was also the work of Ula Kana and her followers. Her being awakened is a clear violation of the truce set in place long ago. Indeed, this agreement has now been officially broken. For this morning it was discovered by the palace that Prince Larkin has disappeared from his bower."

"What the fuck?" Roxana said aloud, and hit the messaging app to start typing to Satsuki and Rafi simultaneously.

Are you hearing this? Ula Kana? Prince Larkin?? Is he bullshitting everyone again or is this for real?

"We are, of course, sending out immediate investigations in order to learn what's happened to the prince," Riquelme was blaring over the shouts of the journalists. "We want to know who has done this, and why."

Seriously wtf?? Satsuki answered. *This is almost too weird and stupid for him to have made up.*

Rafi hadn't responded. Probably across the verge, safe with his benevolent, twenty-foot-tall drake mother. Roxana couldn't bear any other possibility.

"We urge anyone," Riquelme concluded, "to come forward if they have information about either Prince Larkin or Ula Kana. Meanwhile we assure you our emergency forces and personnel stand ready to keep our islanders as safe as possible. We'll update you as soon as we have further news. Thank you." He stepped away from the podium, ignoring the clamor of the journalists.

Roxana went to the living room window. No streaks of fire crossed the blue afternoon sky. No plumes of smoke rose from the piece of Port Baleia visible from here. No waterspouts whipped up over the ocean. So far.

Her father texted: *We're fine, honey! Just busy as heck making sure everyone's got a place to shelter and assigning patrols to look out for trouble. Your mom's turned into a real drill sergeant, haha! She's a pro.*

Roxana responded, *Thanks for letting me know! All quiet up here. Will keep in touch.*

Satsuki sent a link to a post theorizing what had happened: that Riquelme had gotten witches to break the spell binding Larkin and Ula Kana, with the hope that Ula Kana's subsequent spree of destruction would turn more humans against the fae and thereby gain him more support for the idea of pushing back the verge. *Not sure I buy this*, Satsuki said, *but then again I also wouldn't put it past the fuckhead.*

It's hard to believe even he would be that irresponsible, Roxana said. *But I guess we'll see.*

She dropped onto the couch and sank into the tar pit of unfolding coverage and wild theories. Somewhere in the eighth or ninth social media thread, she was startled back into the room by Ester opening the door.

"It's *crazy*." Ester plunked her backpack on the floor and threw herself down beside Roxana. Her greeting hug clung longer than usual, the only sign that she was worried. Outrage colored her voice. "Who would break a spell like that and let Ula Kana loose? Would Riquelme be *that* evil?"

Roxana stroked Ester's shoulder. "It would be a horrible political move.

I doubt he would. One of his followers, though, maybe. Or someone on the other side, trying to make him look bad."

"He already looks bad on his own. Doesn't need any help with that."

A laugh escaped Roxana. "True."

"Is it even really Ula Kana? Is he staging it so he can pretend to rescue the country from her, like Sminu was doing with the ghoul-sylph in Miryoku?"

"That's another theory. Everyone hopes it isn't really her."

Ester pulled herself upright and reconfigured her ponytail. "Yeah, but. Then we wouldn't get to see Prince Larkin awake. And I do kind of want to see that."

Roxana's phone buzzed with another message. Rafi's name gave her heart a kick.

It's really Ula Kana. A messenger came from Arlanuk's realm to tell my mother. I'm back in town to warn everyone, but looks like you all found out already.

"It's really her?" Ester said, reading over Roxana's arm. "Then Prince Larkin is really awake!" She bounded off the couch and scrambled to her room, presumably to get online.

The afternoon tottered past in messages and live streams. Night fell. Roxana made a dinner of reheated leftovers supplemented by a pot of rice, the laptop open to the news the whole time. As she was scraping the rest of the rice into a fridge container, the update flared across the screen.

Prince Larkin had been found. He was back at the palace, alive and well and dressed in modern-style button-down shirt and trousers, to judge from the small bit of footage that had been released. Ester squealed, fists in the air.

"Oh my gods," Roxana said, fascinated, neglecting the pot she still held. "Is it really him? It could be a lookalike they found, to make people feel better…"

"It looks exactly like him," Ester protested.

They'd seen him in person, of course. Just about everyone in the country had. He'd been a tourist attraction in Floriana Palace, asleep behind glass, for the last two hundred and twenty years. Roxana had to admit it looked like his profile, and he had the same shade of deep red hair—now arranged in a casual braid instead of adorned with jewels as it had been in his bower.

"Exo-witches could do that to a person's appearance," she pointed out, just to cover all the bases of skepticism.

"Where is he, then, if that's not him?"

"I don't know. Anything's possible at this point."

"Yeah. I wonder if we'll even have school tomorrow." Ester sounded, predictably, upbeat about the possibility of classes being canceled.

"Again," said one of the journalists on screen, "no word from the palace or from Parliament yet about how the prince and Ula Kana were awakened. That, presumably, is what they hope to find out in this evening's conversation with His Highness."

Roxana closed the browser and finally put down the rice pot. "Let's try to get some sleep."

Not that she followed her own advice. Still awake at midnight, she texted Rafi.

For the next day or so, could you just let me know every couple hours that you're okay? Even in the middle of the night. And tell me if you're going back across the verge so I won't worry.

He answered right away—surely he was not only awake but out patrolling Miryoku.

I promise. And I'm okay. Love you.

⤜⤛

The streets of Miryoku were empty. Had the night been cloudy with a storm blowing in, the quiet might have felt fitting. But under the serene starry sky and budding trees of the first days of spring, the silence was eerie.

Rafi wasn't sure what he could accomplish. The townsfolk already knew as much as anyone else did. Fae messengers had arrived here before him, verifying Ula Kana's identity, and the citizens were following Mayor Wei's advice to hole up in their homes with as many protective spells as they could muster.

He heard a thump and looked up to see an apartment window shutter get slammed and locked. A few people were on the rooftops, too, wading among foliage and casting spells on the building's exterior, or just standing sentinel, squinting into the sky.

He glanced down the alley toward the Bazaar as he passed it, but all its stalls and awnings were folded up or whisked away. Scraps of wrappers and posters blew around on the ground in the lonely beam of a streetlight.

As Rafi reached the street bordering Gusu Park, Tash wandered out of the woods. They stopped in front of each other.

"Looking for your father?" she said.

"Crossed my mind that he and his haunt might take advantage of a mood like this. Offer 'protection' to humans, when in truth they're preparing a welcome party for Ula Kana."

She huffed in agreement. Her gaze flicked to his coat pockets as if she guessed at—or could sense—the cuff tucked into one of them. But she didn't remark on it. "If she does come this way, they'll do something idiotic. That's easy to predict."

"Shouldn't you be keeping out of sight?" he said. "Sounds like she's nabbing any fae she fancies and swaying them to do her bidding."

"I'm not powerful enough to interest her. But I might be able to save a human or two if I'm around. Worry about yourself. You're the mortal one here, and Ula Kana never agreed to your mother's deal preventing other fae from killing you. She could even sway you a little, since you're half fae."

"I doubt I'm powerful enough to interest her either." He scanned the night sky, a check that had become habit in the last few hours. "How will they stop her?"

"That's a task for stronger folk than us. Our job is to keep people safe." She kicked his boot. "So keep yourself safe, all right? Please."

"Please" wasn't a term that came easily to Tash or any shellycoat—laidback, mischievous folk that they were—and it came out stilted, but all the sweeter for it.

"I'll try," he promised. "Maybe she won't even come this direction at all. We're not a big influential city like Dasdemir, why bother?"

"So I hope." But her gaze, too, lifted to the sky.

CHAPTER 27

RAFI HAD JUST BEEN BY IZZY AND JOVE'S house to check on the neighborhood—all was quiet, as it was almost 4:00 a.m.—when the rumbling began.

He could usually tell the difference between a proper earthquake and the ground-rattling of the korreds, and this felt like the latter. He ran to the footpath and pushed his powers into camouflage, melting into the shadows beneath a looming bush. The shaking increased, and fiery gleams flared in the forest.

He had begun to believe nothing would happen. They'd found Prince Larkin, the news said. That seemed like a turn toward order again. But now, in the space of a minute, it *was* happening.

The korreds swarmed out, shaking the bedrock. Above the treetops, half a dozen fire fae blazed across the sky. Not folk from Kepelo's haunt, though at least one was a djinn and one a drake. Their wings were red as coals, their bodies the white-hot of meteors. In the cool March night, the sulfurous-smelling heat rolling off them was a shock.

The faery in the center was the largest, her burning-white glow so bright it stung his eyes. She was long and thin, her hands soot-black, her legs like tendrils of fire, and her face just enough like a human's to chill him with the uncanny wrongness of its perfection. Her gaze moved along the path, right past him, and he glimpsed the fluctuating red cinder glow in her eyes and mouth.

Ula Kana was precisely as she had been described all these years. Potent and terrifying.

He had the crowd of korreds and the darkness to thank for her not noticing him, he supposed. He held as still as he could.

Ula Kana wheeled around to hover over the korreds, who had spilled onto the footpath. It looked to be the entire haunt, as well as the more irascible of the other fae who hung about Sminu's territory. Thank the gods Mukut had been banished and wasn't here. Rafi couldn't have borne it, seeing her gentle strength seized by Ula Kana and turned toward destruction.

"Shall we make it ours?" Sminu called up to her.

Ula Kana's laugh was like flames whooshing high in a gust of wind. "I do not even have to ensnare you to convince you. You're so very willing. But of course. It should all belong to us." She turned, stretching her white arm toward the town. "Take it."

Their roar fractured the night. Windows had already been lighting up in the nearby houses when the ground began shaking, and now Rafi heard voices, too, shouting in warning.

The korreds poured forward and spread like hatching spiders across the path, gardens, walls, and rooftops. The ground flung itself upward and dropped down in erratic jolts. Rafi scrambled over the stone wall into Izzy and Jove's garden. Stumbling on the erupting ground, he sprinted past the cottage and into the courtyard, intent on breaking in if necessary to rescue the three of them. He almost collided with Jove, who burst into the courtyard wielding an iron-coated baseball bat, which he lowered in surprise when he recognized Rafi.

Izzy and Oni ran in, clutching iron chains. They all wore sleeping attire—T-shirts, soft trousers, and bare feet. The four of them stared at each other as the earth trembled and shrieks filled the air. The sky lit up like fireworks had been launched. Ula Kana and her contingent flew across the square of sky above the courtyard, vanishing in another second.

"Oh sweet gods," Izzy breathed.

Breaking stone snapped. A crack raced up the house's wall. A stone statue tumbled off the roof and smashed on the courtyard pavers.

"Out!" Rafi and Jove yelled at the same time, and they all rushed into the back garden.

The garden had already become almost unrecognizable. The trees were wild, unruly, their branches longer, their roots pushing above ground and making a maze of tripping hazards. The bushes and ground covers were tangling together to block what had been paths a minute ago. Even as Rafi watched, in the light of the yellow crescent moon, jasmine vines crawled across the roof of the cottage, covering every tile until he saw nothing but leaf.

Something curled around his leg. He jerked it away and found it was the vinca from the garden bed, extending tendrils and expanding its little empire.

"What the hell?" Jove said.

The building groaned. A root thrust up at the corner of the house, sending another web of cracks across the stone. A thickening wisteria vine crept around the side, squeezing the wall. Flakes of masonry crumbled, falling to disappear in the burgeoning greenery on the ground. A chimney toppled, bricks bouncing away on all sides.

"Our house," Oni said in a whimper.

"You folks okay?" Their neighbor was standing on the wall between properties, waving a flashlight.

They hurried over, picking their way through the tangle, and climbed onto the wall, a wobbling raft held up by the rising sea of plants. "Are there korreds around?" Jove asked.

"A few ran across our roof," the woman said, "then they all took off toward town. I think they're invading."

They looked downhill, toward Miryoku, but roofs and trees blocked their view—especially trees, which were stretching to occupy more space. The flashing gleams of Ula Kana and her minions darted like meteors over the town. Shouts and alarms rose up from one quarter after another.

The alarm bells and sirens, in each case, were silenced in under a minute. The city lights were going out, too, one after another.

The human screams and shouts continued.

"They set the plants growing," Rafi said. "That alone could take over the town in no time."

The story he had invented and told to the korreds as a child: *The trees who stretch their roots and branches all through the buildings so Miryoku becomes an earth fae town—ruled by us!*

He hadn't meant *this*. Not ever.

"Couldn't your mother stop it?" Izzy asked Rafi. "She's more powerful than Sminu. I know she doesn't like to intervene, but wouldn't she now?"

"I...think so, but she can't." Rafi gestured toward the dots of fire in the sky. "Ula Kana would target her, sway her. Turn her toward destroying things.

My mother's in hiding until Ula Kana leaves, for that reason."

"Town's going to be destroyed soon anyway, at this rate," Jove said. "So I guess we just stand here and watch?"

Oni was crying silently, the tears glimmering on her face in the moonlight. "What if they come back this way? What do we do?"

Rafi wanted to say he'd stay, defend them till his last breath. But he didn't think the notion of anyone's last breath would be of much reassurance to her, not to mention he had little skill as a defender, against such fae.

"People will come help," Jove said. "From other towns. They'll be finding out any minute about this. The whole country'll know."

"If it's not happening everywhere else too," the neighbor said dubiously.

Rafi yanked out his phone, but it wasn't getting a signal.

After he tapped at it futilely for a minute, Izzy noticed and said, "They probably knocked out the cell towers."

"Right." Rafi lowered his phone. "Sminu's clever enough to start with that. Probably learned about it from his human buddies."

"So no fae can help?" Oni said. "Because she might sway them?"

"She can't sway everyone at once," Rafi said. "I know Tash is still out there. Probably plenty of others too. And Kepelo has sentinels posted. They'll tell her what's happening. She'll come as soon as Ula Kana leaves."

If Ula Kana did leave. He expected they all thought of it: the possibility of her making Miryoku her new post, her conquered headquarters.

The gleams in the sky flitted back and forth as if gleefully directing the town's destruction. With Rafi's father as head of the demolition crew.

On the outside of his coat pocket, his hand found the shape of the iron cuff.

He turned to his friends. "Get your neighbors together and stay in a group. Keep all the iron and spells around you that you can, and go wherever seems safest. Kepelo's haunt will help you as soon as they're able." He looked out again at the town, the remaining streetlights now a few sparse buoys in a sea of forest.

"Where are you going?" Izzy asked.

"Rafi, stay," Oni pleaded.

Rafi stepped over to her on the uneven wall and hugged her. "I can be fast, and I can blend in," he assured her. "I need to go out and help."

As he withdrew, he let his gaze catch on Jove's and then Izzy's, and he knew they heard his unspoken addition. *I need to stop my father.*

⁓

In the time when Rafi lived in the cottage, Oni had taught him to play some video games. They were vintage, she said, simpler ones, a good beginning for someone who wasn't raised with technology.

As he made his way across the rapidly changing Miryoku, he felt like he was in one of those games, except involving far more visceral panic. Leaping on and off walls and sidewalks that were in the process of crumbling. Dodging branches and putting on fire speed to vault over thorn thickets and piles of debris. Diving into the shadows and going camouflaged when a faery streaked overhead. Pausing when he heard cries for help, and using a burst of endo-witch strength to wrench aside the branches or vines that held someone captive. Carrying the wounded to another human to be looked after. Then racing onward, onward, to find his father.

The collapsing structures, at least, weren't likely to crush anyone. National building code required that houses and other buildings be enspelled so falling debris would sense a human beneath it and freeze in place. The spell wouldn't hold forever, just a few hours or so, but he prayed it would be long enough that people nearby would rescue the trapped. For there had to be so many, far more than he was able to find and pull out on his scramble across town.

He would have said he knew Miryoku's layout as well as he knew the chords of Meloncollie's ten most-played songs. But it was bewilderingly hard to decipher where he was when the majority of the lights were out and the buildings and streets were disappearing under layers of plants. Only the tallest landmarks remained to orient him. The pale spire of the temple near Ti Falls Park. The great rock of the Grotto. And there—lit up by the flashes of fire, witch spells, and weapons—the colorful facades of the five-story buildings along Dragon Street, at the center of town, near Dragonfish River.

Rafi got there via the bridge, which was already close to being flooded. Clearly some water fae had been swayed, too, or had decided to take part in the mischief of their own volition. The river spilled over its banks and was sending a sheet of water across the end of Dragon Street. It splashed over the toes of his boots as he ran toward the commotion.

Korreds climbed buildings, leaped out of windows with stolen prizes, sent vines snarling around every lamppost and railing. The town hall, which housed the mayor's office, was in the middle of the block. Sminu stood on its grand stairs, in the cold glare of one emergency light that remained on. Red light flickered from the glow of a djinn bobbing overhead.

Infusing his skin with camouflage, Rafi flattened his back against the building nearest the river. This street was in better shape than most he had seen on the way. The pavement was as cracked as a jigsaw puzzle, and arms of greenery embraced the structures, but you could still walk through, still recognize everything.

"Yes, keep some of these intact, friends," Sminu called. "Such fine, large creations. So many rooms. A delight for us to play in, and our human haunt-mates will appreciate having familiar spots to live."

"These aren't yours to take, haunt leader Sminu," called a resonant voice. "And we will not be your haunt-mates." Amaris Wei emerged from the shadows of a small park directly opposite the town hall and stepped up onto a bench above the knee-high greenery. "No human made any deal with you for this."

Though she wore a sweatshirt, baggy trousers, and running shoes, since likely she, too, had just scrambled out of bed, she held herself with as regal a bearing as ever. Rafi didn't see Roxana's father, but a slim selkie in human form bobbed anxiously around the bench—one of Amaris's staff. Rafi had seen him at her speeches, organizing folders and podiums. "Mayor Wei, please come down," the selkie begged. "Please, let's get you to safety."

Amaris ignored him, as did Sminu, who opened his arms in greeting and said, "Human town leader Amaris Wei! I've wished to speak to you. But it doesn't matter now. Ula Kana convinced me I could take a different path toward gaining what I want."

"What deal may I offer?" Amaris said. "To stop this, to send you back behind the verge?"

Rafi started forward in alarm—Roxana would be devastated if her mother made some self-sacrificial deal with the korreds—but a cool hand grabbed his arm and held him in place.

"No," Tash said quietly. "Stay hidden."

She had likely come up via the river, which was surging higher now. A chunk of road, at the ragged edge of the bank, broke off and tumbled into the current.

"The verge," Sminu answered Amaris, "is already shifting. Can't you tell? *Our* magic floods this town now."

"A temporary situation," Amaris said. "One that will not be supported by most of the fae."

"Amaris," her aide begged, looking from the river to the djinn above. "Please, it isn't safe for you here. I can take you across the river."

"Your cowering friend seems wiser than you," Sminu said.

Amaris folded her arms. "I'm staying. This town elected me to watch over it, and that's what I'll do."

Sminu sauntered down the stairs and crossed the street.

Rafi tensed, pulling out the cuff. Tash gripped his arm harder in warning.

"By all means." Sminu reached the bench, laid his hand on Amaris's foot, and smiled up at her. "Stand there for centuries, if you wish."

Rafi's breath sucked inward, jagged, even before he saw it happen. He knew, his abused body knew, how terrible Sminu's actions would be. With a burst of strength he yanked his arm out of Tash's grip and ran toward Amaris.

But he couldn't stop it.

Amaris stared at Sminu, her eyes widening. Her face and limbs stiffened. Thickened. Turned reddish-brown and gray. Sminu withdrew his hand with a laugh and wandered back to watch.

She grew downward through the bench, shattering it. Her clothes tore into shreds that fell into the bushes. Branches unfurled and stretched, scaly green needles sprouting at their tips, spreading into wide fronds. Up and up and up the redwood grew, shooting into the night sky.

The djinn bellowed in excitement and darted away, probably to spread the news.

Amaris's aide staggered backward into the shrubs, gaping at the massive tree.

Rafi stopped near Sminu. "Reverse it," he told his father. "Put her back the way she was."

"Oh, you *are* around! I wondered if you'd died yet. No. No, I don't think I will reverse it. She was annoying, always talking about us in such a lofty fashion. Now she can *be* lofty, but without talking. It's funny, don't you think?"

Rafi lunged toward his father, the cuff open, its talons ready to grab.

But Tash's cold arm locked around him and yanked him backward. A red light glimmered close to him, in the air. He twisted to look at her, and his outrage turned to horror. Tash's eyes were distant, impassive. One end of a thread of fire touched her forehead. The other end, he found when he traced it up into the sky, radiated from Ula Kana's fingertip.

She hovered six or seven feet above, close enough that her heat rippled the air. Her face was like a glimpse into an active volcano, the depths of her mouth glowing in all the colors of fire.

"Not much of a prize, this one," Ula Kana said, her voice crackling. "But she can do her part. Sminu, who is this half-breed?"

"My offspring, unfortunately. And what!" Sminu pulled Rafi's hand closer to examine the cuff. "*You* have it? It was you after all?" He looked at Rafi with what almost seemed admiration.

Writhing in Tash's hold, Rafi said, "Try wearing it. See if you're stronger than Brogyo."

"But what does it do? I expect it's more than just the pain of the iron."

"Put it on and see. Kepelo wore it. She was fine. Oof." Tash had added her other arm to the lock and squeezed him around the stomach, expelling the air from his lungs.

The pavement lurched. Cold water spilled around his ankles, rushing over the roots of the giant island redwood that Amaris Wei had become. Her aide hid behind the trunk, becoming a silver shimmer, trying to keep out of Ula Kana's sight.

"Hmm." Sminu tugged the cuff from him, holding it by its exterior, and sniffed it. "Perhaps someday. But at the moment I can think of a better use for it."

He shoved up Rafi's coat sleeve and clapped the cuff around his arm.

Agony exploded through Rafi's body and soul. His skin scabbed over with stone, a useless defense that did nothing but freeze him in place, doubled over. Through the sparks in his vision and the rush in his ears, he witnessed the unfolding nightmare, which now seemed a hundred times worse.

Ula Kana exclaimed in pleasure. Tash let go of Rafi and observed him with indifference. The floodwaters rushed over the end of the street. The redwood had become a hundred feet tall or more, its branches shoving against the sides of the buildings.

Amaris.

Roxana would never forgive him.

"What *does* it do, then?" Sminu asked, curious.

"Causes remorse," Tash said coolly. "Guilt for all the harm one has caused."

"Ah! Well then, you see, Akurafi?" Sminu's voice was pitying. "See what your interference did? Your attempts to toy with such matters? It only hurt you, in the end."

Rafi had hurt so many others too. He saw it now, with clarity brighter than Ula Kana's meteoric glow. His actions had damaged lives—even helped bring *this* about, the destruction of Miryoku. He had escalated hostilities, amped up the antagonism between fae and humans. He had worked up the korreds to a covetous frenzy by his stories, his very existence, then he had stoked them into a fury through his insults.

Hazel's words echoed in his skull: *Follow your love instead.* He hadn't listened. He could have left this mess behind long ago, followed Roxana. Instead he had stayed and made everything worse. Because he was cowardly and spiteful, no better than his father.

"You were going to use this charm on me?" Sminu shoved Rafi to the ground. "This, which pushed Brogyo all the way to regeneration? You aimed to get rid of me!"

Rafi had landed on all fours, his skin stone, his form hunching into gargoyle shape. Cold river water rushed past an inch below his nose as he hung his head, gasping in pain. The stone had sealed the cuff to his body.

He didn't try to change back to soft skin, didn't try to remove the cuff. He deserved this fate. This had always been how it would end, once he had set into motion the making of this wicked thing. He saw that now. Worse still, he had induced the generous, kind Roxana to make it: another crime weighing down his soul.

"A fitting end for him." The hissing voice, the ripple of heat, could only be Ula Kana. "Let us explore what other fun the night holds for us, shall we? Oh! A selkie. There." A sizzle seared through the air. "You can help me as well. See that this flood continues doing its good work. You, little shellycoat, do the same. Come, Sminu!"

The heat vanished with a sound like a torch whipping through the air. Rafi's body shook with nauseating spasms. When he tried to suck in his next breath, the water surged and shot up his nostrils, and he could only cough.

He assumed Sminu left with Ula Kana, and Tash and the selkie departed to wreak havoc with the river. With his eyes shut and his body immobilized, he didn't know.

But then his father said, just a few inches from his ear, "Know that this gives me no pleasure, Akurafi. You are of my creation. But you and I do nothing but antagonize one another, and I am done with my hopes and disappointments when it comes to you. Return to the Spirit, human child."

He sounded more solemn than angry.

Then a foot as strong as a rolling boulder shoved Rafi's rigid body and sent him tumbling into the river.

His limbs tried, feebly and instinctively, to move again, to anchor himself on whatever solid earth they could. But as soon as one of his clawed front paws caught at a broken edge of pavement, the piece crumbled. He fell. Deep into the rushing water, down the steep slope of the riverbank. Bumping underwater against weed and mud and moving creatures and bruising chunks of debris. The chaotic noise disappeared into a peaceful sphere of sounds muted by water.

He couldn't breathe, of course. Even at the best of times, he couldn't use his magic to forge gills for himself. That was a rare ability, not one of his. He could, at most, expand his lung capacity a few extra minutes. But now, thanks to the cuff, his magic was nothing but a weak flicker.

Drowning would be fast. The misery would be over. He would, perhaps, be able to linger as a ghost and tell his mother goodbye. And if he couldn't stay long, Kepelo could pass along his message of love to his friends. To Roxana.

He would see his grandmother again. Maybe. He'd find out soon.

He released the last of his air in a stream of bubbles and sank to the bottom. The current was gentler here. Heavy with stone, his body settled into the mud.

He wouldn't have lasted long even above water. This pain would have blacked him out any minute, and then before long something or other would have killed him. It didn't matter. He didn't matter.

He let his lungs try automatically to take their next breath, and wasn't surprised when he slipped into unconsciousness. He was only a little bit surprised it didn't hurt as much as he expected.

See you soon, Lao Lao.

CHAPTER 28

*I*t's been a few hours. Are you there? Sorry to be *paranoid.*

It was 4:40 a.m., but Roxana still hoped to sleep. A couple hours if nothing else. She had all notifications turned off except Rafi's, and she wasn't daring to look at social media or news—that was a direct road to insomnia.

But he hadn't checked in as he'd promised.

His phone had probably died. These days he relied on a solar charger to juice it up, and it could have easily run out by this hour. She shoved the phone under her pillow, shut her eyes, and tried to meditate, at least, if she couldn't sleep.

A repeated buzzing shook the pillow. Her heart rocketed up against her ribs. She grabbed the phone. Another emergency alert, one programmed to cut through everyone's do-not-disturb settings:

!! NATIONWIDE ALERT !! The town of Miryoku has been attacked by Ula Kana and other fae. Local evacuation is underway. The Great Eidolonian Highway near Miryoku is currently impassable—please plan an alternate route or postpone your travel. Phone and internet communications with the Miryoku region are inoperable at the moment. Please remain in a safe location and await further news.

She had her hand pressed to her chest as if to aid her lungs in functioning. Her breaths were tiny, sharp movements.

No, she thought. Only that one word, a simple yet colossal plea to the gods. *No.*

Rafi. Satsuki. Mom. Dad. Her home. The parks. The cottage. Oni, Jove, Izzy…

Ester's footsteps pounded down the hall. Her daughter hurtled onto Roxana's bed, holding her phone, her face rewritten with panic. "Mom!"

Roxana embraced her. "Maybe it's just a couple of buildings, like with

Dasdemir. And the cell towers. They didn't say. We shouldn't assume the worst."

They took her laptop to the kitchen and started boiling water for tea. But the news coverage, when they found the live stream, confirmed it was far worse than a couple of buildings.

From an air surrey in the pink light of sunrise, a camera panned over Miryoku. Or what was left of it. It was...forest. Thick forest, like the fae realm. With just a few bits of building and bridge peeking through. She didn't even recognize anything until spotting the temple spire above the leaves, then a glimpse of the red-painted Aria Creek footbridge, then the big white M in enchanted ever-blooming flowers next to the highway exit.

Her body felt hollow, scraped out from the inside.

"Oh my gods," Ester whimpered.

Thousands of people milled at the western edge of town, spreading across the roads and highway and into the fields beyond, several lying on the ground, injured and being tended to. From the height of the air surrey, Roxana couldn't recognize any.

Didn't try too hard. Didn't want to.

The flashing lights of emergency vehicles and medic-witches surrounded the devastation, and an occasional blur of magic swept above the treetops, a ripple of orange. Probably one of Kepelo's fire folk. Had it been Ula Kana or anyone in her entourage, the air surrey pilot would have been veering away in hasty retreat.

"We're hearing from the witnesses what happened," the reporter said in voice-over. "In the early morning hours..."

They sat in clammy fear-sweat and listened. Ula Kana had instigated the local fae, korreds mostly, into action, and they had set the plants to growing and engulfing the buildings. Dragonfish River flooded its banks, too, for a short time. Everyone was still trying to account for all the known citizens, a task that would take all day at least, but five deaths were reported so far. (Roxana started weeping. Ester too.) At the start of the attack, the border guards on the two verge stations nearest Miryoku had radioed distress signals before being quickly cut off. They were still unaccounted for.

Sminu, the reporters said, had evidently assumed Ula Kana and her powerful followers would stay to help him hold the territory he had gained, but after a short time she had flown away, back into the mountains. Kepelo had then swept in with the folk of her haunt to stop the korreds' actions. By sunrise all the korreds had fled into the fae realm, and Kepelo had claimed the former town as hers to discourage their return. They and the witches attempting to slow the manic growth of the forest, however, were not achieving complete success. Miryoku was being swallowed by not only its signature vines of jasmine but by honeysuckle, climbing roses, brambles, all manner of trees, and innumerable other plants.

The cell towers and electrical grid were destroyed. Traffic on the remaining roads had come to a standstill, thousands trying to leave while others rushed in to assist. Friends and relatives of those in the area were asked to please remain home and wait a little longer for communications to be restored.

Roxana gripped Ester's hand on the table. "All those people they're showing, they're okay. Chances are really good that Oni and Nana and Papa and Rafi and everyone are fine. We'll wait, okay?"

She called Ester's school and excused her from attending, and sent an email to her own professors, too, explaining she had to stay home and wait for news of her family. Everyone was kind and concerned. They understood.

Ester and Roxana did nothing for a while but pace around the apartment and stare at the news.

"Answer," Ester wailed at her phone in midmorning, after presumably sending yet another text to Oni.

Roxana hugged her. The hot tears on Ester's face dampened Roxana's cheek. "It'll be okay."

"We should go there. We should leave."

"We'd just get stuck in traffic and get in the way. They'll contact us when they can."

Roxana, of course, had tried sending messages too. To Rafi, Satsuki, and her parents all at once. She even added Tash, Jove, Izzy, and Oni to the group text. *We can't believe what's happening. Please let us know asap that you're all right. All we're doing is watching news.*

As if they wouldn't contact her right away. As if they'd have a working phone connection and just let everyone worry.

The hours dragged. Ester lay on the carpet and screamed that this was the longest day of her life and she couldn't stand it. Roxana would have done and said the same, if not for the requirement that she be the adult in the room.

Finally, a little after 4:00 in the afternoon, Roxana's phone buzzed.

"Satsuki," she said on a gust of breath.

Oh sweetheart. A rescuer witch finally hacked a hotspot and is giving us turns using it. I'm OK and I've seen Izzy's family, they're all right too. Don't know yet about Rafi and Tash, no one's sure where they are. But your mother. Amaris got turned into a giant redwood by Sminu. She's still in that form. Your dad's OK, he's with her. But Kepelo says it can only be undone by Sminu, if at all, or maybe another korred, and the korreds all ran away like fucking cowards. She has drakes out hunting for him in the mountains.

Ester was reading over her arm. "Nana? *What?*"

Numb all over, Roxana typed back:

Lord and Lady. Thank you, so glad to hear from you. OK I have to get down there. Tonight.

Technically I'm supposed to tell you not to come, but I know I can't stop you, Satsuki said. *Plus I want to see you!*

You too. No idea about Rafi? No leads?

Jove said he went out early on to rescue people. It's totally possible he's still doing that and his phone fell out or got broken. He knows what he's doing when it comes to wilderness and korreds.

Yet Sminu had a way of wrecking all of Rafi's better judgment. And even if Rafi could handle korreds, no one could handle Ula Kana.

One hour at a time. That was all Roxana could process. In this hour, she had bags to pack.

We're on our way. Let me know if you find out anything else. Love you.

❧

They were on the highway in under an hour. The sun sank into a murky sea mist, staining it red. There weren't many drivers this far north, at least. The Great Eidolonian Highway stretched ahead with only a few other cars in sight.

Night had fallen, and the traffic hadn't increased much, by the time they reached the Amizade Bridge, its lights gleaming through the fog.

As Roxana drove onto the bridge, mist curdled in her headlights, drifting like ghosts over the roadway. "Gods, the fog's thick. Almost like smoke. I can barely see."

Ester shuddered, the green dash lights illuminating her face. "It's creepy."

They reached the southern end, their tires' cadence transitioning from the taps of the bridge road to the solidity of the highway. Something flashed in the darkness, in the edge of Roxana's peripheral vision.

"Was that—" Ester started to say.

Creaking, crashing, squealing, thundering. Fire streaked across the rear-view mirror. The bridge's lights swayed and winked out. "Holy sh—" Roxana pulled over so fast the car fishtailed on the roadside gravel, and she yanked the parking brake.

They both twisted in their seats to look through the back window.

The bridge, towers and road surface and pilings and all, was buckling and collapsing into the ravine, lit by a hot yellow glow from beneath. Roxana got out to stare, mouth open, horror like a blade in her chest. Ester got out, too, and raised her phone to take a video, but her arms were shaking and she was gasping quick breaths. Heat rolled down the highway and across their bodies, the temperature jumping twenty degrees in a second. A car tumbled off the edge on the far side of the ravine, its headlights disappearing into the inferno.

Roxana shut her eyes, covered her mouth.

I just watched someone die. I just stopped my car so my daughter could watch someone die. Spirit be with them. Gods help us.

She spun toward the car. "Ester, get in."

Streaks of pale orange seared along the ravine, back toward the fae realm, the one in the middle the brightest. Pausing at their open car doors, Ester and Roxana watched them vanish into the forest, then looked at each other.

"Did we just fucking see Ula Kana?" Ester said.

"I think so." Roxana dropped into the car and shut the door, all her limbs trembling. "Call emergency services. Tell them what we saw. They probably already know, but...just to be sure." She shifted the car into gear and shoved down on the gas pedal. "I'm getting us away from here."

Within ten minutes, the bridge collapse sent another nationwide alert splashing across their phones. Ester, wiping away tears while spitting swear words, thumbed text messages to their friends in Miryoku to let them know they were safe. No answer came.

As they got near the town, their cell phone coverage dwindled and then dropped out. Traffic slowed. None of the usual city lights sparkled on the hillside. Just dark trees, fae glow, and, lower down, the harsh gleam of emergency floodlights. Police directed traffic, routing everyone onto a detour around the broken highway.

Roxana lowered her window and told the officer, "I'm Roxana Wei. My mother is the mayor of Miryoku. We need to get in. Please."

The officer paused, then directed her to squeeze her car between two supply trucks parked on the shoulder. "Most of the folks are in the fields over there."

Roxana and Ester parked, jumped out, and followed the voices and bright lights. It was a surreal, dreadful scene: a hay field and a strawberry field now filled with tents, makeshift shelters, medic-witch stations, piles of possessions, anxious pets (there was the alpaca family, tethered to a stake), and the entire population of Miryoku.

Minus those dead or missing.

Satsuki spotted them first, running forward with a shriek and squeezing each of them in a hug. She had her hair in a bedraggled bun and was wearing a muddy bathrobe and rain boots.

"I'm so glad you made it. I've got to help sort out supplies, but first I'll take you to Izzy's family."

She brought them to Jove, Izzy, and Oni, who were spreading blankets on the ground under a tarp suspended from trees.

"Oni." Ester's cry was a chorus of joy and misery.

The two girls met in a tangle, sobbing and clinging as if they would never again be separated.

I won't ever make you leave her again, Roxana thought, with a wrenching tug at her heart, and looked up at the looming wilderness where her hometown should be. Somewhere in it was her own lover. It felt unbearably desolate, being apart from him at this moment.

She hugged Izzy and Jove and learned they had gotten out of their neighborhood and hightailed it for the fields not long after the destruction began.

"And Rafi?" Roxana asked. "Any news?"

Jove shook his head. He had leaf stains smudging his clothes, and mud to the ankles, as did nearly everyone. "But I bet you anything he's either crawling through all that, looking for people to rescue, or hunting down his father. We all want the bastard brought to justice, but no one wants it more than Rafi."

"Tash is probably doing the same," Izzy added. "We haven't seen her since last night either, but I know she'd want in on both those things."

Roxana turned to the dark woods. "Then I should find my dad. He's probably with my mom." Her voice broke on the word.

Izzy laid her hand on Roxana's arm. "I'll take you."

Ester came too, as did Oni—the two were adamant about keeping together.

The overgrowth had stopped at the edge of town, where the fields began. A barrier of greenery stood before them, a bit of iron fencing and a house wall visible between branches. Will-o'-the-wisps and sprites perched overhead, lighting the way and keeping watch.

"It's all Kepelo's territory now, officially," Izzy said. "Sminu took it over briefly, then Kepelo took it over from him. Her folk are letting people in." She edged between a bush and a fence.

"So this is the verge now?" Ester asked. "Are we crossing the verge?" She pushed through, pulling Oni by the hand.

"Technically," Oni said. "But they say the enchantment damage isn't really a danger here yet. Neither is the time difference. Because it was only recently overtaken. Well. Retaken."

Retaken. It was a good reminder, Roxana thought as she picked her way down paths and sidewalks that were barely even paths and sidewalks anymore. They were crisscrossed with branches, heavy with buds, and laid with vine snares at ankle level. It smelled like damp forest—it had rained recently—and not at all like a town. But Miryoku, eternal though it had seemed to her, had only stood here a couple of centuries. For millennia before that, it had been this: pure nature, fae territory. Might it soften her trauma to view it as retaking, a return to a natural state, rather than invasion?

Perhaps, when it came to buildings and roads. But the giant island red-wood towering over Dragon Street was not Amaris Wei's natural state.

Standing before it, Roxana actually laughed a little. Out of hysteria and disbelief. How was this her mother? This was a massive tree, thousands of times bigger than Amaris.

"No," Ester said, beside her, sounding similarly skeptical and wretched.

Two people sat in the ridges of its huge roots. Kepelo, in human form but emitting a candlelike glow from her whole being, had one hand on the trunk and was looking up at the tree solemnly. And Roxana's father, with his knees pulled up, was resting the side of his head against the trunk and stroking one of the roots with his hand.

Roxana had seen him recline on the couch with Amaris in just that position, their heads tipped together, his hand stroking her leg.

"Dad." She and Ester climbed the mound of roots toward him.

Timo's face brightened. "Hey! My girls, my honeys. I'm so glad you're here." They met in a three-way hug.

He turned toward Kepelo. "This fine faery neighbor has been keeping an eye on her. It's most kind of you," he added, to Kepelo.

Rafi's mother rose. Roxana had only ever seen her at festivals, years ago, and had never spoken to her. She had a confused moment of feeling flustered to meet her lover's parent—especially in circumstances where she might not be making the best impression.

But Kepelo laid her hand on her heart and greeted, "Roxana, Ester. It's an honor to greet you. I don't have language enough to express how it pains me that my fellow fae caused this destruction to your homes, your kin."

"It's an honor to meet you as well." Roxana dipped her head in acknowledgment. "Thank you so much for taking control of the situation. How is she?" Her gaze climbed to the redwood.

Kepelo looked up at the branches. "Earth is not my element, of course. I can tell she's alive and stable, a living tree. Her curse, however, is a korred curse, and only the one who cast it should try to reverse it. If I or any other tried, I would fear for her well-being. Even her life."

"Sminu," Ester said, teeth clenched.

"Yes. The korreds scattered as soon as they realized Ula Kana was leaving and that they would not be able to hold this territory against me. Given they can become rocks, there are all too many places they might effectively hide in the cliffs and mountains. My folk are out hunting them."

"Nana will live even if it takes a while to find them, though?" Ester asked.

"I see no reason why not. She's thriving and strong."

"No one saw it happen, besides Sminu?" Roxana asked.

"No one we've found," Kepelo said. "I knew it was Amaris only by detecting the spell, and because one of my djinns overheard one of Ula Kana's, crowing that it had been done."

"Her aide was with her." Timo looked off into the former park, now taken up by the tree's branches and dense undergrowth. "Selkie. Poor fellow. He got swayed. I hear he drowned someone while he was under her spell. Then fled out to the ocean when he came back to himself, because he couldn't take the horror of what he'd done." His shoulders bowed. "He was a good kid."

So that was one of the known deaths. Roxana's aching heart didn't allow her to ask for details of the others yet. "And Rafi? Does anyone from your haunt know where he is?"

Kepelo's wings sank. "No. I confess, I hoped he had somehow gone to you, and by finding you, we might find him."

Roxana shook her head and looked down. The long day was becoming too heavy a weight to bear.

"My folk are also looking for survivors in the town," Kepelo said. "As well as...any who didn't survive. They know to tell me at once if they find him."

"I'll look too," Roxana said, but her legs felt weak, and darkness permeated every direction she looked, outside the soft fire of Kepelo's form and the few sparks of fae in the treetops.

"Tomorrow, when it's light." Izzy laid a hand on Roxana's back. "I'll look with you. Kepelo's folk will search during the night. We humans need to sleep or we won't be any use."

Roxana nodded, hating that truth, though she couldn't rightfully contradict it. She took her father's hand. "Coming to the field with us, Dad?"

He shook his head, sinking back down to sit between two gigantic roots. "I'll make my bed here, thank you, honey."

"Then I will too," she said.

CHAPTER 29

ESTER CHOSE TO SLEEP BESIDE ONI, IN THE shelter Izzy's family had set up. Roxana acquired blankets from one of the supply stashes the refugees had put together, along with two sweatshirts that could be rolled up and used as pillows. People had dragged out all the barrels and troughs they could find and collected creek water and rainwater, and matter-witches had treated it with spells to make it safe for drinking. Roxana refilled the water bottles from her car and brought out the food she had packed, ensuring Timo had something to eat for the night.

In the fields, she picked up hearsay of news from Dasdemir that people had seen on their limited time on the comm hotspot: someone had absconded with Prince Larkin. Picked him up off a palace balcony and flew him out into the foggy night. This rescuer was able to fly, it would seem. Now an all-points-bulletin was out for the both of them, prince and flying friend, who was reputedly a distant relative of Rosamund Highvalley—the witch who had engineered Larkin's enchanted sleep in 1799. It all sounded insane. Everyone was abloom with speculation and conspiracy theories.

Roxana didn't care. The whereabouts of the prince didn't matter anymore and wouldn't change the ruin surrounding her. Her lover was missing, her mother was trapped as a tree, and Ula Kana and Sminu were still out there somewhere, presumably free as the wind.

She lay down near her father. The air was rich with the spice of redwood, the ground lumpy with roots.

So this was her first night in the fae realm. It wasn't what she'd envisioned—which had been a scenario of snuggling with Rafi in some cozy, magically glowing cave or fern bower. Where was he sleeping right now? Or, likelier, where was he lying injured or dead?

In her unsettled half-sleep, dreams flung possibilities at her. He could have been strangled by fast-growing vines. Stabbed through the heart by bamboo. Dragged out to sea by a water faery. Incinerated by lava. Grabbed by a djinn, taken up in the air, and flung down.

Something tickled her ankle, crawling over the skin exposed between her sock and trouser leg. She jolted awake, certain she'd find a goblin or a venomous snake faery hulking there.

A harmless brown caterpillar inched away from her leg and slipped underneath the redwood needles.

She let out a gust of an exhalation and flopped onto her back, looking up at the tree. Her mother. This was unthinkable, impossible. Her eyelids ached, her stomach felt sour, her mind was fried. She kicked off the borrowed blanket, which smelled too strongly of someone else's laundry detergent, and got up. Her father still slept, looking faded and broken in the barely-there light of the moon.

Grief for Rafi pierced her. She staggered away and spent two minutes sobbing into her hands. Then she wiped her eyes, blew her nose on a crumpled handkerchief in her pocket, and huffed in anger.

You are a witch! You may not be fae, nor even a witch of the likes of Rosamund Highvalley, but you have powers that would amaze the majority of humans in the world. This island gifted them to you. Use them!

She plucked a cluster of white orchids that had sprouted against a nearby wall. With an injection of magic, the flowers began glowing with the brightness of the moon. She turned the beautiful thing in her fingers and thanked the elements in a whisper. Then she set off on a walk up Dragon Street with her makeshift lantern. Human voices rumbled out in the fields. Fae murmured and sang.

While she dragged her free hand along the building facades, encountering vines more often than masonry, she kept her senses open for her own spells. There wasn't much else she could sense. She had no tracking or summoning magic. In her classes they had worked on learning to detect individual witches' signatures in enspelled items. Everyone began with their own, as that was the easiest to recognize, and that was still about the limit of Roxana's ability. But it might help.

Rafi would likely have had one of Roxana's charms on him. He owned a few of her calming jewelry pieces by now and wore them often. But they were tiny, their spells gentle, so she'd have to be quite close to sense those.

Then of course there was the iron cuff. That would be easier to detect, as it had heft, and layers upon layers of magic. And he'd probably been carrying it last night.

Please, she asked the powers that be, each of them in turn: earth, air, fire, water, Lord, Lady, Spirit. She went all the way up Dragon Street, turned to go around the block, and had to backtrack when she met an impenetrable wall of thorns. *Please*. No sign of her magic anywhere, nor down the other side of the street, nor on what she could reach of the adjacent block before a thicket of bamboo stopped her.

Deep in the thorns and thickets and ruins was where she *should* look. If Rafi were lying in plain sight in the street, obviously someone would have found him already. Plunging into that wildwood alone in the dark, though, would only lead to her needing rescued next. She'd enter the woods the minute it got light.

She dragged herself back down past her mother's tree to the raw gash the river had cut through town. The flood had been brief but forceful, people said, water fae mischief poured on top of earth fae's riotous forest growth. Everything along the banks had been washed away, including the bridge, leaving a swath of mud and broken road-ends.

The river had subsided back to its usual level and burbled along in deceptive innocence, moonlight dancing on its ripples. Roxana stood on the upper bank and shut her aching eyes, absorbing the soothing sound of water.

And she felt…a tickle of magic. Somber but familiar. Her own spell.

Her eyes flew open. Slipping in mud, she scrambled down the bank to search along the river's edge and beneath the dangling remains of the bridge. She found neither Rafi nor the cuff, but the sensation strengthened. She spun to stare at the other side of the river. It wasn't far, perhaps fifty feet, but trying to swim it at night by herself was even less wise than clambering into the forest. How to get across? Was the next bridge upstream broken too?

As she prowled along the bank, about to start yelling for a drake to come help her, the sensation increased in strength again. She had just reached an eddy, a pool curling into the bank, where the current slowed and the water was deep. The ground was washed bare around it; Rafi clearly wasn't lying there. But…

She dropped to her hands and knees and felt around. The magic got even stronger when she reached into the water to grope in the shallows. Nausea swept over her. It was *in* the river. Underwater.

She dropped the glowing orchid on the bank, tugged off her shoes, and jumped into the pool. It was waist deep at the edge and sloped sharply down in the middle. Gasping at the chill, she waded forward. The cuff was down here, close enough that its spell was now like a fishing line she could follow.

The water rose to her chest, to her neck. The silty bottom sank below her socks.

Either scenario was terrible. If she found only the cuff, she still wouldn't have found Rafi. If she found Rafi…

He couldn't breathe underwater any more than she could. They'd chatted about it in the past, the things their magic could and couldn't do. His form-changing extended only to a bit of fire and a bit of earth. "Water isn't one of mine," he'd said. "Not air either. Can't fly—real shame."

If he was in the water, this was about to become the most traumatic experience of her life. But she had to know.

She took a deep breath and dunked under, folding to her knees, stretching both hands downward.

Her hair drifted around her face. Ethereal gurgles and songs wavered into her submerged ears. Slimy weeds slipped through her fingers. Then her hands crashed against stone—wide, curved like a drake's back. Following it down, heart hammering, she found a stone foot with claws, sunk in the river bottom. Then another limb, and on it, the cuff. Though trapped in the stone skin, it still radiated its sinister magic.

Roxana pulled back, kicked to the surface, gasped in a breath, and with her next breath shouted, "Help! Kepelo, someone! Please!"

Wearing the cuff. He wasn't just carrying it, he was wearing it. Had been for hours and hours. That was how his last moments had been spent, undergoing a torture she herself had engineered.

The next few minutes were confusion. Raw despair and grief. Shouting agonized, mixed-up words to the fire sprite and will-o'-the-wisp who appeared. Their attempts to reach into the water—despite their elemental aversion to it—and then their hasty withdrawal.

"If we touch it, or even him, with that thing's magic on him," the sprite explained, "it'll sap our strength. We won't be able to lift him out."

Roxana shoved back her soaked hair in frustration, feeling like an hourglass was draining away precious time. Though surely those sands had run out long ago. She sloshed back in. "I'll remove it."

"There are fish fae with him," the will-o'-the-wisp added before she could duck under again. "At least one I detected, hanging near." When Roxana froze in horror, the faery amended, "Oh, not eating him. The iron and the spell probably keep them from touching him too. We'll pull you out if you're attacked, don't worry."

Far from reassured, Roxana plunged underwater and felt for the cuff. This was his arm, this rigid stone limb, cold from the river. In its warm human form it had caressed her, held her. Never again.

Keeping the scream trapped in her throat, she poured magic into the cuff, forcing it to let go of him and break itself free. Holding it by its outside surface, she pushed above water and dragged herself onto the bank. On her knees in the mud, she caught her breath. "There," she said. "Bring him up."

The two fire fae lowered gingerly to the water. But the pool broke, spilling in a bubble over the large shape surfacing.

"Oh," the sprite said. "The fish faery has him."

The human-sized water faery had her arms around Rafi's stone body and surged up with him, scales and long weedy hair gleaming in the fire glow. She shoved him onto the bank and hopped up after him, then shifted fully to her human form.

"Tash?" Roxana said, stunned.

Tash looked...shaken, Roxana would have said, though it wasn't a state she'd ever seen on her. "I couldn't grab him until the iron was taken away," Tash said. "Couldn't lift him."

"I know. I'm sorry." Roxana laid a hand on the dripping stone of Rafi's back. Hot tears bathed her eyes. "Thank you for looking for him," she said, her voice broken.

She had to tell Kepelo her son was dead. Begin arranging a funeral. Start taking the staggering steps toward the rest of her life without him.

"I kept air around his head," Tash added. She remained at a distance, sitting with her arms latched around her pulled-up knees, her limbs glimmering with sequins. "Even though I couldn't touch him, I could do that. He's still alive. I think."

Roxana sucked in a sharp breath. "He—what?" She put her cheek in the mud, laying it against the nostrils of his gargoyle snout. Firelight gleamed brighter as the will-o'-the-wisp drew near and touched Rafi's side.

The softest exhalation of warmth blew across her cheek. And the will-o'-the-wisp, perhaps feeling for a heartbeat, said, "Yes, he lives."

"Oh my gods." Roxana's tears ran fresh, now from relief. "Tash—Tash, thank you so much. Thank you—"

"Don't," Tash cut in. She looked away with a flinch. "I was there. Rafi was going to put the cuff on Sminu. Sminu put it on him instead."

Roxana stroked Rafi's neck. Unconscious, but alive. *Alive.* "I figured," she answered Tash. "It's all right. No one expects you to have fought Sminu on your own."

"He caught Rafi because of me." Tash still stared aside, at the river. "Ula Kana snared me. Made me cooperate with her and the korreds. I grabbed Rafi and gave him to Sminu."

Roxana sat up on her knees, shivering in her soaked clothes. "And then you saved his life. None of us will blame you for what Ula Kana forced you to do. And if we're talking about reasons to feel guilty—I *made* this fucking thing of my own free will." She held up the cuff.

Tash acknowledged the remark with a tilt of her head. "It's kind of a terrible fucking thing," she admitted.

"Yeah. Now can we get him up the slope and somewhere dry?"

Face still averted, Tash nodded.

ఐౚఐ

Hypothermia and dehydration: those were Roxana's first thoughts. Since the cuff was off and he still didn't revive, it was likely because he'd spent close to twenty-four hours in a cold river with nothing to eat or drink. If Tash had been keeping the water away from his face, he wouldn't have swallowed any—which was probably just as well, given the enchantment flowing rampant in every local element lately.

Tash and the fire fae laid Rafi down in the shelter of Amaris's vast branches. While the sprite zoomed off to find Kepelo, Tash laid hands on Rafi's sides to infuse his veins with water. Rehydrated, he still didn't awaken.

Timo had gotten up by then, roused by the commotion, and wrapped an arm around Roxana. "Oh, my kiddo. It'll be all right. Come on, let's get you some dry clothes."

As Roxana finished changing into a borrowed sweatshirt and a pair of thermal leggings, the pre-dawn sky brightened abruptly with a bloom of fire. Her chest seized in panic. Ula Kana—lightning striking the palace—Amizade Bridge collapsing in lava—

But the dragonlike faery with wide, spark-trailing wings was Kepelo, in full twenty-foot-tall form. She was an awe-inspiring sight, filling the sky, folding her wings to drop to the ground, landing with light grace despite her immense size and the urgency in her face.

As she strode forward, she diminished and changed until she was back to a six-foot-tall human with scaled limbs and small wings. She knelt by Rafi, spread her arms around him, bent to press her cheek to his stone shell. Her orange glow spilled into the shadows.

Finally she lifted her face. "That charm. It wasn't meant for anyone to wear so long, was it."

Never had shame or regret stabbed Roxana so deeply. She doubted even the cuff could take her lower, were she to put it on. "No," she whispered.

"Brogyo gave up his existence after wearing it just a few hours." Kepelo stroked Rafi's shoulders. "It's what ails him. Enchantment, but also despair. I expect seeing this happen to the town would have brought on such a feeling anyway, but the iron and the spells flung him even deeper."

Roxana hid her face behind her hands a moment. Then she picked up the cuff from where it lay atop her wet clothes and brought it to Kepelo. "I saved it in case having it would help unravel the damage somehow. If it does any good to study its spell…"

Fae were extraordinary at healing living things, on the whole. But magic had its own rules—or, more accurately, a lack of consistent rules. Kepelo underscored this point by holding the cuff, pondering it, and then shaking her head. "The damage it's done to him has become something different. Something part of him. At least for the time being." She glanced up at the redwood, and Roxana thought she understood: it was the same way Amaris had become something different, and the tree had become part of her, or all of her, for the time being.

"Then please destroy it," Roxana said. "Melt it. I don't ever want to see it again."

"No," Tash cut in. "Give it to me. I want Sminu to wear it when he's found."

More attacks, more torture, would hardly help, no matter the victim they chose. But knowing that Sminu had put the cuff on Rafi and kicked him into a river—not to mention had transformed Amaris into a tree—hardened Roxana's heart. She didn't protest when Kepelo handed the cuff to Tash.

Satsuki came running—she'd heard, and she brought an exo-witch healer. Roxana would have traded her matter-witch powers for the rest of her life in order to be one of those now. All she could do was sit by him, holding Satsuki's hand, and wait as the healer—an older person who had near-painlessly removed Roxana's wisdom teeth two decades ago—laid hands on Rafi to give him magic.

Though his skin was currently stone, it didn't respond to Roxana's material skills. She had tried it, in a playful moment during their summer affair, touching a patch of stone on his leg, which he had produced for her entertainment. She'd been unable to make it change color or shape. Told him, "Nope. It's still you."

The exo-witch sat back after a while, sweat beading on their forehead. "It's all I can give for the time being. Healers are in high demand today, and I've got a lot of others to see. Let him rest a bit. I'll try again later."

Kepelo's wings drooped, but she nodded to Roxana. "Rest beside him. It could help, having you there."

Satsuki patted Roxana's hand and murmured agreement.

Roxana touched his rough front paw. "I doubt I'll be able to sleep. Though I'm sure I need to."

"May I?"

And before Roxana could ask *May you what?*, Kepelo's hand touched her head, blazing warm, and in a rush of relaxation, Roxana slid down and fell asleep.

CHAPTER 30

WHEN ROXANA AWOKE, THE SUN WAS SHINing between puffy white clouds. Birds caroled throughout the expanded treetops. Roxana rolled over and took stock.

Oni and Ester were sitting and talking on the steps of the town hall. Her mother was still a giant redwood. The town was still wrapped in vines, looking like the ruins of a lost civilization. Satsuki had left, probably to help others. And Rafi was still stone.

Last night they'd taken off his river-dragged clothes, and the healer had tucked him under a shiny foil emergency blanket. Everything still looked the same. She moved over and rested her cheek against his for a few minutes, feeling the soft, regular humidity of his breath. Breathing was good. Warmth and hydration too. But the breathing and circulation proved he wasn't *suspended* in his enchanted coma, the way Prince Larkin had been, and therefore couldn't survive it indefinitely. A human, even one who was half fae, needed sustenance.

How long before they'd have to take him to a hospital and put him on life support? And would that even hasten his recovery better than healing magic provided by people he loved and trusted?

She unclasped the necklace she wore, a chain with a fox-head pendant, silver and enchanted for courage. Maybe it had helped her keep it together at the river last night. She hadn't even given it a thought at the time. Now she coiled it in her palm and infused it with an extra layer, a spell of hope. Nelleke usually labeled it "optimism" when tagging the jewelry pieces, but Roxana felt the word was too confident for the mental state of most people who would buy such a spell.

She looped the chain around one of the curving spikes that covered the back of Rafi's head like hedgehog bristles. "Come back," she whispered, and kissed him on a smooth plane of stone on his nose. "I love you."

Then she hobbled over to the girls.

Ester jumped up and hugged her. "We'll get them both back," she murmured into Roxana's shoulder.

The lump in Roxana's throat blocked words.

Then Ester pulled out of the embrace. "Guess what? People using the hotspot said Merrick Highvalley, the guy who rescued Prince Larkin, posted a video. He says *he's* the one who woke up Larkin—accidentally, he swears, just by messing with old charms Rosamund Highvalley left behind in their house—and now he and Larkin are going into the fae realm on a quest."

Roxana looked in confusion at Ester, then Oni. "A quest to do what?"

"Stop Ula Kana," Oni said. "No one knows how."

"And they're blaming the government for trying to cover it all up," Ester added, "so it doesn't seem like this is some video Riquelme's people put out."

"No," Roxana mused. "None of this has made Riquelme look good."

"So we think it's real," Oni said. "The actual Prince Larkin is in the fae realm, trying to stop the actual Ula Kana."

"With an actual relative of Rosamund Highvalley's," Ester added. "It's wild."

Two humans taking on the fae realm—it sounded beyond hopeless. But Roxana didn't intend to be the one to denounce hope. "Gods be with them, then." Her gaze meandered across the broken street to the redwood and the shape of the gargoyle statue beneath it.

"We're going to fix them," Ester declared again. "And the town. Or build a better one."

"I think if anyone can bring Rafi back," Oni added shyly to Roxana, "it's you. When he lived in our cottage, he talked about you all the time." She smiled. "Apparently there are a *lot* of things that remind him of you."

The words squeezed Roxana's heart. "And most of those things are now somewhere under a jungle." She glanced around at the mass of foliage.

The girls returned to the fields to find food and ask after news. Roxana stayed near Rafi. Caregivers cycled through to visit him. Kepelo came and bestowed more magic on her child before regretfully leaving again to continue consulting with fae and refugees. A different exo-witch dropped in and tried some spells, to the same lack of effect as everyone else. Satsuki came with a three-crystal healing charm that she set on his forepaw. Tash reappeared and gave him a boost of hydration, but, when it did little to change his state, lowered her eyes and slipped away.

Roxana rose to go after her, tell her again she was forgiven and indeed heroic, but Tash crossed the river in a flash of water droplets. In the absence of the bridge, Roxana couldn't follow.

She touched the silver necklace that dangled behind Rafi's ear. Replenished its spell. Not that this revived him either.

Things that remind him of you. Oni's phrase had been wandering through her mind for the last couple of hours, presumably because it was potently bittersweet. But perhaps also...

She frowned at the forest wrapping the ends of the block.

Perhaps also because it suggested one last thing she could try.

The fae were out hunting Sminu because he was the one who had cast Amaris's spell, and therefore he was the best bet at undoing it. Roxana was the one who had created the iron cuff and layered in all its magic. If anyone could reverse its damage, it should be her.

She went to the fields and ate some of the food that rescuers and refugees had collected. No point tromping undernourished through the forest. Then she went to Izzy and Jove's shelter, where Ester was sitting with Oni, and told them where she'd be.

Izzy got up. "Can one of us come with you?"

"I don't know," Roxana said. "I appreciate it, but I feel like it's something I should do myself. A pilgrimage almost."

"All right," Izzy said dubiously, "but at least go to Kepelo and make sure her folk keep watch so you don't get hurt."

Roxana found Kepelo sitting with Rafi, casting a soft net of sparks over his body. He still hadn't moved.

She explained her errand, and Kepelo nodded. "He loves this town," Kepelo said. "Nearly as much as he loves you. It's worth trying. You wish to have someone unobtrusive along. I understand."

She made a whistling sound, accompanied by a call in the fae language. A few seconds later, a will-o'-the-wisp fluttered down, looking like a glowing beetle the size of Roxana's forearm.

"Figo," Kepelo said, reverting to English, "fly near Roxana on her errand. Stay small and out of her way unless she wishes you to help. She aims to revive Rafi with the objects she seeks."

Figo nodded. "Lead the way, Roxana."

∽

She'd had unsettling dreams like this.

I'm wandering through Miryoku, but it's not Miryoku. Or it is, but it's been abandoned and overgrown, like no one's lived here for decades. It's become a dense forest with pieces of buildings showing through in spots. I hardly recognize anything. Fae and animals have moved in—there's a raccoon family looking at me from an apartment window, a cluster of mushroom fae crawling all over a café sign—and it smells like wild plants and earth and flowers. It feels both familiar and unsafe, and it makes me so, so sad.

Grief brought tears to her eyes over and over as she waded and climbed through the untamed landscape that used to be her hometown. The red footbridge over Aria Creek, where she'd walked with Rafi after he'd brought her the first batch of fae-realm metals, was now a curving ladder of tangled roots she had to crawl across. Midspan, she reached down between roots to coax an aluminum nail out of a railing post, tucked it into the pack she had brought, and clambered onward.

Rescuers, human and fae, still searched for the missing. Their voices haunted her, calling through the woods, ragged with despair. ("Tori? … Tori? …" "Mingze? … Mingze? …" "Mom? … Mom? …")

Used to be, you could walk from one end of Miryoku to the other in an hour, even at a leisurely pace. Today it had already taken her an hour just to get from Dragon Street to the red footbridge—a distance of maybe half a mile. When she encountered rescuers, she asked, "What street is this?" to locate herself. When none were around, she asked Figo what landmarks he saw from above. He was quietly following, as promised, in the form of a firefly some ten feet overhead.

But this landmark she knew: a painted phoenix gazing at her with a mournful eye, sunk among building rubble and knotweed. The mural on Starchime Music. Floundering through weed stalks and scattered bricks, she reached the crumbled shop front.

A metal's origins and where it had spent time affected its magical properties, as Roxana and Rafi knew from their experimentation with fae-realm metals. But it was true on a subtler level too. The nail she had taken from the bridge carried the mild aura of countless river fae who had swum beneath it as well as the countless humans who had crossed the bridge—a feeling of motion, meetings and partings, travel, the tranquility of a lunch break. The string of little bronze bells from Starchime's front door, their energy pulling her hand toward them, sang sweetly of music in all its poignancy and joy. Roxana dusted them off and detached three to bring with her.

She forged her way down the street, which had become a thicket of knotweed that soon gave way to blackberry vines forming a mound higher than her head. After attaining a dozen scratches from trying to find a way through, she stopped.

"Figo?" she called. "The Bazaar should be nearby. Can we get to it, or is it all thorns?"

He swooped away to check, then came back. "This way. I'll take you over the brambles, yes?"

Seeing no alternative, she lifted her arms.

Figo expanded, becoming a human-sized glowing bug. He dropped behind her and hooked his two topmost limbs around her middle, then rose into the air and soared with her over the undergrowth. It was a flight of only about fifteen seconds, unnerving yet oddly beautiful: the town viewed from above, greenery and forest shadow rambling in every direction, broken buildings peeking out. Civilization defeated.

Then she was set down in the Bazaar—which now resembled the bottom of an overgrown well. Plants crawled up every wall and choked every alley. Trees interlaced overhead, darkening the space to twilight. Birds and insects chirped. She turned, standing on a fallen wall slab, and sought something to take, a souvenir of this place they had loved.

A copper awning frame, folded near her feet, touched her senses. With her magic, she pulled away a small piece of the metal. It had been the soapmaker's stand—not only did she recognize the awning, but the metal had an air of cleanliness and the art of scent.

With Figo as her personal air surrey, she went next to her parents' house.

Standing on the rubble-strewn front path, she thought: *No.* This couldn't be borne. This was too much.

Her father had told her only the short version. The ground had begun shaking, so he and Amaris had taken cover under a desk, then had run outside after realizing the house was likely to collapse. They had hurried to Dragon Street and onward, to gather their fellow citizens. And Amaris had insisted on going back in, with her aide, after they'd herded most people to the fields. That was the last Timo had seen of her.

So they didn't know, yet, what had become of their house.

The roof had sagged and fallen in on the kitchen side, and a wall had spilled into the garden. The front garden wall and gate had become a giant curb of bristling green. Vines as thick as Roxana's wrist had crawled into the house and splayed across the walls. She only dared view the interior damage from outside, peering in through windows and the torn-open kitchen. A huge toad squatted on their table, next to the knocked-over salt shaker, and blinked impassively at her.

No, she couldn't stay here long. Here she wanted to salvage everything, and that was not today's mission.

Wiping tears off her face with her dirt-stained palms, she took the brass door handle from the front door, as well as a small stone garden gnome her father had made, because she couldn't return without bringing him something. "I need to come back here another time, Figo, all right?" she asked. "You can choose something to have in recompense. Will you be able to bring me?"

"Of course." He sounded aloof, as ever, but his grasp felt sympathetically gentle as he picked her up to fly to their next stop.

But if anywhere would be more painful to see than her own house, it was the place they went next, up the hill and deep in the newly grown forest. Roxana only recognized the property by the statues, most of them no longer on the gray stone roof, instead lying in the saplings that had sprung up in Izzy's courtyard. The grand old house, like most of the town, was now a ruin, sagging and broken and speared through with trees.

Rafi's cottage was almost completely gone.

It had collapsed under the squeeze of the surrounding jasmine and honeysuckle vines, and the nearby trees had expanded to crush it between them. She stood on the overgrown wall, bordering what had once been the footpath (now a dark tunnel below thick trees), and stared in desolation. Finally she stepped onto a massive tree root and followed it over to the porch roof, which lay flat and moss-covered at knee level. She knelt, spreading her hands around the roof's rain gutter, feeling not only the memory of Rafi and herself, but the echoes of many others, from years and years past, taking calm shelter from the rain, daydreaming of gardens and love.

A gleam of glass showed through: a light bulb, from the string on the porch roof. She leaned down and unscrewed the bulb, then coaxed away the metal base to bring back with her.

When she finally returned after several more stops, the sun was going down.

Rafi was still stone, in the same position as before. Timo, Satsuki, and Kepelo, sitting near him, looked to Roxana with worried eyes.

"No change?" she asked.

"No," Kepelo said softly.

Roxana lifted her gaze to the giant redwood. "No news of Sminu?"

"No. They still search."

Roxana swung her pack down and opened it. "I'll get to work."

Sleeping would perhaps have been a smarter idea, but she stayed up crafting her charms long into the night. Oni and Ester brought her food as well as coffee, bland but adequately caffeinated. They also told her that four more people had been found dead, and almost twenty more affected by enchantments.

Roxana's hands paused as she shaped the copper piece from the awning. "Who's died?" she said softly.

"The two border guards," Ester said. "You know how they work in pairs, one faery and one human? Ula Kana swayed the faery who worked with the northern one, and made them kill him. Then she flew to the southern one and did the same."

"Gods. Who else?"

"Someone who worked at the library. And Georgia's dad."

"Georgia?"

"A friend of mine," Oni said. "The girl who was at the Grotto that night."

"Oh." Roxana stroked the copper, an instinctive touch of consolation. "Poor girl."

Ester swung an arm around Oni. "Come on, let's get in line for the hotspot."

Once they had walked away, and Roxana was alone with Rafi, she told him, "It isn't your fault, what happened to the town. No one thinks so. Everyone's only asked if you're going to be okay." She had said it several times by now. Kepelo surmised, when Roxana asked, that Rafi might be able to hear her.

The truth of the cuff had gotten out, every bit of it: Roxana making it, Rafi sending Brogyo to another life with it, and Sminu clapping it onto Rafi. No one had condemned either Roxana or Rafi, at least not that she heard.

"Someone had to do something," a former classmate told her. "If I had the chance to do that to Brogyo, I probably would have."

"Any of us would have tried it," a neighbor admitted. "We were getting our hands on all the iron we could."

"I hope they do put it on Sminu," more than one person said, often appending swear words.

The cuff's cruelty, Roxana supposed, looked tiny now in comparison to what had befallen the town. Her task was merely to reverse what it had done to Rafi, if she could.

She worked for hours, back growing stiff, rear going numb, energy sinking to depletion.

She made loops of each piece of metal—circles, ovals, teardrops—then enhanced the ambient magic the pieces had picked up, the music or conviviality or romance or relaxation or excitement. Atop that, she layered on another spell, the knowledge of being loved. She hooked each loop onto him as she completed it, and related its origin to him aloud. The variously hued loops became a chain that told the story of two lovers.

"This was a bottlecap from near the stage at Gusu Park. Where I first saw you, and later where you sang 'Tuesday Morning' for me.

"This was a nail from the bridge over Aria Creek. I was honored at how you trusted me that day, telling me you were counted human. And this was one of the bells from Meg's shop, where we dropped in.

"This is from the Bazaar. Ever since you told me you loved it as a child, I've thought of you whenever I went there.

"This was from my parents' front door. I'm glad you got to visit, see the house.

"This was a window screen from Hari's shop. I hear Hari's still missing... Do you remember walking along the footpath, sharing mochi? How you put your arm around me? I was thrilled. I wanted you so much.

"This was one of your cottage's porch lights. Oh, the cottage. If we re-build anything, we have to rebuild that, all right? Even just a replica, some-where new. As long as it has plants around it and the same little lights. Do you remember lying there that first morning together, with the rain pouring outside?

"This is a ring someone left at the Lady shrine along the river. I thanked her there once, for bringing us together, did I ever tell you? Then when I came back later, and we had that evening by the river... You have to wake up, all right? I'll be so lonely if I'm the only one left who remembers these things. Please, Rafi."

By the last charm, she was lying on her side, her hand on his stone paw, redwood needles tickling her temple. She had sweated throughout the charm-making, and her mouth was parched, but she was too exhausted to sit up. She managed to drag over the water bottle Ester had brought, drank from it, and fell asleep within a minute.

⚬⚬⚬

But Rafi was still comatose when she woke up in the morning.

⚬⚬⚬

What could a person do, after realizing they are not enough despite hav-ing poured out all their energy and love? What could they do except lie on the ground and weep?

Which was what Roxana did. For ten minutes or so.

Then she felt her father and Satsuki stroking her back. Lifted her bleary gaze to see Tash mutely sending more water into Rafi, and Figo moving his glowing hands down Rafi's stone spine. Kepelo walked into her field of vision. She was holding Rafi's liuqin, cradled to her like an infant.

"He left this in my haunt. I thought I'd bring it, in case it helps. And if he doesn't get better...I think he would want it in your keeping."

Roxana dragged herself up. "Thank you." She hugged her father and Satsuki for a long minute, then blew her nose and blinked her eyes clear. "Right," she murmured. "Right."

It might have helped Rafi to sense the spells that assured him of her love, to feel the tangible truth of their joy together. But mattering to her alone wasn't reason enough for a person to live. Rafi needed to know he belonged to more than just his lover, that many people cherished him and wanted him back. That he had a place in the world, just by virtue of being himself.

Kepelo set the liuqin in her lap. Roxana curled her fingers around the neck.

"You know how to play that?" her dad asked.

"No. He showed me a couple of chords, that's all." She found one of them—G, she thought—and tried strumming it. It sounded tinny and off-key, not the airy, dancing tones Rafi could produce. She tried again with the other chord she remembered. Alternated between the two. Stole a glance at Rafi.

No change.

Roxana sighed and set the liuqin beside him. "I'm going to get something to eat. Then I'll round up a few people."

CHAPTER 31

J OVE AND IZZY WERE THE FIRST SHE AP-
proached. At her request, they collected several townsfolk Rafi had run
errands for, who had been asking after his well-being. Figo darted off to find
the will-o'-the-wisps, drakes, sprites, and other fae who'd been Rafi's longtime
friends.

One by one, people followed the overgrown path to Dragon Street's new
giant redwood and visited him.

Roxana gave them space. She didn't overhear what each said. Some
laughed as they spoke to him. Others talked through tears. Others spoke
steadily and softly, with a calming hand on his back, where the charms still
sparkled in the golden afternoon light.

Tash hung back until the end. When she did approach him and began
speaking, it was with the air of a prisoner giving their last confession. Rather
than kneel at his side, she stood before him, straight-backed but with gaze
lowered, and spoke clearly enough that Roxana, on the steps across the street,
caught some of the phrases. In particular, "I have failed you" and "never forgive myself."

A fine sheet of water glistened on her face. It took Roxana a minute to
realize it was the shellycoat form of tears.

Roxana got up, aching to reassure her. But once again, Tash fled to the
river in a shimmer of speed and was gone.

And Rafi lay where he'd been.

Jove and Izzy were sitting on a curb some distance away, leaning into one
another. Roxana shuffled over to them. "Can we at least make Tash feel better?" she asked.

"We'll forgive her as many times as she needs," Izzy said.

"It's hard for someone who's proud, though," Jove said, looking toward
the river. "She's used to being perfect. She hasn't known till now what it is to

do something really wrong. Even if it wasn't her fault."

Roxana murmured agreement, but thought, *No one could feel more guilt than I do. No one deserves it more.*

The sky faded to pale violet. The fire fae glowed in the trees and set lantern flames burning in the air. The number of refugees in the fields had begun to shrink, people leaving for other towns. Plenty stayed, though. They had to continue tallying up those missing, injured, enchanted, or dead.

When she returned to Rafi after a wander through the fields, Oni and Ester were sitting with him. Oni was speaking quietly to him, and Ester was leaning her head on Oni's shoulder. Giving him their gratitude. Or saying their goodbyes.

Tomorrow morning, if he hadn't changed, Roxana would tell Kepelo they had to move him to a hospital. Even though it would mean putting him into citizen records. Even though he'd hate it. Even though it might do him no more good than staying here. There was simply nothing left to try.

Timo hadn't budged from the vicinity of the tree these last couple of days. He had a chunk of brick in his hands and was shaping it with his magic into something rounded. Several other creations of stone sat between and on the giant roots, a party of figurines to keep Amaris company. Enchanted, of course, with love and encouragement—same as Roxana was doing for Rafi.

Timo had made one for Rafi too. A two-inch-high stone treble clef was propped against his side. And Roxana had strung a long, slender aluminum chain all around her mother's trunk, enspelled it with love, and transformed several links into the shapes of leaves, stars, birds, and houses.

She sat near her father and smiled sadly. "Like father, like daughter."

He held up the brick sculpture. "I'm going to make this one a guinea pig. What do you think?"

"Perfect." Roxana kissed his cheek.

There was no taking a tree of this size to a hospital. Timo might as well settle in here until they knew more.

She bade her father goodnight and lay down on her blanket, near Rafi.

On his other side, Ester and Oni still sat, talking quietly, keeping late teenage hours.

Roxana shut her eyes and drifted into a dream.

They were in a café; Oni, Ester, Roxana, Rafi, and her parents. Clean tables, chairs, a smooth wood floor, a ceiling with electric lights—tremendous luxuries she had taken for granted all her life. Everyone was happy, singing irreverent folk songs. The liuqin was playing, notes and chords weaving in and out of the murmur of conversation.

It sounded better than when Roxana had tried to play it, but still not as lovely as when Rafi did. His hands were unoccupied, interlaced with his chin set on them. Then who *was* playing it?

She twitched and opened her eyes. A string was plucked softly, and another. Oni and Ester were still talking in undertones. Roxana lifted her head and found Oni holding the instrument.

Catching her glance, Oni smiled meekly. "Rafi taught me a little."

Roxana smiled back. Was about to tell her it was fine, sounded good. In fact, maybe Oni should keep it, if…

Between them, Rafi stirred. The spikes on his head softened, folding downward, sending the charms jingling and falling. His front paws tapered into fingers.

"Needs tuning," he mumbled.

Oni gasped. Ester jumped to her feet with a joyous screech. Roxana scrambled forward to grab his hands. Stone softened to grit-dusted skin under her touch. "Rafi," she said, in a squeak.

His face, resting on his arms, changed too, gargoyle features sliding back to human. Black rock dust feathered off his eyelashes; he blinked and blew it from his lips. He turned a hand over and clasped hers. "You're here."

"Hello." She was laughing and crying at once.

He glanced at the loop charms that had fallen around him, then propped himself on his elbows, naked with the shiny blanket draped over him, and looked around. Looked up.

Saw the overgrown street. The redwood.

His mouth fell open. "I'm sorry. Roxana—I'm so sorry. I couldn't stop him—Sminu was—"

"No, I know—I'm sorry, I'm the one who's sorry—"

"Rafi!" Ester hugged him around the neck.

Oni piled on too. "Hi, Rafi!"

Timo popped up, hair askew from sleep, and beamed. "Oh hey!" He hurried off, calling out to someone nearby, "He's awake! Folks, he's awake!"

Even as Rafi twined his arms around the girls, he asked, "Where's Sminu? Is this korred territory now? How did you find me? I was—I drowned—Tash, where's Tash, is she okay?"

"She's around, she's going to be so relieved." Roxana laid her hand on his jaw as the girls pulled away. "I've been worried about you."

Rafi touched his forehead to hers, shutting his eyes. His hair tickled her cheek. "Glad you're here."

"We should tell my parents," Oni said after a pause, in the sensible, aloof tone of someone wanting to give two lovers their space.

"Right," Ester said, in much the same tone. "Let's go find them."

They darted off.

The attending fire sprite of the hour whisked away, too, likely to find Kepelo.

Left alone, Rafi and Roxana kissed for several ardent, long seconds. Then they broke into a simultaneous stream of apologies, paused, asked why the other was apologizing, offered instant forgiveness, finally smiled at their mutual absurdity, and moved on to sorting out everything that had happened.

"It was Oni," he told her eventually, the two of them nestled together on the ground. "She was the last one to talk to me. She said something like, 'You told me once to remember all the things you love that you can't lose. It really helped me when you said that. I know the town's gone and we lost people, but there's still going to be music and festivals and cool things humans make, and we want you there enjoying it.' I was gathering the strength to answer, which took me a while. Then I heard the liuqin."

"Which needs tuning," she finished, cradled in his arms.

Jove and Izzy barreled down the street and tumbled onto him in a hug. Meg and Satsuki followed, along with several of the people who had spoken to Rafi earlier, all of them insisting on repeating their thanks and appreciation now that he was awake.

Ester and Oni brought him some green linen trousers that more or less fit—at least they had a drawstring to keep them on—and a mug of ginger tea, plus an oat bar. He was eating the final crumbs, seated amid everyone's happy chatter, when Kepelo swooped down in a blaze of firelight.

Rafi rose, and mother and son met in an embrace. Her wings, radiating warmth, folded around him so that all Roxana could see for a minute was his disheveled black hair and his bare feet. As they separated, Kepelo wore a sweet smile and a wrinkled brow. Imagining her own feelings if Ester had been imprisoned in such a coma, Roxana's heart constricted in sympathy.

They spoke a minute, then turned toward her.

Rafi told Roxana, "They might be getting closer to Sminu. Aulo found a promising lead."

Roxana nodded, her happiness dimming at the reminder of her mother's enchantment. "Good to hear."

But when Rafi pulled her against him for a warm hug, a sizable portion of the difficulty melted. She would be so much less alone now, whatever happened.

"All right," Rafi said, looking around with a frown. "So where's Tash?"

⁓

For Rafi, the enchantment had been a dark dream. An initiation to the afterlife, he assumed at the time.

In it, he was interrogated by a version of himself who was strong and tall and equipped with drake wings and who was pacing back and forth while he—his current self—huddled on the ground. They were in an underwater cave, a compartment of air in wet rock.

"Now you see the damage you've done," the pacing Rafi said.

"I know. I deserve to die."

"It's supposed to make you want to *fix* it, not want to die."

"I can't fix this. No one can."

"Then you're supposed to want to change your ways. Climb out of this and be there for the survivors. For Roxana."

"I don't think I can. Haven't I died? Anyway, she won't forgive me, not once she sees what's happened to the town. To Amaris."

"Even if that's true, is that the end of everything? Is she the only person in the world who matters? The only reason to live, the only one you could mean anything to?"

"I sometimes think so."

The Rafi with drake wings sighed in impatience. "Think again. Think deeper."

Sapped of strength, he couldn't do much else but think, even if his thoughts were having a way of spiraling into nonsense.

Then the cave shattered and the water drained away. The mind-bending pain dwindled, too, though Rafi still had no strength.

Drake-Rafi walked off after one last instruction: "Listen. Listen to them."

It was hard to listen, to hang on to the words. He was so tired. Were ghosts always this tired? But gradually, with each line Roxana and his other friends said to him—sometimes accompanied by a soothing sensation—his consciousness pulled together a little more.

Then finally he woke up and there she was. Grimy and exhausted but with eyes shining as she held his hands.

And then everyone treated him—quite unexpectedly—to what felt like a fantasy he'd had since infancy: people telling him they were happy he was here, they wanted him to stay, they appreciated him, he belonged. Even with the town in shambles, he was stunned with gratitude.

But one piece was missing: Tash.

After wandering around looking for her awhile, the other band members went to the river and asked the water fae to find her. Given Tash was one of their own, the fae didn't mind obliging, and several of them streamed away in all directions, trailing iridescent ribbons of mist behind them.

It was getting late. Though Roxana insisted she was willing to stay up and help look, she kept yawning and her eyelids were dragging low. Rafi led her back to the space under the redwood. Someone had taken away the emergency foil blanket and brought him a sleeping bag. He unzipped it to spread it wider, and they nestled together on top of it, with a blanket over them in the dewy March night.

"I should make Tash some charms," she murmured into his chest. "To feel better."

He smiled, feeling her exhaustion in the limpness of her body. "In a little while. Rest first."

"Mm." She sounded dubious, but was asleep a few minutes later.

Rafi, having slept quite a lot the last couple of days—if it could be called sleep—lay with his gaze roaming among the redwood's branches. The stars shone between hazy clouds, and glowing fae flitted above the overgrown rooftops. He savored Roxana's warmth, her breathing, the spill of her redwood-scented hair over his arm, and marveled at this powerful combination of love and triumph and remorse and grief all at once.

When a pale yellow dawn was spreading across the sky, a shellycoat finally strode up the street. "We found her," the faery said. "She has that damn *thing* on. You'd better come."

CHAPTER 32

RAFI, JOVE, AND IZZY ALL HASTENED WEST, over the highway, out of the devastation, and into the weirdly unchanged meadows and cliffs bordering the coast. Though Rafi had urged Roxana to come, she had hung back, saying Tash was the kind of person who would only want her closest humans near at such a time—the band.

In the cold wind, Tash sat where the shellycoat had found her, on the cliff where Rafi had taken refuge after his attack on Brogyo, but on top of it rather than in a nook partway down. Her legs dangled over the edge. Waves shattered on the rocks a hundred feet below. She looked smaller, thinner. Her scales were greener and more prominent, and water trickled in a constant seep all over her. Her webbed hands rested on the rock, the cuff latched around her right wrist.

Rafi grabbed it and tugged it off, brushing the iron inside for a moment and getting a sickening wave of misery. Tash, startled from her haze, lashed a stream of water like a whip at him, knocking him back.

Then, recognizing him, she made an agonized sound like one of the shattering waves. "Rafi! See? I can't be trusted." She rose and began pacing precariously close to the edge. It wouldn't hurt her to fall, of course, but he found it nerve-wracking to watch.

"I'm all right," he assured. "Really. Thanks to you. Why would you wear this? You don't deserve punishment."

"I fought for Ula Kana. I was one of her soldiers."

"For two minutes maybe," Izzy said. "Then you spent a whole twenty-four hours keeping Rafi alive."

"I forgive you," Rafi said. "In fact, I'm grateful. Thank you."

"It's good that you're all right," Tash said, still pacing, "but in that two minutes, Mayor Wei was turned into a tree, and her selkie friend was swayed by Ula Kana and drowned someone. If I hadn't been swayed, if I had helped you instead, we could have stopped at least one of those things from happening."

"Against Ula Kana," Izzy said, "it's totally possible you couldn't have done anything."

"But how many humans will suffer," Tash went on, "because of what happened to those two? I've never hurt humans before. I toyed with them, sometimes, getting them to like me. But I would never have done this. They won't accept me now, and they shouldn't."

Hugs and sentiment weren't going to be the right path with Tash. They had all agreed on that on the way here. After exchanging a furtive look, the other three assumed calm expressions, and Jove stepped forward.

"Tash. Everyone already knows, okay? Because you were honest right at the start and said what happened. Guess what? They all think you're a fucking hero for turning around and rescuing Rafi the second your brainwashing was gone."

Tash looked out to the ocean.

"People also want to know," Izzy said, "when the band can play again. No lie, they're asking constantly. And you're a goddamn perfect bassist. We're never going to find a better one."

"You could find an equally perfect one." Tash sounded neutral now, though, and her form coalesced into more of an upright and dry human shape.

"Yeah, but you already know all our songs," Izzy said. "The fans love you. It'd be more convenient if it was you."

"You're pretty good at healing too," Rafi put in. "I know it firsthand. And there's still a lot of people with enchantment damage or other injuries, in the fields. They'd welcome you. I mean, if you want to try."

Tash let out a sigh like a splash in a creek. She turned and began walking toward the town. "You're all very annoying," she informed them.

Behind her back, they grinned at each other, and relief ran through Rafi's limbs like sweet magic.

In the fields, a commotion was underway, people moving toward Dragon Street via the forest path, which had become wider and more trampled in the past few days.

"They caught Sminu," one of Izzy's neighbors called.

The band members rushed to join the crowd near the great redwood and wriggled through to reach Roxana, Ester, and Timo.

Sminu and Unklag were on their knees, held in place by Aulo and three other drakes. Kepelo stood before them, stern and tall, while Sminu wheedled defenses and pleas.

"We've already turned most of it to forest," he was saying. "It might as well be earth territory. Allow me a chance, please. I'll let humans live here! It will be a new type of haunt. I'll be a generous ruler."

Roxana turned to Rafi, her features hard and pale. She flicked her glance to Tash, then held out her palm. "Give me the cuff."

Heart thundering, Roxana stepped up next to Kepelo.

"You will not have this territory," Kepelo said to Sminu. "You *will* reverse Amaris Wei's spell to the best of your ability."

"Of course, of course," he assured. His eyes flickered to the cuff in Roxana's hand, and he smirked, though alarm seemed to tighten his face. "Is that for me?"

"If you fail, yes," Roxana said. She didn't add that she was considering putting it on him even if he succeeded.

"Now." Kepelo flicked her hand at Unklag and Sminu. "Both of you. We want her fully restored and in good health."

The drakes dragged the two over to Amaris.

"Let us see, then," Sminu said, cordially, as if he were at a garden party and offering to heal a friend.

"Very well," Unklag grumbled.

The two of them spread their knobby fingers on the trunk. Roxana prayed silently. Sminu and Unklag grunted, moved their hands around on the tree, muttered to each other now and then.

The tree shuddered, causing a rushing sound as if the wind had swept her branches. Needles rained down, and some of the limbs contorted, jerked. A root near Roxana's feet juddered, splitting the earth. Wood creaked, sounding like a cry.

The korreds retracted their hands, and the motions stopped.

"If you want her in good health," Sminu told Kepelo, "then we cannot restore her as a human. Delicate, these creatures, as you're aware."

"Yes you can," Roxana snapped. "Fix it."

Even as she said it, however, she knew from the despairing drumbeat of her pulse that it was true. For one thing, they couldn't lie. For another, her father's korred curse had yet to be reversed, despite the korreds' own healing attempts, and it was a far milder curse than this one.

"Lovely friend, we truly cannot." Sminu dared sound suave as he addressed her, even on his knees with drake guards ready to bash him. "She is in excellent health as a tree! Never fear. She might live many lifetimes of a human yet. But to compress her from this great form back into the soft little shape of a human—" He made a regretful face and shook his head.

"She'd die," Unklag said, bluntly. "It's how humans are."

Beside Roxana, Timo gave a soft sob.

Roxana rushed forward with the open cuff, a roar emerging from her throat. Sminu jerked backward, but Aulo grabbed him and held him still. Got his arm ready for Roxana, shoved it out so she could reach it.

Taking jagged breaths that stung her throat, Roxana stopped. Stared at Sminu, cowering with his arm forced upward by Aulo's glowing claws. Looked at her mother—the tree—then at her father with his blankly shocked face, Meg's arm around him. At Rafi and Ester and the band members, who all watched, seeing what she would do. Leaving it up to her.

She tossed the cuff on the ground in front of Kepelo. The deep blue enamel shone atop the redwood needles. "There's no point. This is how we got here. Melt it, please."

Kepelo nodded, scooped up the cuff, and carried it out into the street. A hush had fallen, even Sminu and Unklag staying quiet. Kepelo expanded into full drake form, flung the cuff into the air, and sent a jet of fire at it from her open jaws. Later, Roxana supposed, if she wanted to look, she'd find drops of melted and hardened iron, silver, and glass among the broken pieces of the street. They wouldn't hurt anyone. The spell was vaporized, gone. She didn't want them back.

Shaking, she walked to her loved ones. Ester was already in Timo's arms, tears running down their faces. Neighbors and friends touched Roxana gently on the back, the shoulders. A whirlwind had taken up residence in her ears; she couldn't hear anything they said.

Then Rafi was in front of her, and she stepped into his embrace. He held her, his body a shield against everything, a refuge where she could hide. She tried to remember how to breathe. Her mother wasn't dead, but might as well be. They could never talk with her again, see her face again, hear her laugh again. Much as the fury inside her still longed to throw this feeling into Sminu, make him suffer too, that wouldn't bring Amaris back.

Through the pounding in her head, she realized Rafi was speaking, his mouth just above her ear, the words for her alone. She let them filter through.

"I will grieve with you, I will rage with you, I will stay quietly with you, I will do whatever you need. I will be with you."

She sagged in his arms and grieved.

ᗈᑌᕫᘉ

The drakes had the good sense to haul the two guilty korreds far from the redwood. They took them to the edge of town, Rafi heard, where the journalists were gathered, and made sure the reporters took down the accurate truth of what had happened to Miryoku's mayor, including the name of the korred haunt leader responsible. They added his past crimes, too, which Sminu, who couldn't lie, had no way to deny.

He wanted human attention? Let him have it. Adoration, though, he would not get.

After seeing Amaris's family and friends settled in their vigil of grief around the tree, Rafi whispered to Roxana that he'd be back soon, and joined Kepelo. He and she conferred, then went to Sminu and Unklag, still among their audience of reporters.

"This is the deal I offer you both," Kepelo said. "Either return to the elements, or go to live in the interior of the island, in whatever haunt will take you. You will never again, in your current incarnations, live in a haunt bordering the verge. Everyone in the human realm now knows who you are and what you've done. None will welcome you. Many fae, too, will chase you off for your disruption of the truce."

"Just us two?" Standing in Aulo's grip, Sminu bared his teeth in a bland smile. "What of our many followers, our haunt companions?"

"Any other from your haunt who participated in harming humans or the town, without being under Ula Kana's sway, are under the same injunction. There are korreds who live peaceably enough in the mountains. Go learn from them—if they tolerate your presence. Is this deal accepted or must we commission new items of iron?"

Sminu didn't know, of course, that Roxana would never again consent to make such a thing.

The threat was enough. Sminu cut his glance aside at the journalists recording everything. "Accepted."

"On behalf of all your haunt?" Kepelo said.

"On behalf of all my haunt." The words sounded wrenched out of him one at a time.

A short time later, they all stood at the former verge, still the true verge in terms of the strength of magic on the other side of it. The footpath was now more of a skinny trail wreathed in bushes and crisscrossed with roots. Thick rainclouds had spread across the sky, darkening the forest.

Rafi and Sminu gazed at each other a few seconds.

"Did you wish to say goodbye?" Sminu finally asked, sarcastically.

"You tried to kill me. Isn't there anything *you* want to say?"

Sminu shifted his gaze away, looking sulky. "I am not fond of how it turned out, my attempt to become a parent."

Kepelo slipped her wing around Rafi. "I agree the encounter between us was disappointing, but I will gladly take all the treasure that issued from it, if you aren't wise enough to see its value."

Sminu grunted and turned to face the fae realm. Unklag, who had only scowled the whole journey here, did the same.

That was goodbye, apparently. Kepelo nodded to her drakes, who tugged the two away into the hills.

"We might of course see him again," Kepelo remarked to Rafi, still holding him against her side.

He reached up and closed his hand around the claw at the tip of her wing. "But hopefully not for a long time." Then he peered down the footpath, studying the stone walls peeking through the shrubs. "Since we're here, there are a few things I want to look for."

∽

Rafi returned in the evening, the drakes helping him carry the goods he had collected. He brought Jove's guitar, Tash's bass, nearly all the pieces of Izzy's drum set, a pair of drumsticks, a pack of extra strings, a deck of cards, and a solar phone charger, all of which he had managed to pull from the half-collapsed mansion. The flattened cottage no longer held anything of Rafi's: there he had just stood a moment to honor the love he had felt within it. Roxana had spoken of the same, he remembered, while he was in his dream-like coma.

The band was delighted to get the items, despite the instruments' dented and damaged condition, and they set about finding matter-witches to repair them. Oni happily accepted the deck of cards and took them to Ester, to see if a game might cheer her.

Rafi accompanied her, holding up the bottom half of his large borrowed T-shirt to make a sack in which he carried the food he had gathered. Roxana and Timo were sitting at the base of Amaris's tree, her head leaning on her father's shoulder. Rafi dropped to his knees in front of them and gently spilled out the leaves, fungi, flowers, and vegetables. Lifting her head, Roxana hummed a sound in inquiry.

"I did some foraging," Rafi said. "One of the few things I know is where to find edible plants around here. From the safe side of the verge, of course, but matter-witches can treat them to be extra sure. So, fennel bulb, wild asparagus, and oyster mushrooms." He pointed to each. "I'll get a fire faery to roast them. And we can have a salad of miner's lettuce, red clover, and violets. It's actually quite good. I've had lots of spring snacks of violets in my day."

Roxana gazed at the colorful array, then leaned over the foods and hugged Rafi around the neck. "Thank you."

Timo, tears in his eyes, reached out and squeezed Rafi's shoulder.

Rafi found Aulo and enlisted her help in roasting the vegetables on a detached piece of a metal mailbox, in lieu of a pan. It began raining. Still applying a low fire stream to the pan, Aulo spread her wings as a partial umbrella.

Then the ground trembled in steady, light booms like footsteps, a deep voice grumbled, and a huge stone wall tilted itself over Rafi's head and blocked the rain.

He had jolted in alarm at first, but his mood brightened to pure joy when he recognized her. "Mukut!" He turned and spread his arms across her flat front.

She rumbled again, and a stone limb emerged and encased him.

"Oh yes," Aulo said. "We encountered this giant out in the hills when we were looking for Sminu. She offered to help. She knew the places he was likeliest to hide, and could recognize him better than we could. With her assistance, we cornered him that same day."

"Thank you, Mukut," Rafi said. "It's so good to see you again." He looked across to the redwood. "Roxana! Come meet Mukut."

It lifted his spirits to see Roxana's face transform from weary sadness to wonder at beholding her first stone giant. Roxana put her hand on her heart and addressed Mukut. "I've been looking forward to meeting you. Thank you for taking good care of Rafi."

Mukut responded in a mumble, and Aulo piped up, "She says 'I'll protect you both for as long as you need. And I'll try one of the burned mushrooms if you don't have any potato chips.' Burned! Friend, I am *roasting* them, as requested, not burning them."

Rafi and Roxana laughed. The rain came down harder, and they stepped under Mukut's shelter, thanking her anew.

Roxana spent a strange night of crying in her dreams, snuggling blissfully in half-sleep against Rafi, freezing in stark fear of Ula Kana returning, and idly imagining a future that was safe and comfortable and nice again. All of which, she reflected when she awoke, were reasonable things to feel, even if a roller coaster of a mix to feel all in one night.

She made tea with water boiled by fire fae, the mugs and teabags scrounged from a town hall conference room whose corners were now occupied by pink, glowing spider fae—which made eerie clicking sounds but, Rafi assured her, ate only insects.

The rain had washed some of the dust off the faces of the buildings. Sunlight-spangled drops plunked from the tips of the redwood's branches.

While Rafi went to check in with Jove and Izzy, Roxana took tea to her father. He sat on the building steps, gazing wistfully at the tree.

When he took the mug, he looked at Roxana with expressive dark eyes. "Amaris," he said, the word rich and sad on his tongue.

She sat beside him. "I know, Dad."

"No, no. *Amaris.*" He stared at her, waiting for her to understand.

It took her a few seconds. Then she jolted, splashing tea over her hand. "You remembered a name! You can say a name."

He looked back at the tree. "Just hers. I can't remember anyone else's, honey, not even yours. The gods just gave me back this one. Amaris. Amaris." The second time, it was strained, and he wiped his eyes.

They were leaning on each other, crying and smiling, when Rafi came back. After being apprised of the news, Rafi sat at their feet, put his hand on Timo's shoe, and said, "You know, you're about five thousand times better a father than mine ever was."

"If you need a surrogate, I'm here." Timo sniffled. "Gods know I could use as much family as I can get."

"So could I," Rafi said. "I'd be honored." His gaze flicked shyly to Roxana, who smiled.

"Absolutely. We all need that," Roxana said.

"Came to tell you," Rafi said, "the band's hoping to do an acoustic concert tonight. A memorial, to bring everyone together. We're figuring out the set list. Any requests?"

"It's a wonderful idea," she said. "I leave the choices up to you musicians."

"Then I better get back for practice." He stood. "Once we finish repairing the instruments, that is."

Roxana set down her mug. "You need matter-witches? Why didn't you say?"

"I didn't want to bother you two."

"Nonsense. We want to help. Right, Dad?"

"It's what Amaris would want." Timo laid a loving emphasis on the name.

CHAPTER 33

MELONCOLLIE CHOSE THE STEPS OF THE town hall for their stage. The leaf-softened building facades offered decent acoustics, something they had to consider given their lack of electric amplification. But also it felt appropriate, bringing their human lament to Dragon Street, the heart of the old town, where Amaris could hear them. The fae said trees did listen, sometimes at least, so Roxana chose to believe her mother would hear.

People crammed themselves into the street and sat on stairs and railings. Some got into the buildings to perch in windows with a street view—which was discouraged vocally by those who had been appointed safety officers, but they granted an exception for the length of the concert.

The band did have a magic form of amplification: an exo-witch sat on the top step to set her hand on the leg of whoever was singing or speaking and infuse them with a spell that gave their voice extra carrying power. Roxana and other matter-witches had made charms to affix to the instruments, too, to make them louder. Electric amps still did a better job, but the spells were better than nothing.

Standing before the crowd, his voice magically boosted, Jove raised his hands and said, "Hellooooo, Miryoku!"

A roar rose from the street. Everyone wanted to do nothing but cheer and clap in defiant celebration for at least a full minute.

When it finally died down, Jove said, "We considered branching out to-night and playing tunes that weren't from the nineties, but we figured you've all been through enough of a shock, so we'll just stick to what we know." People laughed. He went on: "We've all lost our homes. Many have lost loved ones, or we or someone we love has been injured and we're not sure whether we'll ever recover. We're all feeling it. We're all here. And we're starting by ac-knowledging that. This is our grief song, our memorial."

He stepped aside to let Izzy take the center spot. The exo-witch took hold of Izzy's ankle to amplify her voice. Rafi and Jove set a lightweight chord strumming, a shimmering line without rhythm. Izzy closed her eyes and began singing Sinéad O'Connor's version of Prince's "Nothing Compares 2 U," her voice raw with emotion.

Roxana started crying again. So did Satsuki and Timo, and Ester and Oni, and the band—playing with tear tracks on their faces—and just about everyone she could see. The words and melody, in this setting, were too much to bear, and for a minute or two she wished she hadn't come. But as the song progressed, her mood unknotted and the grief rinsed out, and by the time the song was done—to more deafening applause—the storm had passed. She felt lighter, and genuine hope had filled the cavity that had been scooped out of her.

The band moved next to Collective Soul's "The World I Know," still poignant but more hopeful, and kept stepping up the brightness gradually with each song. The crowd sang along, arms waving overhead, with "Everybody Hurts," and with the finale, "Don't Look Back in Anger."

Under their Mukut-shelter that night, tucked in blankets washed in the river and then heat-dried by fire fae, Roxana said to Rafi, "So we're free of Sminu, but we might be stuck with Riquelme awhile. And possibly even Ula Kana. But..." She stroked the line of scales on his breastbone, between the folds of the faded robe he'd found in the free clothing supply. "Even without knowing the future, I know I want mine to be with you. We can stay here, or move, keep you hidden or not, whatever you prefer. But I want us to stay together. I commit to you, if you're in."

He pulled her close until their foreheads touched. "I grant you this deal."

∞

Aside from that commitment, the next two months were highly unsettled, not just for Miryoku but for the whole country.

With the help of matter-witches, including Roxana, utility workers restored Miryoku's sector of the mobile network and electrical grid, causing much jubilation, only to have it knocked out again some weeks later when Ula Kana's rogue fae returned in a random attack. That cycle repeated twice more over the course of April and May. It was happening all over the island—attacks on towns, pieces of roads getting smashed, water supplies getting hit with dangerous spells, and weather going haywire. Riquelme's government was in a tailspin, his new laws going unenforced as the country focused on disaster response. People criticized him for not only being unprepared but for stoking fae-human hostilities in the first place. His increasingly certain political doom was one of the situation's only bright spots.

Over half of Miryoku's original population had moved away by early May. Among their number were many of the loudest pro-Riquelme faction, who huffed that they felt unwelcome these days. Izzy's parents stayed, but, Izzy relayed to her friends, had shut their mouths lately about their political views and were focusing instead on putting together fruit boxes for those living in the fields.

Hari of the mochi café, and five other citizens, were never found. Hari, people said, was last seen standing outside his café on the night of the destruction, shouting at the korreds, "You were supposed to be on my side! How could you do this?"

Satsuki was among those who ended up moving. Her mother in Kagami was worried about her and had a room available, and it wasn't so far away from Miryoku, after all. She might as well go.

Satsuki and Roxana acquired a bottle of wine, traded with a neighbor in return for repair work, and shared it on a bench overlooking the ocean the evening before Satsuki left.

After lamenting how they'd miss each other, even with only a two-hour drive between them, they became more upbeat.

"Kagami is wonderful," Roxana said. "You deserve a fresh start. Maybe a hookup with a cute lagoon faery."

"I am very much keeping that option open. And you, meanwhile, are completely on the right track by making it official with Rafi."

"Yeah?" Roxana said, grinning, as if she didn't already feel the rightness in her bones.

"You two *glow* around each other. Like, literally, in his case."

Rafi and Roxana lived together now, in a hut they called a cottage, which they had styled as much like the original cottage as they could. It was set into the newly grown woods between Dragon Street and the fields. Next to it was a matching cottage for Timo and Ester, and on the other side, one for Izzy, Jove, and Oni. Mukut stood guard as a large wall every night, and helped with tasks requiring muscle during the day.

None of them felt they could leave Miryoku anytime soon, not with Amaris and their whole childhoods rooted there. Besides, they had work to do: Rafi and the band helped find possessions and pets in the overgrown town, Roxana repaired things, and everyone helped build shelters and distribute supplies.

The owner of the fields had lost her best friend in the destruction—one of the missing, probably caught in the flood—and, desolate, had no desire to reclaim her agricultural lands and resume work. She donated the fields to the town as a residential area, setting up the paperwork that would make the transfer official as soon as the case could be handled. The nation had an avalanche of property damage reports coming in, and sorting it all out and recompensing those who had been displaced would likely take years.

No one showed up to inquire after Rafi again, nor after any fae living among humans, nor any other witch with rare abilities. Jove and Izzy did get a few inquiries—on days when the internet was working—from people around the country wanting to hire the band for gigs. Their memorial concert had been recorded by journalists and had become a national sensation. They politely declined the gigs for now. Maybe in a later month, they said, when the country wasn't under occasional random attack and all that.

Roxana's grief for her mother went through cycles. Some days she was able to pay attention to the news from other parts of Eidolonia—a tsunami decimating a seaside neighborhood in Port Baleia, a landslide wiping out the highway near Sevinee, another tower of the palace in Dasdemir destroyed—and mentally send her compassion to the people affected. *What you feel, I feel too*, she thought, and the empathy eased her own pain. Other days it was too much to take in, and she had to turn inward, just herself and the giant tree, with Rafi and Timo and Ester as cherished consolation.

As for Prince Larkin and Merrick Highvalley, despite everyone expecting them to have been swiftly killed in the fae realm, news arrived every now and then reporting they were still alive and making their way through some of the most dangerous haunts in existence. What exactly they were planning to do was a mystery, but the fae who carried the reports assured everyone that they seemed determined to put a stop to Ula Kana's attacks. Many fae had taken a liking to them, finding them interesting, and public opinion among humans grew in their favor too.

The pair were also doing the rest of the island the favor of drawing Ula Kana's fire. Hearing of their mission, she periodically dove back into the fae realm to seek them out and try to vanquish them, which resulted in days or weeks of relative peace on the human side.

Then in late May a marvelously strange event occurred: during another lull in sightings of Ula Kana, two hundred and seventy-nine humans, ragged and weak, came across the verge into the human realm, not far from Kagami, escorted by fae of all varieties. They had been prisoners in a ghoul-sylph's realm, they said, some of them having been missing for as long as two centuries on the human side. Their rescue had been the work of Merrick and Larkin.

The country burst into hopeful speculation again. The freed prisoners were taken into homes and hospitals and reunited with all their loved ones that could be found. The calm stretched out for days.

Then on a misty evening, Figo shot in like a fiery arrow. "Ula Kana's been captured," he said. "She's confined on Pitchstone Mountain within enchanted barriers. It was witches and fae together who cast the spell—the two humans managed to arrange it. I would hardly have thought it possible."

They jumped to their feet—the whole circle of Roxana's family, friends, and neighbors, who had all been sitting around the cooking fire after dinner.

"Are you sure?" Rafi said. "Absolutely sure?"

Figo pressed a skinny insect limb to his own chest. "This word comes from an unbroken line of fae who cannot lie. It is true, or at least was true a short time ago."

"Are Merrick and Larkin okay?" Ester shouted.

"Injured, healed, and now being escorted safely back to the human realm. I expect the news will reach this side soon."

No one quite dared to give in to joy, though, until the announcement flashed across all the phone screens in the nation a couple of hours later.

Ula Kana has been imprisoned in the fae realm. Prince Larkin and Merrick Highvalley have returned across the verge and are safe. The palace will address the nation at 10 p.m. The nationwide alert is now lifted. Please celebrate responsibly!

"Responsibly? Screw that," Jove said.

And the remaining citizens of Miryoku joined the rest of Eidolonia in a jubilant, ongoing cheer so loud it echoed off the sea-cliffs five miles away.

‹ ∞ ›

Larkin and Merrick dominated the news in ensuing days, surrounded in the video clips by swarms of journalists and guards. They were obliged to stay in Dasdemir and undergo extensive questioning about their unauthorized journey. They had, after all, violated several laws regarding magic use and endangered the whole country. On the other hand, they had succeeded at stopping Ula Kana and set free all those human captives—which, Rafi and his family agreed, should ameliorate any sentence they got.

By "family," Rafi now meant not only Kepelo but Roxana, Ester, Timo, Oni, and the band. They insisted on the word and used it themselves. It felt strange at first, but he had settled into it.

Merrick and Larkin weren't the only ones undergoing investigations. Lawfolk had caught up to Riquelme and his cabinet, bringing all kinds of career-ending charges involving fraud and embezzlement, and the long-deferred referendum was finally held. He was voted out in a landslide and would soon be put on trial. His "anti-witch-cult" laws were revoked, and the incoming prime minister and her new cabinet replaced them with programs allowing for flexible employment, education, and housing options among humans and fae, including for those choosing not to be recorded as citizens.

"Harmony and unity, on this utterly unique island of ours," she said in her inaugural address, "must always be our guiding aims."

In the interests of harmony and unity, in fact, and in recognition of the offenses caused by humans toward fae and not just vice-versa, the government, after a special countrywide vote, returned a few parcels of land to the fae. The largest was Miryoku. The administration, as well as the local citizens, recognized Kepelo as a benevolent neighbor to have, and the former town land was now under her control. Rebuilding the town would be more expen-

sive than recompensing the citizens for their loss, and not many people wanted to stay anyway. More and more had moved away or, like Rafi and his family, had resettled west of the ruins. Dragon Street, the redwood, and almost all
the buildings were now fae territory, becoming a little more saturated with fae
magic every day, and thus a little more prone to a time slip when one visited.

"Crossing the verge a lot more often than I ever thought I would," Roxana remarked to Rafi on a mid-June day. But she said it with a smile, and
started humming a song as they walked among the trees.

In July, Roxana and Timo received an email from Merrick Highvalley.

Dear Timo, Roxana, and Ester,

*I've been reviewing the details of the damage caused in the human realm by
Ula Kana these past months. I am so sorry for the permanent transfiguration of
your family member, Mayor Amaris Wei, and in particular for my part in releas-
ing Ula Kana. While I know there is nothing I can do to change the situation, I
would like to visit and offer my apologies and condolences in person if you are willing. I hope for our island to heal as much as possible, and this is one of my small
attempts toward that aim.*

*I plan to be in the former Miryoku on August 4 to meet with all the bereaved
who still live there and wish to come. Prince Larkin will accompany me.*

Best wishes, and may the gods be with you,

Merrick

While Ester and Oni screamed in delight and clutched each other's arms,
Roxana reread the email.

"The poor man," she said. "He's going to talk to everyone? That's a lot of
hurting families to face."

"It's brave and noble," Timo said. "I respect him for it."

Rafi tried to imagine facing that much guilt, that publicly. "Brave" didn't
cover the half of it.

"And he's bringing Larkin," Ester said archly. "Things must be going well."

Oni batted her arm, but grinned.

After giving a ceremonial speech a few weeks back, Larkin had taken his
seat beside Merrick and kissed him on the mouth, knowing full well they were

being nationally televised. It had looked like an established-couple kiss, Rafi and Roxana had to admit, not a first kiss or a staged kiss.

It had been a savvy move: people already loved Larkin, the enchanted prince, so they were inclined to soften their views on Merrick if Larkin esteemed him so highly.

But some clearly still held grudges.

On the day of the visit, Rafi stood back with Amaris's family, waiting their turn, as Merrick and Larkin spoke to the other bereaved folk first. The event took place in what had become the central square of the village in the fields. Though the ground was still beach gravel and dirt, a café with an awning had been built on one side, electric lampposts and light strings had been erected, and market stalls made a cheerful border around the square, with residential huts behind them. People had dragged out some of the public art from the town and installed it here, along with planters full of summer flowers. The jasmine in one planter was already starting to climb the wall of someone's hut.

In the warm afternoon, Merrick and Larkin wore lightweight black trousers and silk shirts with the fluttery tatter-style hems of Eidolonian formalwear, Merrick's shirt a vivid lava red, and Larkin's a sea blue that contrasted with the russet of his long hair. They each wore sashes to indicate their witch affiliations: Merrick's in red, as an endo-witch, and Larkin's in yellow, as an exo-witch. Larkin also came with royal attendants, three unobtrusive people in dark blue suits.

Standing under the shade of the café awning, Merrick spoke quietly to those who came forward. Larkin waited beside him, hands folded, silent unless anyone addressed him, at which point he gave a gracious nod and soft words.

Most of the family members spoke softly too. They shook Merrick's hand, wiped tears from their eyes, said things Rafi couldn't hear from where he stood. A few held themselves stiff and spoke with tight jaws. Merrick didn't look away from them, though he grew paler as he nodded and listened. When one man, whose spouse had been killed, started getting loud enough that Rafi and his family could hear some of it—"...fucking irresponsible...all your fault..."—Merrick still didn't flinch. Larkin, however, gently stepped forward to touch the man's shoulder, speaking quietly, compassion in his eyes.

The man's tense shoulders, and his volume, lowered within seconds.

"Exo-witch," Roxana murmured to Rafi. "Handy."

Rafi nodded, too stricken by all the pain he was witnessing to say anything.

When that family moved along, Larkin twined his arm into Merrick's with a focused look. Some of Merrick's color returned, and he gave Larkin a grateful flicker of a smile.

Then it was their turn.

Merrick greeted Roxana, Ester, and Timo by name even before they introduced themselves. He had evidently done good research. Rafi and Oni, hangers-on to the group, gave their names too, both in a shy mumble.

"I am so sorry," Merrick said after the greetings, his smile fading. "Amaris was a wonderful mayor. We've been reading her records, and it's clear she loved Miryoku, and her residents loved her back. How have you been coping?"

Roxana, Timo, and Ester piped up with interweaving accounts of building the village, repairing things, recovering items from the ruins, making friends with the fae from Kepelo's haunt. "Not too bad really," Roxana concluded. "We have each other."

"That is good to hear," Merrick said. "Genuinely."

"It wasn't your fault," Rafi blurted out. "What happened to Miryoku. It was my fault, really."

Larkin and Merrick looked at him, bemused.

"Given I was the one who woke up Ula Kana," Merrick said carefully, "I have to insist it was my fault."

"But you didn't mean to," Rafi said. "You should be forgiven for that."

"I'm sorry, friend, you said your name was Rafi?" Prince Larkin asked. He sounded sincerely sorry for not being sure who Rafi was.

"Yes. I'm a wanderer. Counted human, born to haunt leader Kepelo, raised in the fae realm."

"Oh, a fellow half-fae." Merrick smiled. He was half fae too—Rafi remembered that from the articles.

Larkin murmured something to one of his attendants, who picked up a folder from a table.

"I'm also related to the korreds who had a haunt along the verge," Rafi explained. "And this was their doing. Ula Kana didn't even have to sway them. She just encouraged them, and they went out and took over the town. I should have stopped them. I knew for years they were hurting people and would probably try something like this. But I wasn't quick enough or strong enough. I failed."

Looking unconvinced, Merrick was about to answer, but Larkin spoke up instead, perusing a stapled sheaf of paper from the folder. "Rafi the wanderer. Yes." His hazel eyes lifted to Rafi. "We have an extensive report on what happened in Miryoku, and many of the residents testified that you saved their lives that night. Pulled them from places they were trapped, carried them to safety. You also suffered great enchantment damage yourself, which made everyone most anxious. They were relieved indeed when you were healed. Nowhere would it indicate, friend, that you failed. Quite the contrary. You seem a highly valued member of the community."

"But—I wasn't enough. I should have done something about them long ago. I tried, but I went about it the wrong way."

Roxana wound her hand around his arm. "Not your job," she said softly.

"I'm sure you didn't mean for any of this to happen," Merrick said. "Right?"

"Of course not," Rafi said miserably.

"Well, if you think I should be forgiven because I didn't mean to do what I did, then shouldn't you be forgiven too?"

Larkin, arms folded elegantly around the folder, gave a decisive nod.

Rafi had no answer for that. "I guess?" he finally said.

For some reason that made everyone laugh.

"May I?" Larkin said, reaching a hand gently in Rafi's direction. When Rafi nodded, confused, Larkin set his fingertips on Rafi's forearm, and a sensation of serenity washed through him. "Be at peace," the prince said, with a twinkle of a smile.

∽

"It's true, you know, it wasn't your fault," Kepelo told Rafi later, as they wandered the overgrown town, picking peaches, plums, and grapes from abandoned gardens and putting them in a bag. "Your existence wasn't what caused the korreds to be obsessed with the human world. Sminu and I ourselves could be blamed, and plenty of fae similar to us. We were fascinated with humans. Everyone was, in our haunts. I kept you—a human child—when I shouldn't have, because of such fascination."

"But it's not your fault either," Rafi said. "What about your parents, or his, making mixed-breed children, blurring the lines? Though I suppose that kind of thing's been going on since humans came to Eidolonia."

"Since the fae *let* them come. Because the fae were interested in them. This mixing, this living side by side, no, it hasn't always been harmonious. Sometimes the mutual interest has been obsession rather than love, violence rather than cooperation. But those dark times are the exceptions. Our many types of people here—we've made it work, on the whole, have we not?"

She extended to her maximum height to reach the peaches from the topmost branches of a tree and handed them down to him. Watching a mighty drake pick peaches for a mere mortal, Rafi found he couldn't help agreeing.

EPILOGUE
APRIL 2021

ON A SUNNY SPRING DAY, ON THE ROOFTOP deck of a building on Dragon Street, Roxana leaned her elbows on the parapet and looked eastward. She stood on a foot-thick tangle of sylph jasmine that covered the roof with a layer of vines and fragrant white flowers. A full year had passed since the town's destruction, and the buildings were essentially off limits these days, prone to collapse, but a few on Dragon Street had been shored up enough to stand for a handful of years yet. They were beyond the verge, of course, and humans weren't exactly supposed to come here anymore. But the people of Amaris Town, the new village, still visited now and then.

This rooftop, accessible via a nerve-wracking stairwell with holes in it, served as an observation deck and a memorial site, or at least Roxana viewed it so.

Rafi leaned his shoulder against hers as they watched a cloud of yellow butterflies swirl over the forested ruins. They settled in a treetop, resembling a temporary bloom of flowers. In a rooftop garden below, a blaze of bluebells and red tulips had shot above the tangle. Beyond the woods, the mountains of the fae realm rambled across the horizon in a rugged stone-blue line.

Roxana stretched her arms up, then dropped one around Rafi. "Is it wrong to look at this and think it's beautiful? It seems like it should be wrong."

He tucked her against his side. "It's ridiculously beautiful. That's what April's like."

"Silly us, about to go off where it's autumn."

"Oh, that'll be beautiful too. I'm quite certain."

They had plane tickets and lodging reservations in New Zealand for a fourteen-day trip starting next week, just the two of them. The generous government payout awarded to each displaced citizen had finally come through, and a portion of it was funding their vacation. Roxana had at last completed her final quarter of schooling, long put off in the chaos, after a few week-long trips back to Port Baleia. With Nelleke's help she had packed up her and Ester's belongings from the apartment, said goodbye to the north, and returned to Amaris Town.

Ester did want to travel to New Zealand, too, but was equally interested in staying with Oni's family, who was planning outings in Dasdemir and vicinity, so ultimately she had chosen that.

Crosswater travel for any Eidolonian required special arrangements involving white lies (such as the passports that would show them as being from Canada) and the bringing of memory charms to preserve their knowledge of Eidolonia while off its soil, but the arrangements always worked, thanks to the fae magic that concealed the island flawlessly.

Roxana and Rafi had taken the leap and made the plans because they needed to get away, not only from the Southwest Peninsula but from the whole island. The break would be only temporary, though. Of course they would return. More domestic than the fae realm, yet wilder than the human realm, Amaris Town suited them both. They had deep roots now with the band, as well as with their fellow citizens, plus they had undertaken new projects—including writing their own songs, which so far they only dared play for each other. They knew their future would involve more charms to make, festivals to celebrate, and friends to spend foggy winters and humid summers with. There would be new songs to perform, perhaps even the ones they had written, and after a while, new decades to become nostalgic for.

And over it all would grow, for centuries to come, a magnificent island redwood, the tallest tree for a mile around.

Read the story of Larkin and Merrick in *Lava Red Feather Blue*, available now.

ACKNOWLEDGMENTS

I STARTED PLANNING AND WRITING THIS STOry in late spring of 2020, in lockdown, and wandered slowly through it for the next two years. I finally put on enough speed to finish it by Halloween 2022, when the world was starting to feel a bit more normal again—except for the exhaustion we all dragged along with us. Given the stress and distractions, I didn't expect anything I wrote during that time to make any sense, nor for anyone to have the energy to read or understand it. So not only am I profoundly grateful to my faithful beta reader team for taking on that task, I'm amazed that, according to them at least, it did end up making some kind of sense. Kit, Melanie, Tracey, Annie, Jennifer, and Addie: you each made my day with your messages about the book! I especially valued our discussions about how to tackle issues of gender and sexuality in this universe—which may be non-issues in Eidolonia but which affect many of us daily in the rest of the world.

In addition: Addie, this is not at all the gargoyle romance you wanted me to write, those many years ago, but thank you anyway for planting that idea! One way or another, it grew into Rafi.

Thank you also to the editing clients I've gained over the last few years. Studying and tinkering with your beautiful stories always helps me learn more about constructing fiction, at both the word level and the overarching plot level, as well as keeping me employed. Thank you so, so much to Michelle at Central Avenue Publishing for being a longtime friend who believes in my books more confidently than I believe in them myself. To Beau at Central Avenue as well: thank you for the invaluable proofread plus sensitivity read— your loving eye for nuance gave this book the perfect final touches! And the biggest thank you goes to my family, who struggled and improvised alongside me during lockdown. I'm so glad it was you all I was stuck with.

Finally, a pertinent question people might have: is there a Spotify playlist for this book with way too many nineties songs on it? Yes. Yes, of course there is.

Molly Ringle was one of the quiet, weird kids in school, and is now one of the quiet, weird writers of the world. Though she made up occasional imaginary realms in her Oregon backyard while growing up, Eidolonia is her first full-fledged fictional country. Her previous novels are predominantly set in the Pacific Northwest and feature fae, goblins, ghosts, and Greek gods alongside regular humans. She lives in Seattle with her family, corgi, fragrance collection, and a lot of moss.

She is the author of *Persephone's Orchard, Underworld's Daughter, Immortal's Spring, The Goblins of Bellwater, Lava Red Feather Blue, Sage and King,* and *All the Better Part of Me.*